THE
BONE

'A murder mystery story with a
modern twist. **Enjoyable read**.'
The Times+

'**Blisteringly fabulous** dark crime'
Northern Crime Review Book Blog

'Intensely creepy . . . **truly addictive**'
Lizlovesbooks.com

'**Outstanding** . . . Perfect for readers who like
their police procedurals fast paced, twisty-turny,
and served with a side order of grit. I loved it,
and **can't wait to read the next in the series**.'
Crime Thriller Girl

'A **great** read'
Swirl and Thread

'a contemporary thriller that **keeps you on your toes**'
Rachel's Random Reads

' fast-paced and exhilarating plot . . .
I can't recommend it enough.'

Alex Caan was born in Manchester, has spent over a decade working in information systems security for a number of government organisations, and is currently specialising in terrorism studies. A lifetime passion for writing was sparked by the encouraging words of an English teacher in school, and eventually led to Alex successfully completing an MA in Creative Writing and writing *Cut to the Bone*.

CUT TO THE BONE

ALEX CAAN

twenty7

First published in Great Britain in 2016 by Twenty7 Books

This paperback edition published in 2016 by

Twenty7 Books
80–81 Wimpole St, London W1G 9RE
www.twenty7books.co.uk

A CIP catalogue record for this book is
available from the British Library.

Export trade paperback ISBN: 978-1-7857-7050-0
Paperback ISBN: 978-1-7857-7049-4
Ebook ISBN: 978-1-7857-7048-7

Typeset by IDSUK (Data Connection) Ltd

1 3 5 7 9 10 8 6 4 2

Printed and bound by Clays Ltd, St Ives Plc

MIX
Paper from
responsible sources
FSC® C018072

Twenty7 Books is an imprint of Bonnier Zaffre,
a Bonnier Publishing company
www.bonnierzaffre.co.uk
www.bonnierpublishing.co.uk

To MKAZURHZZI, because they asked.

PART ONE
THE AMERICAN

Chapter One

Ruby is running. Her eyes pop, bright like a cat's. She is looking over her shoulder as she moves, which causes her to stumble. Her breathing is heavy; when she falls she moans, she cries out. There is blood on her face, there are cuts on her body. Her clothes are gone. She wears a sack, tied at the waist. Each time her bare feet step on sharp objects she whimpers. The scene is holding those watching it in thrall. The trees around her are black, dense. She falls again, to her knees.

Help me.

Who is she speaking to? Does she call on God? Or is someone there with her? Or is she simply pleading, hoping someone will hear, come to her rescue? Does she know they will be watching her?

Loud screams as someone grabs her. Ruby struggles and is dragged backwards, kicking out with her damaged heels. Ruby is gone. Only her screaming remains.

Ruby is seated in a chair. Her arms are strapped, her legs are bound. She looks straight ahead. Her mouth is taped.

Her eyes squeeze out tears that crawl down her cheeks.

Then there is darkness.

Ruby thinks she will die. She hopes she will die. Death seems like an end, like peace. Cessation of pain, no more fear.

The walls are coming in. The darkness has icy fingers. Her skin is on fire.

She wants her mother.

She can't breathe.

She is drowning.

She opens her eyes. Her body has slumped forward, her face is half buried under putrid sludge. The tape on her mouth has been removed; she tastes foul liquid, and spits. She pulls herself out of the mire, and she screams. She knows no one will come. Because no one can hear her now.

Something grabs her ankle, tugs at her, pulls her into the darkness.

She tries to escape, tries to break free. She can't; it has clamped its jaws on her soft flesh, gripping her bones, which it can crush.

She wants to die.

And then the rats come.

Chapter Two

Blood-red, rust-orange, liver-brown. A riot of colour pricking at her senses, unlocking her memories. Kate Riley was sprinting through a New England forest. It was fall. The world around her beginning to mulch and rot. She was alone, and then he was there. Out of nowhere he appeared, and she knew what would happen next.

Kate opened her eyes, stared into the darkness. Head against her pillow, her senses alert, her heart hammering. Familiar aftershock, from a familiar nightmare. She checked the baby monitor. It was silent. She checked her phone. Three missed calls. It was 2.38 a.m. She checked the caller ID. Unknown.

The phone rang again in her hand.

'Riley,' she said.

'Detective Chief Inspector, it's Justin Hope. Apologies for disturbing you at this hour.'

This wasn't going to be good.

'What's the emergency?' said Kate.

'Missing girl. It's sensitive,' said Hope.

'Message me the details. I'll head out now,' she said, pushing her sheets back.

'No, send Harris,' he said, quickly. 'He can open for us. He needs to get his fingers burnt.'

The garden was shadowy, dim and obscure. Kate kept her kitchen lights off, didn't like the idea of being visible to anything out there.

Pitch black. Watched, but not seeing. That old paranoia.

She rubbed the backs of her legs with her bare feet, trying to soften the goosed skin, warm herself up. There was a draught. Or maybe it was just her imagination, conjured up by the situation she was in.

The display on her phone showed 2.46 a.m. Her body, shivering and slow, still held on to its stolen sleep. But her mind was alert. She rubbed her face, gulped back freshly made black coffee, scalding her throat. Then dialled.

There was no answer. She let it ring. It was 2.51, her fifth attempt, when he finally picked up.

'Harris,' he said.

'It's DCI Riley,' she said. 'I'm texting you an address. Missing girl, name of Ruby Day. I need you to speak to the parents, get some background, open the investigation for me.'

She heard herself talking. It was the same clipped voice she put on for all work calls. Holding back the American teenager she had been, and forcing herself to speak with a British accent. It was an old trick, a politician's trick. Speech alignment; copy someone's way of speaking and they are immediately drawn to you.

'How old is the girl?' Harris asked.

'Early twenties,' she said.

'Missing since when?'

'Seven-thirty, or thereabouts,' she said.

Silence. She knew what he was thinking. She had thought the same.

'Are you serious?' he said. 'Why have we been called in? That's, what, under eight hours?'

'It came from Justin Hope. The call. He wants us there.'

'I'll head over. Text me the address now,' he said.

'And, Harris, I have no idea why Hope is involved, but he is. So let's not give him a reason to screw us over, OK?'

'No worries.'

Harris would hate it, of course. He thought being part of her team beneath him. This would irritate him further. Called out for a missing persons case. Not even a child, but an adult. Kate didn't like Justin Hope being involved. Things were always murky when he was around. He spoke in riddles and myths. He spoke as though he was on a pulpit, as though they had been chosen to serve him. He liked to boast about his 'team', about relying on them. Conferring status on them, because they were his.

Kate imagined a small child squeezing a soft toy too hard to its chest. The toy inanimate but silently screaming.

DS Harris was new, only two weeks on Kate's team, but he would learn the power dynamics quickly. And if he didn't, Justin Hope would simply get rid of him.

Chapter Three

There had been demons in his brain, tearing at his throat, clawing at his skin. Blood was soaking him and his bed. His eyes had stung, and in his mouth was the taste of iron.

The spasm that had woken Detective Sergeant Zain Harris from his nightmare had caused a cramp he was massaging and walking off, so at first he didn't hear Riley's calls. When he was done speaking to her, he wished he hadn't picked up.

He had showered after Krav Maga the night before, so made do with washing his face, applying deodorant and brushing his teeth. He pulled on jeans, a V-necked khaki T-shirt, and finished with a black jacket. Riley encouraged her team not to dress like accountants. He didn't know if this look had the desired effect; this was the first time she had called him to be part of an investigation.

Investigation. It seemed like a loaded word, inappropriate. Woman in her twenties goes missing for eight hours. What was that about? Why was there a panic? She was probably at a party, or hooked up with someone at a party, or asleep from drinking too much at a party.

Is this what he had become? Some top brass lackey?

A quarter of a million people went missing every year. Ninety-one per cent turned up within forty-eight hours, ninety-nine per cent within a year. He didn't get the urgency, or Justin Hope's involvement.

Zain pulled open the drawer in the bureau behind his front door. He let his fingers rummage through the brown and white envelopes, containing bills mainly, until they grazed the metallic sachet.

Green pills in plastic bubbles on one side, smooth foil with Chinese writing on the back. It could be alligator testicles or snake venom for all he knew. The Tor site had simply told him what the pills did, not what the ingredients were.

He popped a tablet through the foil, the green pill falling into his hand. He placed it on his tongue, and swallowed. He felt it kick in as he slammed his front door behind him and headed to his car.

Driving through sparse traffic, turning off from Lower Marsh, he hit a block of buses at the top end of Waterloo Bridge. Traffic bottlenecked around Aldwych on the other side. It was late, or early, depending on your point of view. Why were so many people out? Maybe the missing girl was on one of these night buses. Or folded up in the back of a taxi.

His satnav was taking him down the official route, the big roads. Up Kingsway, towards Euston, through Bloomsbury. Then on to the A501, Euston Road followed by Marylebone Road. It was like a tourist trail, heading past Madame Tussauds, the green syllabub of the Planetarium, Baker Street, Regent's Park. He should have navigated the smaller roads, cut straight through London's heart.

He felt humiliation needle him again. Seriously, this is what they were making him do? With his background, his skills, his experience? And why the hell was Justin Hope involved? What was so special about this girl? Was she the daughter of a friend? Was this Hope pissing over his patch, showing how much clout he had?

If it turned out to be a favour for one of Hope's golfing buddies . . . Then again, Zain was in no position to argue. Not with his past. However he felt personally, this stint with Riley and Hope, it was a favour. Another loaded word that. It implied a debt would be called in to repay it.

Zain turned onto the A5, heading up the Edgware Road. The restaurants were mainly closed, but the shisha cafés and shawarma outlets were still open. He felt hungry, but decided he'd get something on his way back. This wouldn't take long. He wouldn't let it.

At least the car was running smoothly. Audi A6. Sleek, black. A gift from Hope for the newest member of his team. Being someone's bitch had perks, then.

Eventually, beyond the flyover, he arrived at his destination. Windsor Court, a late-Victorian mansion block, red brick, white-framed windows. It sprawled across two buildings, with two entrances. There were metal posts blocking the driveways, no parking allowed. Zain drove his Audi onto the pavement at the front, got as close as he could.

He saw a sign for flat numbers 1–26 painted over one of the entrances that was lit up from the inside, so he headed for that door. There was a security panel listing flat numbers. He pushed at the button next to 1A.

A man's voice, urgent, panicky. Was he expecting it to be his daughter?

'This is Detective Sergeant Harris,' said Zain. 'I've a report of a missing –'

The door was buzzed open before he could finish.

Chapter Four

Kate watched the sleeping form. Still, dreamless. Vulnerable.

Ryan would be here in a few hours. Ryan – a stranger, to look after something so precious, so irreplaceable. Officially he was her housekeeper/sitter. Unofficially . . . what was the term for someone who guarded the thing you cared about most in the world?

Kate closed the door softly, padded back to her own bedroom. She slept with the door open, always. Just in case. Who needed the guilt if something went wrong? The baby monitor was top of the range, discreet, metallic. It looked like a digital radio. Kate turned it up; listening to the stillness she had just seen for herself.

She pulled back her bed sheets, crisp, smelling of pine and fresh air. One of Ryan's jobs. Laundry, cleaning . . . minding. That was the term; it hardly seemed big enough. As for the smaller tasks, Kate used work pressure, erratic hours, as justification for shirking them.

It had been true once. But since Justin Hope, things didn't fit into that cliché anymore.

Hope was a trial run, an idea dreamed up by the prime minister and home secretary. The police crime commissioners, PCCs, had been successful nationally. Well, that was the spin, so they wanted to give London a taste. Westminster was created as the first PCC set-up, powers taken from the Met's commissioner and given to Justin Hope. He had been an MP in a previous existence, a somebody at the Foreign Office, followed by the Ministry of Defence, then the Home Office and finally the Ministry of Justice.

On his appointment, lines were drawn hastily across London. The existing boroughs of Southwark and Lambeth had their prime landmarks taken. Hope was allegedly keen on jurisdiction over

Thames House and Vauxhall Cross. Most of the existing City of Westminster being swallowed whole, he had an area of nearly thirty square miles to govern. Drawn up in seven days, again allegedly.

Unofficially, he had jurisdiction over all 609 square miles of London.

When Kate had been offered her role, she'd thought it would be a promotion. Not just in title terms – she was already a detective inspector, now bumped up to detective chief inspector – but in terms of casework. She'd imagined the PCC would want the biggest, most complex crimes himself. She in turn would be given the opportunity to really make a difference, utilise her skills.

Skills gained in the past, before she'd had to leave.

Who was she kidding? She didn't leave.

Run away. Hide. Search for a new beginning. That was more like it. They said they'd find her a new state to live in, on the other side of the country from Massachusetts, somewhere she could start again. And she had tried it, for a year. A year that meant obscurity, nothingness: her career, her passion, all of it deadened.

She'd watched as they made plans for her, around her. Then she'd taken the initiative, taken control over her own life, and decided she would change country. She needed to get back to what she did best. Be a cop.

So London happened. And in London, she'd found she could start again. They'd snapped her up, dazzled by her Criminal Justice Ph.D. from Brown, her time with the United States Capitol Police, the Department of Homeland Security. Her fabricated references.

And things had been fine. For a while.

Until Justin Hope and his Special Operations Executive 3, unit without portfolio.

She felt as though she was holding her breath under water, waiting to let her lungs fill – or rise to the surface. She had been in this post for three months, and she was still waiting.

ALEX CAAN | 13

It was approaching 4 a.m. Kate closed her eyes, turned off the bedside light, counted the fifty states, their capitals. Sleep evaded her. She dialled Harris's number.

'Update?' she said when he answered.

'I'm with the parents now, just looking round Ruby's bedroom.'

'Call me when you leave.'

In the silence, she thought she heard the baby monitor buzz. Kate raised herself on her elbow and stared at it. No light, no sounds. She let it go, closed her eyes. Even if she couldn't sleep, she could rest them, and rest her limbs.

She tried to picture where the girl might be. Was she alive? The parameters of probability said yes. Had she been in an accident? Or just in need of some alone time? People often were.

Missing people were like a knife edge. Most came home, unharmed: blunt. Some didn't, which cut to the bone. What was this going to be?

Ruby Day. Who are you? Where are you? Why have you gone? And why is the commissioner looking for you?

Chapter Five

Detective Sergeant Zain Harris stood in Ruby Day's bedroom, taking in her life.

Her father – 'Call me Mike' – was in the doorway. The mother – 'This is Laura' – was sitting on the bed, brushing her daughter's duvet cover, smoothing creases that weren't there. Zain saw Mike's eyes dart around, checking, looking. For what?

Laura Day was dressed in a camel cardigan, white trousers. She had white-blond hair, pale-blue eyes. Mike Day had thick brown hair, gold-rimmed glasses. He was barefoot, wearing long shorts, a striped blue shirt over a white T-shirt. Zain thought they looked like a couple of people playing at being 'the Days'. It was as though they had plucked images from a catalogue instructing what they should wear, how they should behave.

Laura had a soft voice; she sounded tired. Her eyes were red, her skin blotchy. She kept swallowing when Zain was speaking to her, refusing a drink Mike offered her. Nerves? Fear?

They had given him a short list of friends, including a boyfriend, Dan. Ruby was an only child, so not much family to mention. They said she didn't have any medical conditions – nothing that required medication, anyway – that might put her in danger.

'She has a lot of computers,' Zain said, looking at Ruby's desk.

There was a desktop, a PC from HP, a netbook from Acer and a MacBook Air. He also saw a Kindle and an iPad.

'Is she a developer?' said Zain, eyeing stacked textbooks on HTML, XML and web design. The parents had said she worked from home, an online business.

The Days exchanged looks. Mike took his phone from his pocket; it was a red Nokia Lumia. Zain watched him slide his finger over the screen, tap away. Music started, followed by the voice of a girl. She was welcoming people.

Mike handed the phone to Zain. 'That's Ruby,' he said.

Hi guys, so welcome to my regular update. Can't believe it's been a week since I did this, but it has. And this time it's a Ruby special, as in something a bit more personal. I got a message from someone and, yes, you shall remain nameless. I won't go into the details, oh, hang on . . .

Ruby picks up a piece of paper and waves it at the camera, before scrunching it up and throwing it over her shoulder.

Anyway, the basic gist was, why do I bang on about having a positive attitude, and all that crap. Yes, people, that's a kinder version of the word actually used. So why do I go on about this? Because you know, it's still important. If everyday I log on and I say you can do anything, it's not enough. Because there are still too many people that are living half-lives, and there are still too many of you that think they're not good enough.

And I know how that feels. I remember back in the day, when stuff was happening to me, how low someone can make you feel. Worthless. As if you are a waste of the air you breathe. And into that, if someone had said to me, everyday, that actually that's not true. That I can do anything I want to, I would have loved it.

So that's what I'm doing now. Any of you feeling crushed by negativity, let me tell you this. You are strong enough to get beyond that state, and in your head, you can stay positive.

And I'll be that voice for you that I never had. So look at me, look right into my eyes now.

Ruby zooms in closer, so her face fills the screen.

And let me tell you this. You are not on your own, and you can do anything you absolutely want to. All of you watching this, take this message away. From me to you.

Ruby had thick brown hair, glossy. She was attractive, but not beautiful; no model but definitely loved by the camera. Maybe it was the angle but she seemed to dominate the screen. It was her eyes, Zain thought: they were green, saucer-like, drew you in.

'She vlogs?' he said, handing the phone back. Mike nodded. 'What else does she do?'

'Vine, Snapchat, Instagram. But mainly YouTube proper,' said Mike. 'That's her job. Lifestyle tips, make-up tutorials, fashion advice.'

'That explains this,' said Zain, pointing at Ruby's dressing table.

It was covered with make-up. Rows of polish, eye shadow, mascara, eye pencils. Bottles, pots, boxes, all sorts of items Zain had no clue about. The array of colours put him in mind of the counters he walked past in Boots, the overall smell like wax, mixed with cheap air freshener.

Zain saw a webcam had been set up on top of the dressing-table mirror, connected to nothing, its wire hanging loosely.

He looked over the bedroom walls, studied the posters.

The closets had floor-to-ceiling mirrors for doors. In their reflection, he saw Mike subtly shake his head at Laura. In the lounge they had been fraught parents. In the bedroom they seemed on edge.

He chided himself; he was doing it again. Making assumptions. He had to remember he was a regular cop now. He could ask questions; he didn't have to fill in gaps, work through opaque lenses.

Zain slid open the mirrored doors, revealing Ruby's closet. It looked like backstage at a fashion shoot. It was a mess. He eyed some designer labels. Ruby must have a healthy allowance, he thought.

'She gets given a lot. Because of her videos,' said Laura. She sounded defensive. Was she seeing Zain's judgement in his eyes?

Zain smiled thinly, taking in designer clothes, accessories, shoes. It would be a teenage girl's fantasy, he imagined. He closed the doors, hiding away the chaos.

There were bookcases against another wall. Zain studied the spines. The titles gave away their content.

The flat itself was in the basement of Windsor Court. Ruby's bedroom had two windows. Zain shifted the blinds to look out onto a square courtyard, with a door leading off it. He looked up at the flats on higher floors. They were all in darkness.

Along the windowsill were Disney figurines. There was a heart, squashed, made from rubber or Plasticine. It had sad eyes and a turned-down mouth. Next to it he saw several occult pentagrams. The same symbol appeared as pictures on the wall, patterned into a cushion cover.

He turned back for another glance around the room. The posters, the books, the figurines, especially the make-up . . . they were all lined up, neat. OCD levels of neatness. Yet the closet . . . it was like rage, an artist experimenting in free fall.

And something was missing. Paper. There was none. No bills, Post-its, notepads.

'Is her passport here?' he said. 'Do you know where she keeps it?'

Laura opened one of the closet doors. She moved aside bunched-up clothes, revealing a safe.

'Do you know the combination?' Zain said.

'No,' said Laura. 'Everything is in here, though. Passport, bank documents, cards she's not using. I think there is some jewellery she inherited from my mother, too.'

'No clue what the code might be?' said Zain.

'She went for a walk, she didn't abscond,' said Mike.

Zain suggested they go back to the lounge, letting the Days leave first. He bent down, on the pretence of tying his shoelaces, so he could scan the room from a lower level. Nothing.

But then he caught sight of something, under Ruby's desk. Left alone in the room, some instinct kicking in, along with a perverse drive to ignore protocol, he reached underneath.

Pushed away from sight was a wastepaper basket. Made out of black metal wire, it was empty except for a shredded document. Zain reached in and pulled the shreds out, hiding them in his jacket pocket before joining the Days in the lounge.

Chapter Six

'Do you have any idea where she might have gone?'

'No. It's not like Ruby to disappear. I think . . . I don't even want to voice my thoughts,' said Laura.

'We started calling the hospitals,' said Mike. 'If she's had an accident –'

'I can put an alert out for you,' said Zain. 'Save you having to go through red tape and petty bureaucrats.'

'Thank you,' said Laura.

'What were her precise words before she left?' said Zain.

'Just what we said earlier. She said she was going out,' said Mike.

'Out? Or for a walk?'

'Yes, a walk. She said she was going out for a walk, that's all,' said Mike.

'What was she wearing? When she left?'

'We didn't see her. We were watching a soap on TV, and she left without coming into the lounge,' said Mike.

'What was she wearing when you last saw her?'

Mike looked to Laura.

'Jeans and a black top. It had white stars on it. She also has a ring. It's her birthstone, tourmaline,' she said.

'Was she wearing a jacket or coat? It's freezing out there.'

'She has a patchwork red and grey coat. And a black woollen hat,' she said. 'I presume she put them on before she –'

'I understand she's been missing since about seven-thirty.'

'That's right,' Laura confirmed.

'It would have been dark already by that time,' Zain said. 'Is it usual for her to take walks in the evening?'

'Sometimes she does,' said Mike. 'Not often, but occasionally she takes the walk through St John's Wood down to Regent's Park and the back of London Zoo. It's a nice walk, a safe walk; it's a nice neighbourhood. That walk takes you past Lord's Cricket Ground, too. Laura and I also do it, when it's warmer.'

Zain watched Mike's mouth move, the words tumbling out. He was thinking how out of touch and deluded people became, believing that their Georgian houses, their cream and red mansions, their tree-lined streets and their proximity to affluence, could protect them. No one was immune from risk, ever. The only way to get through life was to not think about it.

'How long is that walk?' he said.

'Maybe an hour. Sometimes it takes less, sometimes more.'

'And she didn't say she was going for a walk and then going out?'

Hesitation.

'No, she just said out for a walk. I think. Laura?'

'Yes, I remember her voice. Only . . . is that just what we thought we heard, because that's what she normally says? No, she would have told us if she was going anywhere else. If she's back late from dinner, going to the cinema, any delay. She tells us. We know. And if we don't, she has a tracker on her phone.'

'An app,' said Mike. 'It feeds back her location. If you're registered, you give people access, so they can see where you are.'

'Why did she get that?'

'It's just an app; she's into them. She thought this one was nifty.'

Nifty? Zain was sure Ruby didn't use words like that.

'And she gave you access?' he said.

'Yes,' said Mike.

'Voluntarily?'

They exchanged those muted glances again. Were they prompting each other for answers? He had that sense again that they were playing a part, that their responses were scripted. He had to switch it off, this paranoia.

'I can't remember. Why is this an issue?' said Mike.

'Is the app still working? Have you checked?'

'It says she's at home. It hasn't changed since she left.'

The battery may have died, thought Zain. Or the phone was purposely switched off.

'Have you been worried about Ruby?'

'Of course. We are her parents. Do you have kids?' said Mike.

'I mean specifically,' Zain said, ignoring the question. 'Any over-zealous fans from her vlogging? Has she had any trouble with any individuals online?'

Again the subtle, quick looks.

'No,' said Laura. 'Nothing specific. Not that we know of, anyway.'

'And if she decided to go clubbing with her friends for the night, or just wanted to take off, she would let you know? Or the app would let you know? What if she just wanted some alone time?'

'She isn't that sort of girl,' said Mike.

'I'm always surprised by how little parents know their children,' Zain said.

'Not us. Not Ruby. Why do I feel like we are on trial?' Mike said, frowning. 'Our daughter is missing – why aren't you out looking for her? She could be lying injured somewhere.'

Most people turn up, usually within hours. Ruby will, too. I'm trying to take this seriously. The response ran through Zain's mind. He kept it to himself, though.

'Knowing her movements, what she gets up to, who her friends are . . . all this helps us do exactly that.'

Laura raised her eyes to her husband. He sighed, backed away.

'So this walk . . . does she ever deviate from her usual route? Any cafés or places she might have stopped off?'

'I don't know. Not usually, no. She normally goes out and comes straight back. That's why we were worried.'

'What time did you start worrying?'

'Maybe half nine? It's unusual for her not to be back by then. We tried calling her about ten, just after the news had started. It kept going straight to voicemail. Then I went out to look for her.'

'What time did you get back?'

'Around midnight. Laura was contacting Ruby's friends, people she knew.'

'Mainly on Facebook,' Laura said. 'I don't have their phone numbers. I sent messages to friends on her page.'

'Her friends list isn't private? From you, I mean?' Zain asked.

'She added me as a friend a while back, but with limited access. I can see her friends, but not her posts.'

Even with limited profile view, Zain wouldn't add his parents to his Facebook. If he had one.

'What time did you call the police?'

'Maybe half one? A few of her friends had replied by then. None of them had heard from her,' said Laura.

'You called the commissioner?' Zain said.

They didn't register his words.

'Justin Hope?' he prompted.

Again, nothing.

'We called 999,' said Mike. 'And then you turned up.'

And did sod all, was the end of that sentence, thought Zain. His mind was reeling, though. Why had an emergency call operative escalated this to the commissioner?

'Has Ruby been depressed at all?'

The bluntness of the question as it fell into the room, as the Days picked up on it . . . the way they reacted. They denied it, but Zain knew then that there was something. They were hiding something.

Zain's phone rang when he was back inside his car, warming his engine up.

'Harris,' he said.

'Detective, I need you to do something for me,' said the voice.

Zain felt his insides tighten.

Chapter Seven

Kate flicked on the bedside lamp, checked the baby monitor again. A cough sounded from it. She held her breath, staring at the monitor, willing for it to cough again or be silent.

A few moments later, she called Harris for an update, too impatient to wait for him to call her. He was eating, and driving.

'Shawarma. Café Helen. It's open all night. They do the best. Clubbers' paradise,' he said, sucking at his fingers. She heard him scrunch paper.

'Should you be doing that while driving?'

'I'm an expert at one-handed driving.'

'So what did you find out?' she said.

'Ruby Day, only child of Mike and Laura Day. They live in a basement flat, pretty nice, walking distance to Little Venice.'

'I already know all that, Agent . . . Detective Sergeant Harris. I sent you there,' she said.

'Sorry, boss.'

'What do the parents do?' said Kate.

'He's a management consultant, she's a home maker.'

'Management consultant? Who for?'

'He was quite vague on the details, said he's freelance.'

'How do they manage to afford a flat in W9?'

'Not sure. Might be family money; Laura's quite well spoken. Might be Ruby's money.'

'Ruby's money? What do you mean?'

'She's a vlogger,' he said.

'Blogger?'

'No. Video blogs. They call themselves vloggers. She does videos on YouTube, mainly.'

'What does she do in these vlogs?' said Kate.

'Things aimed at teenage girls. General advice, especially about body image, make-up, relationships, how to deal with parents, the world. Navel-gazing teens, you know what they're like.'

Kate stretched herself under her bed sheets, wrapped them closer. Cold air was filtering through from somewhere; she needed to get that checked out. The house had central heating; it should be warm all night. Did she forget to set it?

'What else does she do?'

'That's all she does. She's a full-time vlogger.'

'How can that be a full-time occupation?'

'It's the new celebrity. The news is always full of how much vloggers are earning. The ones at the top anyway.'

'How many videos is she posting?'

'Fortnightly.'

'That can't take that much time. Or earn her enough for a Little Venice flat.'

'Who knows? Vloggers earn from all sorts. Product placements, personal appearances, books. Ruby's got over two million subscribers.'

'As in views of her videos?'

'No, boss, as in people who follow her videos on YouTube. Like fans. They sign up for updates from her. She has over two million of them.'

Kate imagined what that would look like. She couldn't. It was a ridiculous figure.

'And any one of them could have been getting off on her, obsessing over her,' said Harris. 'It would be so easy – some sad, twisted fuck out there, stalking her. And he could do it without even leaving his room. Ruby came to him, every two weeks.'

'Why haven't I heard of her?' said Kate. She didn't want to think of disturbed individuals, not just yet.

'She's famous online, on YouTube, to her fans, her subscribers. But not really to us mere mortals. She's not a pop star, or movie star. It's the same notoriety a dancing cat might get when it goes viral. She's an odd one, though.'

'In what way?'

'You'll think I'm being harsh. She had these posters on her wall. There was One Direction, of course, but also Five Seconds of Summer. Teenage artists. And her bookshelves – from what I could see, they were all young adult novels. It's as though, well, like she's in a time warp, infantilised,' said Zain. 'My step sisters are into this stuff. And they're twelve.'

'Plenty of people Ruby's age indulge in all of that,' said Kate.

'And her room, it didn't make any sense, either. She had freakish levels of order – her computers, make-up. Oh, she has over half a dozen computers and devices. Her books, everything – all incredibly neat, and the carpet was super clean.'

'Sounds ideal.'

'Yes, until you look in her closet. That was a mess. It looked like somebody had rummaged through it in a burglary.'

'It's early, you're probably tired, maybe you're being paranoid?' said Kate.

'Maybe. And her parents, they were no better. They were terrified for Ruby. I first thought you'd got the details wrong, that she was a child, a two-year-old.'

'Parents worry, Harris; it's their job.'

At least, it's supposed to be, she thought. Normal parents, normal people. Experience told her that normal seemed to be less homogenous than people might believe. She looked again at the baby monitor.

'When did they last see her?'

'They said around half seven. The mum, Laura, remembered a soap she was watching. Ruby said she was going out for a walk, wouldn't be long. Around ten they started worrying. They called her phone, it kept going straight to voicemail. And she has this app, it tracks her location. Her parents have access to it, but it said she was at home still when they checked. It probably stops working when you switch your phone off. Her father, Mike, went out looking for her. When she wasn't back by about half one, they called the police.'

'Six hours gone – sure they're going to worry. Her mobile is still off, I take it?'

'Yes. It's an Android operating system, so her apps are pretty much dead with the phone. I've requested last location from her network provider, asked them to ping the phone as well. See if we get a hit.'

He didn't have to explain it would only work if the battery hadn't been removed.

'Have her friends been contacted?' she said.

'The Days said Ruby doesn't have many. I've got a list.'

'She has two million people watching her – doesn't seem as though she'd be short of friends,' said Kate. 'What about a boyfriend?'

'They said there is a boyfriend, Daniel Grant. He's another vlogger. They aren't too keen on him, I'd say.'

'Not keen how? Unsuitable boyfriend or cause for concern?'

'They didn't really say much, more the way they said it.'

'Possibly she's gone to see him, then? Knows her parents don't approve, so she didn't tell them? Can you arrange contact with him, see if she's with him?'

'I've already tried. It was ringing through to voicemail, so I left him a couple of messages, asked him to contact the office. Ruby's parents said they tried calling him earlier on, but he didn't answer. He probably recognised their number.'

'That might be all it is, then,' said Kate.

'Her parents were adamant, though. Kept saying it's not like her to just go off. They were being weird too, especially in her bedroom. They kept looking around, checking it. You know what it reminds me of? People checking a crime scene, making sure they cleaned up.'

'What are you saying? They're involved in their own daughter's disappearance? They called us in, remember?'

'It sounds ludicrous, I know. The whole thing is off. And there was all this occult stuff around her room. Pentagrams, just placed randomly.'

'She might be going through a phase. Did you ask her parents about it?'

'No. They want to check all the hospitals. I said I'd put an alert out.'

'How did they get Justin Hope involved?'

'They don't have a clue who he is. They said they called 999, asked for the police, and I showed up.'

'How did this case end up with Justin, then? Routine emergency calls don't get routed to us.'

The silence was heavy between them, acquiring layers of something unspoken. There would be a logical explanation in the morning, she was sure.

'How did you leave them?' she said.

'I told them we'd put out an e-notice. Circulate Ruby's picture and particulars, and alert hospital accident and emergency departments. I'll look into her bank and credit card activity back at the office.'

'Are you worried at all, by what you saw and heard from them?'

'Honestly? I don't know. On paper, no, I'm not. She's a grown woman, in perfect mental and physical health, as far as we know.'

'Your doubts?' said Kate, sensing them.

'Why switch off her phone? And why just go? Her parents keep saying it's out of character for her. But what if she's running from them? They think she's had an accident. I can't help thinking it might be worse than that. If she was unhappy, thinking of ending it all . . . and we always have to consider the other possibility. Someone else may have taken her.'

Kate told him to call the boyfriend again, then go home and get some rest; they would re-evaluate everything in the office later this afternoon. She heard a cough, followed by her name, coming from the baby monitor.

Kate put on her red towelling robe and was on the landing before she realised, but came back in time. She took the blond wig from her dressing table and adjusted it on her head, checking her appearance in the mirror.

Now she was ready.

Chapter Eight

Zain let the cold water run, dipping his fingers into the spray until the sharpness hurt, until the shower was freezing. He stripped off his shorts and slowly walked into the icy cascade, letting it pelt his body. He smiled through it. It was a trick; it was training he had learned. Fool your mind: smile when it hurts and your brain will think you're happy; it won't register the pain. Even when they're pulling your toenails off. One by one.

He closed his eyes, and the water winded him. Immediately another image filled his brain. He turned the temperature up. The fear he would keep for another day.

Zain lathered his hard body. Skin, muscle, bone. He was taut, always crouched, always waiting. Working for Riley would only be a blip, he was sure of it. He would be on the frontlines again soon enough.

Riley had told him to come in for the afternoon shift. He had emailed the list of Ruby's friends, including her boyfriend, to the office. Riley said she would get one of the others to follow them up. Did she think he was weak? One 3 a.m. wake-up call and he would be crushed?

Zain decided to go in earlier. Just because people told you to be one thing, didn't mean you had to follow through.

He pulled on black trousers, tucking an olive-green shirt into them. His combat boots and black jacket stopped him looking polished, kept him looking casual. Although DCI Riley herself seemed to favour suits. Maybe she had to meet the upper echelons more. Maybe she liked to show she was different. In charge. He let the thought flit through his head, the one telling him how good she looked. She was his boss; she was off limits.

For now.

Zain poured skimmed milk over Weetabix, throwing in a handful of cashew nuts to add flavour. A glass of grapefruit juice to go with it, and green tea. He tried to avoid caffeine.

Maybe the green pills were loaded with it, anyway. Alligator balls, snake venom and caffeine.

He laughed into his empty kitchen. His flat was on the top floor, but the traffic along the main trunk road running past Waterloo sounded a constant background. It was subsidised accommodation, practically opposite the Old Vic Theatre, on the doorstep of the South Bank. Built especially for key workers. His neighbours were other police officers, along with nurses, teachers, ex-armed forces, some civil servants. In London's jacked-up property market, they couldn't afford these flats on their wages alone. So the city stepped in. Thank you, Mr Mayor, he thought.

Zain's phone buzzed, followed by a leopard's growl. His incoming text message ringtone.

The message was from Riley.

Am at the Days' apartment. There's been a development. Get here asap.

Zain felt his heart pounding as he ran out of his flat.

Chapter Nine

Laura's whole body was shaking as she sobbed, visibly devastated. Mike tried to comfort his wife, handing her a tumbler of something amber. It smelled like liquorice, but the alcohol permeated the air.

Their initial paranoia, their conviction that they knew their daughter and that something was not right, had now been justified. They had seen footage of Ruby running for her life, pleading for help. Only to be captured and imprisoned. A video sent to Mike's phone, anonymously.

Mike poured himself some of the drink he had used to calm his wife.

Kate breathed in the pungent vapour and felt a touch of nausea. Her stomach was empty, with only black coffee swilling around in it. There had been no time to eat. She'd barely had time to bring Ryan up to speed and race from her home in Highgate to the Days' flat in Warwick Avenue.

'I'm sorry, Laura, Mike,' Kate began. Using their first names was standard police practice, to engender familiarity and openness. It felt clinical in the face of their tragedy to follow textbook procedure, but that rigidity was essential if Kate was to do her job properly. 'I know you've just had a great shock, but we need your help.'

Kate was trying to distract them as much as anything.

Yet all three of them would be thinking the same thing. The reality, the awful truth.

Ruby Day had not disappeared; someone had taken her.

'Do you recognise the location in the video clip? Is there a rural place you have ever been to? Can you think of anyone that might want to do this to Ruby?' said Kate.

They shook their heads.

'What about your work, Mr Day? Anything that might lead to something like this?'

'I manage projects for the government.'

'Anything sensitive?'

'What? No. Projects for the NHS, nothing like that.'

'Anything in your own personal history? Anyone who might hold a grudge?'

Kate thought of Ruby's two million subscribers and about what Harris had said about the sicko out there watching Ruby. Had someone got tired of watching her from the privacy of their home, and found out where she lived? Turned their fantasies, in which Ruby spoke to them through her videos, into something else?

Kate was familiar with cases like that. She had studied the psychopaths, the sociopaths, the uncategorised, at Brown University. She knew how sometimes it could be a passing encounter in the street that sparked something. The colour of someone's hair, eyes, the shape of their mouth, the way they walked, what they wore. One man she had hunted had stalked women based on their footwear, and what it reminded him of.

And from that transient second, that initial spark, that innocent person became the centre of someone's universe, and they had no idea. No idea until it was too late, until someone else was mining their body, mining their life. With Kate trying to figure out why and how and who. All the time knowing that the victim was arbitrary. A hieroglyph that someone had interpreted.

Is that what had happened to Ruby? Had someone interpreted her, projected their own fantasies onto her, made her into something else? Was Ruby chosen because she reminded her kidnapper of someone else? Or had she been chosen for her own sake?

Kate wanted to mine Ruby's life, before she was stripped of it. On the video, Ruby was still alive, and she wanted to find her before that changed. Stop her becoming an object, a mere body that was worked on for clues.

Laura stroked Mike's arm; it was a comforting gesture, although it might have been a signal.

'Your colleague, Detective Sergeant Harris, he kept asking us why we were so worried when Ruby didn't come home,' said Mike. 'We said it's natural concern, and he looked at us oddly. I knew what was going through his mind: Ruby is a grown woman, why were we panicking so much. It's just that Ruby is different from other women her age – she wouldn't have just gone off. That's who she is – no trouble, sensitive to our feelings. She wouldn't make us worry unnecessarily.'

'Of course, and as it turns out, you were absolutely right to be worried.'

'Yes. And last night that's all it was. Parental worry. We assumed something had happened to her. An accident, or she was in a situation where she needed help. We didn't think it could be something like this . . . not really. But now, the video, seeing that . . . someone has her, and this changes everything. Now it makes sense in a way that is terrifying for us.'

'You have my complete support, Mike, we will do everything to find her.'

'No what I mean is, we think we know who might have taken her,' said Mike.

Chapter Ten

Mike looked embarrassed, unable to meet Kate's eyes.

'We think it's her boyfriend, Daniel Grant,' he said.

'That's a pretty serious accusation, Mr Day. Why do you think he would be involved in this?'

'He's not well,' said Laura.

'In what way?' said Kate.

'Mentally,' said Laura. 'He has an unpredictable temper.'

'Has he ever taken that anger out on Ruby? Has he ever harmed her?'

'No, not that we know of,' said Laura.

'How did it manifest itself in that case? His temper, I mean?'

'We had arguments with him,' said Mike. 'I'm not proud of some of them, but we thought we had Ruby's best interests at heart. Dan's bad news, he's not good for her. And when she started going on about living with him, even marriage ... the rows escalated. That's when we saw how ugly he could be.'

'He's not good enough for her,' Laura echoed, 'and more than that, he's trouble.'

'Ruby was so blinded by what she thought was love, she just let him come between us,' said Mike.

So Ruby the perfect daughter wasn't so smooth a ride. *Come between us.* That suggested to Kate there might be a rift. Rather than the breezy, 'I'm off for a walk, see you in a bit,' Ruby might have been an, 'I'm going out and you don't get to know where or why!' type of daughter. She might have been in a sulk; distant, even.

'Was he the first boyfriend you had issues with?' said Kate.

'Yes,' said Mike. 'She's had boyfriends before, but not like Dan.'

'The last one, James, he was perfect,' said Laura. 'Ideal, so sweet, polite, and he treated Ruby with respect. She ended it with him, though, and went after Dan. It broke my heart. I get it – I was her age, once. I went after the bad boys; it's why I had her the way I did. They wasted my time, and I was terrified she would do the same.'

'What do you mean? You had her the way you did?'

'She's not mine,' said Mike. 'She's Laura's daughter. Ruby was six when we married.'

Kate looked at Laura, who was leaning her head against the sofa, looking up at the ceiling. So Mike was Ruby's step father. Kate wondered at the relationship they might have shared.

'Her father? Where is he?' she said.

'Mike is her father.' Laura's voice was harsh, sudden, defiant.

'Her biological father?' said Kate.

Laura looked away, colour rising to her face. 'There was a donor,' she said.

'I don't understand,' said Kate, understanding perfectly, but wanting to be sure.

'I was single, chronically single. Kept making the same mistake again and again, the unsuitable boy, the unsuitable father. So I decided to take things into my own hands.'

'Artificial insemination?' said Kate.

'Yes,' said Laura.

Mike held Laura's hand, covering it with his own larger one.

'So you see, Mike is her father. He's the only father she ever knew, and there was no conflict. No biological father turning up, or Ruby going off to find one.'

Kate knew the law had changed in 2005, long after Ruby's birth, to allow a child to trace their biological father at the age of eighteen. It was why so many women were heading to Denmark, where anonymity was still guaranteed. That and the fact it was cheaper. More sperm donations, for some reason.

'Thank you, Laura, I appreciate your honesty,' said Kate. 'I want you both to feel comfortable enough to tell me anything. Anything that might possibly help.'

Laura took a sip of her drink, tears filling her eyes. Kate focused her questions on Mike.

'You told DS Harris that you called Dan last night. When Ruby didn't come home. Did you suspect his involvement in Ruby's disappearance then?'

'No, not at all. We tried him as a last resort, we were calling all her friends,' said Mike. 'It sounds so naive, but until we saw the video, we really didn't think he was involved . . . '

'I'm still not sure I fully understand why you think he would do this,' said Kate.

'The arguments my husband described were in the past,' said Laura. 'Ruby was waking up to Dan. She told us she was going to leave him.'

'When was this?' asked Kate.

'A few weeks ago, maybe a month. She'd had doubts for a while. They were together for nearly a year, but the last few weeks . . . her mood changed. She became very insular, sullen, quiet. She seemed to have a lot on her mind, and then about a month ago, I think, she just said it. Told me she had a decision to make, and then later she said Dan wasn't going to be part of her future.'

'How did he take it?'

'I have no idea. The thing is, that's why I'm so worried,' said Laura. 'Ruby didn't tell me exactly when she would break up with Dan. But I can imagine his reaction . . . he's not a well person. Oh, God . . .'

'You keep saying he's not well, Laura. Why would you think that? Please help me understand,' said Kate. She leaned forward, closing the space between them. Pressure or intimacy, both yielded results. It was standard Reid interview body language. Standard for US law enforcement.

'He's a psycho,' said Mike. 'If Ruby had dumped him, I don't think he would have just let her go. He was obsessed with her, and he manipulated her.'

'How?' said Kate.

'Well with the vlogs she did. He made her start doing them with him. She had her own success, but he started to say things like she didn't love him, and to prove that she did, she should make videos with him. So her vlogs started to become ones in which Dan would feature with her.'

'When we tried to reason with her, remind her how much her vlogging was a part of her, she just accused us of hating Dan and interfering,' said Laura. 'And one particular row I remember. Well, I don't remember what it was about, but Ruby was livid. She was screaming at us, hurling accusations at us. And all through it, Dan sat there, and on his face . . . on his face was the biggest self-satisfied grin. As though he had orchestrated the whole thing, and was sitting back to watch Ruby do his bidding. Oh, God, why didn't we stop her from seeing him?'

'Laura, Mike, why are you so convinced Dan would be capable of something like this? Causing arguments with your girlfriend's parents is a far cry from kidnapping. Do you really feel you have reason to believe Dan might be behind this?'

Laura looked at Mike, and nodded.

Chapter Eleven

'Yes,' said Mike. 'When Laura said he wasn't well, it's an understatement.'

'What has he done to make you think that?' said Kate.

'A few months ago, back in July, I think, Dan had a birthday party,' said Mike. 'Don't you see, this makes sense ... it has to be him. The fucked-up little bastard.'

'Mike, please, as soon as I leave here I will find Dan. But I still need to know why you think he might be responsible. You were saying about his birthday party?'

'Yes. He had his birthday party ... He's only twenty-one, although he's got enough evil in him ... He had it in a hotel, one of the expensive ones, I can't remember which now. Anyway, it was one with a swimming pool. His party was in the penthouse suite, so about twenty floors up, or something ridiculous. You know the sort. Alcohol, drugs, sex. It was crazy, from what we heard.'

'Heard from Ruby?' said Kate.

'Christ, no, she didn't go. She wasn't invited. It was for his gaming pals, his boys.'

'So what happened?' said Kate.

'Dan, the crazy little shit, was stoned and drunk. And he wanted to know what happened if you tried to fly out the window.'

'From twenty floors up? Did he try?' said Kate.

'Did he fuck,' said Mike. 'Little coward.'

'Then what happened?' Kate got a sense of what he would say next.

'He threw a woman off the balcony instead,' said Mike. 'Into an empty swimming pool.'

Kate jumped as Mike's phone rang.

He answered it automatically. 'Hello?' He listened, wide-eyed, looked at his wife. 'Thank you for telling us.'

He looked at Kate, disbelief on his face, then began sliding his fingers over the phone. He froze when he found what he was looking for.

'Oh, God,' he said. 'That was a friend of Ruby's. Someone's just posted the video online.'

Kate felt a crushing sensation in her chest.

Zain watched the video without showing any reaction, handed the phone back to Kate. 'That was emailed to the father?' he said.

'Sent through Viber,' said Kate.

Zain sat down next to her, a strong citrus smell drifting from his body. They were in Ruby's bedroom. 'Was there a message with the video?'

'No,' said Kate. 'Mr Day tried to message back, but the number came back as being out of service. Someone sent the video, and then somehow deleted their account?'

'It would have been sent through an online texting service, I think. You can set them up anonymously; it would come to Viber as a message that looked like a mobile number. You can delete the account you set up immediately after you're done.'

'Is that readily available?' she said.

'If you know what you're doing. But that sort of anonymity would require at least a bit of knowledge – specialist knowledge, I mean. Usually when you text online they need your mobile, or the message comes from a random number assigned by a site. It's usually longer than a normal mobile number, and you can't delete the account straightaway. This looks like a regular mobile number.'

'I don't like what you just told me, Harris,' Kate said. 'And the video posted online?'

Zain played the video, this one on YouTube. The same images. Ruby running, begging for help. There was no message, no reason, no demand. The subject heading of the video was simply: 'Ruby's Dilemma'. Zain clicked into the account posting the video. It was registered to INVISIBLE. Joining date and time was literally a few minutes before the video went up. No links, no contacts, just the one video.

'I need my laptop,' he said. 'I can't do this on my phone.'

'I'll get back to the parents.'

'How are they?'

'Convinced the boyfriend is behind this. We need to leave soon; I want to speak to him. And see if you can get more details about the girl he allegedly pushed into a swimming pool.'

'Has he responded to my messages?' said Zain.

'He called the office this morning, said he hadn't seen Ruby for a week.'

'Shit. He better not be involved. We didn't exactly go after him last night.'

'There was no reason for us to treat him as a suspect,' said Kate. 'Until now.'

Chapter Twelve

Outside, the day was bright, but chill, the sun filtering through the conifer barrier screening Windsor Court. Zain's Audi was still parked up on the main road, Kate's midnight-blue Ford Focus ST in front. She had been given a BMW by Hope, but kept it parked at HQ in Victoria. Zain's laptop was under a layer of carpet in the floor of his car, in a built-in compartment, secured with a passcode. He headed for his car in long strides, discreetly checking that he wasn't being watched as he retrieved his computer.

Back in Ruby's bedroom, while his laptop booted up, Zain decided to see if he could get into Ruby's desktop. It required a password.

Cracking passwords. He had software he could access though his laptop, but it would take a while. He thought about Ruby's room, looking around for clues. In the meantime, he was on YouTube trying to track the IP address the video was uploaded from. Using software he had brought with him to the police, he managed to look into the back end of the video channel. The IP address revealed, Zain tried to track it. His laptop started hurtling through locations, scrolling through random addresses. Five minutes later, the software crashed.

The server used to upload the video had sent it through hundreds of proxy servers, making it virtually impossible to trace. Zain couldn't even tell the country of origin.

'Fuck,' he said.

His eye caught Ruby's books, her posters. No, too random for a password. It would have to mean more. Ruby was internet savvy, computer literate. How would she think? It wouldn't be a word, or a date. Possibly a word written in letters and numbers? Or a phrase?

Zain made a request to YouTube, asking for a trace at their end for the INVISIBLE account, but more importantly for the video to be taken down. It was always a hassle. These social networking companies all said they didn't want nutters posting, but it was rarely simple getting them to close down an account on Twitter or Facebook, or remove a video from YouTube. They always claimed freedom of speech.

Formulas. It was the new 'in' thing for secure passwords. Algebra – the toughest thing for a password cracker to break through. Zain tried to think, scanning Ruby's room again.

DCI Riley came in.

'Anything?' she said.

'The account is new, and it's been bounced through so many proxy servers I can't get a handle on it. I've asked YouTube to take it down.'

'The account isn't Ruby's?'

'No.'

'The friend that phoned Mike to alert him   how did she find out about the video?'

'Maybe she was sent an alert or something? It's obvious this is related to Ruby's online presence. Why else choose YouTube to upload?' Zain stopped. 'You don't think this is a stunt?'

Riley looked at him intently. Her eyes were sapphire in the dimness of Ruby's room.

'She is one of the new internet stars; isn't this the sort of thing they might do?' he went on.

'We can't assume that, and if her parents suspected a planned stunt, they wouldn't have raised the alarm. Clearly, this isn't something that's happened before. Are those the pentagrams?' she said, edging towards Ruby's window.

'Yes.'

Something clicked in Zain's brain; he remembered something about pentagrams, about the isosceles triangle in them.

'The golden ratio,' he said.

Kate looked at him briefly. 'They're inverted; this one is, at least,' she said, picking up a five-point star in a circle of metal. 'It's used by Wiccans. And Satanists.'

Zain searched online, and found the formula. He typed it into Ruby's desktop. It accepted it.

'I'm in her computer,' he said.

Chapter Thirteen

DS Harris was in the bedroom, mining Ruby's computers.

Kate sat with the parents in the lounge. It was decorated in whites, creams, pastels. The coffee table was thick glass, Scandinavian, expensive. She'd seen it in a catalogue she'd picked up, or one her mother had. The plasma TV stretched across one wall; it must have been fifty inches. HD, possibly 3D. A Bang & Olufsen stood to one side in the corner.

Laura and Mike looked dazed. Laura was still sipping from her tumbler. Outside, they could hear the dense traffic along Edgware Road, despite the double glazing. The road was hidden from view by thick evergreens shielding Windsor Court.

'Did Dan make any specific threats to Ruby?' said Kate.

'What do you mean?' said Mike.

'I'm just trying to build a fuller picture, before I speak to him. Has he said anything that might give you particular cause to worry he's involved in this? Targeting Ruby, I mean?'

'Are you for real? That sick bastard has Ruby, and you're here talking about fucking specifics?' said Mike. 'Why aren't you out there rescuing our daughter? We've told you about Dan, why isn't he being hauled in?'

'Please stay calm. Panicking about this, it won't help us,' said Kate.

'That's easy for you to say. It's not your daughter out there, having who knows what done to her. Find her!' said Mike.

'Mike,' said Laura, gently.

'We are trying, and anything you can tell us will help.'

'We've been telling you everything we know and it's getting us nowhere.'

'Mike, please,' said Laura. Her calm tone began to have an effect; he started to breathe deeply.

The sound of the doorbell broke through the tension.

DS Harris put his head around the lounge door.

'Pelt's here with Forensics and Tech,' he said. 'And Family Liaison.'

Detective Sergeant Robin 'Rob' Pelt was in charge of operations. He must have struggled to find support from one of the Met's police stations, otherwise he should have been here much sooner.

'Tell FLO to wait outside for a bit, until I've finished here,' Kate instructed Zain.

DS Harris disappeared, and they heard him open the front door, heard voices from outside the flat. Someone cracked a joke, someone else laughed. Zain shushed them, as footsteps walked past the lounge door.

'They'll search the flat. It's just routine but, as I explained, it can feel very intrusive,' said Kate. 'It's important to do a thorough search, though.'

'Why? She's not here, she wasn't taken from here,' said Mike. 'Find Dan, and you'll find Ruby.'

'It's procedure, Mr Day, and please don't worry, we are completely focused on finding Ruby. Tech are here to set up traces on your phones, in case you receive another video. Or in case whoever has Ruby gets in touch.'

'A ransom?' said Laura.

'And there's a Family Liaison officer; they'll stay with you. Any questions you have, direct to them, and they'll get in touch with me.'

'The only question I have is why you're still sitting there when we told you who has our daughter,' said Mike.

'Mr Day, I understand your frustration and your suspicions around Dan. And if he has ever said anything, or done anything, that can help us verify those concerns, it would be useful.'

'He threw a woman into an empty swimming pool. What more do you need? Laura told you Ruby was about to end things with him.'

'So there were no threats of violence or intimidation to Ruby that you know of? Made by Dan?'

They both stayed silent, Mike bristling. He got up and paced the room, while Laura stared at a spot on the floor.

Kate checked her phone. Zain texted to say he had Dan's address, and had tracked down the emergency call made by the woman he threw into the swimming pool.

Mike sat down, leaned towards Kate. She caught the scent of stress from his body, and the alcohol on his breath. He seemed calmer.

'Ruby is our world, detective. Please bring her back,' said Mike.

Kate was hoping there would be something, not just the view of parents who thought Dan was an unsuitable boy. Something she could use to put pressure on Dan, to make him give up his secrets. Give up Ruby if he had her.

Instead she would have to treat him with a detachment she didn't feel. And all the while, whether he was involved or not, Ruby's chances of survival were lessening by the minute.

Chapter Fourteen

After passing on DCI Riley's instructions to wait for her to conclude her interview, Zain slipped past the rest of her team and sat waiting in his car, on the phone with the team manager at Despatch. Gill Leake was checking her database, pulling up the file Zain needed.

'OK, so I think I have it. It was Sunday the sixth of July. The call came in at three-seventeen in the morning. From a Hotel Chrome – it's a new five star up by London Bridge.'

'Who made the call?'

'It was from the hotel itself, room 2001,' she said. Her voice was monotone, direct. Zain supposed she needed to maintain this cool manner, in case of distraught callers and in order to make tough decisions, immediate decisions. 'A woman, there's no name.'

'Send the audio over to my email,' he said, giving her the address. 'Who was on duty when the Ruby Day call came through?'

Gill tapped away, Zain able to hear the gentle keystrokes.

'An operative called Tom Williams,' said Gill. 'Is there a problem?'

'No, just curious. What time did he take the call?'

'It was one thirty-nine in the morning,' she said.

'Is there a log of who the emergency was directed to?'

'Yes, an Officer Miller, down in Southwark,' said Gill. 'Arnold Miller.'

'Thanks,' said Zain.

He looked out into the Edgware Road traffic, his thoughts circling. His phone made the sound of a letterbox. Email from Gill Leake. He would open it when Riley was there.

Zain called Southwark police station, asked for PC Arnold Miller. He was off duty, did the night shift. Zain asked for his home number, said it was PCC business. That got the supervising officer's back up. The Westminster commissioner was managing stretches of their patch. They resented him something twisted.

Constable Arnold Miller was asleep when Zain phoned.

'This is Detective Sergeant Zain Harris, from the Police Crime Commissioner's office.'

Miller coughed, a smoker's cough, and Zain thought he heard the click of a lighter, confirmed by a momentary intake of breath on the other end.

'How can I help you, Sergeant Harris?' said Miller, yawning.

'You took the despatch call Ruby Day early this morning,' said Zain.

'Yes,' said Miller.

'What did you do with the call?'

'Usual – logged it on the system, started a case file. Then got ready to head out there.'

'After the despatch call, how come you didn't go to investigate? I was the first officer on the scene. Did you flag it up to the commissioner's office?'

'No. I was heading out, but Despatch called me back. Said the call had been escalated. Hope, I mean the commissioner, had asked for his office to lead.'

'You didn't think this was odd?' said Zain.

'Saved me a trip out, and who's going to argue with the big chief, right?'

'I take your point,' said Zain.

'I was surprised, though, that he was getting involved in the case,' said Miller.

'Golf buddies, you know how it is. Don't worry about it. I'm taking charge of the files, so will restrict access.'

'As you wish,' said Miller, a long drag, smoke blown out. The adult version of the raspberry.

'What's your username and password for case files?' said Zain. 'So I can assign ownership to myself?' A beat. 'Alternatively, you can come down to the station, right now, and do it manually?'

'I'm not sure about this, fella,' said Miller.

'Look, save us both some hassle, mate. I'm not going to implicate myself, so you're fine.'

Thinking time. Smoke being drawn and released.

'Username is MILL73. Password is MPC1783942,' said Miller.

Zain repeated it back to him to confirm. 'You kept the default password?' he said.

'Hey, I have enough problems remembering the one for my computer. Bastard changes every two weeks. So shoot me if I didn't change the one for the database.'

'No, it's fine. Thanks, Miller. Go back to bed.'

Zain logged into the central database storing case files using Miller's details, bringing up Southwark police station's. He had credentials giving him access to most of the Met's databases to some level, with full clearance for the majority of those in Hope's patch. But he couldn't reassign the case to himself without Miller's login.

Ruby's file was flagged as current. Tom Williams in Despatch had assigned the file to Miller. Zain made himself the new owner, and locked it down. He logged out and then logged back in again as himself, amending the record to show that the call to investigate had been flagged to him.

The case records now showed that the Days had called Despatch, and Tom Williams had sent the call through to the PCC's Office. DCI Riley was called by Justin Hope, and then Zain called by her. Flawless chain. False chain.

Zain made a call.

'It's done. I've changed the database. The only part I couldn't get to was Despatch records. They still show Miller's involvement. But I have software at home, so I'll do it later tonight.'

'Very efficient, Zain,' said the voice on the other end.

Zain felt a sliver of guilt, but shook it off. Convince yourself what you're doing is justified. He didn't say thanks, ended the call quickly instead. Riley was heading his way.

Chapter Fifteen

It was a woman's voice. Shaken-up, drunk, hysterical.

'Oh, God, please, we need an ambulance,' she said.

'What's the emergency?' said the emergency operator.

'She's hurt, I think she's dead,' said the woman.

It was interspersed with sobs, hiccups.

'Who is? What's happened? What's your name, caller?'

'Millie, it's Millie, she's Millie,' said the woman. 'She fell. She jumped. I don't know. She's down there, just not moving.'

'You are calling from the Hotel Chrome?'

'Yes. I'm in . . . doesn't matter. Can you get here, please? We need a doctor, an ambulance. Hurry, please!'

The line went dead.

'Is that all?' said Kate.

Zain nodded, playing the call again on his phone.

'Did you pull up the case file?'

'Yes. Doesn't say much,' said Zain.

'Why is Dan not in prison? If he threw her off the balcony?'

'The charges were dropped,' said Zain.

'Why?'

'Doesn't say. I only downloaded the summary. Will review the full case file in the office.'

'Is the girl, Millie, alive?'

'Yes,' said Zain.

'How is that possible? If she was pushed from the tenth floor, into an empty swimming pool?' said Kate.

Zain shrugged.

'Let's see what Dan Grant has to say about all this,' said Kate. 'Where does he live?'

'It's a flat in Borough,' he said.

Zain started the car, plunged into the London traffic. He could smell the amber and ginger scent of Riley's perfume.

'You smell good,' he said.

She ignored him, and called in to her boss, Detective Chief Superintendent Julie Trent.

'The Days are with FLO and the Tech team now. If anyone gets in touch, we'll know and start a trace, ma'am,' said Kate. 'We're on our way to interview the boyfriend, Daniel Grant. The parents think there might be an issue with him. He's got some form, possibly.'

Form. It sounded so public school, Zain thought. History of bad behaviour, more like. He beeped at someone cutting in front of him.

'Yes, ma'am. And, ma'am, do you know yet why the commissioner called me directly? Why didn't he run it by you? Yes, ma'am, I'll report once I'm back,' she said.

Have a nice day, thought Zain. That's what she should say. Although Riley seemed to temper her American accent, tried to sound out the vowels as though they were local. It just made her sound even better, as far as he was concerned.

'What did she say about Hope?' said Zain, trying to keep his voice steady.

'Doesn't know. Somebody must have gotten him involved. He probably called Despatch and asked for the case to be sent to his office, and then he called me.'

Once again, Zain felt apprehensive about his involvement, about doctoring the database case files. DCI Riley seemed to have integrity, and he didn't like to think how she would react if she ever found out.

Chapter Sixteen

Zain was heading over Waterloo Bridge for the fourth time that day, despite it being just after eleven. Eight hours since DCI Riley had first called him.

The traffic was moving, but he had to stop every few seconds. He switched on his car sound system, music bursting around them.

Kate was tapping away on her phone while drinking a coffee – which she had made him stop to buy – out of a styrofoam cup. It was non-branded; she said she had a thing against globalisation. Ironic coming from an American, he had thought. Was that racist?

His music pitched high, as the piece reached a crescendo.

'What is this?' she said.

'It's spiritual music, from Konya in Turkey,' he said. 'A present. If it's annoying you, we can listen to something else.'

'Can we have silence?' she said.

'Yep, no worries,' he said.

He switched the music off. Silence filled the space between them. Uncomfortable, heavy and oppressive. He wanted to break it.

'So what brought you to London?' he said, unable to take the quiet any longer.

'Does it matter?' she said. 'What made you come to London?'

'I was born here,' he said. 'I am London.'

Silence again. Normal people would ask him to explain.

'What about you? Why London? Whereabouts in America are you from?' he tried again.

She sighed, sipped her coffee.

'Massachusetts,' she said. 'A small town you would never have heard of.'

'Try me,' he said, grinning at her. Someone blasted their horn at him. The traffic had moved; he hadn't kept pace. A few seconds later, they stopped again.

'So why London?' he persisted. 'Isn't America the land of milk and honey?

'I'm pretty sure that's Israel,' she said. 'How did you decide on this posting? Were you bored with SO15?'

So she wasn't the type to do small talk.

'Haven't you read my personnel file?' he said.

'I like to hear it from the source,' she said.

Zain stayed quiet. The car was now directly outside Waterloo station, near his flat.

'Waterloo,' she said. 'That's why I came to London. The history you find on almost every corner. I walk the streets, and it brings to life all the books I've read, all the things I've learned. I watch people, and they fly around London, taking every inch of it for granted. Me, I came as a teenager with my parents, and it stayed with me. I fell in love with it, so I made it my home.'

Zain was surprised at the intimacy of her words.

'So why did you make the move? From SO15?' she said.

Zain laughed. She'd given up something only because she wanted him to give more. 'You must know why,' he said.

'I told you, I like it from the source.'

SO15 was the Met's counter-terrorism command. Zain had been drafted in following a stint with GCHQ after university, but soon became enamoured with police work. There was an honesty to it. He smiled as he thought this, reflecting on what he had become in the end. He had retrained at Hendon Police College, done his duty as a rank and file, then been drafted into SO15.

'You did well,' said Kate. 'I saw how quickly they moved you along.'

'I was ideal for it. I knew London, and I don't mean on the surface, but the grit in its claw.'

'Until it went wrong,' she said.

Fuck, she was cold, he thought. 'It didn't go wrong. Let's just say I was wounded in the line of duty.'

'I read the occupational health report,' she said. 'It seemed clinical. It talked about injuries, mental trauma. Sustained while on duty. Is that the line you're going to spin me, too? I thought we were becoming friends?'

She said this with a set face, looking out of the car window.

'What I want to know is, should I be worried? Are you over it? I'm curious, you see, because if you are so completely fixed, why did they send you on secondment?'

Zain ignored her, enjoying the rare free flow of traffic down the London Road. They drove past Elephant and Castle, and then hit Newington Causeway, where they caught more London gridlock. Borough wasn't far away now; he could have just not answered. Instead, something compelled him to. She compelled him to.

'We were staking out some al-Qaeda operatives,' he said. 'They were planning an attack, a hit on St Pancras station, the Eurostar. It was the usual set-up, a small cell, but they were weakned. Easy to keep tabs on, and they were leaking information badly. We were aware of their every move. It was a joint operation; we had an agent from MI5 with us.'

Zain remembered the agent; he had disappointed all preconceptions about spies. No James Bond, just a very ordinary, grey man, not memorable physically. Yet his mind was acutely tuned into the situation, the cell, SO15, and he had conveyed that intelligence in a low, authoritative voice.

'The main part of the cell shifted location to another safe house,' said Zain, 'close to King's Cross. I stayed at the primary location, running surveillance on the cell member left behind.'

They were at Borough Market now, and Zain found the street they were looking for. He parked his Audi outside the building Dan Grant lived in. It had a glass turnstile front door, with an access code and a security camera. Higher up were huge windows, giving the residents views out across the city.

'What happened?' said Kate.

It was a whisper, her breath warm with coffee as she spoke.

'It was a trap. I was ambushed, dragged from the stakeout van. The cell we had been monitoring, they were just a decoy. The rest . . . well, you've read my file.'

The sun was almost blinding him through the windscreen, warming his face, creating a bright glow in the car. It wasn't the day to delve into the darkness of his past.

'How do we play this?' he said, ending their conversation.

'Sympathetic,' she said, taking the hint. 'Let me see what Daniel Grant's about. I want to see his reaction when we talk about Millie.'

Something moved inside Zain as he watched Kate get out of his car. She pushed her hair over one ear, the dark brown flecked with auburn and copper as it caught the sunlight. Her eyes were bright as she looked out across the street, waiting for him to move.

Zain took his time, trying to shake off the feelings running through him.

She dulls my senses like wine, and stirs them like a storm. Was that Rumi? It should be.

'Let's see what the boyfriend has to say,' she said, as they buzzed his flat.

There was no answer.

'Maybe he's not home,' she said.

'He's home, or in the area,' said Zain. 'His mobile is, anyway.'

Kate gave him a look that said: *Who authorised that?*

'Did we get a trace on Ruby's?' she said instead.

'Yes. It pretty much stopped transmitting close to home at seven thirty-nine last night. Someone removed the battery, I think.'

'Yo? Who are you?' said a voice from the intercom.

'Mr Grant? This is Detective Chief Inspector Riley and my colleague Detective Sergeant Harris. We need to speak to you about a friend of yours, Ruby Day?'

The door buzzed open.

Chapter Seventeen

A security guard at reception watched them walk through the foyer. Zain asked him if he could get hold of the last twenty-four hours of CCTV from the entrance. The security guard said it was digitised; he could email the recording over, if they wanted.

'Do you know Daniel Grant, lives in flat 115? You know where he was yesterday?' Zain asked.

The guard claimed ignorance. Kate saw astrophysics textbooks on his desk. Foreign student making extra cash, not wanting to get involved with the police.

The flat was on the fifteenth floor. As they exited the lift, they had to pass through a second security door, which someone had propped open with a box. It had a picture of a gaming control on it.

The corridor in front of them was carpeted in blue. It felt like a student hall of residence. Flat 115 was the second door on the right. The door was open, but Kate knocked anyway. A voice from inside shouted for them to come in.

Kate's shoes, heeled, were noisy on the wooden floors of the entranceway. A hall led off to the other rooms in the flat, and immediately to the right was an open-plan kitchen/lounge. A young man, presumably Daniel Grant, was seated on a brown ergonomic sofa. The room was sparsely furnished, with just the sofa plus one other leather La-Z-Boy chair, and a glass table in the centre of the room.

Against one wall was a unit on which sat a TV, similar in size to the one the Days had. From it ran numerous cables into every gaming device Kate had ever seen.

'All right?' said Dan.

He was casual, dressed in shorts and a grey T-shirt, the sort of stuff you'd wear to bed. He looked dozy, yawned, scratched himself.

'Mr Grant?' said Kate.

'Obviously, this is my place. Thought detectives were meant to be bright,' he said.

Zain bristled, tension bouncing off him.

'I'm just messing,' said Dan. 'You're Harris, right? You left me them messages this morning? How can I help?'

'We need to ask you some more questions,' said Kate.

'Poor Rubes. This is crazy what's happening. I saw the vid on YouTube. Someone's playing a sick game.'

Kate nodded when Dan indicated the empty La-Z-Boy for her to sit. Zain took a space next to Dan on the sofa, sitting a bit too close to him. Dan shuffled away slightly, looking uncomfortable.

Dan looked young to Kate, in the way that everyone below twenty-five looked like a teenager to her. Light-brown hair cut simply, close to his scalp, and big green eyes. There was still acne on his chin in places, and the room was heavy with the scent of sweat and food.

'You just woken up?' said Zain. 'Late night?'

'Something like that. Had a friend round.'

'All night?' said Zain, sounding solicitous.

'Yeah. Think till about six, or something. Why? You checking for my alibi already?' said Dan.

Zain smiled at him. There was steel in it.

'I called your office before. Told them I didn't know where Ruby was. What else do you want to know?'

'You saw the video on YouTube? How did you find out about it?' said Kate.

'Someone emailed me, sent me the link. We all got it – Rubes' crew.'

'You were deliberately targeted?' said Kate.

'Yeah, think so. Be too random otherwise.'

'How are you feeling about it?' said Kate.

'What, the video, you mean? I'm majorly disturbed, obviously, how would you be feeling if it was someone you knew? We have to help her, get her back.'

Dan stayed immobile on the sofa; glued to it, almost. He didn't convey distress, and his half-awakened state suggested he hadn't lost any sleep over the situation.

'I've been on YouTube all day. Been trying to see if I can get the handle. I put it out on Twitter, Facebook, Vine, SnapChat. Even my Instagram. I got people looking for her. Asking if anyone knows where she is, or if they see her, to get in touch. I don't know what else I can do.'

'When did you last meet with Ruby?' said Kate.

'Don't know, it's been a week, I think. A bit over, maybe.'

'A week?' said Zain. 'Thought you were dating?'

'We are. It's complicated. I just haven't seen her, nothing weird about it.'

'Why not?' said Zain.

'Just busy. Time slips, we don't get together. Nothing major.'

'Did you guys have an argument, or something?' said Zain.

'No, I told you, just busy.'

'When did you last speak to her?' said Kate.

Dan leaned forward, picked up one of three phones he had on his coffee table. He started scrolling through.

'Texted her yesterday.'

'What did you say in that text?' said Zain, looking over at the phone.

'I just asked her how she was, when were we hooking up. She said she couldn't say, would be in touch.'

Zain took the phone from him. Dan tried to grab it back.

'Give it back to me, man, what is this?'

'Just having a look. Interesting, some of these messages. Do you mind if we hang on to this, Mr Grant?' said Zain.

'Yeah, I do mind. You can't come in here, taking my stuff. What is this? North Korea?'

'We're trying to build a picture of Ruby, anything that might help us locate her.'

Kate threw Zain a look; he gave the phone back to Dan.

'Apart from texting her, when did you last have a proper conversation?'

'Dunno, probably a week ago when I saw her.'

'When was it exactly?'

Dan flicked through his phone.

'Last Thursday, at 5 p.m. We met for a drink in a pub called The Garter, off Charing Cross Road.'

'Just the two of you?'

'Yeah.'

'What did you talk about? How did she seem?'

'Usual stuff, about our vlogs and shit. She was all right, normal.'

'She didn't seem different at all? Worried about anything?'

'No, just normal, like I said.'

'Her parents seem to think she had ended her relationship with you.'

Red crept up Dan's thin neck, into his face. Anger and embarrassment, she thought.

'Those jealous twats, you wanna watch them. They can't stand me, they've been trying to get between me and Rubes for ages.'

'So they made it up? You and Ruby didn't break up?'

'We were just going through some stuff, that's all. Rubes is mine. She isn't going anywhere, we were meant to be.'

Interesting turn of phrase, charged with the idea of ownership, thought Kate. 'Do you feel Ruby belongs to you in some way?' she said.

Dan glared at her, but didn't deny it.

Chapter Eighteen

'Do you have any idea who might wish to harm Ruby in this way? Did she ever speak about anyone, a fan possibly, somebody she might have been afraid of?' said Kate.

'No. Well, yes. Look, we are all out there, us Youtubers, we are the future. People, they leave all sorts of comments online, proper fucked-up, hateful shit. But they're just trolls, jealous and bitter, cowards. Hiding behind their keyboards, so we just ignore all that.'

'Any persistent trolls?'

'A few, but they get smacked down by our fans.'

'So she wasn't concerned about her safety at all?'

'No, not that she said. Looks like she should've been. Fuck, to think some sicko was planning this shit, right?' Dan looked more animated than upset.

'Yeah, some real sicko,' said Zain, not very subtly.

'What do you mean? You think I'm involved with this shit?' Dan turned crimson again, staring wildly at Kate, turning his body away from Zain.

'Nobody is saying anything of the sort,' Kate said. 'We are just trying to build a picture. Anything you can tell us will help. Was there anyone Ruby was in communication with? Any new friends she'd made online?'

Dan laughed at this. 'She's not ten or an idiot. She's not gonna chat to some random freak online. I used to get it, all these old pervs pretending to be girls. We're not stupid, we got wise to that stuff quickly. She didn't get groomed, if that's what you're thinking.'

'Is it possible she turned to someone, if she was depressed, for instance?'

'She would turn to me, turn to her friends, turn to her millions of fans. Not some loner serial killer. Fuck's sake.'

Zain leaned closer to Dan, making him shift away again an inch.

Kate tilted her head slightly in Zain's direction. They had agreed on the way up that they would spring it on Dan, see how he reacted.

'Ruby's parents told us a little story,' said Zain, almost speaking into Dan's ear. 'About you, a birthday party and a swimming pool. And the woman you threw into it.'

Dan jumped away from Zain, red and sweating.

'What? What do you mean?'

'They said that back in July, you had a birthday party, in a flash little hotel not too far from here. Said you threw a woman off a balcony. Is it true?' said Zain.

'No, that's typical of them, fucking liars. You think I'd be sitting here if I did that? What the fuck! Those bastard parents are just . . . aaargh. They'd say anything, just to get rid of me.'

'You're saying they made it up?' said Zain.

'Too right. I'm going to sue them, spreading shit like that. Fucked up.'

'Why would they invent something so . . . graphic?' said Kate.

'I told you, they want to get rid of me, split me and Rubes up. They're sick, like real-life trolls.'

'So it's a lie? The Days lied to the police? The police looking for their missing daughter?' said Harris.

'You think because they have nice middle-class accents, live in a posh flat and dress in M&S, that they're decent? They're scum. And they're liars.'

Zain moved away, looking at Kate. His blue eyes were bright against his olive skin, and he was smiling behind Dan's head. The boyfriend that had just lied blatantly to the police.

'You have no idea who might have wanted to harm Ruby?' Kate said.

'No,' said Dan.

Kate wanted to keep this, have a hold over Dan in case she needed it going forward. She thought about the recording of the 999 call when Millie had fallen. Dan had just shown himself to be deceitful. His words meant nothing and, right now, he was fast becoming her prime suspect.

Chapter Nineteen

Kate got up, stretched her legs, walked to the window of Dan's apartment. Her head was mulling over his denial of something they had proof of. She tried to sift through the things he had said, picking out anything that might show further fabrication.

The view looked across towards the City. The aircraft warning light on top of One Canada Square, the building commonly referred to as Canary Wharf, was dim in the sunshine. Its towers faint, surrounded by a light mist.

'Her parents said she doesn't have many friends,' said Kate.

'She has two million,' said Dan. 'Her parents are just deadbeats, need to get out of Rubes' space. They stifle her, and they don't know jack about Rubes.'

'What don't they know? Enlighten us.'

Dan shrugged.

'Who would you say are Ruby's closest friends?' said Zain.

Dan opened his mouth, closed it without speaking. Close friends, he should rattle off some names. His silence corroborated what the Days had said. Ruby was a loner. Lonely in the glare of two million people watching her.

'Ruby's parents didn't have any numbers, said they used Facebook mainly to contact her circle. Can you help us out?' said Kate.

You better help us, before I make you face up to your lies, she was thinking.

'I got numbers somewhere.' He gave Zain a side look as he went through his phone. 'You got an email address? I'll send you a list.'

'Does she have anyone she is particularly close to?' said Kate.

'There's some of us, YouTubers, we get together now and again. Go to VideoCon and stuff like that. There are so many awards now, people trying to tap into what we do. They don't get it, a lot of them, and they hate that. We did it without them, you see, just us and cameras in our rooms. No budget, no advertising, we just clicked. It's perfect democracy; the people choose what they want to watch. And they want to bottle us.'

'Who are *they*?'

'All of them. Companies, film studios, brands. Anyone out there trying to make money. They want us fronting it.'

'Had Ruby been approached by anyone, to front anything?'

'Yeah, tons. She gets free stuff every day, almost. People send her stuff, ask her to use it in her videos. It's like advertising, but without advertising. People watch her, and they watch what she uses. Last year, she used this eye shadow, right, and it sold out in a month all over. A month. Beyoncé has that sort of power, and here's little Rubes doing the same. The Americans love her, they love her accent.'

Dan looked at Kate; she didn't react. She'd heard it enough times.

'So she was sent random things? She didn't have a contract with anyone?'

Dan looked furtive, started stroking his arms, drawing his hands into his stomach. Classic concealment, comfort grooming: Kate had hit on something.

'No,' he said.

Your body is saying something else to me, she thought. What exactly was he hiding?

Chapter Twenty

They were getting ready to leave. Dan Grant had been exhausted; he didn't have anything useful left to say.

'What do you do, then? On YouTube? What's your talent?' said Zain. He rolled the word talent in his mouth, heavily mocking.

'I have a gamer channel. I play games.'

'What do you mean?' said Zain.

'I play games. All the latest games that come out, I play them. And I film it, and I do commentary, and I give tips to people. So when people struggle, they come to my videos, and they get through levels.'

'A tutorial?' said Kate.

'Sort of. I film myself playing the game, and I talk over it. I literally review every second of it.'

Kate didn't grasp it; she would have to watch a video later, get a better idea of what Dan did. Why would anybody want to watch somebody else play a video game? Wasn't the thrill, the escape, in playing yourself?

Dan didn't make a move to show them out.

'You literally just make your own videos, filming yourself?' said Zain.

'Used to, that's how we all started. Now it's different. We have them produced for us.'

'Who by?' said Zain.

'It's a company we signed to,' said Dan. 'MINDNET.'

'MINDNET?' repeated Zain. 'What is that?'

'Just a media company. In Soho. They produce our videos, so they look professional, better quality editing and all that.'

'And what do they get from it?' said Kate.

'A cut of our money,' said Dan.

ALEX CAAN | 65

'Your money? People pay to subscribe to you?' said Kate.

'No, from ads. We put ads on our stuff, and we get paid. Rubes gets paid in goods, but sometimes she gets money too for advertising shit. And games companies pay me. I got nearly two million regular viewers. And any ads I run, MINDNET take a cut.'

'Why would you let them? If you can make your own videos at home, why do you need them?' said Zain.

'Better quality product. And they use their tools. They have weird software and shit, helps raise our profiles. I only had half a million people last year, and within months they got me up to two million. They think I'll be hitting five or eight million in another year.'

Kate felt her head filling with information, new and odd, parallel to reality. She had to separate the bits that mattered, that would be useful to her investigation.

'Ruby has a contract with MINDNET?' she said. 'You said a moment ago she didn't have a contract with anyone.'

Dan opened his eyes wide, child-like, feigning innocence. Trapped and nowhere to go.

'I thought you meant something else,' he said. 'Like sponsorship, branding. L'Oréal, that sort of stuff.'

'What's in her contract with MINDNET?'

Dan shrugged.

'We never discuss it. It's personal. Like asking someone how much they earn – not my business. We all get different cuts.'

'You must have a general idea?'

'No, we all get different deals,' he said.

'What do they do? Just manage her videos, then? Her online profile?'

'Yeah,' said Dan. 'Sort of. They help with the clothes and make-up ones. Rubes still does diary-style stuff by herself.'

'Do they script the videos they produce?'

Something Harris had said . . . Was this a stunt? Would MIND-NET set something like this up?

'No, we are real, they don't script us. Sometimes though, just the odd phrase maybe. We've got to be what our fans want – the MINDNET guys just remind us.'

'Ruby OK with them?' said Zain. 'She happy with the way they were treating her?'

'She is having some issues with them,' he said. 'I don't know what, but she isn't feeling them as much anymore. She's talked about ending with them, but she wouldn't spill. Said it didn't concern me.'

'Was she afraid at all?' said Kate.

'Seriously, I don't know what's going on, she never said. Might just be money. I know one of my YouTube buds is going through the same with someone else. Not happy with the cut they're giving him. I don't know if it's the same. Ruby's never said.'

'Keep your phone on. We might need to speak to you again,' said Zain.

Kate smiled thinly at Dan as they left his apartment.

Chapter Twenty-one

'Drop me back at HQ,' said Kate. 'I'm going to find out where MINDNET are, and what their issues with Ruby might be. Can you go and find Millie, the girl Dan pushed from the hotel balcony?'

'Sure. He was weird, my instincts are telling me he's all wrong.'

'He was lying throughout that interview, or hiding something,' said Kate. 'He knows a lot more than he told us.'

Zain checked his phone. 'Ruby's last tweet: "*Every man/woman is guilty of all the good he/she did not do.*" It's a quote from Voltaire, according to her.'

'Very profound,' said Kate.

'Typical teenagers, full of their own self-importance.'

'She isn't a teenager,' said Kate.

Zain swiped his phone, opening an email from Dan Grant. List of Ruby's friends, he told Kate.

'Send it back to HQ,' she said. 'Get Stevie to call them. Find out Ruby's movements yesterday, any concerns she may have mentioned recently.'

Detective Sergeant Stevie Brennan would love that, thought Zain. She was part of Kate's team, with DS Rob Pelt and Zain, and already seemed to hate him. Making her do legwork would piss her off further no doubt.

'Got another email. Rob's done a search on CCTV,' he said. 'He has Ruby walking home from Warwick Avenue station, approximately 4 p.m. yesterday. She wasn't hurried, just calm. The last image is her coming through the main doors to Windsor Court. Nothing after that.'

'And he's sure she didn't leave through either of the exit points to Windsor Court?'

'Yes.'

'How else could she get out? Have someone examine the building, see if it's possible to get in and out any other way.'

'I'll get someone to do a walk-through, every scenario,' said Zain. 'See if Tech want to stretch their legs.'

'Where did Stevie find them? Tech and FLO?'

'Paddington Green station,' said Zain.

Justin Hope didn't have his own police force, just a handful of small teams like Kate's. Any case requiring specialist skills like forensics meant borrowing manpower from the Met Police themselves. Their commissioner, Sonya Varley, was less than reticent about how unhappy she was. She had openly clashed with Justin Hope many times. Hope had the Home Office and Ministry of Justice backing him, and the Met were currently undergoing a trial by fire with parliament. While Varley was being forced to police smarter with less money, Hope was being given her budget, splurging on designer cars and their HQ in Victoria.

Kate felt uneasy thinking about it. A turf war was a danger. And she had a feeling she was on the wrong side.

'Ruby must have left that building somehow,' she said to Zain.

Kate didn't believe in the impossible. There had to be an explanation.

The pentagrams flashed into her mind. She pushed them aside. The day was bright, hitting its stride. No room for the shadows for that type of irrationality to hide in.

Chapter Twenty-two

Fifth Avenue. Zain smiled as he walked down it, images of New York reeling through his mind. Images of Kate Riley, her voice, her history. An American girl in London. Sounded like a movie.

This Fifth Avenue was in north-west London, near Queen's Park tube station. It was a street of Victorian terraces, each identical in build, with slate roofs, brown brick walls. He found the one he wanted and buzzed.

'I'll be, down in a minute,' came a woman's voice.

The woman who opened the door made Zain catch himself. She was stunning at first glance. Brown hair, hazel eyes, sharp cheek-bones. She was wearing a thin nightgown, orange, the shape of her body visible beneath.

'Detective Sergeant Harris?' she said.

'Call me Zain,' he said.

'As in Malik?'

'As in Harris, and I had the name first,' he said.

She smiled, revealing dimples in her cheeks. Zain looked away, mentally pulling himself together.

'Please come in,' she said

Millie Porter looked out onto her street, her head tilting right and left, scanning to see who had witnessed Zain's arrival.

The house was split into four flats. Hers was on the top floor. Standard wooden floors throughout. Millie asked him to remove his shoes, and left Zain in the lounge while she finished dressing. There were white and cream rugs placed on the floor, an assortment of chairs around them. Replica prints on the walls. Monet, Picasso.

A picture of a Buddha with his head turned away on one wall, three golden circles falling in a pattern on another.

Millie returned dressed in black trousers and turtleneck jumper. She'd made them flavoured tea. His was lemon and mint; hers was vanilla with cinnamon. His smelled better than it tasted.

Millie took her place in a rocking chair; Zain opted for a bean-bag. He sat cross-legged on it.

'Thank you for seeing me,' he said. 'I know you were hesitant.'

She looked into her tea, then at him. 'It's still very raw. I didn't want to rake it all up,' she said. Her accent was clipped, as though she came from a finishing school somewhere.

'I'm sorry if that happens,' said Zain. 'I wouldn't have insisted unless I thought it was important. And that you could help.'

Millie moistened her lips with her tongue, drank her tea. 'You promised none of this would re open anything. I don't want our conversation to get back to . . . certain people.'

'You have my word, on my honour as a member of Her Majesty's finest,' he said, smiling. She laughed lightly. 'The file summary was so clinical. It said you were thrown from the tenth floor, into a swimming pool. The Days said it was empty. The report didn't mention how full it was.'

'I doubt I would be alive if it had been empty.'

'The Days were embellishing, then?' said Zain. Millie shrugged. 'I interviewed Dan today, about Ruby. He denied ever having pushed you.'

Millie's eyes flared and her nostrils did, too. It was brief, her expression neutralising quickly, her temper drawn in. Is that why she was interested in Buddhism? Was she learning to tame that anger?

Zain understood. Maybe he should try meditation. Might be better than the pills. The ones that might contain alligator testicles. Why was he fixated on that concept?

'Why would Dan lie so blatantly? To the police, as well?' said Zain.

'In his head it's over, a closed case. He thinks because he didn't end up in prison, it's not real. He's damaged, detective.'

'Please: Zain.'

'Zain, he's damaged,' she said.

Zain ran the sentence over his tongue, in his head. Someone might say that about him. 'And for you? Is it real?' he said.

'I have metal splints in my legs; I fractured my ribs, my collar-bone. It will be real for years, maybe even my whole life.'

'I thought the swimming pool wasn't empty? I don't understand?'

'Falling at the speed I did, hitting the water the way I did . . . it was like hitting an ice sheet,' she said. 'Luckily, I had some sense. I managed to shield my head, turn to my side. In those seconds, hundredths of a second, even, a survival instinct kicked in.'

She held her mug to her chest, the hot tea comforting her no doubt.

'I'm sorry, that sounds horrendous,' he said. 'I don't understand – why did you drop the charges?'

Millie looked away from him, staring at the Monet replica he had noticed on arrival. It was above his head. She seemed to feel the art, looked lost for a few moments. Then she turned her eyes to his.

'It's complicated,' she said.

'These things always are. Try me.'

Millie lowered her eyes, recalling what had happened? Zain tried to lighten the atmosphere.

'How did your parents feel about it? When they saw you in that state.'

'Let's just say we aren't the closest of families. They kept me in a boarding school most of my formative years. They visited me in hospital, of course, played the role of concerned parents. But even then it felt as though I was an inconvenience.'

Zain thought about Ruby's parents. Were they playing a role?

'Surely even more reason to sue him for everything he has? If you are alone, in a sense, I mean.'

'And dredge the entire incident up in court, relive the hor-ror of my injuries and face him again? It sounds so easy, suing people.'

'I suppose it does to me. I still don't understand why you didn't.' Millie stared through him, then directly at him.

'Your honour, Zain, is it intact? This conversation won't end up on a record somewhere? Can I trust you?'

'Yes,' he said, knowing it was a lie. If anything she said could be used to help their case, of course it would be used. 'You can trust me. Anything you say, it won't come back to hurt you. I can promise you that, at least.'

She mulled over his words as she swilled tea in her mouth. He watched her swallow, imagining the liquid moving down her jumper-covered throat.

Zain arched his back, stretching his neck from side to side. The tea was beginning to taste sour, so he put his cup down gently on the wooden floor, lacing his fingers as he watched Millie.

'You probably should start at the beginning,' he said. 'What were you doing at the party in the first place?'

Chapter Twenty-three

Millie looked into the distance, pulling together her story. Zain thought the process of recollection was like inserting a DVD and watching it in your head.

'Young man, has some cash, hormones raging. Invites his friends to occupy a hotel suite. It was an executive room on the tenth floor, the sort corporations book for meetings. He had the penthouse suite booked, too – that's where the real party was, on the fifteenth floor.'

'What was happening on the tenth floor, then?'

'Food, cake. He even had jelly. They were casts – medieval – of forts and castles, but still just coloured jelly.'

'And on floor fifteen?'

'Open bar, champagne. An alphabet of drugs. A DJ. And to finish it all off . . .'

'Escorts?' said Zain.

'Escorts,' confirmed Millie.

He smiled, kept his eyes on her, didn't want her to think he was judging her, looking down on her in any way.

'There were half a dozen of us, hired for the occasion. Dan had invited his YouTube friends, some specially selected fans. And the weirdest ones were old school friends of his. You should have seen him. He was lording it over them – the school friends, I mean – really showing off. I got the feeling he invited them as a form of revenge.'

'I get that,' said Zain.

'He was manic. One minute he would be hugging them, kissing them, plying them with drinks. The next he would berate them, tell them how this was his party, they were somehow diminished because they were there. It was a strange night.'

'How did you end up back on the tenth floor?'

'I was getting a headache,' she said. 'We weren't there to sleep with anyone – I have to be clear about that. We were there just to help them enjoy themselves.'

'The headache, did something trigger it? Something you took?'

'Would I admit that to a police officer? But no. I don't do drugs. Ever.'

'The atmosphere, then? The music? That's what caused the headache?'

She nodded. 'The room on the tenth floor was empty by that time, but the doors were open to the balcony. I stood there, breathing in the air, trying to clear my head. I heard someone come into the room. It was Dan. By that point, he was wasted; he'd taken a bit of everything.'

'What did he say? When he saw you?'

'He said he'd followed me, saw me leave the main room. Said I was being paid to be up there and who did I think I was. I could tell he wasn't right, and it frightened me. My first instinct was to head back up, not argue. But he blocked my way.'

Zain saw the ire rise into her face, the same flashing anger he had seen before. This time it wasn't temporary, it stayed as Millie carried on speaking.

'He was out of it, shouting in my face, grabbing my wrists. Then he . . . he tried to kiss me. I pulled away. I know what you're thinking: I'm an escort. I still didn't want to; I was only there to play hostess. He made me retch, as in actually want to be sick. He was disgusted by it, as I was bent over, trying to heave my guts out. And he couldn't handle it, started shouting how he owned me, how I was his.'

Zain felt the words burn themselves into him. He had said the same about Ruby. She was his.

'And then?'

'I struggled with him, told him I wasn't his property. He said it again, kept saying it. I was his; I was his. *You are mine*, and he grabbed me, and was pushing me towards the balcony. I fought him off as best I could. He isn't strong, but it must have been the drugs, I don't know. And then he picked me up and threw me over. And all the way down, as I fell through the air, while I was screaming, I swear to you, I could hear the bastard laughing.'

Chapter Twenty-four

Kate drove past the *Miss Saigon* signs, past Balans. Seeing the restaurant made her hungry. She had breakfasted there at 3 a.m. once. Scrambled eggs, bacon bits, maple syrup, washed down with hot black coffee.

From Old Compton Street, the heart of Soho, she turned sharply onto Frith Street. A 'No Entry' sign barred her way. She ignored it.

The MINDNET offices were a block away from Ronnie Scott's. The glass doors and clean lines of the lower floors were topped off by listed red brick above: a building from two different centuries.

The wind picked up as she stepped out of her car, blowing hair into her face. She pulled it away, over her ear, smoothed down her suit.

Ruby Day was out there somewhere; somebody must know her location. Truth was, Kate was paddling. Her instincts were directed towards Dan, yet she was worried about ignoring the other possibilities. It felt like going through the motions, picking up everything she could, throwing it up in the air and seeing what landed.

Would MINDNET land? She was about to find out.

The receptionist had been chosen for her looks, Kate could tell. She was blonde, perfectly made-up, wearing a smart shirt that revealed her figure. Kate caught the look of slight judgement crossing the girl's face as she took in the detective's sombre ensemble.

Kate felt a burning rush through her. Even now, even from the heights she had reached, the things she had done, some chit of a girl was going to judge her for hair, make-up and clothes. Really? I have a doctorate from Brown University, she shouted in her head, and it helped her to smile and be polite.

'DCI Kate Riley. I would like to speak to your CEO, please. Jed Byrne?'

'I'm sorry, but Mr Byrne isn't available,' the receptionist said.

Kate looked at the nameplate on her desk. 'Carrie, is it? I don't think you understand. This is a formal police matter. I'm sure if you informed Mr Byrne, he would be more than happy to oblige me with some of his time. It concerns Ruby Day.'

There was a look of recognition, then excitement, on Carrie's features. 'Please, take a seat. I'll check for you,' she said.

Kate perched on an uncomfortable chair in a corner given over for waiting clients. Magazines, mainly media and trade titles, were spread like a fan over a small table. Kate checked her phone and answered a couple of emails. DS Rob Pelt with confirmation that Windsor Court only had two exits. Unless Ruby abseiled down the building. Possible, but unlikely.

Unless it was indeed all a hoax? Kate didn't understand this world, where young people posted videos online and it was an actual profession. Where was the talent? What were viewers and subscribers buying into?

Shadows formed in her mind, then fell across her face, as a woman in jeans and a smock dress held out her hand.

'I'm Siobhan Mann,' she said. 'MINDNET's head of communications. Mr Byrne isn't in the office today, but he left instructions for us to help in any way we can. Such a tragic case. We were all so shocked when we saw the video. Anything we can do to help get Ruby home safely, please just ask. I've arranged a room for us to talk in, and I've asked our head of security, Bill Anderson, to join us.'

'Thank you, Siobhan,' Kate said, following her past the security barrier that Carrie released. Kate felt the receptionist's eyes burning into her back as she headed to the elevators, and deep into the MINDNET offices. To discover what secrets they kept about Ruby Day.

Chapter Twenty-five

Bill Anderson was in his late forties, hair silver and black, eyes grey. He had a hard jaw, his square shoulders giving away his weight-lifting regime. He was dressed in a standard dark suit, sleeves too short, a tie falling above his belly button. He squeezed Kate's hand with a noticeable pressure.

They sat in a conference room, a spider phone on the oval table, a videocon screen at one end. It was a space designed for twenty people; with the three of them occupying only one corner of it, it felt like they were trespassing. A coffee machine, with real china cups instead of throwaway paper ones, stood on a small wooden cupboard.

'Can I get you anything?' said Siobhan.

'Coffee would go down well,' said Kate. 'Black, no sugar.'

'Bill?' said Siobhan.

'I'm fine,' he said, his accent Scottish, but the sort Kate could understand clearly. 'Tragic case, all this. We were all shocked this morning when we heard Ruby is missing. Any resources you need, we will provide.'

'Thank you. Yes, it is worrying, but I'm hoping I can avert a tragedy,' she said.

'Of course,' said Anderson.

'Her parents must be suffering,' said Siobhan.

'They are. I spent some time with them this morning. I'm trying to understand Ruby, and why someone might have taken her. It's why I'm here. I need to understand more about her online profile. Explore that as a possible motive.'

'It's a worry, isn't it? The internet. I know it's our business, but still. I keep my own kids off it,' said Siobhan.

Kate didn't think she looked old enough to have kids that had to worry about online predators.

'What exactly do MINDNET do?' said Kate, after Siobhan handed her a cup filled with coffee and sat down.

'We provide a global online resource,' said Siobhan. 'It sounds woolly, I know, mainly because it is. It's an ever-changing marketplace; it's impossible to define yourself. The market defines you. Needs change, we adapt.'

'And currently? What have you evolved into?'

'Our main focus is on harnessing the power of personality online, trying to channel a generation. There are hundreds if not thousands of online stars out there, with millions of followers, billions of video views. We are aiming to hone that power, and provide a quality control to it. Giving the viewers what they want, but better, and allowing the content providers to really make a living from it.'

'And Ruby? How does she fit into this power dynamic?'

'Ruby Day is one of our biggest assets; she's key to our future. She is on a plan to take her from where she is now to become one of the biggest female stars on YouTube.'

While Siobhan spoke, Anderson was watching Kate intently. He had a Bluetooth in his ear, and Kate got the distinct impression he was recording the meeting. It would explain Siobhan's scripted approach, at least.

'Interesting piece of equipment, Mr Anderson,' said Kate. 'Is it entirely necessary? Are you expecting a call?'

He didn't flinch, but made a show of pulling it out and switching it off. The room probably had some sort of in-built conference recording facility anyway.

'From what I've gathered, Ruby came to you fully formed,' Kate said. 'What exactly were you providing for her?'

'Numerous things. Video production is the most obvious service: we record her videos in a studio, and use effects on them. Nothing flashy – we want to keep the raw, one-to-one relationship in focus.

Lighting, hair and make-up, some touching up, slicker pacing to keep the content engaging and fresh. It's a feat to release a video so regularly. Imagine a fortnightly soap opera with only one character; it would take a team to make it work.'

'Ruby seems to have managed without your help. Built herself quite a substantial fan base.'

'Subscriber numbers are one thing. It's easy to subscribe; it's a mere click. People of that demographic click because they want to feel part of something. It doesn't translate into anything unless those subscribers are watching your content regularly. The more eyeballs you get on your videos, the more advertisers are willing to pay in revenue.'

'And you do what for Ruby? In terms of revenue?'

'We formalise it, produce detailed breakdowns of who is viewing her channel and we work with the advertisers to make sure they are paying a fair price and receiving the maximum return.'

'And how much of that return are MINDNET retaining?'

Siobhan didn't flinch, but instead laughed as she gave a scripted reply. 'We don't disclose our client contract terms; we are legally bound not to.'

'I think we can waive that, surely?'

'Not without a warrant and Ruby's consent.'

'Then how about we explore the idea that Ruby was dissatisfied with what's in this contract you gave her? That she wanted more revenue – because you weren't actually creating fans for her; she was bringing them to you.'

Siobhan lost the nice, robotic image. She became colder. Anderson shifted in his chair, moving forward, his hands folded in fists on the table in front of him. Kate wanted to arch an eyebrow and ask them if eyeballing was all they had between them.

'Rumours like this always abound,' said Siobhan. 'For all the success stories, there are thousands more that have tried and failed. For every Ruby, there are thousands of girls who barely even get into double figures in terms of subscribers and view counts. That hatred leads them to slander.'

'So you're denying Ruby was unhappy with MINDNET?'

'Categorically. She was one of our flagship personalities; she is also dating one of our other flagship personalities. Why would we antagonise her?'

To pay for your offices in Soho? To pay for your expensive coffee machine? Your ex-SAS security chief? Your model receptionist?

'And how far would you go, Siobhan, to ensure that Ruby gave you a return on investment? To ensure she got you and your advertisers the views? Something like this video of Ruby . . . it could go viral, right?' said Kate. 'I mean to say . . . would you do something so audacious, so mercenary, as to stage a kidnapping?'

Kate watched as Anderson and Siobhan exchanged uncomfortable looks. A long second ticked by, before they spoke again.

Chapter Twenty-six

Millie was in the bathroom. Zain suspected she was fixing herself. Her composure had been rocked. She was back in that room, Dan Grant pawing her, treating her like an object, screaming in her face, twisting her wrists, and then . . .

Zain had almost felt the impact, he'd pictured it so clearly. Like an ice sheet, Millie had said.

There was a small voice inside his head, nagging at him: *Well she's an escort, what did she think would happen?* But the louder voice, the voice that was really him, said: *No means no. Doesn't matter who you are, what you wear, where you are.*

Millie's face looked freshly washed when she came back.

'Can I get you more tea?' she said.

Zain looked at the dregs in his mug. Untouched, cold, soapy. 'No, I'm good for now,' he said.

Millie went to a cupboard, pulled out a bottle of bourbon. She filled two tumblers. 'Drink with me?' she said.

'Too early. On duty,' he said.

'More for me, then,' she said.

She sat back down in her rocking chair, gently moving it with her bare foot. A practised, deliberate movement. She sipped from her glass, stared into the distance, picked up the story from where she had left it.

'I blacked out,' she said. 'After I hit the water. People say they forget the moment of impact. I didn't, I haven't. I thought I was going to be split in half. The only thing I did – as I say, maybe it was survival instinct – I flipped. Through the pain – and I was in agony, and in tears – I managed to twist in the water, so I was face up when I passed out. If I hadn't . . .'

She sipped from her glass.

'And I swear, and you'll think I'm imagining things, hallucinating. I swear I heard his laughter still, just before I passed out. And they watched. The people in the penthouse suite, stoned out of their brains, they watched. Like I was a fireworks display to end the night. Not a single person tried to help me.'

'Somebody called for an ambulance?' said Zain.

'It was one of the other girls. One of the other escorts. I never knew which one; none of them were willing to testify or be witnesses. I understand, though; we're not exactly like characters out of *Call the Midwife*, are we?'

She laughed. It was hollow, her eyes still pained.

'What happened after that?' said Zain, determined to keep her speaking. Here was one person who wasn't enamoured by Dan, who would reveal his reality.

'I was taken to hospital. They induced a coma; I had swelling on my brain. Luckily, it subsided quickly. I was left with bruises, broken bones. You know about the splints. I'm still being treated.'

She rolled up her right trouser leg. Zain saw the scarring. It was raised, pink and red. Like someone had trailed bits of butchered meat over her skin. She flinched as her finger went down it.

'I'm tanked up on painkillers most of the time. Sometimes, though,' she said, indicating the drink, 'they just aren't enough.'

She covered her leg up and pulled up her jumper. Her stomach was flat, the size zero look. Closer to her chest there were yellow, black, purple marks. Not bruises, something more permanent.

'I'm like a mutilated piece of art,' she said. 'No buyers.'

'I'm sorry,' he said. 'I hate putting you through this again.'

'It's fine. It feels cathartic.'

She drained her glass, set it down beside her chair. She eyed the second glass, the one she had filled for him, resting on her table. 'Do me a favour, will you? Pour that down the sink for me?' she said. 'And then I need to show you something.'

Chapter Twenty-seven

Zain headed to the bathroom, emptying the bourbon into the plug-hole. He checked the cupboards, saw the prescription medicines. The creams, lotions, bandages, compresses. Millie had a pharmacy to support her. And Dan was doing what? Chilling with his friends, playing computer games?

Millie was curled up in her chair when he went back to the lounge.

'Can you get me a glass of water?' she said.

He got her a beaker and one for himself from the kitchen/diner. It was clean, the sort of space that barely got used. Millie didn't look like she ate much.

Zain sat back down on the beanbag, stretching himself.

'I can tell you work out,' she said.

'Have to, in this job.'

'You have nice eyes,' she said. 'Blue, green. They change colour. Do you know that?'

'I've spent a few years with them; I picked up on it,' he said. 'If you don't mind me asking, no offence, but why did you not pursue this? You're intelligent and articulate. You seem like a decent person.'

Millie's face coloured slightly, red flushing up her neck, her cheeks. 'How did you end up where you are?' she said. 'Nobody wakes up one day and life is already lived for them. Life is made up of thousands of tiny steps, minute decisions. Today I'm here; you're there. Tomorrow, in five years . . .'

Zain bit the inside of his cheek, winced, tasted blood. It was true. The steps he had taken, the journey through SO15 to where he was now. And before that, the day his parents met, in the unlikeliest of places. A sense of alienation growing up, a peripheral existence.

The need for belonging. He understood what Millie was saying, the journeys people took.

'The injuries, they must have stopped you working?' he said.

'Partly. I only escorted in the evenings and weekends. During the day, I worked as a translator. News articles – financial, mainly – from English into Russian and vice versa.'

'Russian?'

'My degree. It was in Russian.'

'You're fascinating,' he said, before he could stop himself.

She held his gaze; he felt desire course through him as though he had swallowed the bourbon. His stomach tightened and he heard his heart hammering inside his ribcage.

There was a moment, just a second, maybe two. He could have reached over, and she wouldn't have objected, might even have instigated it.

Then something about her, just a hint, reminded him of Ruby. Like a blunt force, he remembered why he was there, what he was doing.

'Dan has obviously had a deep affect on your life, and not in a good way. I know I keep asking, but why didn't you press charges?'

Millie circled the rim of her glass with her fingers. 'Like I said, London is expensive. When I knew what had happened . . . I was worried. For all the glamorous façade, I have bills and a mortgage to pay.'

'Dan paid you off?'

'You make it sound dirty, like blood money. It was compensation. What would I get by him going to prison? Justice? When what I really need is money to get me through this.'

'Isn't justice important to you?'

'Is it what drives you? Gets you out of bed in the morning?' She sounded scornful. 'Trust me, justice doesn't feel as good as keeping the wolf from your door does.'

'How much did he pay you?'

'Enough. This place . . . let's just say the mortgage is almost done.'

Zain whistled. The flat must have been worth at least half a million, if not more. He must check it out.

'It's nothing to Dan; he can afford it. What he can't afford is what I would have done to him.'

For a moment there was fire in her eyes.

'I thought about it. It's all I did lying in hospital, thinking how I would like to destroy him the way he had tried to destroy me. I thought about taking him for every penny he has, a public humiliation, expose him for what he really is.'

'Why didn't you?'

'Because in the coldness of reality, when the morphine haze was wearing off, what had really happened that night? I had fallen, Dan was in the room. Nobody saw him do it. They were so off their heads, they only noticed when I was screaming. And that was sheer luck; some of them were on the balcony above already.'

'You could have tried the justice system . . .'

'I started to imagine the two of us at loggerheads, exchanging bitter accusations. My private life on display. The nightmare being relived again and again. And all for what? The chance he might walk away with no consequences? Instead I chose the rational option. I took as much money as I could get out of him. And kept my silence.'

'I don't get it – how was he able to offer you so much? His parents? I mean I know vloggers earn a lot, but I'm never sure how they do from just YouTube. And I can't imagine Dan getting a shampoo to endorse.'

Millie laughed. It was part sardonic, part bitter.

'Sorry, I said I would show you. Follow me,' she said.

Chapter Twenty-eight

Kate considered how different the dynamics would be if she wasn't protected by her badge. Siobhan Mann and Bill Anderson thickened the atmosphere with blustered denial. Siobhan began her spiel again. *Ruby is an asset, MINDNET are a reputable company, the suggestion was absurd, defamatory . . .*

'You can't deny it's possible, though?' said Kate.

'DCI Riley, I am no longer comfortable with your insinuations. We have nothing to gain from wasting police time, from causing so much stress and unhappiness for Ruby's parents. We are not mercenaries; we are pioneers.'

'You should be careful what comes outta your mouth,' said Anderson, 'Detective.'

'Likewise, Mr Anderson,' said Kate.

'I think things may be getting a little heated. I can understand why. We are all under pressure – Ruby has been kidnapped, some sick bastard is holding her somewhere, doing who knows what,' said Siobhan.

'Why are you under pressure?' said Kate.

'I meant collectively. The media have already started hounding us with queries.'

'And I'm sure they found you extremely helpful,' said Kate.

'We are not so callous, detective,' said Siobhan.

'It was not an accusation,' said Kate, looking pointedly at Anderson. He bared his teeth at her, a forced grin. Aggression, and warning.

'Is there anything we can do to help?' said Siobhan.

'You monitor her online channel? Any specific or rep

'Aye, we keep a log, run all these fancy bits of software. We look after our clients,' said Anderson. 'I can provide your team with them, in case that's where your investigation is heading.'

'Thank you, that would be useful. Any threats in particular we need to be aware of?'

'Not really. Most of these are from kids. You know how it is – they get riled up in their bedrooms, have a rant, probably regret what they say in a day or two,' said Anderson.

'Anything else? Anyone with a vendetta against MINDNET? Any reason why one of your clients might be targeted?'

'We're a media company,' said Siobhan. 'Not the Mafia.'

Standing back outside in the bright autumn daylight, Soho crawling around her, Kate wasn't convinced she had been afforded the complete truth. She looked around her. She loved London in the daytime; so much was going on. Free of the rush-hour commuter crowds, she marvelled at how people existed in the times when so many were at desks or doing nine-to-five shifts.

Kate had a searing sensation in her back; it was an intuition. Pure rot, she thought. She didn't believe in invisible energy streaming through the world. She might as well believe in the god her mother worshipped, if that was the case. Still, sometimes, her gut worked. She turned her head, scanned the MINDNET offices. As her eyes scanned the building, she saw, on one of the upper floors, a movement, a shadow falling back into place. Someone had been there, she was sure. Someone had been watching her.

Chapter Twenty-nine

Jed Byrne was standing at his window, staring down at DCI Kate Riley. She seemed to sense him, turned around and looked directly up at him, although he was hidden behind the blinds.

He listened to the recording of her interview with Siobhan Mann and Bill Anderson, playing it aloud in his office.

'It's not normal,' he said. 'Why would she suspect we had any sort of involvement?'

Anderson shrugged, switching off the recording. Jed returned to his seat behind his desk. It was the expensive glass and chrome one he felt entitled to have. He had seen it at head office, had craved it.

'Just looking at all avenues,' said Anderson.

Jed looked at the man from Edinburgh, into the coldness of his eyes. 'She's hit too close to the mark,' he said. 'It makes me uncomfortable.' He tapped at his desk. 'How good are our technical team?'

'For what you pay them, I would hope they're the best.'

'I need them to do something for me. I want them to start destroying any incriminating messages sent between Ruby and us. Especially . . . well, you know which ones.'

'I've already had it done,' said Anderson. 'We have an algorithm picking up key words, and I will do a manual check on any that are left myself.'

Of course he will, Jed thought.

'And . . . are they able to delete problem messages from Ruby's accounts? Her emails, her computer?'

Anderson grinned, and Jed reflected that he would be frightening, if he weren't on his side.

'All sorted,' said Anderson.

Jed nodded. In his mind, he pictured the detective. She was too attractive to be a detective; they should be dour and dull and angst-ridden. Her voice sounded in his head, her New England accent. She was interesting; mesmerising, even.

Jed remembered a time when he had felt the same about Ruby. When he'd first seen her videos, when he'd first made a beeline for her. Interesting and mesmerising.

But look how that all turned out, he thought.

Kate was seated in Balans, having ordered coffee and an all-day breakfast, when her phone rang.

It was Ryan.

'Hey, sorry to bother you. I know you said only in emergencies during the day . . . She's not doing too good. Any chance you could maybe swing by for a bit?'

Swing by? From Soho to Highgate? She couldn't disappear off a case, not when it was so live. Especially if her office was about to be harassed by press enquiries.

'How bad is it?'

'Enough to make me disturb you,' he said.

Kate weighed up her options. It would take her a couple of hours, at least. She would have her phone with her, could leave it to Harris and the rest of her team to keep things moving forward for a bit . . .

'OK, I'm on my way,' she said.

She left money for her order, took a gulp of the coffee, and headed home.

Kate sat in her car, sending emails and text messages to her team. She diverted all calls; she didn't want to be disturbed. She felt weak, letting her personal life interfere like this. Still, she had obligations bigger than her career, ones she chose to have.

Was Ryan overreacting? He was prone to do that sometimes, but he had never called her unless it was a genuine emergency. Thankfully, they were rare, but getting more frequent. There were tough decisions Kate had to face, options she needed to explore.

She turned her key and let herself into the silence of the house. No alarm, which was odd. Ryan kept it on when they were home. She had made him. He never understood her paranoid insistence on so much security.

He came out of the kitchen, flour on his face and laundry folded in his hands. Her clothes.

'Hey, detective,' he said. 'I flipped the alarm before you came. I know, don't look at me like that, you've warned me so many times. It was only for a few minutes.'

'One issue at a time?' she said.

'Sure,' said Ryan.

He was from Ohio. A small town, not so dissimilar to her own, except a whole lot more conservative. Men like Ryan didn't do well in those sorts of towns. Like Kate, he had found himself drawn to London. A seething metropolis where you could be whoever you wanted to be.

'Where is she?' said Kate.

'In her bedroom. She threw a lamp at me.'

'Did it hit you?'

'Uh-uh. I was on the other side of the room.'

'Have you given her anything?'

'No, I left that task for you.'

'Thank you,' said Kate.

She went upstairs into her bedroom. She pulled the blond wig from her dressing table, where it sat moulded to the mannequin head. She removed her suit jacket, her claret shirt still smooth, thanks to the special synthetic fibres.

She moved quietly back onto the landing, knocked gently on the second bedroom door and turned the handle.

'It's me,' she said, loudly and clearly.

She saw the figure huddled in a corner, saw she had been crying. The lamp fragments lay forensically correct to match Ryan's story.

'Winter?' said the voice, small, weak. 'Are you home?'

'Yes, I'm home,' said Kate, closing the door behind her.

Chapter Thirty

A double bed stood in the centre of Millie's bedroom, looking almost like an altar, draped in white sheets and duvet. On a bookcase Zain spotted Tolstoy in Russian, along with a dictionary and grammar tome for the same language.

There was a desk in front of a window looking over Fifth Avenue. A laptop, MacBook Air, sat idle. Millie rolled her finger over the mouse pad, entering a password when prompted.

She called him over, and as Zain crossed the room, he brushed past the bed. Millie leaned over his shoulder and stared at the screen of her laptop. Standing so close to Millie, he could smell her layered scent.

'This is Dan's YouTube channel,' she said.

Zain watched as the screen was filled with a quest game, medieval in setting. The selected protagonist was a giant, built with square muscles, blond hair flowing in his face. His eyes were purple, a hefty sword in his hands.

Dan Grant appeared in a little box in the corner. He was filming himself, the purples and reds and blues of the game reflecting in his face.

So this is Medieval Space Bandits. The graphics are good but not great, guys, if I'm honest. And you know me, I'd never lie to you. Still, it combines the best, don't you think? Medieval warfare and alien warriors. Plus you get to choose from a series of avatars.

Dan freezes the screen and scrolls through the various avatars. The first is a bulky male, in chainmail, with a sword as his weapon of choice.

This is SyCo. He's got 130 points melee attack, and 100 melee defence. His ranged attack is crap, 43, but he has good ranged defence of 73. You can upgrade him later, increasing his defence. He's all right, but a bit bland.

The next is another male, this time thinner, with a hood. He has a bow across his back and daggers in his hand.

Like they didn't copy this from Assassin's Creed, right? Still, this is Jerome. No idea why they picked such a retard name for him, probably one of the developers' own name or something. He's, yeah you guessed it, the archery supremo. 128 points ranged attack, and 100 ranged defence. His melee is decent, he has 70 melee attack points, probably his dagger skills, and 45 melee defence.

The next is a female. She wears chainmail in a bikini fashion, and is armed with a curved sword and giant shield.

This is Tiana. But I don't like playing female avatars, so you can work out her stats for yourself. There's a hack somewhere to make her get it on with Jerome, if you know where to look. Not for me to share that though, I'm too decent, as you know.

The next avatar is also female, again scantily clad. Dan skips over her completely, with a *meh*.

So this is the one I've gone for. Balthazar. He looks like a badass, and has a top sword, don't you think? Plus he has something else. He's got secret powers. Yeah, that's right, he does wicked tricks, shoots lasers from his hands.

Balthazar is a demon, with red horns, and fire for eyes.

He has 150 melee attack, 140 ranged attack and 110 melee defence. So you're asking me, what's the downside? I won't lie to you. He has no defence against ranged. You shoot him up with an arrow, and you're looking at him with 40 ranged defence. No armour. Cos like I said, he's a bad ass.

OK, so got my avatar, time to play this. Are you with me, guys? I got your back, just like I know you have mine. Oh, and if you get bored, don't forget to click on the link appearing below, yeah I know it's some dumb advertising, but hey it keeps me online for you. And if you get really bored, click on the link to the right to my website. And don't forget to subscribe.

'So he literally talks through a game? That's the attraction?' said Zain.

'Yes, for his fan base. It's mainly young guys, trying to see if the game is worth investing in, or trying to work out where they are going wrong if they keep failing levels.'

'Or lonely young gamers wanting some company? Dan becomes their friend as they play their games. A pseudo big brother, and I don't mean Orwellian,' said Zain.

'We all get by how we can,' Millie said.

'I get this. I know how YouTube works. I can see his two million subscriber figures there. Pretty impressive. But they don't pay a charge.'

'No, he gets paid for this.'

Millie refreshed the page. It started with an annoying advert that you were allowed to skip after five seconds. Zain barely paid attention to these ads when he was watching videos.

'Each view of this, Dan gets money,' she said. 'I had a channel a few years ago, when I tried to do make-up tutorials. I wasn't very successful. It can be anything from one cent to fifty cents per view, sometimes higher. If the advert is set to play fully, meaning you can't skip it after five seconds, they pay you more. And while the actual video plays, you see all these adverts scrolling across the screen? Again, he gets paid for them.'

'Still, how does one cent, or half a dollar – what's that, thirty pence? – earn him enough to live in his flat or pay for yours?'

'Look at his view counts. I think he has hundreds of millions of them. Not all of them earn him cash, but just think how many do. He earns a lot.'

'Fuck me,' Zain said. 'So, guy makes videos, posts online, and earns millions. The yoof of today.' He stepped away from the laptop.

Millie laughed, sitting down on her desk chair. 'Seems unfair, doesn't it?' she said, looking up at Zain. 'But they had the balls to do it, put themselves out there. Got in on the rising surf. It's an endless supply. Young people around the world turn into teenagers, and some of them turn to people like Ruby and Dan. And there will always be Ruby and Dan, or someone else like them.'

'Thank you. I had an idea, but it helps seeing it,' said Zain. 'Do you know anything about MINDNET?'

'Not really, they're one of these companies that are realising the potential of online stars. Helping them somehow. Dan's agent mentioned it to me.'

'Dan has an agent?'

'Had. Karl Rourke. His agent, accountant, manager. Like a theatrical lawyer. I hate to say it, but Karl's actually a nice guy. Married, two kids, lives in the suburbs. Can't believe he used to represent trash like Dan.'

'Used to?'

'MINDNET manage him now. They do all that for him.'

'So why did Rourke get involved with you? Let me guess,' said Zain, moving back and sitting himself on the edge of Millie's bed as she turned in her office chair and looked back at him. 'Karl Rourke is the one that arranged the cash?'

'Yes. He came to see me, told me how I could destroy Dan – that actually there was a better option. He was so apologetic, and it was genuine. Said if someone did that to his daughter, he'd rip them to pieces. He understood, said I was someone's daughter. Sounds cringe, but it worked.'

'The cleaner. Comes to shovel up Dan's shit.'

'Everyone has to make a living.'

'Why didn't MIDNET get involved? Why did Dan send Karl?'

'Maybe he didn't want MINDNET knowing. Or maybe they wouldn't do what Karl did. Maybe Karl did it as a favour?'

'Do you know where I can get hold of Karl Rourke? I think I need to speak to him. You think he could be involved?'

'I don't think so. He might be willing to sort out Dan's mess – even hire people like me for his parties – but he wouldn't do something like this. He was also Ruby's agent, before MINDNET.'

'Dan and Ruby shared an agent? How romantic. How did that happen? Who signed up first?'

'I have no idea,' said Millie. 'You think Dan's done this, don't you?' she said.

'Don't you think he's capable?'

Millie considered for a moment, then nodded. 'Yes, I do,' she said. 'I've seen the evil in him. He is an absolute monster.'

Chapter Thirty-one

Ryan was poking something in a cake tin when Kate went into the kitchen.

'We need to talk,' he said.

Kate sat down at the kitchen table. She had called Harris from this exact spot during the night. It seemed like a lifetime ago.

'I don't have long. I'd better get back,' she said.

'You can't keep running from what's happening,' said Ryan. 'This is the third time in two months.'

'I know,' said Kate.

'You need to have a conversation with her. Or at least get it checked out.'

'I know,' said Kate again.

'Do you want me to book something?'

'I'll get on to it, later today. It might just be a seasonal thing.'

'The pull of the full moon?' he said, laughing. 'That New Age bullshit is my mantra, not yours. She's going to hell in a hand basket, as my dear old mother used to say. Although that might have been after she was admitted to the funny farm.'

'Don't, Ryan; don't even joke about it. It's too much today. I'll sort it, I promise.'

'OK. But if she damages my pretty face, you're paying for the cosmetic surgeon.'

He kissed Kate on the top of her head and went back to his baking.

He was right. Kate needed to face up to some truths.

Kate walked slowly back upstairs to the second bedroom, and knocked on the door again.

Too late, Kate realised she wasn't wearing her blond wig.

Kate felt part of her curl up in despair at the look of vulnerability, panic, fear she saw.

'I'm sorry, Mother,' she said. 'I didn't mean to frighten you.'

'Oh, sweetheart, you could never do that. This is all me, I know that. It will take a while for your new hair colour to register, that's all.'

Jane sat up in bed, patted the space next to her. She seemed so in control sometimes.

'I was very bad today,' she said.

'Yes. Poor Ryan.'

They both giggled, like children in on a practical joke.

'Do you remember what happened?' Kate asked.

'I'm not crazy, and I'm not losing my mind. Or my memory. God knows, I've lost enough of my brain.'

'Mom, you threw a lamp at him . . .'

'It wasn't . . . I wasn't . . . has he gone? Has he run fleeing from the Norma Desmond upstairs?'

'Mother, don't be cruel. He cares, he's just worried. So am I.'

'It kills me when you say such things,' said Jane. 'I feel like such a burden. Look at what I've done to you. Sometimes, I just feel like . . . like making it all over with.'

Kate looked up at the woman with grey hair, whose eyes were still as blue as her own. 'Don't you dare,' she said.

'It would make things easier for everyone,' said Jane.

She slumped where she was, running her hands over her face. Desperate for the tears not to fall. But they did anyway, and she silently shook. Kate reached out, laid her hand palm up on her mother's stomach. Jane clasped it, and they held hands for a while.

'If you go, I'll be left alone,' whispered Kate.

'You're so vital, so alive. You should be with a husband, with a family of your own.'

'Why did you get angry? With Ryan?' Kate said, changing the subject.

'You'll think I'm being silly. I was remembering something. A vacation we took. Remember Branson? The cabin?'

Kate laughed. It was for an anniversary. Twenty-five years of marriage for her parents. A rental cabin in the Ozark Mountain range in Missouri.

'Yes, I remember,' she said. 'What about it?'

'I just . . . it just came to me. I was looking out back, at the colours on the trees. And it just came back, all of it. I remembered it so clearly. I remembered you all so clearly . . . and I wanted to stay there, in that moment . . . and Ryan, he just pulled me away from it. And it made me angry. And then there was the lamp, broken.'

'It's OK, Mom, we'll get Dr Lyons to have a look.'

'Yes. That would be nice.'

'I have to get back. Are you going to be all right?'

'Yes, of course. I'm sorry. You shouldn't have come home. I'm a nuisance, I know.'

'No, you're not. And if you ever talk about ending things again . . .'

'We have to talk about it sometime,' said Jane.

'Not today,' said Kate.

Kate knew her mother was right. Truths had to be faced. It was not confronting them in the first place that had led them all to where they were.

Chapter Thirty-two

The air was fresh when he stepped outside. An old lady with a terrier and a shopping trolley walked by. Zain patted the dog, scratched its ears. The dog barked, but seemed harmless enough.

'Don't touch the bugger, he'll bite you,' said the woman.

Zain laughed. 'I'm a detective, don't worry, I've been bitten by worse than him. You need help?'

'No.' A terse response. 'Thank you.' More mellow.

He'd also be suspicious if he were her. Random stranger, dressed as though going for a pint, tells you he's a police officer.

In his car his phone burst into life, the theme tune from *Knight Rider*. The office.

'Harris,' he said.

'Hey, it's DS Pelt. I checked the CCTV the guard sent over. Dan Grant wasn't home from about 5 p.m. until 8 p.m.'

'So he was missing during the time Ruby disappeared?' said Zain.

'If we work on a timeline from when she left her parent's place, then yes.'

'Little fucker. Give him a call, ask him where he was.'

'That's not all,' said Rob. 'He left again about 9.30 p.m., and didn't come home until just after eleven in the morning.'

'Thanks. Get onto his network provides. He has three phones that I know of. We need to monitor who he calls or texts. Speak to the security guard. I want to know if Dan leaves his flat, and if he does, track him through CCTV, see where he goes, and if that doesn't work, get someone to tail him. Ask Brennan to get you some back-up. Don't ask Paddington Green station, though; she stole a team from them this morning.'

'Whose turn is it next?'

'Try Southwark. They already hate me today. They're also on Newington Causeway, close to where Dan lives.'

So Dan was out there somewhere when Ruby was in trouble, and he definitely had the psychosis, according to Millie.

Zain sent a text update to Riley. It was odd she had just disappeared like that. Still, he would worry about that later.

Zain typed Rourke's postcode into his satnav instead. He wanted to know what the ex-agent had to say.

The traffic was sluggish. Mid-afternoon London. Zain envied the cyclists, whipping through the cars and vans, leaning on the back of buses at traffic lights to rest. He made it through Chandos Place, and turned left into Agar Street, passing the police station. There was a private door, off to the side and rear, accessed from William IV Street. A vehicle, police patrol, was coming out of the underground car park. Zain waited for it to leave before approaching the intercom. He gave his security passcode, heard the voice at the other end groan – a typical response to anything to do with the commissioner. A few seconds delay and Zain was in, heading to an empty parking bay.

Karl Rourke's offices were off Leicester Square; the parking round there would be atrocious, even with police privileges, so Zain decided to park and walk. The desk sergeant at Charing Cross police station looked at him the way he would a turd on his shoe. Zain winked at him.

Back out on Agar Street, Zain's phone rang. He picked it up immediately.

'An update please. Where is Riley?'

A beat. Zain thought about the right thing to say. The truth seemed the best option. And the worst option.

'She's gone off radar,' he said. 'Left us to it.'

'Where to?' said the voice at the other end of the line.

'A family emergency or something. Don't know the details. There was no warning, she just took off.'

'What's your focus now?'

'The boyfriend,' said Zain.

'You're doing well,' said the voice.

Zain didn't know what that meant. And he sure as hell didn't feel well. Only, some debts he had to honour, even if it meant betraying Riley and his new team. Zain ended the call, feeling filthier as he did.

Chapter Thirty-three

You'd miss St Martin's Court unless you were aware of it. It was a narrow turning off Charing Cross Road, close to the Wyndham Theatre.

Rourke's office was in the basement below a model train shop, down some spiral stairs. The owner of the train shop looked up briefly, but barely acknowledged Zain. He was too busy polishing a green engine.

At the bottom of the spiral stairs was a glass door, no lettering. Zain knocked and pushed the door open. There was no waiting area, no secretary, just a man Zain presumed to be Rourke at his desk.

Karl Rourke confirmed his identity and beckoned Zain into his office. He was in his early forties, possibly late thirties. He had dark hair, but it was receding at the temples. His face was fake-tanned, his teeth very white. He was wearing a suit, tailored, expensive, and Zain caught the feel of a manicure when he shook his hand.

'Please sit, detective,' Rourke said.

When did people start using that term? Detective Inspector, Sergeant, Detective Sergeant. American crime shows now meant everyone called him Officer, or Detective.

'Can I get you a coffee or tea?'

'I'm OK for now,' said Zain. 'Have you seen the video of Ruby?'

'Yes. I couldn't believe it. When her parents called, I thought they were being paranoid, but they were right to worry. It was out of sync for Ruby to disappear on them, and they were spot on. Unfortunately.'

'How long was she a client of yours?'

'A while – maybe a couple of years, eighteen months. During the time she wasn't with MINDNET. They're a company that has her under contract now.'

'Yes, I am aware. My DCI has spoken to them. Dan Grant was your client as well?'

'Yes, he was. They're good kids, work hard. Lots of sharks out there, though, and to protect themselves they need an even bigger shark.' Rourke showed his teeth off.

'And MINDNET?'

Rourke lost his jovial manner. 'They're the biggest shark of all.'

'Why did they switch? From you to them I mean?'

'Money, prospects, exposure. MINDNET offered them more than I could. In the end I was like those old people hanging on in council flats. You know the building is going to be bulldozed, with you in it. So I sold them my client list, for a reasonable amount of compensation.'

'Why did you get compensated?'

'Ruby and Dan were under contract to me. MINDNET bought out the contracts. I hated doing it, but I did it for my clients. They wanted to go.'

'When was the last time you heard from Ruby?'

'Yesterday.'

'She still contacts you? But she's not your client anymore?'

'We're still in contact. Usually she asks for my opinion about work, sometimes about personal issues. Let me check.'

Rourke went through his phone.

'Yes, I messaged her at six-thirty in the evening, and I called her a few times after her parents told me she had gone missing.'

'What was the message?'

'Just about some issue with MINDNET. Ruby wanted some advice and we were trying to get together to discuss it.'

'You don't know what the issue is?'

'No, we were arranging a time to meet and talk. She wanted to deal with it face to face.'

'Are you a lawyer as well?'

'I am aware of enough law to satisfy my client's needs. I also do their accounts for them. And PR.'

'And you take how much?'

'A measly seven per cent,' said Rourke, turning his mouth down.

'Seven per cent seems low, since you do so much for them,' said Zain.

'They are in a position of power; they bring the audience. It's as simple as that. Economics.'

'Have you got any clients left? Or did MINDNET take them all?'

'They took everyone I had at the time. I've got some more since. Building my list again.'

'You didn't set Ruby up with MINDNET, then?'

'No, MINDNET approached her.'

'Before that, did Ruby come to you directly?'

'No, through her ex-boyfriend. James Fogg. He was on my books, too. He was a vlogger as well.'

'Was?'

'MINDNET didn't want him. And I didn't keep him on. James is one of those kids, they don't really have a talent. He did some goofy stuff online, made a few people laugh. His audience outgrew him. He stopped doing it, moved on.'

'To what?'

'I have no idea. We lost touch.'

'Must have been tough for him. Losing his online career, and then his girlfriend.'

'James is made of stern stuff. He's normal, already has a new girlfriend, I believe. If anything, Ruby was the one struggling to get over him.'

'The personal stuff she confided in you about?'

'Yes. She saw me as a father figure.'

Zain looked around the office. There were a couple of filing cabinets – steel, old school. A coffee table with magazines, and a comfy sofa. A door at the back led to the WC.

'You must pay a premium for this place.' said Zain. 'The MIND-NET money must have helped?'

'I pay nada,' said Rourke. 'I inherited the lease, and I rent upstairs to train man. Just pay bills.'

'How does he survive?' Zain said, referring to 'train man'.

'Don't be fooled by his dinky engines; some of them go for hundreds. He's a specialist; serious collectors and enthusiasts come to him. He does a lot of international sales. India is surprisingly obsessed with classic British trains.'

Zain feigned interest, then dropped in his key information. 'I spoke to Millie Porter today. Came directly from her flat, in fact.'

Rourke's mouth opened into a grin, but his eyes darted sideways, and Zain detected the start of perspiration on his lip.

'Do you know her?' said Zain.

'No, I don't think I do,' said Rourke.

Chapter Thirty-four

Zain asked for water, which Rourke got from the sink in the toilet. He gulped it down before speaking again.

'Lying to a police officer is a serious crime, Mr Rourke. Millie Porter claims you booked her for a party for Dan. She's an escort.'

'Not true. I haven't booked escorts for any of Dan's parties, or for any of my clients, past or present. I'm not their pimp, detective. She's lying.'

'Why would she?'

'God knows. Maybe ask her?'

'I did. I saw her. Saw the injuries, too, the ones that Dan gave her. The ones that you paid her off for.'

'Dan has never been charged with anything, so all you say is conjecture and hearsay.'

Zain liked the man's confidence, but he needed to convince his face: colour and moisture were all over it.

'I spoke to Dan this morning. He claimed you supplied him with the drugs he was high on,' Zain said, deliberately lying. 'I'm guessing he would say the same about the alphabet of drugs available at his party. The birthday party, you know? The one you didn't book any escorts for? The one Millie wasn't pushed out of the window at?'

Rourke wiped his face with his sleeve.

'Don't worry, as per your agreement, Millie won't be pressing charges. Her conversation with me was off the record. Just like this one. Come on, Karl.'

Zain picked up a photo frame on Karl's desk. A boy and girl, with a woman who looked like summer. Chestnut hair, blue eyes, a naturally straight-toothed smile.

'Are those your kids? You really want to jeopardise their happiness for Dan's habit? I'm just trying to work out who he is, and if he had anything to do with Ruby being kidnapped.'

Rourke hesitated, eyeing the picture of his children, clearly gripped in a mental struggle. Zain gave him time; he even moved his chair back, pretending to stretch his legs, to give Rourke physical space.

'We are running out of options, and time,' Zain said evenly. 'I'm not trying to cause trouble. I just want to know as much as I can about Ruby. I'm hoping some little detail will turn up, that somehow we'll make a link and find her.'

'You saw the video, you saw what state she is in. Dan is not capable of that. I'm not, either. Whoever has her, it's not someone from our world. Vlogging isn't a prelude to kidnap and torture, detective.'

'Then help me. Right now, Dan's name is screaming at me. Shut him down as a suspect, so I can focus elsewhere. You know supplying class A drugs is against the law? You must do, you have enough law to work that out, I'm sure.'

'The drugs are a lie. I'm not crazy. Like you said, I have two kids to think about. And, yes, OK, I hired Millie and a few other girls. As waitresses, not escorts. Just to serve drinks.'

Zain held his smile in check.

'Dan has a clean image. He's the boy next door, the all right guy everyone wants to hang with. He's not cool, but he's funny, genuine, a mate. That's his appeal: he's approachable and he's relatable. Millions of guys out there think they can be him.'

'And if they saw him wired and off his rocker?'

'It's a tough call. Some might think it's wild, edgy. Most wouldn't, and his fan base is teenage kids, mainly. The older ones make a show of getting wasted, but drugs . . . and escorts . . .'

'A step too far?'

'Something like that. It's not just Dan, though. It's Ruby, too. MINDNET have engineered their romance. It's not organic, or real. It's them trying to enthral their captive audience. Everyone loves a love story, right?'

'Ruby's parents seem convinced she's genuinely dating Dan.'

'How much do parents really know about their kids these days? They do date, but I don't think they're in love. I don't even think Ruby likes Dan very much. It doesn't matter, though. They make videos in which they play silly games. They make cute comments about each other. Act like a young couple in love, and their fans watch them. Millions of them watch their videos. And MIND-NET . . . well have you seen *Twilight*?'

'The vampire stuff?'

'Yes. MINDNET have a blueprint. They want to turn Dan and Ruby into the Edward and Bella of YouTube. They want people to root for them that way. The potential earnings, it's something, right?'

'Ruby went along with all of this?'

Rourke looked embarrassed now more than angry or worried. He didn't meet Zain's eyes, started scratching at a spot on his desk.

'MINDNET didn't like the existing set-up with Ruby and James. I'm not sure how, but they convinced Ruby he had been cheating on her. I don't know the details; I just caught the tail end. Ruby was heartbroken, distraught. You know what young people are like; they think their relationships are like something out of *Titanic*.'

'So Ruby is heartbroken, and MINDNET push Dan into her path? It's classic in its simplicity, but sickening in its execution. They used her?'

Rourke didn't respond. The implication was there though. Then again, was Rourke just bitter at the loss of his former clients? Is that why he was helping Dan with his escort issues? He just couldn't let go?

'And if Ruby wanted out of everything? What would Dan and MINDNET do? How far would they go?'

'You'd have to ask them.'

'And you? Must be difficult seeing someone else managing them now? Did you resent them? You gave them a start, and when MINDNET turn up, they drop you. Must have hurt.'

Rourke swallowed hard, before denying it. But he was hiding something, Zain was sure of it.

Chapter Thirty-five

Zain was feeling uneasy when he left Rourke, and also feeling sorry for Ruby. These men had orchestrated messing with her emotions, for their own gain. She was barely out of her teens. Zain tried to remember how unprepared he was for the world at her age, how sheltered a life he had led.

His phone rang as he made his way through the Covent Garden crowd.

'Harris,' he said.

'We've been trying to get hold of you,' said DS Rob Pelt.

'What's the urgency?'

Zain stopped, letting people walk round him, like water circling rocks in a stream. He was on the piazza, people having coffee and food al fresco, even in the chill.

'Check your email. Another video's been uploaded, this time to Ruby's website. And it's not good.'

Zain felt adrenalin prick his skin, run through him, as he opened up his email . . . and stared, frozen, at the horror on his screen.

Kate checked in with her mother, then with Ryan.

'I might be late,' she said.

'That's OK. Chloe will be, too,' he said.

It was a condition of employment. Ryan got to use Kate's kitchen to make dinner not only for Kate and Jane, but for his wife as well. A commodities trader in the City, Chloe's hours were more unpredictable than her own.

'She feels awful about the lamp,' said Kate.

'Me too. I'll make it up with her later. Gonna watch *Gone with the Wind*. That's torture for me; she'll know it means I forgive her.'

'Thank you. Sometimes I don't know how I'd manage without you.'

'I know when I took up this post that I agreed I didn't want to know the details. But if she's gonna start attacking me . . . we need to talk. I need to know now. You said there was a past that you didn't want to divulge. But you have to trust me. I'm here in your home, and I'm looking after her. You need to trust me, Kate. If you want me to stay, you will have to tell me what happened.'

Kate knew he was right, but she was loath to comply.

'I'm in a rush now. But I promise I will.'

Kate's phone buzzed as soon as she turned it on to receive calls. 'Riley,' she said, walking to her car.

'Boss, I hope to fuck you are sitting down,' said Zain.

'What's going on?'

'There's another video. Shit just got nasty.'

'Have you sent it to me?'

'By email,' said Zain.

Kate put her phone on loudspeaker, settling into her car seat. She opened the email, played the video.

'Oh, God,' she said, jumping as it ended. 'Get this taken down, now. I want her website offline immediately. I'm on my way to HQ.'

She was shaking as she tried to put the car in gear, her mind reeling as she headed back into London.

Ruby is on her knees. She is seen through a night-vision lens. Monochrome. Green and grey. She is no longer screaming for help. She is still. As though to move will mean death.

Her hands are tied behind her back. The camera zooms in on her face. It is streaked with dirt. Her dress is white, pure white. It is clean. She has been made to wear it. When she looks into the camera, her eyes are bright. It looks like someone has coloured them with luminous paint.

Behind her is a figure. Male, female, it's difficult to tell.

The figure wears a jumpsuit; it is dark in colour. On their head, they wear a cloth mask, tied at the neck. On the mask is drawn a smiling mouth; there is no nose, and two holes are cut for the eyes.

The figure creeps up behind Ruby. She senses it, her eyes roll to her shoulder, but she doesn't turn her head.

The figure bends down, says something to Ruby, staring straight into the camera. Ruby nods. The cloth face's mouth is smiling obscenely.

The scene cuts to dark.

The lights fade up.

Ruby is still on her knees. The cloth-faced figure stands behind her. This time it is holding a gun. Holding it to Ruby's head. Ruby's eyes are closed; she is shaking. Her mouth is now covered with tape.

A lightning flash as the gun goes off. Blood, skull, brain fly from Ruby's head. She slumps to the floor.

The scene fades. Letters appear on the screen. One by one.

Ruby Day. R.I.P.

They fade, replaced by more letters.

You're Next.

PART TWO
THE INVISIBLE DEAD

Chapter Thirty-six

There was silence in the room. Five people, and no one moved, or spoke. Kate Rilcy's team. Special Operations Executive Unit Three.

Detective Sergeant Robin Pelt. Responsible for the CSIs, CCTV, liaison with other agencies.

Detective Sergeant Stevie Brennan. In charge of Met liaison, responsible for getting boots on the ground, organising interviews, searches.

Detective Sergeant Zain Harris. Her second in command. Information and intelligence expert. Responsible for analysis, database mining, cyber expert.

Michelle Cable. IT and systems analyst. Responsible for their network, hardware, software and technical structure.

Zain was seated closest to Kate, his eyes alert. Rob next to him, red triangles in his cheeks, reflecting his mood. Stevie was seated across from them, looking away from the group.

'We failed, then,' said Rob.

They were in a meeting room, large plasma screen across one wall. Michelle was operating the tablet computer running the video of Ruby.

'You're next? What does that even mean?' said Zain.

'You saw it, didn't you?' said Stevie. 'She's fucking dead. And now he's after someone else.'

'What if she was dead all the time?' said Rob.

'She only disappeared last night; she's been gone twenty-one hours,' said Zain.

'And Sack Face could have whacked her in an hour, made his bullshit videos, and watched and laughed while we've been chasing a ghost,' said Stevie.

'There's no body. Shall we still treat this as murder, boss?' said Zain.

Kate stared at the frozen frame on screen. At the white of Ruby's dress. 'Officially, it's an investigation into a kidnapping, a missing young woman. Unofficially, yes, we treat this as homicide. Even without a body.'

'Who is he warning?' asked Stevie.

'Until we know why Ruby was killed, I don't think we can answer that,' said Kate.

'Let's just assume Dan Grant is behind this,' said Zain. 'He has a bad history and he's a possessive, sick little twat. He'd get off on this, doing this to Ruby, and then posting it where his fans could see. Threatening the ex-boyfriend.'

'I need proof, not theory,' said Kate. 'Michelle, can you get me some background on the video? I want to know if you can trace it. Make sure any channels or sites that still have a link take it down. And break down the first video; get a forensic arborist or forester to have a look. See if there's anything specific that might tie down a location. And have a look at the list MINDNET sent over. Any of those trolls make specific threats, or more importantly, any of them in the area, I want to know.'

'I have some software you can use, Michelle. It runs an algorithm on comments. Can check for users trolling under different handles, picks up on key phrases and repeated abbreviations of words. I also have one that can cross-check IP addresses with mobile phone numbers.'

Zain's words were met with a cold stare from Michelle Cable. Even in his first two weeks on the team, Zain had shown off his techie skills. Michelle was paranoid, and felt as though he might be judging her. Kate was aware of the tension but didn't have time for fragile egos; she was about to head up a murder investigation.

'Pelt, comb the Days' flat again,' said Kate. 'This time look at everything, including the communal gardens. I'll head over there with Harris and speak to the parents again, keep them out of your way for a bit.'

FLO had said the Days were a mess after the video was sent to them. Again anonymously, from the same source as before.

'Brennan, I need you to get me manpower. Question the Days' neighbours. Any cars seen around Little Venice around that time, see if Ruby got into any of them. Send Pelt any suspicious registration plates, get them tracked on CCTV. Start interviewing her friends again. Any anomalies, you bring them to my attention.'

There was a knock on the door. Lia Chan, one of the admins, opened the door nervously.

'Just thought you better know, it's hit the news and the press are going crazy. BBC just ran it on News 24, and #RubyRIP is trending on Twitter.'

Lia closed the door quickly behind her.

'Fuck's sake,' said Stevie. She ran her fingers through her short brown hair. 'We're a media circus now?'

'Let it be. It's happening away from us. Stay fixed on what I've said. I'll speak to Hope and get him to deal with them. It was only a matter of time; this was always going to happen. I would suggest our perpetrator intended this from the start. Without a ransom request, an apparent motive, I think they wanted the media involved. We can use this to our advantage, though.'

'How?' said Stevie.

'We play by the rules of whoever is behind this, and make one move ahead of them.'

'How are we going to look? No suspects, no idea where Ruby is, or exactly what's happened to her. We know as much as those guys do,' said Zain. 'I say we haul Dan Grant in. Let's just make him sweat a bit. He might be innocent, but at least we look like we're doing something.'

'Is that all you give a fuck about, Harris? Maybe you should be on YouTube instead. Fame whore,' said Stevie.

'We used to be so happy together,' muttered Rob.

'There's a direct threat at the end of that video. It's about instilling confidence in the public,' said Zain.

'Is that what you used to do before? Pretend there was a terror threat, haul a few bearded robe-wearers into jail, and then tell us we were all safe?' said Stevie.

'Why are Mummy and Daddy fighting?' said Rob.

'They haven't shagged since you came along,' said Zain.

'Some urgency, please. I don't want a second murder on my hands. Do any of you? Pelt, why aren't you in CSI overalls? Brennan, where are my bodies on the ground? Michelle?'

The three of them left, Stevie narrowing her eyes at Zain as she did.

'Don't wind her up,' said Kate.

'Who?'

'Both of them.'

'I don't know what you mean. Brennan has a stick up her rear, has done since I turned up,' he said.

'Since you turned up promoted to the role she wanted,' said Kate.

'She can speak to Hope about that. And yourself. You both hired me.'

'Just be aware; she's sensitive.'

'And what about Cable? What's her problem? I'm just trying to help her,' said Zain.

'By showing her up? How do you know she doesn't have her own software?'

'Because she doesn't. I didn't write this stuff; I just borrowed it from SO15.'

'Give Michelle a break. This isn't SO15. Get used to the pace.'

Kate didn't have to say anything else; Zain should realise the implied threat.

'Now go and make peace. I want you to spend the next half hour making calls for Brennan. Including the ones you think are beneath you. And then I want you to think of something nice to say to Michelle. Praise her skills. Even if you have to lie.'

'Yes, boss,' he said.

'And have a think; who might be next, who is the video referring to? Meanwhile, I'll go and brief Justin Hope,' she said. 'He's finally hit the headlines, I'm sure he wants to know all about it so he can have his fifteen minutes.'

Chapter Thirty-seven

The Westminster Police Crime Commissioner was having bespoke offices built at Scotland Yard for his teams. Until then, they had rented out office space in Regus House, on Bressenden Place. A skyscraper, cutting twenty floors into the London sky. From the rear side, the windows looked into Buckingham Palace's gardens.

The PCC occupied the top two floors of the building.

The uppermost floor was split in two. Exiting from the lifts, you turned left to the hub of law enforcement staff. The Special Operations Executive teams, plus a number of others under Hope's control: Transport, Security, Diplomatic Protection, Immigration, Fraud, Business. Units like hers, manned by specialists, with an opaque agenda.

Turning right out of the lifts, you came to a section for the executive offices. Justin Hope's plus those of Kate's own boss, Detective Chief Superintendent Julie Trent, along with the other DCS staff and the assistant commissioner, Mark Oakden.

Kate used her electronic fob to access the executive reception area. The doors opened up to reveal two police officers, carrying Heckler & Koch MP5SFA3 semi-automatic carbines. Behind the armed women was a receptionist with patrician features and iron-grey hair, to match the steel in her eyes.

'Deborah,' said Kate, approaching her for the second round of formal identification. 'Is he in?'

Deborah Scarr checked Kate's badge, scanned her fob card again, and pressed a button that opened up inner glass doors.

'Yes. Dreadful, isn't it? I saw it on the news,' said Deborah. She was whispering, which was pointless. The armed officers could hear every word, no matter how quiet she was.

Kate walked through the open doors, which glided shut behind her. The corridor that lay ahead of Kate had offices leading off it on both sides. She first tried Trent's door, got no reply. She would have liked some moral support.

Justin Hope's was the last door on the right. Kate knocked.

Kate felt bile rise in her throat and the heat pulse through her. It was searing, anger shooting through her brain, her heart hammering in her ribcage.

'I appreciate your concerns, commissioner, and your desire for transparency, but I have to object. I am heading up one of the most complicated cases I have been involved in. There are scant leads or information, and my team are already under tremendous stress. We are doing our best.'

'Tremendous stress? Interesting choice of words. Try dealing with the stress that comes from the home secretary calling, raising concerns from the prime minister.'

Hope steepled his fingers in front of his face, rested his chin on them, looked at her expectantly.

'Not to question those in authority, but why are they so interested in Ruby Day?' said Kate.

'She is news. It is as simple as that. And it's time for me to justify what we do, the funds they send our way. I am relying on you and your team.'

'And they will deliver; exerting pressure on them will not help. It runs the risk of compromising my investigation, sir.'

'Make sure they do deliver. All our necks are on the line with this one.'

Hope relaxed his hands, wiped them over the surface of his desk. Drawing a line under their 'discussion'.

'So how do we compare to Washington DC?' he said, his voice slimy.

Kate narrowed her eyes. She didn't mean to.

Did he know why she had to get away?

No, she must not think like that, she must not let paranoia in.

'A sprawling metropolis with government at its heart? I think our patch is similar in some ways,' Kate said instead.

It was like playing tennis. The way he started and stopped elements of the conversation.

'You must trust your team?' he said.

'They are the best at what they do. I trust them to do their jobs without being monitored as though in kindergarten,' said Kate. 'You sat in on the interviews; you know what each one brings. Did any of them strike you as incompetent?'

'How is the boy wonder getting on?' he said.

'Which one?' said Kate.

'Don't be obtuse, you know which one.'

'I have two detective sergeants that are male,' she said.

'Harris. How is he getting on?'

Why was he interested? Why him in particular?

'Hard to be objective at this stage; this is his first case with me.'

'Do you trust him?'

Shouldn't I?

'I have no reason not to,' she said.

'Any concerns, I want you to flag them up to me directly.'

Surely she should flag them up to Trent? As her immediate superior in the hierarchy? It was Trent's job to inform Hope. There was a long pause as unspoken awareness of this chain of command hung between them.

'DCS Trent has had to take a leave of absence,' Hope said. Slowly, carefully.

Kate felt her lungs fill, the air clogging them like molasses. She swallowed back a cry as the shock took a second to pass through her.

'I spoke to her earlier today, with an update on the Ruby Day case,' she said. 'She didn't mention it to me.'

'I asked her not to. Wouldn't want your attention diverted from the investigation.'

Kate felt the force of his sarcasm. She bristled, wanted to snap back. Held it in. She needed to speak to Trent, find out what had gone on.

'Is it health-related?'

'Data protection; I wouldn't like to say. There should be no effect, for now. Any duties she performed, you can rely on me for. Starting with a press conference. I want the Days primed; I expect them on the news tonight, making a plea for information. I'll get Comms to draft a statement.'

Where was Trent? Kate didn't like the sensation of not having a buffer between herself and Hope. He made her skin prick. Like a needle on a sewing machine hammering through silk. And if Trent could so easily be set aside, what chance did she have?

Chapter Thirty-eight

Justin Hope looked out of his window into the gardens of Bucking-ham Palace. It was a prestigious view; it conveyed gravitas to any of the MPs and ministers parading through his office. The mayor, and not to mention Met commissioner Sonya Varley. He loved watch-ing her taking it in and remembering that he had a huge chunk of her budget.

Not bad for the son of immigrants from St Lucia. His bus driver father and care home worker mother had instilled a self belief in him that had helped propel him to the top. And he made sure he worked twice as hard as everyone else around him. He didn't want the accusation that he got where he was because of a quota or his skin colour thrown at him. He got there through his own hard work and determination.

Yes, the view was something else. A manifestation of his suc-cess. Hope was half tempted to cancel the refurb secretly taking place at St James's, to stay put at Bressenden Place. The rumour that they were moving into Scotland Yard HQ was pure fabrica-tion. He would never allow the Met to control his access and security.

DCI Riley was an interesting choice, he thought. Trent had been keen on her, so he had acquiesced. She had too much of something he hated, though. Self-righteousness. It poured from her. In her narrowed eyes, the confidence with which she sat and spoke. Part of him was glad to see her so confused by the Ruby Day murder.

In just over a day it had gone from a missing person's case to a kidnapping, and now it was murder, verging on serial killing. A high-profile investigation, one to win him plaudits and recognition. He had heard the whispers, the sneers, the seething resentment.

Why do we need a commissioner? It was a waste of public money. For too long he hadn't been able to show them otherwise, but now he could.

Trent was thorny, was asking too many of the right questions. He felt a burning anger again at the audacity of the woman, and the sheer ignorance. He was her boss; she wasn't paid to question him. Getting rid of her was easy. He didn't owe her or anyone else an explanation.

As long as she kept quiet, and if she was as smart as her career trajectory suggested, she would. Wait it out, let him calm down. She could be back when the time was right. Now she had tasted his power, she would be less inclined to contradict him.

Trent, just like Riley. Women with integrity. The worst kind.

He poured himself a Scotch. Diluted it with water. A small celebration.

'To Ruby,' he said, toasting his reflection in the glass of his window. Ghostly against the fading light of London.

He opened his desk drawer, took out his scrambler. It was technology spooks used. Hope attached his phone to it, dialled.

'You took your time,' said the voice at the other end. 'I don't take kindly to delays, commissioner.'

'I had some housekeeping I needed to attend to,' said Hope. 'Trent is gone; I'm controlling this investigation now. I've kept to my side of this little arrangement. I hope I can assume the same of yourself?'

'I want to see how this plays out. Once the boyfriend is locked up, I will,' said the voice.

'I can't promise that. He might be innocent.'

'His innocence is irrelevant. Just get him arrested and charged.'

Hope thought of Riley, the assurance that the investigation was heading just that way. Daniel Grant was their only vaguely suspect person. Hope would push it. It would be a distraction, at least.

'I will try,' said Hope. 'I have to be careful, though. There's now a direct threat to someone else. It's a risk.'

'I don't appreciate people who let me down. You should know that by now.'

'Of course. And I hope you reward those who help you appropriately?' said Hope.

There was silence on the other end. The call had ended.

Chapter Thirty-nine

Rob Pelt could tell she would look good naked. Quite a feat since she was buttoned up in CSI white, digging through the rubbish bag in the Days' kitchen.

'Jess, is it?' he said.

She looked up, hands full of decaying vegetables, baked beans. The smell was rough. Her eyes were dark. Long lashes.

'That's not me, that rotting stench,' he said. 'Unless it's the new aftershave I'm trying. Here, have a sniff.'

He presented his neck, tapping the plastic overall covering it. Was she smiling? Hard to tell through the face cover. She started sorting through the detritus in her hands.

Rob let her be; he would pursue her later.

He looked out from the kitchen window into the courtyard of Windsor Court. His mind searched for exit points. How could you get out of this building unseen?

A detective constable came in, uniformed, part of Brennan's team of recruits. 'The caretaker's back,' he said.

'Cheers. Don't miss me too much,' said Rob, but Jess ignored him.

The caretaker, Charlie Grey, was in his early sixties, forced by recession and draining pensions to keep working. Rob had no interest in the guy's life story, but sat patiently listening, the CSI suit pulled down from his head, his face mask in his hands.

'You're responsible for the CCTV?' Rob said, when the guy was done with stories about his wife and kids. Who didn't live with him.

'Yeah, I just keep it running. It used to be on tapes, but they changed it. The building company, they got all fancy. Now I push a button, and check the light is green. Don't ask me to explain.'

Rob asked to see it instead. It was set up in what must have been a boiler room at one time, a small hall cupboard. There were two screens monitoring the two main doorways, and a green light on the control.

'Cheers,' he said. 'You know the Day family well?'

'Yeah, they've been living there for about eighteen months. Polite when I see them. Don't have much cause to, though.'

'Ever heard anything odd? Shouting, arguments?'

'No, they're good people,' said Charlie.

'All families argue,' said Rob. 'Even good ones.'

'I keep to myself, detective, until I'm needed.'

'They ever need you?'

'They had a problem in the bathroom. The waste water disposal under the tub started leaking. I fixed that.'

'Notice anything unusual?'

'No. I fixed the disposal, they made me tea, I left.'

'No strange visitors? You ever see Dan Grant, Ruby's boyfriend?'

Charlie shrugged. 'Can't say I ever did. I have a lot to do. Keeping the communal areas clean, the gardens. All the things that go wrong, get broken.'

'The Days close to any other residents?'

'Can't say I've noticed, but nobody is in this place. They say hello when they pass each other, but generally they ignore each other. You know how it is these days. Not like it used to be.'

Rob groaned inside. Charlie Grey was sounding like his dad. Rob asked him to play, on fast forward, the video for both exits for the half hour during which Ruby was meant to have left.

'How could Ruby get out without using those doors?' said Rob.

'I have no clue. Unless she didn't leave?'

Rob looked at the old man hard, looked at the live screens in front of him. People were moving in opposite directions, mainly CSIs and ground troops.

'She left,' he said.

Unless she really didn't. Something formed itself inside his mind. What if the videos had been recorded previously? What if her disappearance was a hoax? Or Ruby was made somehow to take part in their recording, and actually she disappeared in the building and was being held somewhere in Windsor Court?

'If she was,' he said to Charlie, 'holed up in here somewhere, which one of your dozens of flats would you say she would be in? Which of the residents is a nut job?'

Charlie shrugged, shook his head.

Jess was no longer in the kitchen. Zain and Kate were with the parents in the lounge. FLO was asleep in a police car out back. She said she only needed twenty minutes, a power nap.

Rob thought more about the idea he was starting to believe in. The online videos of Ruby as a double bluff.

Looking out of the kitchen window, he saw the flat opposite, one floor up. It had a direct view into the Days' flat. Rob headed over.

Chapter Forty

The woman who opened the door was a type. A woman married to a man who earned a lot, who spent time perfecting their home. She was in her early fifties, late forties, maybe. Although with moneyed women, Rob couldn't always tell.

'Sorry to bother you, I'm Detective Sergeant Robin Pelt. I'm here about Ruby Day?'

'Of course you are. It's shocking, isn't it? Something like this happening to someone in this building. Come in.'

'Thank you,' he said.

The flat was as he expected. Wooden floors, thick white carpets. She made him take his shoes off.

'I'm Vanessa Tan,' she said. 'Can I get you a drink?'

'No, I'm OK, thanks. Odd question, but do you mind if I have a look out of your windows?'

'Of course, help yourself,' said Vanessa, looking perplexed but not offended.

Rob looked out of the lounge windows. They faced Edgware Road.

'Do these open?' he said.

'Yes. They have locks on them; let me get you the key,' she said.

Rob saw pictures of Vanessa with her husband and their children. They must be out. At piano or ballet practice, whatever kids growing up in places like this did.

Vanessa unlocked the middle set of windows, which Rob pulled up. She even smelled expensive, as she stood next to him.

The drop from the window wasn't so high you would damage yourself. Maybe eight feet. You'd have to calculate your landing, and there was gravel all around the building. Using the window, Ruby could have made it out to the main road.

Rob pulled the window shut, moving aside to let Vanessa lock it.

'Your children, do they know Ruby?' he said.

'No, I don't think so. They are away at boarding school most of the time. We have a house in Guildford during the holidays. This is our London flat, for Lee's work.'

Rob tried to keep his voice neutral. Sure, it was normal to have kids in boarding school and a flat in Little Venice as your crash pad. This was some whacked normal.

'And you? Did you know her?'

Vanessa looked hesitant at first.

'I feel as though I did,' she said. 'And not in a pleasant way.'

They were standing in the Tans' kitchen. Dark wood surfaces, a dining table, chrome cooker and fridge. Not a single glass or plate was out of place.

Rob shared his flat with two other guys. He wanted to take Vanessa home, get her to organise the mess.

Through the kitchen windows you could see into Ruby's bedroom and the Days' kitchen. Jess was back in there. Other CSIs were in the bedroom. The darkened November sky made their white suits pop against the dull backdrop.

'I know her, in that I've observed her.'

Vanessa twisted her wedding ring.

'Sometimes, when I load the dishwasher or finish up in here after dinner, especially if we've had a small gathering, I look out. I'm not spying, but my eyes are drawn to the light. She occasionally doesn't drop her blinds, so she stands out brightly in the darkness. I see the back of her head, usually; mostly she's either at her computer or her dressing table. Sometimes she's on her phone, on her bed. It always reminds me of my own daughter, of my own youth. Lying on your bed, playing with your hair, talking away. Of course, back then I had to make the phone cord stretch.'

Vanessa looked to him for acknowledgement.

'Have you ever seen anything unusual?' Rob said.

'Once. Some things stay with you, don't they? I saw her with her young man. At least I think it was him.'

'Dan Grant?' Rob Googled him on his phone, brought his picture up. 'This him?'

'Yes. He was there. I was switching the dishwasher on, I think. I can barely remember. I didn't have the kitchen light on, I remember that. They couldn't see me. I saw them clearly, though. They were having a conversation. A heated one. Ruby was shaking her head, gesticulating with her hands. Her friend, he was shouting, angry.'

'You could see that from here?' he said. He looked out, tried to make out anyone's features. They all had masks on. He tried to see if Jess's eyes were visible.

'It was more the way he was acting, his body language. Ruby pushed him away at one point, and it really affected me. He grabbed her wrists. Held them by her sides, then behind her back. She struggled. He put his face into hers, so I couldn't see the expression, but Ruby turned her face away, over her shoulder. It just looked wrong. And, you will think I'm crazy, but I shouted out. I shouted out into the darkness. *Let her go,* I said. *Let her go.*'

'What happened then?'

'It was strange, but he heard me. I know he didn't, obviously, but it seemed that way. He looked up. He must have seen my silhouette, or something, but in any case he let Ruby go and left her. She sat on the bed and . . . she sobbed, her face in her hands.'

'When was this?'

Vanessa's eyes turned to the left as she recalled her dates and times. 'Just over four weeks ago, I think,' she said.

'Had you seen them fight before? Or since?'

'No, not that I recall.'

'Anything else odd?'

'No. Except . . . it's nothing, just scared me a little.'

'Scared you? What did you see?'

'Ruby, I saw her one evening, at her dressing table. The lights were all off, but she had two candles burning in front of the mirror. She was rocking back and forth. It looked as though she was praying, or chanting. For a moment, it seemed horrific.'

Rob stared back into the bedroom. You could make out the dressing-table mirror. In the dark, with candles burning, it would be clearly visible.

Jess cornered him when he went back to the Days' flat.

'I knew you couldn't resist me for long,' he said.

'Don't flatter yourself, detective,' she said. She pulled her mask down. She had a mark above her lip, a scar. It looked like she had had a cleft palate. Her eyes didn't meet his as she spoke, already determining he wouldn't want to know. Rob Pelt, with his blond hair, grey eyes, boy-band looks? He wouldn't be interested in her.

Rob hated being judged, defined, by his outer shell; it had happened all his life. Sure, he played up to it when needed, but inside, he had some depth.

'Investigating is making me thirsty,' he said. 'You sure you don't want that drink with me?'

She blushed. Was she embarrassed at the assumptions she had made about him, or was she genuinely interested?

'There's something you need to see,' she said instead.

She laid out a series of plastic wallets for him, containing bits of paper. Rob checked them all, reading the contents. Something clicked, something DS Harris had said. He said it looked as though Ruby's room had been cleaned out, tidied up, all paper removed. Rob realised he was looking at evidence proving that's exactly what had happened.

Chapter Forty-one

Laura and Mike Day had moved beyond the hysteria they must have suffered. They were in the resigned phase, the worst phase. It was like drowning in tar and realising you couldn't save yourself.

They had rehashed everything Kate had heard earlier. She couldn't believe it was only hours earlier. A week squeezed into a day. The sky was now purple-grey, the sun burnt out. The atmosphere in the lounge was heavy with the pungent mix of food, coffee, sweat and chemicals from the CSIs.

Laura was hanging on to the thread of possibility that the video was just a thing of illusion. The bits of flesh, brain tissue and blood that flew from Ruby when the gun fired ... it was all special effects. She was beginning to parrot Kate's earlier theory, that it might be a stunt.

Kate let her. If there was hope, there was lucidity.

Zain checked his phone. Whatever he read, there was no change to his expression. His blue eyes were dark, thinking.

'Dan is the one you should be questioning,' Mike said, again.

The same place, the same conviction, thought Kate. She couldn't arrest people based on personal dislike; she needed more.

'Is there a motive?' said Zain. 'I agree with you guys that he's a piece of work. Wouldn't trust him with a pet snake. But why would he do this to Ruby?'

'Because he's sick, and because Ruby was going to leave him,' said Mike.

'A break-up? It happens, but he would surely try to convince her to come back to him first? A cooling-off period?' said Zain.

Kate felt Laura move; it was sudden, jolted her.

'Not if there was no hope of that. Not if Ruby had already moved on,' Laura said.

'Moved on how?' said Kate.

'A mother picks up on these things,' said Laura. 'I can't say why, but I'm convinced of it. Ruby was getting back together with James.'

James Fogg, the suitable boy, Kate recalled.

'And you think Ruby told Dan?' said Kate.

'Yes. She must have,' said Laura.

Was this it? Was James the second name on Dan's list? She couldn't think that, make assumptions.

'Save yourselves a lot of time, detective. Dan is the only one who could do this,' said Mike.

Zain was staring at his phone. Kate arched an eyebrow when she caught his eye. He nodded, confirming he had read something of interest.

'Has anyone else been in this flat since you reported Ruby missing? Apart from us?' Zain said.

'No. No one,' said Mike.

They were standing outside the main entrance to Windsor Court. The Edgware Road traffic was loud, constant. The temperature had plummeted as evening had fallen, spits of rain flecked Kate's cheeks and hair.

She folded her arms over her chest, trying to draw her body in, get some warmth into herself. Zain was wearing a thick jacket, Rob was still in CSI overalls. The rain made slapping sounds as it hit him.

'It was in a black plastic bag, in the communal bins,' said Rob.

'What did they find?' said Kate.

'Bills, statements, doodles. It looks like every bit of paper in Ruby's room. Either she did a clear-out before she left, or someone else did,' said Rob.

'I knew it,' said Zain.

'We have two possibilities, then,' said Kate. 'Ruby left home, purposely. The end result may be the videos, but her intention might have been genuine. She might have been leaving home, possibly with someone. This was her deleting her life.'

'Or her parents did this when they reported her missing,' said Zain. 'Why the fuck would they do that?'

'People with money,' said Rob. 'They're messed up more than the rest of us.'

'I don't want them knowing about this discovery yet,' said Kate. 'Let's keep it to ourselves, in case we can use it.'

It was her standard MO to gather evidence you could use later. Criminals gave themselves up eventually, and then you could derail them and hammer down their defences with shots out of the dark.

'I've got Forensics piecing together a document I took from her wastepaper basket,' said Zain. 'It had been shredded. Someone missed it. If Ruby was clearing out her shit before she did a runner, she'd surely remember something that took effort to destroy.'

'Why am I only hearing about this now?' said Kate. Was Harris concealing evidence from her? Doing his own thing?

'There was a lot going on,' said Zain, not looking at her. 'It must be significant, though.'

'I agree,' said Rob.

One of the female CSIs walked past, distracting him. He mouthed two minutes as he held up his fingers towards her.

'You got some game, Pelt,' said Zain. 'Picking up women during a murder investigation.'

'Don't hate, Harris,' said Rob. 'Imitate.'

'Trent has gone on a leave of absence,' Kate said.

'What? Why?' said Rob.

'No idea. I've left her messages to call me, but nothing so far. Means Justin Hope is now leading on this, acting as senior investigating officer. He's hosting a press conference in a couple of hours. The Days will be with him.'

'I bet they'll love that,' said Rob.

'Keeps them busy,' said Zain. 'They're not worrying about Ruby if they're doing interviews.'

Kate's phone rang into the cold evening air between them. The display show'd it was Brennan.

'Hey,' said Kate.

'We have a problem. The boyfriend, Dan, he's in A & E.'

'Accident and emergency? Why?'

Zain and Rob looked eager, tried to get close to her to listen in. Kate turned her back to them.

'He's overdosed on something.'

Chapter Forty-two

'Little fucker, he's done this on purpose,' said Zain.

'A bit harsh, dude,' said Rob. 'Why would he overdose to avoid us?'

'Because he's hiding something. He has no alibi, I bet,' said Zain, letting out his frustration as a deep groan.

'I agree with Pelt,' said Kate. 'Seems a bit drastic to risk his life.'

She checked her watch. It was already 7 p.m.

'Pelt, finish up here, and then get some sleep. I'll get Hope to get us a warrant to search Dan's flat tomorrow, so I want you in early.'

'No worries. Even if I stay up all night,' he said, winking at Zain.

'I'll chase up Forensics, see if they can't get my document done. I'll get them to check the papers from Ruby's bedroom, too, dust for prints in case the Days are behind their dumping. And I want to mine her computer, and Dan's phone messages. Ask Brennan if she can get hold of it.'

Kate pictured Harris blustering in, working on Ruby's computers, while Michelle Cable sat rocking in the corner.

'Make sure you use Michelle,' she said.

'If she's still there,' said Zain.

'She's not a nine to five gal, not when something is kicking off,' said Rob. Kate was touched by his loyalty.

'I didn't mean to imply that she is. She's got a husband and young kids, right?' said Zain.

'Women don't have lobotomies when they get married or have children,' said Kate.

'Hey, chill, guys. Don't gang up on me,' said Zain.

Kate ignored him, aware that she needed to make a call of her own to Ryan, to see if he could stay with her mother for a bit longer.

'I'm heading to Essex,' said Kate. 'Going to speak to the ex-boyfriend, James Fogg. I want to know just how close he and Ruby were becoming, and whether Dan made any threats to either of them that he knows about.'

Kate used her hands-free as she headed into gridlocked traffic. Chloe, Ryan's other half, picked up after a couple of minutes.

'Kate, I'm heading into an online meeting between two clients. New York and Abu Dhabi. You have about ten seconds.'

Typical Chloe; she was always like this.

'I need to borrow your man,' said Kate. 'Murder case. Ruby Day. On the news. Possibly until 2 a.m., so he might have to stay the night.'

'Yes, yes, it's fine. I'll eat here, get a cab home. Doubt I'll be home before midnight, anyway.'

'I hope you appreciate him,' said Kate.

'I'm taking him to Rio for a week,' said Chloe. 'This is how I pay for it all.'

Kate felt a rush of guilt and selfishness. If Ryan disappeared to Brazil for a week with Chloe, she was stuck. She'd have to take annual leave, or hire someone from an agency. Her mother would hate that.

'Got to go,' said Chloe.

Kate called Ryan to let him know.

'Already made up the spare bed,' he said. 'It's all over the news, so I guessed what was coming next.'

'Your wife sends her love,' said Kate.

'I'm sure she does,' said Ryan. 'I'm a war widow, just like your mom.'

'Don't be so dramatic,' said Kate. 'She said she'll eat at the office.'

'OK. I'll leave you something for when you get back,' he said.

Kate marvelled at him. She felt a stab of envy at Chloe's luck, but it passed quickly. It was a familiar ache, and she had learned to deal with it.

She thought of her father, then. Another, sharper pain, one that lingered.

Kate turned up the volume in her car stereo, letting the voice of Sarah McLachlan surround her. She fixed her protective walls, let her guilt and loneliness solidify like cement. And then wondered what Ruby's ex-boyfriend would have to say.

Chapter Forty-three

The estate James Fogg lived on was typical of the commuter places built in the nineties. Yellow bricks, red pavements and small, neat gardens. There was a mixture of houses on one side, apartments on the other. With a twenty-minute journey into London Liverpool Street station from Goodmayes, it was a favourite for those who worked in the City, especially.

James lived in a house in one of the corners of the estate nearest to the train station. You could see the station from his front door, hear the announcements, the trains themselves. Not loud enough to cause a disturbance, but background noise for sure.

Inside, the house was small, with an open-plan kitchen/lounge/diner that would fit into her old bedroom back in Massachusetts. A staircase led directly from the lounge to the bedrooms upstairs. Patio doors led into a garden that was in darkness. Neighbouring houses cast yellow rectangles of light into it.

The lounge had black leather sofas, and Kate and James assumed positions on opposite sides of the room. He had made her a weak coffee; not used to making drinks, she could tell. A giant television occupied one wall; it seemed standard, these days. Kate saw it was a 3D model.

The greasy aromas of cooked meat and tomatoes hung in the air, making Kate's stomach demand food.

Kate looked James over. He was attractive, but in the same way Dan Grant was. If the camera picked up on his grey eyes, the angles in his face, his smile, he could look good on screen. He was wearing a baseball cap, turned backwards, loose jeans, his boxers on show. His waist was tiny.

'You're twenty-three now? When did you start vlogging?'

CUT TO THE BONE | 144

'I was fifteen – one of the first, really. I didn't have a clue what I was doing, none of us did. There were no blueprints, we just grabbed our cameras, started posting things. Stupid things. I used to put up videos brushing my teeth. Or filming the hair in my nostrils. And still got views.'

'You posted to YouTube?'

'Yes. It's strange, isn't it, that it's such a big part of our lives now? It didn't even exist ten years ago, and now look at it.'

Kate couldn't hide her shock. Is that how recently it had all started? She thought of her own existence back then, the transition she had been going through.

'How popular are you? How many subscribers do you have?'

James's faced darkened; his eyes became cold. 'I left it. I had half a million last year. Built them up over the years.'

'Why did you leave?' Kate didn't comment on how half a million fans, impressive at any other time, now seemed paltry compared to the figures she'd been exposed to earlier that day.

'It's complicated.'

'Does it involve Ruby at all?'

Kate knew there was an angle, from Harris's meeting with Karl Rourke. The agent had made allegations about Ruby's feelings for James, and she wanted to know what his version was.

'Why would you say that?'

'Ruby's my primary focus; she's the reason I'm here, and also why you agreed to meet me.'

'Yeah, it involved Ruby. Me and Ruby, we met online. She was a fan, sent me messages on YouTube. We got talking, started dating.'

'How long ago?'

James calculated in his head. 'We met years ago – online, I mean. Think I was seventeen, eighteen. We didn't start dating until 2010, though.'

'That's very precise.'

'We brought in the new decade together, I remember that. New Year's Eve, 2010. We were together then.'

'Describe your relationship with her.'

'It was normal; we loved each other. I was her first boyfriend. It was good. Really good. We had been mates for ages, online, sending messages to each other. When Ruby started her own vlog, I helped her out. Simple stuff like how to register and all that, how to upload videos.'

'Did she feel an obligation towards you?'

'In a way. But we were dating, it didn't matter.'

'You were already dating when she started her vlogs?'

'Yeah. She got the idea from me, I reckon. It's normal.'

'Did you meet a lot of your fans?'

'No, not really. Although I went through a phase when I did. I was a horny teenager, so yeah, I guess I did. Girls would message me, desperately in love with me. I met a few. Ruby was my first proper girlfriend, though – from online, I mean.'

'When Ruby started her own channel, how did that affect the relationship?'

'It made it better. We started posting videos together. Stupid stuff, but people loved it. Thought we were so cute together.'

'And what about Karl Rourke? When did you meet him?'

James bristled, turned his cap so it faced forward, hunkered down into the sofa. Protective body language, the sharp end of the cap facing towards Kate. A shield, a weapon, a spear ready to pierce.

'Do we have to talk about that bastard?' he said.

Chapter Forty-four

Kate checked her phone, giving James some time to compose himself. To calm the anger that had flashed through him at the mention of Rourke.

'Not a fan of Karl, then?' she said gently.

'He's a piece of shit,' said James. 'He owes me. I was the first one to sign up to him, when he was nothing. I showed him the potential of vloggers, how much we earn, how much he could earn. What we need. I was his gimmick, like that dog in the insurance ads? I would turn up to meetings, and nod and grin, get others comfortable and persuade them to sign with him.'

'Things turned sour?'

'Yeah. He got others, with more . . . whatever, you know, subscribers and shit. So he started to pay less attention to me. I didn't get him enough revenue.'

'What were you doing by then? On your vlog? Surely not nostril hairs still?'

'It was a comedy thing by then. I would play pranks on my mates, slap their faces with shaving foam, jump out at them and scare them. Then I started reviewing films, taking the piss out of them.'

'Why did you stop?'

'Lots of reasons.'

'Such as?'

'Karl sold out. His clients got bought by this company, MIND-NET. They were going to take us places, said they'd get us millions of fans, make us global.'

'Sounds like a good deal.'

'It was all bullshit. Karl didn't include me in the final deal. Said MINDNET couldn't work out how to market me, how to sell me.

They wanted Ruby and some of his other clients instead. And when he sold his list to them, Karl let me go. Said he wanted a fresh set of vloggers. It hit me pretty hard, being dropped. And I just thought, I'm nearly twenty-five, I'm getting old, I need to do something else.'

Kate fixed a smile on her face. She was looking back at forty, and he was claiming twenty-five was old?

'You blame Karl for how things turned out then?'

'Yeah, I do. Greedy fucker. He just wanted the money MIND-NET offered him, didn't give a fuck about any of his clients. And when they said I wasn't good enough, he lost interest as well. Got scared. Forget all the money I'd made for him, all the clients I'd got for him. I mean Ruby, for fuck's sake. She was only on his books because of me, and she was the one that really got him the deal. It was her they were after.'

'How did Ruby feel? About you not being included? And about Karl dropping you?'

'She was angry, had a go at MINDNET. Threatened them, said she'd walk unless they signed me. I persuaded her to stay. There was no point her leaving them. She was their star, they were going to turn her into Miley Cyrus, or some such bullshit. Karl, though, he should have had some loyalty, but he didn't. Chased the big fat corporate pound sign, didn't care what he did to me.'

'It must have been tough for Ruby, working with them. Did she stop making videos with you?'

'It was. She had so many arguments with them all. I had to calm her down, tell her not to get mad, said it wasn't worth it. We had to stop. It was in her contract, a clause she didn't read properly. They got to say what videos she could and couldn't make. It takes away the revolution, the freedom. I was glad in the end, not to be some corporate whore.'

'Ruby was, though?'

'Ruby did what she had to do. I didn't blame her. I loved her.'

'Is that what caused your relationship to suffer? Her career?'

'No. I'm not some jealous halfwit. Ruby was my world. She was separate to the arseholes she worked with.'

'You were both happy, then?'

'Yes. Very.'

'So what happened? Her parents seem to love you, so did Ruby. Why did you break up?'

'Yeah, her parents are cool, good people. Me and Ruby, we were fine, happy. It wasn't what they wanted, though. MINDNET. They wanted Ruby to have a boyfriend they chose. I wasn't good enough for them.'

'What did you do afterwards? What do you do now?'

'I use my IT skills, provide computer support. Small companies, people that can't afford to have in-house IT. I learned it all while I was vlogging. Plus I have some cash set aside from the vlogging. I do OK. I can't afford to live in central London, but I'm happy.'

His mouth smiled, the smile that must have melted teenage girls, but his eyes were moist. Kate lowered her voice, almost whispered her next question. 'So tell me, why did things go so wrong between you and Ruby?' she said.

Chapter Forty-five

James turned his cap back around, pulled his jeans up. He spread his hands on the sofa.

'I was set up,' he said. 'Ruby was told I cheated on her. Someone gave her evidence, all these emails between me and some girl. They claimed I was cheating on her for ages.'

'Were you?'

'No. It was all bullshit and made up. She never said, but I know it was MINDNET. And she just wouldn't believe me, said she had the messages. Anyone can fake emails. But she wouldn't listen. They must have been there, picking away at her, telling her I wasn't to be trusted.'

'So she ended the relationship? How did that make you feel?'

'I was devastated. She stopped all communication – no more emails, texts. Blocked me. I got depressed. I even tried to see her. Her parents let me into the flat, but she went ballistic. Started throwing things at me, screaming at her mum and dad. I ended up on pills for a bit. From my GP, not illegal stuff.'

'How did you get out of that phase?'

'Met my current girlfriend. Rachel. She was nothing to do with the vlogger world, just ordinary. Goes to uni, normal stuff. We live together now, and she pulled me out of it all. Saved me, if you like.'

'Is she home?'

'No, she's gone to meet a friend. Gave us the place to ourselves.'

'Why do you think MINDNET did that? Lied to Ruby?'

James laughed, scratching his scalp through his hat. 'It's obvious. They wanted Ruby to be with that twat, Dan. They wanted a love story they had put together, so they had to get me out of the way.'

'Sounds mercenary.'

'They are. It's all about money with those guys.'

'You don't like Dan?'

'No. He's fucking mental. The way he treated Ruby.'

'How would you know? I thought she stopped all contact with you?'

James looked caught out, unable to meet her eyes. He pulled his legs up onto the sofa under him.

'Ruby got in touch again, a few weeks ago. A couple of months, maybe. She said she'd made a mistake, that she knew now that what she'd been told was a lie. Said she loved me, wanted me back.'

James had a glow as he spoke.

'What did you do?'

'I told her about Rach, said I'd moved on. I still love her, though. When I saw the videos today, it killed me. Rach, though, she saved me. I could never walk away from her. Not even for Ruby.'

Caught between a game of Rs, thought Kate.

'How did Ruby take that?'

James looked uncomfortable.

'Look, I don't want you to think I'm making myself up to be something. I'm not like that. Ruby was determined, though, kept calling me, sending me messages. She wouldn't take no for an answer. I ended up speaking to her parents, said I was worried.'

'Why?'

'She wasn't herself. Ruby isn't some desperate girl; she wouldn't chase me like that. Not the Ruby I knew. I was worried about her, and I didn't want Rach to find out, get paranoid. Think I might be going back to Ruby.'

'What did you think was wrong with Ruby?'

'I think she was battered. Dan wrecked her confidence, made her like that.'

'Battered?'

'Not physically, but mentally. Her mother agreed, said Dan was a mind fuck. I think Ruby had no self-worth left. He made her feel like nothing. And he turned her into the desperate girl who was trying to get back with me.'

'You were worried about her mental state, then? You think she was vulnerable?'

James looked into her, through her. Kate shivered.

'Yes. I think she was. Ruby was badly bullied at school, she was always an outsider. I don't think she was thinking straight, because of Dan. I think she would have behaved in ways she normally wouldn't. If someone approached her online, or something, maybe gave her some comfort. I don't know, I think she might have become naive, because she was so unhappy.'

A stranger that used her vulnerability and lured her away into a dangerous situation. One she had no control over, and which led to her apparent death.

'When did you last see her?'

'A little while back. We met for coffee a couple of weeks ago. We messaged yesterday, though, just normal stuff. She was asking me how I was. I always kept my messages neutral, in case she read anything into them.'

'No indication she may have met someone?'

'No.'

'Do you have any idea who the message on the video referred to? The threat at the end? You're next?'

'No, sorry.'

'Do you personally feel threatened by it?' said Kate.

'Why should I?'

She didn't answer him. The message was personal. Someone reading it knew it referred to them. If James was scared, he wasn't showing it. He looked distracted, then pulled his phone out. He scrolled through his messages, handed the phone to Kate. It was a message from Ruby, sent over WhatsApp.

U kno we need 2 sort this.
I'm not giving up on u. It's not right.
I need 2 spk 2 u

'That's how I know she hadn't met anyone else. You can see, nothing had changed. She was still determined.'

It was sent at seven-fifteen the evening she disappeared.

The car was freezing when Kate got in. She turned the heating up. It was 9 p.m. Tiredness crept in, filtered behind her eyelids, into her shoulders and back. She needed to eat something. The home-cooking smells from James Fogg's house clung to her.

She was about to pull away, ready to head back to Victoria, when Stevie Brennan called.

'It's Dan. He's awake,' she said.

Chapter Forty-six

Forensics occupied a basement floor of University College London, in Bloomsbury. It was part of the UCL Hospital, used to train future specialists, and a refuge for medical professionals who wanted to spend their lives in research. Perish the thought that they would want live patients.

Dr Kavita Mehta was the forensic pathologist assigned to the PCC, although Zain had met her before in his old life. She was in her early thirties, attractive, and way too happy to be dealing with rotting bodies. Her team of scientists ranged from morgue assistants to fingerprint specialists, and even included an expert on putting together shredded documents.

'He's a PhD student,' she explained over the phone to Zain. 'Very committed, keen to impress, which is why he didn't mind doing such a painstaking job.'

'I appreciate it, anyway,' said Zain. 'Time is precious; anything that might help us catch this sick killer. Before they strike again.'

'It's difficult not being able to give you anything concrete – forensically, I mean. I don't think there will be much from Ruby's apartment. CSIs have checked for blood, but only minute traces have been found.'

'You're not worried, then?'

'If I searched your flat, or anyone's, I'd find the same traces, I'm sure. Could be nosebleeds, menstrual, paper cuts. It all adds up.'

'Any foreign DNA?'

'We're checking her bed, but the sheets are clean, so unless anything has seeped through to her mattress, I can't say. When we have the body, we can kick ourselves into gear.'

Zain didn't like to think of Ruby dead somewhere, her body being disposed of, hidden.

'You got the document with you?'

'Yes. It's a contract. I'm surprised how people think shredding something, then keeping the shreds in one place, will protect them or destroy evidence. Burning is the best way, in my opinion.'

Zain laughed. Mehta would know how to commit the perfect crime and get away with it. 'What does it say?'

'It's between Ruby Day and MINDNET. A contract for royalties.'

'Can you email it?'

'Yes, I'll get it scanned. Wanted to let you know as soon as I had it, though.'

'I appreciate it.'

'I saw your mother, by the way,' said Mehta gingerly.

Zain did a double take. His mother wasn't in town; he would know.

'She was in *Society* magazine, at an opening in Mumbai for something or another. Says she's getting married again.'

Of course. His mother, the socialite.

'I'm surprised you read such magazines, doctor,' said Zain.

'I have to escape somehow. Bollywood and gossip magazines are all I have.'

The reconstituted document came through five minutes later. Zain read it carefully, looking for the relevant sections. He did a double take, and re read key parts of it. He highlighted those.

'Greedy fuckers,' he said.

Michelle Cable grimaced as soon as she saw Zain. Bit harsh, he thought; he wasn't going to attack her.

'I got the shredded document through,' he said, sitting down in an empty chair next to her. He pulled Ruby's laptop towards him, entered the password he had hit on earlier. The golden ratio.

Michelle ignored him, busy with Ruby's desktop computer. Zain saw she was running scans on relevant search terms, checking for files that had been permanently deleted.

'They were screwing her over,' he said in a friendly tone, remembering Riley's admonition.

'How?' Michelle responded without looking at him, but curious all the same.

'They wanted seventy per cent of her royalties, anything she earned from her videos or endorsements. Proper avarice. No wonder she shredded it. If indeed she did. How far are you getting with her computer?'

'Nothing so far. There are thousands of documents, videos, pictures. I haven't started on her online profile yet, nor her emails and history. Still mining her hard drive.'

'Anything she deleted that looks suspect?'

'No hits so far, but I'm still recovering a lot of it. She's had this for eight months, so there's a lot to go through.'

Zain opened a command window on Ruby's laptop. He typed in code to get him into the back end, but it revealed very little. Her internet history was clean, deleted recently. Right before she'd left home, from what he could see.

He plugged in a USB stick, downloaded a software programme. Someone had dubbed it Grave Digger. It checked for her deleted files, pulling them out of memory spaces not yet overwritten. Lines of alphanumeric data flittered across his command window, so he let it run. The software would try and make sense of them. It wasn't always clean, read like a book full of spelling mistakes, or words the software assumed should be there.

'You want Grave? It will get through the deleted online stuff quickly.'

'No, I have my own programmes. Official programmes from NCA.' The National Crime Agency.

'Mine are official, too. Well, developed on company time, anyway. NCA only share the stuff they've beta tested.'

Michelle tapped some keys angrily, probably wishing it was his head. Zain was used to working with people who welcomed any assistance, any correction. If you let people behave in ways that weren't cutting edge, you risked lives, risked operations. He couldn't deal with egos and domains. Kate had told him to learn.

Ruby's laptop beeped. Grave had finished its job.

'Let's see what you just dug up for me, then,' he said.

Chapter Forty-seven

Ruby's erased files opened up in Notebook. Zain copied them into Word, saved them to his USB stick. Included in the list were her email account details. She had Gmail, Yahoo and Hotmail. Yahoo seemed to be the one she used most – it had the most hits – so he tried to work out the password.

He tried the golden ratio again, but it didn't work this time.

'You have any password-cracking software?' he asked Michelle.

'Yes, from the NCA. It will take a while, though, Yahoo's encryption isn't easy to break. Even for us.'

Zain nodded, looking for clues in the thousands of lines of data dumped to his screen.

'Try to reset her password, it will be easier,' said Michelle.

Zain logged into Yahoo on an official work terminal. The first prompt for password reset was 'favourite novel'. He recalled the titles on Ruby's bookshelves, scanning them in his mind. Which would be her favourite? He remembered one set in particular; she had it in paperback, hardback and a special edition. He typed in *Northern Lights*. It didn't work.

'You remember the Philip Pullman books?'

'*His Dark Materials*?' said Michelle.

He typed that in. Yahoo said it was successful, so prompted him with question two. 'Name of your favourite uncle.' He tried Karl Rourke, Mike Day.

'Is there an uncle character in those books?' he said.

'Lord Asriel,' she said.

'That's it, I'm in,' he said.

Zain scanned the emails, but they were general ones. Nothing stood out as he started combing through them.

'I better get someone to read all these,' he said.

'I'm busy,' said Michelle.

'No, one of the admins,' he said. 'Is Lia still here?'

'They leave at normal times, do normal office hours.'

'OK,' he said. He emailed the details to Chris Lewis, who managed the admin teams, and asked her to get one of them to go through Ruby's emails. He searched instead for emails from Dan or MINDNET. There weren't any.

'Can I use your cracking software? For her Hotmail?' he said.

Michelle came over, gave him a USB key. She smelt of tangerines; it was pleasant.

'It's called PITO57095,' she said. 'From when it was all done through the Police Information Technology Organisation. They haven't renamed the software yet.'

He set PITO57095 to crack Hotmail, YouTube and Facebook. Zain used the Yahoo password to change the Gmail account. Ruby had set up a password recovery email from her Gmail to her Yahoo.

Zain scanned the same empty emails. Again nothing from Dan or MINDNET.

'This doesn't make sense,' he said. 'They must have sent her something.'

Zain plugged in his USB stick again. He had tools that would allow deleted emails to surface if they hadn't been overwritten on the hard drive yet. He started the software running, but it pulled up fragmented data. Most of it was meaningless. He ran a cleansing tool, which gave him better results.

'This is more like it,' he said.

There were emails that Ruby had read on her laptop, which had opened as internet pages, which she had then deleted. Messages from Dan included.

Zain read through recent ones. His heart started racing as he did, excitement in his blood.

'Fuck me,' he said. 'I think we've got the bastard.'

Chapter Forty-eight

DS Stevie Brennan was pacing, trying to keep her blood flowing. Her nails were turning blue, her nose threatening to leak. She was wearing a three-quarter-length black jacket. Underneath, she only wore a dress, stockings and ankle boots.

She sat down on the plastic chair they had given her, rubbed her thighs to warm them, then picked up the styrofoam cup with hot tea in it. She held it against her skin, which burned under the intensity of it.

The ward was dark, patients put to bed. Dan had his own room, the door closed. Heart monitors provided a ticking clock. Nurses gave her curious stares as they passed by. She should be home, having a hot bath, catching up on a box set.

Her phone buzzed. A nurse from the nurse's station looked over at her. Stevie looked back. It was on vibrate; it didn't exactly ring and wake the whole ward up. She pressed a green button by the main door, went out into the even colder main corridor.

It was Harris. She thought about not returning his call, but put the idea aside. It wasn't his fault she had been passed over. She hadn't given him a chance, seeing in him her failure personified. He hadn't exactly set their unit ablaze, though; she was still confused why Hope and Riley had picked him as second in command on the team.

'What?' she said when he picked up.

'You still at the hospital?'

'Yes.'

'I think we may have something.'

Was he crapping her? Trying to act as though he was having a breakthrough, while she was left on guard duty? PC Plod could have sat in a chair; she didn't understand Riley insisting she stay here.

'Emails he sent to Ruby. She deleted them, but I managed to recover them from her hard drive. Some nasty shit; he's a demented fucker. And now I have him in his own words.'

Stevie felt a spasm of annoyance. Why did he have to have a breakthrough? She felt bad then, thinking of Ruby.

'You told Riley?'

'Not yet. I need you to do something. I need access to Dan's phones.'

Dan Grant was dozing in bed, propped up, topless. There was a drip, taking care of his dehydration. His skin was yellow, with areas of pale green and pure white. A bruise on the side of his face, his shoulder and arm. It was where his body had hit the floor when he collapsed in the reception of his building.

Stevie moved closer to the bed, the sour smells of illness pungent around it. The phones were lying on the cabinet to the side of the bed, where Dan's top was folded. They had been in his pockets when he was brought in.

His heart was beating at a rapid rate, she thought, checking the monitor. A hundred bpm. Shouldn't it be seventy?

Dan opened his eyes as she approached.

'Feeling better?' she said.

He stared at her, his big eyes bloodshot, grey circles around them.

'We'll need a statement if you are.'

He didn't blink. Stevie was used to oddballs. A messed-up kid wasn't going to freak her out.

'It's just a statement, not an interrogation. You won't need a lawyer.'

Dan's eyes closed and his head fell forward; he whipped it back. It was the sleep you sometimes fell into on a train, your body waking up before your head fell too far forward. He followed her with his eyes as she walked to the side of his bed.

'Is there anything I can get you in the meantime? Anyone you want me to contact? Your parents?'

The door to the room opened, the duty nurse came in. She was just as frosty to Stevie as she had been before. Smiling at Dan, she said she had to check his vitals. She deliberately came to the side where Stevie was standing, took out her digital thermometer. Stevie had coached her before she came in, told her exactly what to do.

Distracted by the nurse, Dan couldn't see Stevie. She slipped his phones into her pocket.

'I'll be back when you're done,' she said to the nurse.

'No consideration,' muttered the nurse, engendering an alliance with Dan, despite being embroiled in Stevie's plan.

Chapter Forty-nine

Stevie closed the door of the main office the nurses used for processing paperwork. A terminal sat in the middle of the leaning towers of files and paperwork. The computer was logged on, the internet switched on.

She called DS Harris.

'What do you want me to do?'

'Describe the phones to me,' he said.

She did.

'OK, he mainly uses his Android one for personal stuff. Ditch the iPhones. Is there a cable to connect the phone to the computer?'

Stevie looked around, but couldn't find anything. 'No,' she said.

'Shit. OK, we'll have to do it the hard way. Is the phone pin-protected?'

'Yes,' she said.

'Double-fuck,' Zain said.

'Does it matter?'

'Depends if he's switched on the encryption,' he said.

'Explain,' Stevie said.

'They encrypt the data on them by default now. Makes it impossible for anyone without the pin code to access. Even Google can't get to the data on the phone without the pin code.'

'Great. I get protecting privacy, but not for fucktards like Grant,' she said.

'Have you got wireless on your phone?'

'Yes,' she said.

'OK, I need you to open your wireless connection manager, and see what networks are available.'

Stevie did, a list of half a dozen appearing.

'Any of them look like they might belong to Dan's phone?'

'No. They're all generic.'

'OK, have you got Bluetooth switched on?'

'No, it's not secure,' she said. 'Michelle forbids us from using it on work phones.'

She heard the accusation in her tone, the defence of her friend. She had to stop being so prickly; it couldn't be easy being the new guy.

'Switch it on, and see if you pick up Dan's phone,' said Zain.

Stevie changed her settings, and immediately Dan's phone appeared as a connection she could make using her Bluetooth.

'He's called himself Wolf,' she said. 'WolfDan and WolfDaniP.'

'Ace. OK, can you connect to his Bluetooth for me? The WolfDan link. I'm guessing the IP is one of his iPhones. I'm emailing you something to your phone, and I want you to run it. It will force his phone to connect to yours,' said Zain.

Stevie did as she was instructed, once Zain's email had come through, and sure enough she had her Bluetooth request accepted by Dan's phone.

'I'm sending a second lot of software. I want you to transfer it to his phone,' said Zain.

Stevie did this. Dan's phone came to life, and she saw his password prompt disappear, allowing her full access.

'You've impressed me,' she said, monotone.

'OK, now open up an internet connection on his phone. Is it 4G?'

'Yes,' she said.

'Log in to the IP address I'm sending you,' he said.

She was focused, following what he said. She typed the address into a browser on Dan's phone. There was a commotion outside, shouting.

'I think he's realised I've got his stuff. We don't have long,' she said.

'No worries, shouldn't take long,' Zain said. 'Just downloading from his phone now.'

It took another five minutes, by which time the nurse was in the room, shaking her head. They were going to claim the nurses had taken Dan's phones when he had been admitted. If he claimed they were by his bedside, they would say he was delusional because of the drugs.

'OK, done,' said Zain.

Stevie disconnected the internet from Dan's phone, and switched off the Bluetooth.

'Thank you for your help,' she said to the nurse, handing the phones over.

Chapter Fifty

Zain watched as the data downloaded to his screen. Text messages, thousands of them, sent and received by Dan Grant. Zain had managed to access those that Dan had deleted from his handset, but which had been backed up by his provider to the cloud.

He couldn't access the data files or photos on the phone; the pin code protected them. He needed the phone physically to get to those.

As the text messages opened up, he glanced at Michelle. She was sitting with arms tight across her body.

'What?' he said.

'I get that you have to lead on cyber protocols; I understand you are a cyber crime expert. Downloading from phones, technical support, though. That's my role.'

Zain opened his mouth, but nothing except air came out.

'I think I'm done for the day,' Michelle said.

She shut down her computers, grabbed her coat, and was gone.

'I'm sorry, I didn't think,' he said, as she walked past him. It sounded feeble even to him. 'Shit, fuck, damn,' he said.

'Everything OK, Zain?'

Zain turned to see Deborah Scarr walking into the room.

'Sorry,' he said.

'Genuine question. I just saw Michelle Cable storm out of here.'

'Thinks I'm stepping on her toes,' said Zain.

'And are you?' Deborah said, with knowing overtones.

Zain thought for a moment. Should he be candid with Hope's right-hand woman? She had inducted him on his first day, shown him around. She had seemed genuine. Then again, would she repeat everything he said to Hope? Fuck it, he decided, he needed to vent.

'Probably. Yes. It wasn't intentional. She should be happy, any-way. I was getting stuff done so she doesn't have to do it.'

'Remember she has been doing this job for four months, in this unit. And she has been working for a decade in law enforcement. It is probably difficult for her.'

'Don't take her side. I'm the new guy being ostracised,' he said, smiling.

'Being facetious won't help,' she said, putting an envelope down on his desk.

'You sound like Riley,' he mumbled.

'The warrants you needed to access the phones and computers . . .'

Zain grinned at her. She raised her eyebrows in response.

'Just pretend you had them before you did whatever it is you did. And brittle toffee with cashew nuts. Fortnum and Mason. Expensive, I know, but Michelle melts when she has them in her mouth. Just a tip.'

Deborah patted him on the shoulder, then squeezed it.

Zain did an online search, found the toffee she was referring to. It cost the same as an expensive bunch of flowers, but if it would ease the tension with Michelle, then it was worth it.

His laptop told him it had reached the end of its download and search. Zain filtered for Ruby's texts, and Dan's replies to her.

'You can hide, but you can't be invisible,' he said into the empty office.

No one was there to see his results, his handiwork. He didn't feel a sense of triumph, though, just emptiness. A pocket of darkness enveloped him, and he felt himself fall through a series of ten floors. He ran to the bathroom, emptying his guts out into the sink.

He was shaking, and feeling anxious as he looked at his face in the mirror.

He checked his pockets, but he didn't have any of the little green pills on him.

Chapter Fifty-one

The house was loud in its silence. The rafters stretching their muscles. Central heating gushing through radiators.

Kate reset the alarm, left her shoes in the lobby. She walked up the stairs in darkness. Gently opened the door to her mother's room. Loud breathing, but confident, assured. No nightmares tonight. She hoped.

Kate went into her own bedroom. She stripped off her clothes, switching on the en suite light, walking on the cold tiled floor. She peeled off her bra and underwear, dropped it into the laundry basket.

The water was hot. She stood under it for five minutes, letting it scald her. Washing away the grime of the day, the tiredness. Kate massaged soap into her skin, her scalp. She dried herself, brushed her teeth.

Kate climbed into the bed, her body still damp, her hair still wet.

Ryan was awake. She reached out for him, his skin warm, smooth. He let her pull him closer, let her feel her way in the dark. Kate found his mouth, salty from sleep, his tongue hard as it sought her own.

He kissed her neck as she grabbed at his T-shirt, pulling it over his head. It got stuck and they laughed as he struggled. She tasted him, her mouth on his chest, following the line of hair down his stomach. He pulled her back up and they locked mouths as his fingers found their way inside her.

Kate gasped as he pushed her onto her back. He moved his hands back between her legs, his tongue in her mouth, his feet rough against her legs.

She pulled his lips down to her breasts, let him explore, felt soft hammer blows through her body, explosions she craved.

He whispered into her ears, phrases her mother would term blasphemous. She undid the string on his shorts, and, naked, he covered her, then was inside her.

They sunk into the mattress, covered by the duvet, trying not to cry out.

She thought of Chloe then. The wife. The other woman. Something borrowed. A husband borrowed, to dull her desires.

And sadness filled her, as Ryan did. Lonely in the arms of another woman's husband, in a bed where her ghosts made love to her as much as any man of flesh.

Ryan fell into a deep sleep soon after, having shifted to the guest bedroom. For appearances' sake.

Kate sat downstairs with hot cocoa, her laptop switched on. Darkness beyond the kitchen window. Shadows moving in the corners of her eyes. The wind picked up, the rain tapping on the glass. Don't look; don't let it disturb you.

She called Stevie Brennan.

'The duty nurse, Becky Molloy, she's been great,' said Brennan. 'But Dr Kureshi, the consultant ... guy's a dick. Won't let us near Dan. I said to him, what you going to do, call the police? He didn't see the funny side. Said Dan's too fragile. If we want to question him, we come back in the morning.'

'So we will,' Kate said. 'Go home, get some sleep. I need his flat searched first thing.'

'How? We're not charging him yet?'

'Yes, we are.'

Harris had found incriminating messages and emails on Dan's phone, saved to his cloud, or something. There were gaps, but on particular days Dan had sent enough vile words for them to start building a case against him.

Kate scanned them now.

If I can't have you, no one else can. You think you're going to be OK without me?

You will regret leaving me.

I'll fucking hurt you, make you feel the pain you're giving me.

I never loved you, this was all a game, you know it was. Are you that stupid? Ugly and stupid. Girls like you don't deserve to live.

You might as well kill yourself. Before someone does it for you. Useless cunt.

Was it enough? It might just be anger, high emotion, a spoilt brat losing his toys? Could she use these messages as a foundation, create a noose from the sentences swimming before her eyes?

Dan had also cut and pasted cases from the internet, serial killer court cases. Detailed forensic minutiae on how women had been stalked and kidnapped, then, layer by layer, had their skin, hair, dignity taken from them.

No messages accompanied the extracts. No explanation. Just random poems of hatred, sent to Ruby via email.

Kate closed her eyes, imagined Ruby, in her bedroom, reading these. What must she have felt? Was she trapped, unsure, caught between letting Dan rant and just ignoring him, and reporting him? Had she told anyone? She must have been terrified, as the man she loved turned.

It happened to women all the time. Every day. Kate knew. She had been there, seen it happen.

Little girls growing up thinking of heroes, knights, men who would make them the centre of their universe and love them. So they let them do it, let them in. Only to find the doors locked, and the monster was in the bedroom, not the basement.

Other messages about James. Saying Dan would like to stick a hot poker into him, then watch his flesh melt and fall off his bones.

The darkness, it angered her. Men thinking they could control women, scare them. Angrier still at women so beaten down, so insecure, they didn't fight back. Until it was too late.

Kate had been too late.

For Ruby, and for herself.

She shut the laptop, finished the cocoa. A movement outside. She looked up, through the glass. She thought it was *him*, staring back at her. She dropped her cup, stepped into the shattered pieces, her feet pinching on sharp ceramic edges and points.

It was nothing. Not *him*. How could it be? Only her own reflection. She switched the light off, looked out into the garden, tried to make sense of what she was seeing.

It was late, nearly 2 a.m. She was due at the hospital at ten. She messaged Harris, told him to meet her there.

Kate looked again out of the kitchen window, just to make sure. She was being absurd. She left the cup where it was, her skin goosed, her heart beating. She was unsettled, and felt as though she wasn't alone in the room. She went quickly to her bed, trying to find sleep under her heavy bed covers.

Chapter Fifty-two

Zain read the text from Riley as it came through. Didn't the woman ever sleep?

He was calmer now, another pill dulling his instincts and paranoia.

Two in one day; he hadn't been there for a while. It had been a full-on day, though, maybe a trigger day. He still couldn't work out why he had fallen so quickly. It was the old anxiety, the sense of purpose lost, a useless existence. What was he?

Underlying it all was the remembered pain. Not just a memory. It was tangible, visible. He lifted his right foot into the air. It cast a shadow on the wall behind him. Zain stared at the hardened flesh where his toenails should have been.

He turned onto his side, trying to relax. He needed to. He would have another busy day tomorrow; he couldn't be tired. The pills only achieved so much. If he stared at his bedroom wall long enough, he would fall into sleep. It was always temporary, fitful, but it happened. And was enough to rest his body. His mind. His nightmares.

He checked his phone again. Again that sense of betrayal. Riley was a good person. All the team were.

So why do this? Why disappoint himself so easily? Because he had no choice.

No, that was crap. Everyone had a choice, always. He had decided to be part of this, because he wanted what was on offer. It was self-preservation. And was what he was doing so bad?

Zain thought he had a gut instinct for right and wrong. That was before his time with the shadow world of SO15. Dealing with spooks and undercover operations, when all the players were bathed in grey light. You started to blur the lines between right and wrong, it became about something else.

Was he letting that experience cloud his judgement now?

He imagined what Riley would say if she knew.

In his dreams it was her. Pulling the nails from his feet. One by one. Hearing him scream, and laughing as he did.

Chapter Fifty-three

Rob Pelt wore plastic boots over his shoes, his fingers sweating inside latex gloves. The flat was being checked, square metre by square metre, being marked off on a shared file drive. He held an iPad in one hand, watching entries appear as the CSIs made their discoveries.

He was in Dan's bedroom, with its views across to Canary Wharf. The sky was blue, clear. The warmth from the storage heater made it feel like a summer's day. His jeans and V-neck jumper clung to him, making him uncomfortable.

Boxes were piled up on one side of the room. The contents were mundane. Roller skates, school notebooks – Rob had laughed at that, at the idea of Dan being still young enough to be proud of achievements at school. CDs, DVDs. All empty cases, the discs kept in plastic index folios. Weights, 10 kg the heaviest, with spiral bars and locks to keep them in place.

A row of trainers, shoes, Converse, lined up in a straight line against one wall. A cloud of foot funk suspended over them. The flat smelled of boys. Sweat, food, rubbish bags not emptied. He wondered if his own flat gave off the same stench.

He felt a twinge of envy at the idea of being as young as Dan, having a flash pad in the centre of London. Money at an age when you could have some serious fun with it.

At Dan's age, Rob had been holding down shifts at McDonald's and Gap, while trying to study chemistry at Birmingham. After that he had been fast-tracked in the police, and nearly a decade into his career, here he was, detective sergeant for SOE3, working for the PCC himself. Not bad for a boy from Manchester, born below the poverty line.

Dan's bed was against the wall under the windows. The mattress still in the manufacturer's plastic.

'Lazy git,' said Rob to one of the CSIs. 'He couldn't even be bothered to tuck the bed sheets in.'

They were spread over the plastic, a duvet rolled up in one corner. Pillows on the floor.

'How could he sleep with all that going on?' he said.

The CSI ignored him, checking and tapping away. Another called him over, indicating Dan's dresser drawers.

Rob looked in, whistled. 'And we have a winner,' he said. 'Freaky little perv.'

The CSI put his hands in, pulling the contents out, individually. Rob held them up to the light coming in through the window, turning them around. He put one closer to his nose, taking in the faint smell of perfume and body odour.

'They've been worn?' Rob asked him.

The faceless man nodded behind his mask.

'Bag them,' said Rob.

'There are fifty-six pairs in all,' said the CSI when he'd finished.

'Either Dan's got a fetish,' said Rob, 'or he's been collecting trophies. My bet's on him getting his fans to send them in. Like Tom Jones, only by post. I hope.'

Rob sent a message to Riley, telling her what he'd found.

Chapter Fifty-four

Kate met Zain in the hospital cafeteria, where he sat drinking a rare coffee. That was her addiction; normally, her second in command didn't touch the stuff.

'You look tired, Harris,' she said.

His skin looked washed-out, pale. His eyes were lined with ribbons of red, smudges under the lids.

'I feel wrecked. You, on the other hand, look like you just came back from a mini-break.'

Kate was feeling relaxed. Ryan did that to her. For her. She had weighed up the moral arguments long ago, decided she was a better functioning individual this way. A better daughter, a better police officer. She wasn't trying to take Ryan from Chloe; neither of them wanted a shared life.

'Where's Brennan? Thought she'd be dragging Dan in. Like a cat with a dead bird. Or rat,' said Zain.

'She's interviewing.'

'Still? She must have interviewed half of London by now. She going to start on the two million psychos stalking Ruby?'

'No, she's interviewing, as in applicants. Hope signed off an expansion of staffing, so we're getting a set of detective constables.'

'How? Is someone shitting diamonds and giving them to him?'

'There have been some acrimonious allegations and confrontations. About us using Met resources. So Hope applied for budget a couple of months ago, and the home secretary signed it off.'

'Nice,' said Zain.

It was murky, not nice. She didn't like opaque management; she wanted the sort of transparency Julie Trent gave her. She had managed to grab her DCS that morning. Trent claimed she was suffering from sciatica, and had been signed off work by her GP.

'I know it's tough, just play along. Do what you have to, and focus on the case. Promise me you won't care about the politics?' Trent had said.

Kate never lied, so hadn't responded to that. Instead, she'd said, 'I'm going to ask you again. You might not be able to say now, but I'll come and see you soon.'

She wanted that conversation with her boss, to find out what had gone on between her and Hope, and why her boss had really ended up at home with a fake illness. Not once in four months had Trent mentioned issues with her back. Sciatica didn't just happen, Kate was sure of it.

'Shall we head up?' she said.

'You want a coffee first? I don't think I can handle Dan Grant without being pumped full of something.'

'No, I had some before I left home.'

Zain followed her out of the cafeteria with his coffee, its aroma then filling the lift as the doors closed. He looked her over from where he stood in one corner; she felt his eyes trailing over her. The heels, the legs in sheer tights, the maroon dress falling to above her knees. She had her jacket hanging over her wrist, her arms bare in the sleeveless outfit. The shape of her body on display.

She turned her face and Zain was caught out in his appraisal. Kate saw his eyes on her calf muscles. He looked up at her. Unembarrassed. His mouth twisted into a half smile. She was conscious of his judgement of her body. She hadn't been to her mixed martial arts or Pilates for a couple of months now. She would have to go back to classes, as soon as she got a break.

Kate gave Zain a direct stare, putting her jacket on and shaking her hair out over the back. As the lift doors opened, she walked two paces in front of him, her shoes clacking on the hard floor of the hospital.

Jerk, she thought.

Dan was sitting up in bed, wrapped in a blue dressing gown.

'You have to wait,' he said to them.

'Why? So your doctor can save you again?' said Zain. He pulled up a chair, leaning back into it, then put his feet up on Dan's bed.

Kate stood at the foot of the bed, looking through Dan's vitals on a clipboard. The room smelled like the ward outside. Old food and decay, with an overriding hint of bleach and alcohol.

'What's the hold-up?' said Zain.

'I'm not speaking to you without my brief,' said Dan.

Zain rubbed his eyes, slurping his coffee.

Swallowing his irritation, Kate thought. 'You are, of course, entitled to have legal representation, now that you are in our custody,' she said.

'Oh, yeah, silly me, I forgot,' said Zain. 'So where is this lowlife?'

Dan looked to Kate; he was afraid, shifting his body subtly away from Zain. She had seen him do the same back at his flat, when they had first met him.

Dan looked younger than she knew he was; his widened eyes looked infantile. Her instinct was to reach out to him, comfort him, save him from boorish Harris. Until she remembered the texts, the emails, the stories of dismemberment, the collected underwear.

'What you got on under that dressing gown?' said Zain.

Dan didn't look at him, pulled it tighter, bent his legs under the blanket, pulled them close to his chest.

'How long do we have to wait?' said Kate.

'He said he'd be here for ten.'

There was a knock on the door. Dan's legal representative came in. He was dressed in a tailored suit, had a fake tan and very square white teeth. He held out a hand to Kate.

'Sorry I'm late,' he said.

'Fuck me,' said Zain.

'Nice to see you again, too, Detective Harris.'

Zain didn't hide his feelings as Karl Rourke took a seat at Dan's bedside.

Chapter Fifty-five

Michelle Cable looked at the box on her desk, read the note again.

'Sorry. Z. xx.'

How did he manage it? He must have picked it up as soon as the store opened, dropped it off, then headed to the hospital to meet Riley. That took effort, sincerity. She sighed, unsure now of her own emotions.

She had spent the night unloading to her husband. She had gone home to find her children asleep, and she had felt something inside her tear apart. She hadn't seen them since breakfast, wouldn't speak to them until the morning now. She had lost twenty-four hours of their lives.

Somehow she made that Harris's fault. She should have left early, on time. Even when there was a case, she did that. Riley understood; they all did. She often logged on from home, after the kids were asleep, once Aiden was vegging in front of the TV or playing a computer game.

Only last night she had stayed in the office, because *he*, Harris, had made her feel inadequate. Because *he* made her feel as though leaving on time would be some measure of failure.

A night of complaining had followed – of advice, of imagining what she would say, how she would prove her worth. She had come into work armoured, shielded, armed. Only to find he had sued for peace already.

The tension bottled up inside escaped through her sighs.

She opened the box. She knew she should wait, share it, keep it for a special occasion. But having a shit day at work, getting stressed by office politics, and then coming out the other end, well, that was an occasion, wasn't it?

Michelle chewed on the toffee, letting it fill corners of her mouth, under her tongue, savouring its feel against her palate, before finally swallowing.

Harris was still the enemy. But she decided to sheath her swords. For now.

She went to work instead, looking through Dan's hard drives. They had been dropped off by Forensics earlier, under Rob Pelt's instructions. She marvelled at how it had become the norm to have multiple hard drives. Made it twice as complicated to get results.

Although Harris probably had some software that did it in a nanosecond.

She put another piece of toffee into her mouth. It was like Pavlov's dog, she thought. Eventually, she would think of Harris, and her mouth would taste toffee. Not yet, though.

An hour later, Michelle was on the phone to Pelt, who was still at Dan's flat.

'Nice one,' he said when she told him.

'Can you have a look, see if you can find the paperwork?'

'Do we need it?' he said.

'You know Riley; she'll ask. I've only found references to it, not the exact location.'

'I'll try one of these boxes; it must be here amongst this junk. How did you find out?'

'The good old-fashioned way. I checked his Facebook, Twitter, some of his YouTube videos and files on his computer.'

'Who needs spooky stuff, right?'

'Call me when you find it,' she said.

Michelle flexed her fingers, cracked her knuckles, then started looking again. There was a faint hope, just a glimmer, but she might just be on her way to finding where Ruby was.

Chapter Fifty-six

Zain set up the digital camera to record, tilting it until he had the perfect angle. Karl Rourke sat by Dan. He had a tablet in his hands.

'The new Surface,' said Zain. 'Expensive bit of kit. How does it run?'

'Fine,' said Rourke.

'So how come you're here, anyway? I thought he wasn't your client anymore?' said Zain.

'Later,' Kate said, interrupting them.

She took a seat on the opposite side of the table to Rourke, with Zain next to her.

They were in an interview room at Southwark police station, on Borough High Street. Zain had been reluctant to use them, said they were already complaining about the resources she had pulled from them.

'They get paid for anything they do for us,' she had reminded him. 'And we get priority. For the moment.'

Dan was now dressed in jeans and a T-shirt of thin material. She could see the outlines of his ribs through it. He had asked for a wheelchair to transport him from his hospital room, and was limping when he walked. She didn't know if he was exaggerating, trying to garner sympathy, or if he was still suffering from the aftereffects of his overdose.

It all seemed suspicious to her. He had collapsed in the reception area of his building, where he would be seen and helped. Why not alone in his flat?

'I was home all night. I was having a party, with my friends,' Dan was insisting.

'No you weren't,' said Kate. 'CCTV showed you left your building at 5 p.m., and didn't return until around 8 p.m. on the day Ruby disappeared. You left again at 9.30 p.m., and didn't come back until just before 11 a.m. the morning after she disappeared.'

'CCTV is lying. I was home.'

'The security guards also confirmed what we saw on camera,' she said.

'Those illegal immigrants? Did you threaten them with deportation or something?'

'Are you accusing us of corruption?' she said.

'Yes. I saw the hacking trial. You're all at it, getting backhanders. I should've done that.'

'Are you offering to bribe a police officer?' she said.

'Go on, then, pretty boy, bribe me. See what happens,' said Zain.

Dan looked at Rourke, who was making notes with a digi-pen on his tablet. He seemed bored. Dan turned back to them, but avoided looking at Zain.

'Can you name these friends you were with?' Kate asked.

'I was with him, with Karl. Tell them, I was with you.'

Rourke was obviously startled at the sound of his name, taking a few seconds to rewind what Dan had said. He smiled apologetically. Shook his head.

'Your lawyer can't be your alibi, you dumb fuck,' said Zain.

'Is that an official term, DS Harris?' said Rourke.

'Well, speak to your client. Are you his alibi?' said Zain.

'No. Dan, tell them where you were,' said Rourke.

Dan pretended he didn't understand, his eyes widening, then narrowing again.

'I wasn't with Ruby, that's all they need to know. No comment,' he said.

'What?' she said.

'No comment. To everything,' said Dan.

Great, thought Kate. He definitely had something still in his system. And junkies on 'no comment' highs were her favourite.

'Fine, let's just put you in a prison cell. With someone who likes pretty boys,' said Zain, sneering at him.

'You don't fucking scare me,' muttered Dan. 'This is fucking bullying and harassment.'

'Are you using abusive language to a police officer?' Zain said.

'No comment,' Dan said, looking at Kate.

'He didn't mean to swear, or accuse you of bullying. He is under obvious duress, fresh from a hospital bed. Might still have morphine in his blood,' said Rourke.

'You mean class A drugs. That's a criminal offence right there. Who's your dealer?' Zain was doing nothing to conceal his loathing, Kate observed. She didn't believe in playing good cop, bad cop. She believed in intelligent cops using their experience to get results. Harris seemed intent on being a cardboard villain, and stressing out her interviewee.

'Did you realise the amount of drugs you took would lead you to overdose?' she said.

'No comment.'

'Guilty conscience?' said Zain.

'No guilty conscience here. I didn't hurt Ruby.'

'Let me read you examples of the messages you sent to Miss Day,' Kate said.

She read some of his emails and texts. His face was shiny with sweat when she had finished, scarlet patches all over it. Rourke had stopped doodling; he was looking disgusted.

'That's not me, not from me, no comment,' said Dan, in a whisper.

'You sent these to Ruby. Are you saying somebody else had access to your email account?' she said.

'Yes. No comment.'

'They were sent from your computer, you dumb –' began Zain.

'Shut up, you just shut the fuck up. What? You're going to punch me now?' said Dan. He looked at Rourke, who looked back at his screen, fidgeting.

'Was Ruby frightened of you?' said Kate.

'No, she loved me.'

'Did you threaten her?'

'No.'

'These messages are very threatening. If I was Ruby, I would be terrified of you.'

'Conjecture,' said Rourke, half-heartedly.

'You're not in court, Rourke. Are you really a lawyer, even?' said Zain.

'I am a qualified solicitor, yes.'

'Joker of all trades, eh?' said Zain. 'Do MINDNET know you're here?'

'Why did you send her these messages?' Kate said to Dan.

'I didn't.'

'Mr Grant, they were sent from your computer, using your private email. Unless someone hacked into your system, or compromised your account . . .'

'Yes, they must have.'

'We know you opened Ruby's replies to these messages, sent directly to you. Did you not then realise your account had been hacked?'

'Detective, how did you get access to my client's emails? Have you got a court order?' said Rourke.

'Yep, check it out, legal eagle,' said Zain, pushing an envelope across the table to Rourke.

The benefits of Hope. He had judges on speed dial; they got warrants signed off in minutes. No need for applications to court.

'And your text messages? Saying that you would destroy Ruby if she left you? Is that what happened? Did Ruby leave you? And did you destroy her?'

'No, no comment, I didn't harm her. I just said it, I was angry, I didn't do it.'

'Do what?'

'Anything.'

'Like scaring young girls, do you?' said Zain.

'No, I didn't do this. I was just . . . no comment.'

'You look like you're going to wet your knickers,' said Zain. 'All fifty-six pairs of them.'

'What?' said Dan, alert. He looked even more frightened than he had been, sheer panic all over his face.

Chapter Fifty-seven

'We found your stash. Are they for you? Do you get off on it? Is that why Ruby left you?' said Zain.

'I'm not a faggot. I don't wear them. I just . . . they send them to me. My fans.'

'Your fans are teenage girls. You better not have got them to send you any,' said Zain.

'No, they just send them. I don't ask them to.'

'We'll check your YouTube channel. If you have anything on there, I'll find it. So you better start telling us the truth,' said Zain.

'My fans send them. I don't know who they are.'

'How do they get your address?' said Kate.

'Him. Karl gets them. They send them to his office.'

'That's true. I used to get sent gifts for my clients,' said Rourke. 'Since Dan left, some still send them to my office.'

'Maybe he tells them to send them to you? Maybe MINDNET don't put up with his perversions? Maybe that's why he uses you? His old pal, Karl, do anything for a quick buck?' said Harris.

'Am I being interrogated, detective?'

'Used underwear though?' said Harris.

'On occasion.'

'So why keep them?' said Kate, turning back to Dan.

'No comment,' he said.

'Did Ruby know about them? Is that why she dumped your whiny little backside?' said Zain.

'She didn't.'

'We know she was getting closer to James Fogg. Her ex-boyfriend. He told us she had been messaging him, wanting to resurrect their prior relationship. Did you know?' said Kate.

Silence.

'Is that what tipped you over? Took you from your angry, vile fantasies, the email descriptions and text messages, and pushed you to turn them into reality?' she said.

'No. You are setting me up,' said Dan, flushed and angry.

'Was it jealousy of James? Is that why you did this?' said Kate. 'Is he next?'

'James? James is a cunt. Ruby fucking hated him. You're lying; you're setting me up. He's nothing, nobody. He's scum. Ruby would never choose him over me.'

'I think she did. Her parents preferred him, too. It must have hurt when she left you?'

'She didn't leave me.'

'Dumped for someone with no subscribers. Ouch,' said Zain.

'No fucking comment,' said Dan.

'Is that why you threatened to do him in? You killed Ruby, posted the video, and left a threat for James,' said Zain.

'No comment,' said Dan.

'Mr Grant, yesterday, when myself and Detective Sergeant Harris interviewed you, we asked you about Millie Porter. A woman you allegedly pushed from a balcony at your birthday party. Do you remember us asking?'

Dan stared into her, as though he was imagining what her kidneys would taste of.

'And do you remember your reply? You denied the incident occurred, that any charges were ever pressed. We have access to the police file from then. We know it happened, that a case was opened.'

'Those charges were dropped,' said Rourke.

'I'm not bringing up the details of the case, but the fact that you lied to us yesterday. Without there being a need to. You were not under suspicion. So can you see how I might decide not to believe you today?'

'Millie, she's crazy. Just greedy for money, stupid slag. She jumped, that's why she dropped the case. Why would I tell you that?'

'Lying little prick. I spoke to Millie, I saw what state she's in. Metal splints in her legs. You're lucky you have her under contract, or I swear that, if she told me to, I would have hunted you down for her.'

Kate felt a stab of jealousy. It was irrational. It was the devotion Harris displayed for Millie. Why did it matter? A small voice in the back of her head asked if they had slept together after he interviewed her. Why did she even care? She let it pass, allowed her subconscious – the friend with the dagger always to your throat – to subside.

'Mr Grant, how am I expected to believe what you tell me, when you have lied to me already?' she reiterated.

Kate's phone rang. It was Michelle. Kate sent it to voicemail. Zain's phone rang. They both got text messages. Zain stood up and left the room, went into the corridor. He was back a minute later, came up to Kate, whispered in her ear.

She looked into Dan's eyes. The eyes of a psychopath and a killer.

'Mr Grant, do you own a property in Hampshire? A small freehold cottage, between Winchester and Otterbourne?'

Dan looked between them both, then to Rourke.

'We found the deeds to the property in your flat.'

Dan stared as though he didn't understand what they were saying.

'We have officers from Hampshire police heading over there now. Myself and Detective Sergeant Harris will be joining them. I believe this is where you held Ruby, and where you made the videos you posted.'

'Sick fuck,' said Zain.

'You are still unable to provide an alibi for the time Ruby disappeared?'

'Last chance. Where were you?' said Zain.

'Dan, tell them – where were you?' said Rourke.

'No comment,' said Dan.

He looked cowed, and put his head down on the table between them. His shoulders started shaking as he sobbed.

'Daniel Edward Grant, I am arresting you on suspicion of abducting and murdering Ruby Day . . .'

Kate read him his rights.

'I'll make sure you get a really nice cell, with a nice roommate to keep you warm,' said Zain. 'For Millie.'

Dan looked up, his face covered in tears. He grabbed Kate's hands. His were sweaty, made her flinch. Zain grabbed his fingers and pulled them back, freeing her.

'No, please, I didn't do it. Please. Don't let him do this to me.'

'Suck it up,' said Zain.

Kate felt excitement, and foreboding apprehension. What state would Ruby's body be in when they finally found it? She shuddered as the images ran through her mind. Followed by a whisper of doubt.

Dan locked up would mean he couldn't carry out the threat at the end of the video. If the murderer wasn't Dan, then the real one was still out there. Free to kill again.

PART THREE
INTO THE WOODS

Chapter Fifty-eight

The cottage was a ninety-minute drive from London. At least, that's
what it was supposed to be, according to the satnav. Nearly two and
a half hours later, Rob Pelt finally found the place. It was at the end
of a muddy road, down a turning so small you could easily miss it,
even if you were aware it was there.

Rural Hampshire was green, yellow and red. The air smelled of
mulch, manure and smoke. Rob kicked at loose conkers, put one in
his pocket.

Dan Grant's cottage was situated on the edge of farmland, that
itself sat on the edge of the South Downs National Park. The nearest
neighbour, the farmer who owned the land, was at least two miles
away. In each direction, thick wooded areas. It would freak out a
normal person, being so cut off.

Rob checked his phone signal. Nothing.

The local DS, Helen Lowe, met him by the gated entrance to
the property. She was five eight, blonde, petite. Just his type. He
thought of Jess. That had been fun. Hampshire was a different
county, though, right?

'Thanks for locking this place down,' he said, shaking her thin
but strong hand.

'Easy to lock down when there are no people about,' she said.
Her accent was smooth, Home Counties smooth. It made him conscious of his own rough Manc tone.

'At least we don't have to worry about crime scene contamina-
tion. Are the CSIs inside?'

Helen nodded.

Rob hadn't wanted to bring his crew down from London, so had
asked Hampshire police to send their finest. Or their spares, anyway.

'The cottage is quite self-contained,' she said. 'Open kitchen-diner, separate lounge. Two bedrooms, a bathroom. It's built like a bungalow, no second level.'

'Any signs of recent occupation?'

'Plenty.'

He followed Helen through the thick mud, his shoes squelching, dirty water seeping over the sides and into his socks. Man up, he said to himself. He was a northerner. Bit of mud and water never killed anyone.

'I should have said that it's been raining this past week. I have spare wellies in my boot, if you want them.'

'I'm great. We'll be inside soon enough.'

'Put these on,' she said, handing him plastic booties from Forensics.

The door to the cottage had chipped wood, with creases in the paint. There was a rusted old lock, just the one.

'Not exactly secure, is it?'

'Crime rates are pretty low round here,' she said. 'Too much effort to get to, and the farmers have guns.'

'Sounds like Peckham. Only without the farmers.'

It was lost on her.

The front door opened into the kitchen diner. There was an Aga, flagstone floor, wooden table in the centre. Dust and damp filled the air. A microwave sat on top of a work surface, looking out of place.

'Guess Dan doesn't do much cooking when he's here,' said Rob as he pulled open the Aga doors. The shelves were clean.

A mini fridge sat on top of a side table. There were cans in there, Heineken, but nothing else.

'The important things, right?' he said.

'The cupboards are empty, not even a pasta packet or can of baked beans.'

'They eat baked beans round here?'

'I do,' Helen said.

'You live nearby?'

'Yes, in the middle of the forest, in a tree.'

'Nice,' he said.

'I live in Otterbourne,' she said, rolling her eyes.

'I came the other way, through Winchester. Didn't see it. Maybe you could give me a tour later?'

'Through there is the lounge,' she said, ignoring the question.

The lounge had various loose-covered sofa chairs, all old and well used. A wood burner sat under the chimney mantle.

'You can smell the wood,' he said. 'Recently lit, do you think?'

'Possibly. Forensics will test, see if they can confirm.'

There was a bookcase containing magazines, mainly computer game tomes.

'The place isn't very lived in, is it?' he said.

'He comes here to escape the cluttered London life, maybe.'

'Yeah, but you'd expect something. A TV?'

'TV's in the bedroom,' she said. 'Forensics found some beads in one of the sofa chairs. Turquoise and maroon. Possibly from a broken necklace or bracelet. Do you know if the victim had anything like that?'

'I'll send the details to my colleague, Detective Sergeant Brennan. See if she can follow up with the parents. Although I'm not sure how I'll get a signal.'

'You won't, until you're closer to Otterbourne or Winchester.'

'Is that an invite?' Rob was nothing if not persistent.

Helen moved on to the bedroom. There was a bed, the TV mounted on a cabinet. No wardrobe.

'You got a signal?' he asked.

'There's a digital connection, built into the TV set, and a DSL line.'

'Was wondering how he connected to the net; it's his lifeblood.'

'Mobile signals are an issue, but he has broadband. No wireless.'

'Explains how he posted the videos online, and why he used a web service to send the messages. His phones wouldn't work out here.'

'If it's him,' Helen pointed out.

'It's him,' said Rob.

The second bedroom had a bed, another set of drawers, nothing else.

'The bathroom is worth a look,' she said.

Rob saw it as soon as he walked in. A dark stain, the size of a human head, in the wood of the floor.

'Blood?'

'Forensics tested, said it was. They're working on a DNA match.'

Rob saw sploshes of blood in the sink as well, and some in the bath tub.

'Water is ropey. Hot water is on demand only,' she said.

Rob felt his toes freeze, the mud from earlier seeping through his socks.

'Where are the CSIs?' he said.

'In the basement,' she said.

Of course. There was always a basement, he thought.

Chapter Fifty-nine

Zain thought about using police privileges and driving down the emergency lane.

'It is an emergency,' he said, when Kate objected.

He tapped his sound system. Ariana Grande.

'My step sisters,' he said. 'I downloaded it for them last time they were in London.'

He tapped again. Puccini, without words. *Si, Mi Chiamano Mimi* from *La Bohème*.

'They don't live in London? Your step sisters?' Kate said.

'No, Scotland. Dad's involved in Trident, and my step mother's from Edinburgh.'

'Your parents' marriage ended?'

'Yeah. When I was nine. They were a bit doomed from the start, I reckon.'

'How so?'

'He's the son of English Catholics from the south – east; she's the daughter of a Turkish diplomat and an Indian journalist. My parents met by accident in a war zone, fell in love, then found they had nothing in common when I was born.'

'Sounds exotic. How old are your step sisters?'

'Twelve. They're twins. I have a step brother, too. He's eighteen. From a different woman, though, not my current step mother.'

'Your mother didn't have other children?'

'Too busy raising me. Waited till I was twenty-one, then got re-married. Then divorced, then married again. And divorced again. She's getting married again in a couple of months.'

'She sounds fun,' said Kate.

'She's great. Unless she's your mother, when she becomes a monumental embarrassment.'

Zain got blasted by drivers behind when he cut across two lanes of the motorway.

'The crime scene's not going anywhere; let's not become road accident statistics,' said Kate.

'Yes, boss. How did Michelle find this place?' he said. He wondered if the expensive toffee was having any effect at all.

'She found pictures on Dan's hard drive, got the scent. Trawled through his social media. She found references to it, pictures. She alerted Pelt, who found the deeds in Dan's flat.'

'Dan must have known we'd find out eventually. Why did he buy a place out there, anyway?'

'His parents live in Winchester.'

'He doesn't strike me as being the family type,' he said.

'How can you tell? Family ties lie deep; they're not always obvious on the surface.'

'You going to interview them?'

'I haven't made up my mind yet,' she said.

'What else did Michelle say?'

'Interestingly, Dan gave himself away on Twitter. The cottage was bought as a wreck. He fancied himself an architect, wanted to build his dream house.'

'*Grand Designs*? It's a TV show,' he clarified, when Kate looked blank.

'He had to have his DSL installed, but BT got the timings wrong. He boasted on Twitter that he'd had to rush to the cottage and back, to make it to a meeting. He said he used his knowledge of back roads and country lanes, and cut across private tracts of land. He got there in just over an hour, had his internet installed, then got back to London. Within three hours.'

'Meaning he could easily have driven Ruby down there, done . . . whatever, then got back to London? In the time he was missing from his place, I mean?'

'Precisely. I know I lambasted you earlier for pursuing him, but it seems he had motive, means and a place to act out his murderous intentions.'

'Sick fuck,' he said. 'I swear, if this was a different country, I'd batter him to get a confession.'

'Well, luckily for us all, we have the rule of law, and protection for the rights of all citizens.'

Zain stayed quiet and gripped the steering wheel tighter as he stared at the road ahead. Some people didn't deserve rights. He didn't care about the human rights brigades when it came to rapists, paedos, wife beaters and child killers. That was his list. And Dan Grant was now on it, too. He just felt wrong.

'South Downs National Park is six hundred and twenty-eight square miles,' said Kate. 'I just hope Dan had the decency to keep her close by, and she's not in some random place we'll struggle to get to her. I don't want her rotting in an unmarked grave; I want her parents to have closure.'

Zain wondered again at his boss. The attractive woman from America, with plenty of charisma and strength. He didn't buy her story about coming to London because she loved history. She was hiding something. He was a cop, he had instincts too, and he knew she was keeping things to herself.

Still, he would figure out Kate Riley another day. Today, they needed to scour a forest to find Ruby's body.

Chapter Sixty

Justin Hope filled two glasses with bourbon shots, handed one to his guest. At twenty-eight, Paul Newton was one of the youngest MPs, and already a minister for the Home Office. They had spent the morning interviewing potential detective constables for the team. With the brash Stevie Brennan.

'She is quite something,' said Newton. 'Very forthright.'

'Yes, she is. Riley made a mistake sending her to do the job though. Riley's been making a number of mistakes of late.'

'Anything we need to take action over or be concerned about?'

Hope swirled his drink in his glass, imbibed it through his nose first, before swallowing. It felt warm, energising, as he did so.

'I'm watching her carefully. I think possibly Trent gave her too much free rein. Let's see what happens with me micro-managing her. And she has Harris now, so he'll keep an eye on her, I'm sure.'

'You have a lot of faith in him.'

'You don't?'

'I think he's unstable. You know what he went through, don't you? There are a lot of rumours flying around about him.'

'Hearsay, old wives' tales. I am far from being influenced by such peculiarities. Anyway, he is dispensable, like most people. If he, as Brennan would say, fucks up, he will be got rid of.'

Newton tipped his glass to him.

'To Brennan,' said Hope, draining what was left.

'How is the investigation into Ruby Day progressing?' asked Newton.

Hope took a moment to consider. This was a stealth mission in itself, he had no doubt.

'Very well. We think we have the location she was taken to, where the videos were made. Riley and her team are there now.'

'So the boyfriend is likely for it, then?'

'Yes, I think so. I can't see him getting out of it, to be honest. He's made threats, he has no alibi, and soon they'll find the forensics to seal the case.'

'Sounds positive,' said Newton.

Yes, thought Hope, you can scurry off and report back. Tell them it's all done with, that MINDNET will soon pass out of all suspicion. That Jed Byrne is safe. For now. And whatever debt Newton owes them won't be called in today, at least.

Back in the office, Stevie banged her drawers shut, bashed her computer keys, and flung her suit jacket across her desk.

'Rough day?' said Michelle.

'Get dressed up in this crap, and sit and listen to those two pricks, while doing pointless interviews. Sorry, I know you don't like swearing.' Stevie pulled her shirt out of her skirt. 'I'm sure I had some spare jeans or trousers somewhere in here,' she said, hunting through more cupboards.

'You look nice.'

'Fuck off, I feel like a fake in this. Normal clothes, that's what I need.'

'What is normal anymore? You want some toffee?' offered Michelle.

'No, I'm heading to the gym later. Isn't that the posh stuff you like?'

'Yes. Harris got it for me this morning. As an apology.'

Stevie tried to bite back her resentment. Who was he to start stealing Michelle from her? This was her team before it was his.

'He's given me jack for stealing my job,' she said.

'I might have overreacted with Harris,' said Michelle, turning back to her screen.

'So he's charmed you, then? Slimy wank. I knew he would.'

Michelle ignored her. Stevie found some jeans in a drawer under mandatory health and safety documents she'd been given. Which she'd never read. There was a T-shirt, too.

She stopped by Michelle's screen on her way to change. 'Fuck off,' she said, reading what was on it.

'It's his fans, they've found out. Hashtag FreeDan is trending,' said Michelle. 'And check this one out: PoliceState is also trending, as is DanStitchUp.'

'Sad bastards,' said Stevie.

'FindRuby is still trending, though, but pretty low down.'

Stevie didn't say anything. She hoped there was good news from Hampshire. If finding a dead body could be called good news.

Chapter Sixty-one

Rob Pelt led the way to access the basement, through a door off the kitchen. Zain had thought it might be a utility room when they initially saw it. Now it was a gaping black rectangle, leading to the underbelly of the house.

There was a steep set of stairs going downwards. Zain took a moment to let his eyes adjust. He sensed Kate look back up at him.

Zain had become used to the dark when he had been taken, trying to figure out what the movements of air meant around him. The experience had stayed with him.

He felt something touch his spine, and his nerves tightened. It was just sweat, brought on by the forensics suit, but it was enough. His anxiety was let loose and it was crawling through him.

The darkness was complete as they made it to the bottom of twelve steps. Zain walked as though on a wire in a circus. The room turned blue as Rob switched on the torch on his phone.

They were in a small space, another door in front of them.

'Bit brighter in there,' said Rob.

Rob pushed at a door that, as it opened, sounded the way Zain was feeling. The CSIs were combing the room behind it, busy in their phantom drone outfits. Tasks Zain knew the technical details of, details read from enough forensic reporting forms.

Someone brushed past him; he jolted. Just a faceless figure, with plastic evidence bags in their hands.

The cellar smelt of mould and damp. The sharp feral smells of animal, like cat piss, probably rats. Did foxes hide away in country basements?

The room had been lit scantly, low lamps set up where the forensic staff were working. A hum of evidence collection. Someone opened a water bottle and drank from it.

There were two lamps shining up at the object in the centre of the space. It cast a shadow angled over the walls and onto the low ceiling. It expanded in dimensions, but when he was close to it, Zain saw what it was. He recognised it.

The final frame from the first video.

The chair belonged to the set of used furniture he had seen upstairs. It was splintered, the nails in it rusted. Over the arms were two loops of silver tape, looking like bracelets that didn't join. He recognised those, too. They would find Ruby's skin and hair on them, he was sure.

'Did they find the camera?' Kate asked.

'No, not yet,' said Rob.

There wasn't much to see. Just trails of dirt.

'She must have been brought back here after she was running out there,' Zain said. 'You can see the mud.'

'They think they found blood traces, think her feet were lacerated while she made a run for it,' said Rob.

'I don't see how. She was locked down here. We saw the bolts. Unless she was waiting? Managed to release herself, and then jumped whoever held her here?' said Zain.

'Possible,' said Rob.

'Unlikely,' said Kate. 'She was filmed running away. It was planned. I think she was let go, to heighten the sense of pleasure for the perpetrator. It was always their intention, part of their game.'

'Well, we can ask him,' said Rob.

Rob moved away from the chair, towards the back wall. He stopped some distance from it. Lamps lit the floor. Yellow markers were spread out across it.

'There's no light,' said Rob. 'Someone removed the only bulb.'

'She was kept in darkness?' said Kate.

'We saw from the video that she was filmed in that grey-green colour,' said Zain. 'It's what they use on *Most Haunted* and crap like that. Fuck.'

Another memory, coldness in the pit of his stomach. A light trilling sensation began in his temples. He felt the base of his skull, as though it was detaching itself from his spine. Making him nauseous.

'Stuck down here, tied to a chair, waiting for that sick bastard. Might explain what they found. She pissed herself. Sitting there,' said Rob.

Zain looked back at the chair, feeling sicker, but also angrier. He couldn't help the images in his head; he'd seen Ruby taped to the chair. He remembered the fear in Millie's eyes. Dan would never get the sort of punishment he deserved. Zain wanted to hurt him.

'Do we know where she was shot?' said Kate.

Her voice was calm, unaffected. She was a visitor to a museum, keeping her emotions in check.

'Not yet,' said Rob.

'I think we'll find her body wherever she was shot, just dumped,' said Zain.

He was feeling pressure build inside him, felt sweat on his hands inside plastic gloves, on his face, throughout his body.

'Any signs there might have been a second victim?'

'You thinking he might already have done someone else in?' asked Rob. 'Forensics haven't found anything yet.'

'I need to breathe,' Zain said, rushing from the basement, his legs giving out under him.

Chapter Sixty-two

Outside, there was peace. The sort of country peace he wasn't used to. Birds and stuff, background noise. A tractor or some other farm machine.

Zain took in deep breaths, to clear his system. He needed something to clear his mind as well.

Kate joined him. She was dressed in black again, but wore boots like his, and a maroon shirt. Her face still had the fresh hue he'd seen that morning.

'You OK?' she said.

'Yes. Just a bit claustrophobic down there. Kept seeing her, and when he said about the piss . . . fuck, people are just twisted, sometimes.'

'I understand. At least we can do something meaningful about it,' she said.

'Can we?'

She looked out at the trees, thick and black in places, that surrounded them.

'If he took her through, there will be a trail,' she said. 'Broken tree branches, disturbed foliage. I don't think Dan would be strong enough to carry her; she must have walked.'

'At gunpoint,' he said. 'Did she think she was going to live? If she kept walking, I mean?'

'Yes,' said Kate. 'Always. It's how the power plays out. People do whatever they are told, hopeful of release, survival. No matter how slim the chances, our desire to live is stronger than anything else. Even rational logic and experience.'

He knew all about that. He had done the same. Believing they would let him go. Even when they told him what they were going to do to him.

Zain massaged the back of his neck. He often did when he thought of that time.

'What now?' he said.

'Dogs. I want to catch her trail. You have her T-shirt in the boot? Let's see where the dogs lead us. Get the local police to start searching.'

'That would be us. Detective Sergeant Helen Lowe,' the petite blonde officer said, stepping forward to shake hands with them both. 'Sorry I missed you when you arrived. I was updating HQ, had to drive until I found a signal.'

'You think we can get access to a decent-sized search team? I want the dogs to hit a direction, and then I want the area scanned inch by inch,' said Kate.

'Dogs are on their way. Search team will follow.'

'Any sign of a vehicle?' said Kate.

'Yes. We found tyre tracks. The whole area is pretty dense with mud, as I'm sure you can tell.'

'Yeah, Pelt told us to park right up by the entrance,' said Zain.

He saw some colour shift into Lowe's face. Had Pelt been asking her out already? Last he heard, he was shacking up with one of the CSIs. Just last night. A mixture of envy and irritation shot through Zain.

'Any idea what type of vehicle?' said Kate.

'Small, from the measurements of space between tyres.'

'Very perceptive,' muttered Zain. 'Sorry. Been a long drive.'

'Put out an alert, see if anything comes up,' said Kate. 'I don't think you get a great amount of traffic around here. Someone might have seen something.'

Zain wasn't sure. When you asked the public for anything, you usually got hundreds of crank calls. It just built up intelligence, more to be sifted through. The important pieces always got lost.

'Did the press conference with the parents deliver anything?' said DS Lowe, as though running on the same track as him.

'Nothing concrete,' said Kate.

They heard the sound of tyres screeching as a Transit van came towards them. Moments later, the sound of dogs barking filled the air.

'I'll get Ruby's T-shirt,' said Zain.

Chapter Sixty-three

Hampshire police had sent two female dog handlers. Kate was impressed by the representation of women in the force, and commented on it to Zain.

'You think? I reckon there's a man up there somewhere, though, sending the women, because they're not as good. In his opinion. I'm laughing, though; they're better.'

'Are you trying to kiss my ass, Harris?'

'Is it working?'

The dogs, bloodhounds, had caught Ruby's scent from the T-shirt they had brought with them from her flat. They went crazy inside the cottage for a while, where she had been recently. In the bedrooms, the basement. Something odd happened, though. When one of the dogs got near to the chair Ruby had been tied to, it panicked. The dog yanked its chain, started whimpering, scared.

'Fuck me,' said Zain.

The handler looked around, asked for light to be brought, and a magnifying lens.

'Cayenne pepper,' she said. 'Someone's put it down, to affect the dogs.'

The dog was taken back to the holding van. It always surprised Kate how animals of strength, with the ability to tear a new throat for a man, could be rendered passive that way. The other dog, Diva, picked up Ruby's scent, its handler avoiding the chair, back up the stairs to the kitchen, through the back door and into the woods.

Diva started a light canter, her handler trotting along with her. She darted through a break in the trees, invisible from a distance. When you got close, you could see the disturbance in the natural alignment of forest.

Kate followed with Zain and Rob at a brisk walk. Her boots fared better than Rob's shoes. She glanced at them meaningfully.

'DS Lowe offered me a spare pair of wellies, but I'm good,' he said.

'You should have taken her up on her offer,' said Zain.

'I have a reputation to maintain,' replied Rob.

'These country gals probably like men in wellies.'

'She's not country; she's from a town.'

'Is she indeed? What happened to the forensics woman?' said Zain.

'We had a nice time.'

'Do you think work is a dating agency?' said Zain.

'I hear jealousy in every syllable, mate,' said Rob, slapping Zain on the shoulder.

'Can you check what stage the moon was at in its cycle,' Kate cut in. 'I want to know how dark it was the night Ruby went missing.'

She pictured Ruby with no awareness, brushing branches across her face, tripping over loose rocks, fallen bits of wood. To be filmed, to be led.

'Dan must have used night-vision glasses,' she said. 'He knew where he was taking her. Her scent leads this way for a reason. There are no tyre tracks; he didn't drive.'

They walked on, Diva barking softly ahead of them. They caught up with her, eating treats from her handler's palm, about a half hour later.

'What happened?' said Kate.

'Take a look,' said the handler.

Kate walked forward, and saw why they had stopped.

Chapter Sixty-four

She was sitting in the passenger side of Zain's car, the door open.

'Any joy?' she said, when Rob walked past her.

'They're bringing another dog, searches for cadavers. Tomorrow we can access one that searches under water. In case.'

'Sounds like a circus act,' said Kate.

'The rest is going to be a manual job for now,' Rob said.

'We'll stay and help,' she told him. 'Get DS Lowe to recommend a hotel in Winchester, then get Lia to book us in.'

Diva had run until she reached a creek. She lost Ruby's scent there. A rowboat was moored to the side. It reminded Kate of home, a boy she had loved. He used to take her sailing at night, the banks lit by fireflies. Had it been love? Probably teenage hormones confusing her feelings. She remembered the ache he used to cause in her body, just seeing him, knowing he was near.

Ruby must have been put in that boat, and taken somewhere. Diva could track over water, but the stream was running. She had set off in one direction along the bank, but had then become unsure, headed the other way.

'I'll take her across, start on the other bank,' said her handler.

Diva had run along, trying to pick up the scent, until the creek hit a bank of trees that acted as a dam of sorts. The dog then became excited, picking up speed, and headed onwards. Until it reached a minor road.

'She got into a car here,' said her handler.

Kate looked on, seeing nothing but road in either direction. Planning. Dan had known what he was doing. He was taunting them, wanted them to be part of his game. To be part of the chase.

The curse of the internet. Too much information on how to commit crimes undetected.

It meant the search area for Ruby was expanding further. Until they knew where Ruby had been taken, where she got out off the car, the dogs would be of little use. Kate wasn't taking any chances, though; she was dealing with someone who was meticulous. The body might have been dumped in the water, buried somewhere nearby. A painstaking, intensive, laborious search was starting. Rows of officers and volunteers had agreed to search while there was still daylight. The officers would search on into the night, but she wasn't hopeful. It felt like filling the time, doing something because doing nothing wasn't an option.

Hope was arranging a second press conference with the parents.

And through it all, Twitter was being used as a weapon to criticise her and to campaign for Dan's release. It seemed that if you were famous or vaguely attractive, you couldn't possibly be guilty.

Back in London, Stevie Brennan had interviewed Dan, confronting him with the facts of what they had found at his Hampshire property.

'He was shitting it,' she said when providing an update. 'His eyes kept widening, on cue, every time I mentioned something. The cottage, the cellar, the chair, the stream. He denied it, said it was someone setting him up. I asked him who hated him that much; he said half of YouTube did. The jealous, failed half.'

'Was he really that articulate? Last time I saw him he was in floods of tears,' Kate said.

'Yes. I think prison is sobering him up,' said Stevie.

'Still no alibi?' asked Kate.

'Still no alibi,' said Stevie.

Chapter Sixty-five

Lia had booked them into a Holiday Inn, outside of Winchester. It was midnight when they checked in, Kate's legs feeling as though she had climbed twelve flights of stairs. Through her window she looked into a black shadowed copse, the tops looking like broken glass shards.

Kate kicked off her boots and lay back on the bed in her room, curled up and started to fall asleep. She woke up a few minutes later, her room phone ringing.

'Riley,' she said.

'They've opened the restaurant for us, if you want to get something?' said Zain.

'You're going to eat at this hour?'

'I'm starving,' he said.

'I need to shower. I'll be another half hour yet,' she said.

'That's fine, I'll wait.'

'Where's Pelt?'

'Asleep,' said Zain.

'Alone?'

'No idea.'

Liar, she thought.

They were seated in the bar, sated after a rough and ready dinner. Zain had opted for a tuna and red pepper Panini, while she had gone for steak.

'You don't drink?' she said, as he sipped his lime and soda.

'Rarely,' he said.

She was on her second vodka. It felt indulgent.

'Don't think we've ever done this,' he said. 'Just hung out.'

They weren't alone in the bar. Executive types were drinking amiably around them. She noticed inebriated heads turning her way, becoming more blatant as the time wore on. She was the only female there.

The bartender was black, with short hair and a French accent. He stood with his hands behind his back, leaning against a tall stool, when he wasn't serving.

'You haven't been with us long enough,' she said.

'Or am I just not welcome at Friday night drinks?'

'There is that as well,' she said, smiling.

He didn't bite, or take it badly, just stared into the distance. His blue eyes gave him a lupine quality, smouldering against his olive skin.

She checked her phone. Ryan had sent her a joke, making her smile.

'Boyfriend?' said Harris.

'Why would you say that?'

'No reason.'

'My sitter, actually,' she said.

The word hovered; Zain pulled it out of the air and ran with it. 'Babysitter? I didn't know you had kids.'

'I don't,' she said. Her face was hot; she tried to cool it with the ice in her drink, but failed. What could she say? House-sitter? Dog-sitter?

The tiredness, the intensity and the drink were all loosening her up, and she said to Zain, regretting it as soon as she did: 'No, a sitter for my mother.'

He raised his eyebrows slightly.

'Like a carer?'

'Yes. In a way.'

'Body or brain?' he said.

'Brain,' she said, draining her glass. 'Get me another vodka, will you? Straight up.' Zain returned a few moments later, long enough for her to carry out a discourse in her head. Should she tell him the details? Would everyone else find out? Would it affect how people saw her, her ability to do her job?

Her mind was clouded, and she had an urge to confess. See his reaction. If he was OK, then maybe that was a start? She could peel off the layers of deception with the rest of the team?

'Were you all right today?' she said instead. 'You went a bit quiet in the basement.'

He didn't meet her eyes, looked away at the other drinkers. 'Yeah, I was OK. Just had a flashback to something, that's all.'

'Anything to do with what happened with SO15?'

'It always is,' he said. 'Everything is to do with what happened.'

'What did they do to you?'

He ran his fingers through the hair on his face. What was that? It wasn't quite a beard, but was too long for stubble. She caught herself imagining what it would feel like, running her fingers over it. She remembered doing that to her brothers when they had shaved their heads, feeling the prickly new growth. She didn't think it would feel that way if she reached out and touched Zain Harris. The sensations in her fingers would be the least heightened part of the process.

He caught her staring at his mouth. She smiled with her own.

'You really want to know?' he said.

Kate felt awake suddenly. Excited, even.

'Yes,' she said.

Chapter Sixty-six

Zain went to the bar, ordered a Scotch diluted with ice and a splash of soda water. His father's drink.

The bartender was obviously tired, his movements laboured. He struggled to pick the ice up with a fork and spoon. He filled another glass with vodka, diluted it with Coke, for Kate.

It was nearly 2 a.m. The bar was empty. Just the two of them left. A heater was pumping warm air over him when he sat down, making him uncomfortable. It was prickly. His mother used to say that about British summers. The heat is prickly. She was used to summers in Istanbul and Delhi.

Zain was wearing a navy T-shirt he had in his car, with jeans. Pelt had borrowed a second T-shirt from him. He thought of the cocky sergeant, wrapped up in his sheets, wrapped around DS Lowe. The feeling of resentment and disapproval twisted in him again. As did a sense of arousal.

Zain took a sip, feeling the fire in his throat. The heat made him sweat as he watched Kate leave her drink untouched. She already had three vodkas swimming around in her. She seemed eager, a willing audience.

'You told me you were taken, caught in a trap?' she said.

Caught in a trap. Like an animal. That fit.

'Yes. They grabbed me, blindfolded me, bound my hands with plastic ties, my legs, too. Kicked my head a couple of times. Out of sheer hatred or to cause me to black out. Probably both.'

'You were alone?'

'Yes.'

'Where did they take you?'

Zain remembered snatches of a drive, some moments awake, some not. The smell of greased cloths, the taste of the metal. The hardness of the van floor.

'I still don't know. It was a holding cell, a basement somewhere. I was left shackled to some pipes. My eyes were never uncovered. Even when they beat me.'

She moved her chair closer to him. He caught the scent from the body wash she must have used earlier.

'I lay there, and I didn't have a clue what was happening around me. Time, it just goes. I tried, I mean I tried to count the seconds, the minutes. But you give up after a while. And I was never awake all the time.'

'Did they ever speak to you?'

Conversations he couldn't repeat. Ones he had shared in his debriefing. The relentless questions, the breaking down of Zain Harris. He wasn't a spy; he wasn't trained to deal with interrogation techniques. He didn't have a cyanide capsule. He'd had to learn the hard way.

'No,' he lied. 'They were trying to trade me. It was hopeless. They weren't in some Middle Eastern dugout; they were operating on British soil. Where could they go?'

'What did they want?'

'Safe passage, destination of their choice. It was all bollocks. They were on a suicide mission; they wanted to take as many people like me with them they could.'

He remembered the electrodes. Attached to his feet first, his nipples. Then his testicles. The pain, it got so intense he'd passed out.

'How long did they hold you?'

'A week I found out afterwards.'

The words seemed inadequate to his ears. A week. Is that all it was?

'Portsmouth. That's where I ended up.'

'Why there?' she said, her voice a whisper now.

'They had a shipping container. They were going to use it to smuggle me out.'

'What happened then?' said Kate.

Visions flooded his head. Zain felt anxiety in his bloodstream. The pills. He didn't have any. Fuck, no. Panic joined the anxiety. His heart started hammering inside his ribcage, loud and fast and strong. So strong he thought it would burst. He imagined it exploding, the way Ruby's head had exploded, the way the brain matter spattered out from her skull. His heart spattering out from his chest.

Kate held his wrist, put a hand to his face.

'Zain,' she said. 'You've turned pale; you're sweating. What's wrong? Shall I get you some water?'

Zain looked at her. 'I don't think you've ever called me Zain before,' he said.

Illogical, but it was enough. It drew him back, he took a drink of his Scotch, his heart still playing drums, but the loss of consciousness that threatened had abated.

'Can we go for a walk?' he said.

Chapter Sixty-seven

The hotel was surrounded by forest. They stood at the back of the hotel building, looking out over a lawn, staring into the black trees.

'You got a smoke?' he said, shivering.

'No,' she said.

The sky was clouded, but stars flashed like coins between them. The moon was almost full.

'At least you know where the moon was in its cycle,' he said. 'It looks so different, doesn't it? Without all that light pollution in London.'

'Yes,' she said. 'Reminds me of home.'

'Do you miss it?'

'Always,' she said.

'Why don't you go back?'

'Sometimes you can't,' she said.

'Why not?'

She looked up, over the forest line. Her eyes caught the stars, shone in their light, her head tilted back, her mouth slightly open. Zain felt the urge to kiss her. He imagined it.

'What happened at Portsmouth?' she said.

Zain looked into the sky now, all thoughts of Riley's mouth gone.

What had happened at Portsmouth? He was in a shipping container, one of thousands stacked up along the harbour.

'Desperate acts happened there,' he said. 'They took my toenails off. One by one.'

Kate shuddered next to him. He had no jacket to offer her, so he moved closer until their arms were touching. His bare arm against the cloth of her shirt. Heat sealed the place where they touched. Desire rose in him.

'I gave them nothing,' he said, lying.

They weren't there to disagree.

'They found us, though, the SAS. I got rescued, the terrorists got killed, imprisoned.'

Zain remembered those moments. He'd thought it was all over for him.

'Fuck, you must be depressed. I've depressed myself, and I went through the whole shitty experience.' Zain laughed. He heard only a trace of mania through it.

'And you got over it?' she said.

She looked into his eyes, her face blue in the glow of hotel security lights and moonlight. Kate reached out, her fingers running over his forehead, his cheeks, his lips. She was as tall as him, and leaned forward to kiss him.

Zain did the same, closing his eyes, feeling the adrenalin, the sheer lust. He felt himself respond to her, and for a moment it was OK. They were hungry, raw. He lived in those seconds, when two people were giving in to something. He kissed her neck, his hands going under her shirt; he sucked at her breast through her shirt.

She reached her hands back, over the nape of his neck, through his hair, and that's when he started to panic. The touch against his neck. And then they weren't two people kissing anymore; this wasn't a prelude to sleeping together.

He felt trapped, the heat of their bodies cloying. He tasted her tongue, hoping it would ease the anxiety, but it felt fleshy, like meat. He gagged, pulled away, and threw up.

'Well, I've never had that effect on a guy before,' she said.

Outside her bedroom door, he tried to explain. She brushed him off, said it didn't matter.

'I'm sorry,' he said, again.

'Goodnight, DS Harris,' she said.

She opened her door, but before she could close it behind her, he put his foot in to stop it. He pushed the door back, and shut it softly. Kate didn't pay attention to him. She took her boots off, sat down on the bed. She stared at him, daring him to watch her. She started unbuttoning her shirt, then took her trousers off. She got into bed, in just her underwear.

He felt stirring again; he should be all over her.

She lay staring at the ceiling, then switched the light off.

'Please go away,' she said. 'You're making it worse.'

He took his own boots off, and lay down on the bed next to her, on top of the duvet. The downy material separating them.

'I haven't been able to,' he said. 'Since they did that. When I get close . . . when you touched the back of my neck like that . . . they were going to behead me. In that container, they had a sword to my neck. They were going to stick me on the internet.'

She didn't reply, but turned around so she was facing in his direction. He had his hands under his head, looking up at the darkened ceiling.

'Being touched, like that, I can't explain it. I freak out, and I panic, and I can't do it.'

'You could have said, told me to stop. You didn't have to demonstrate your disgust.'

He laughed. 'If it makes you feel any better, I've never done that with a girl before, either.'

'Great,' she said, sarcastically.

'I was pushing through it, because I wanted you so badly. I ignored the warning signs.'

'Probably for the best,' she said. 'I am a little drunk right now. I think we both would have regretted it in the morning.'

He agreed in his head. When she found out he had betrayed her, and lied to her, it would feel a thousand times worse if they had slept together.

'I don't think I would regret it,' he said.

Chapter Sixty-eight

The grainy images played out in front of him. He froze, then zoomed in. Pressed play again.

'Who else has seen this?' said Jed Byrne.

'Just the two of us, internally,' said Anderson.

They were in Byrne's office in Soho, the blinds closed, all calls being held.

'How did you get hold of this?' asked Jed.

'Used some pals of mine. They logged into the city-wide grid for me, did a facial recognition search,' said Anderson.

'How did you know where to look?'

'I keep tabs on all our clients. I knew exactly where to look.'

Jed wondered if a tab was being kept on him, too. 'Have you covered our tracks?' he said.

'Completely,' said Anderson.

'I need you to be sure. I can't let this go public until there's not even a hint of our involvement.'

Jed looked at his head of security, trying to find a flicker of doubt. There wasn't one. Anderson was ex-SAS, a security veteran. When had he gone bad, wondered Jed. There must have been a turning point when he lost his way. What was it? Too much death, a love story, or just good old-fashioned greed? Jed didn't have much time for people like Anderson, but his father had insisted. If he was going to fund MINDNET, then he wanted one of his own men on the inside.

That raised the question of trust. How much could he trust this man, his father's man? Was he reporting back, divulging Jed's failures? That couldn't be the case; Jed would have surely felt the fallout by now.

'I don't make idle promises, and I don't do half measures,' said Anderson, his accent strong when he was trying to be sincere. 'When I say we're safe, we're safe.'

Jed liked the 'we' in that sentence. Anderson was aware that his own balls were in the shredder if things went badly for them. How ⟩yal: dirty their hands as

⟩ling two days' sweat and ⟩ad been too wired, nerv-⟩r. He went through bouts ⟩rst, his nerves shot. Bile ⟩ic energy, pacing. His life ⟩ic.

⟩ace to breathe?

out.'

Anderson.

e right, though.'

tly,' said Anderson. 'That rself. She'll be here asking

all links to us?' Jed hated the thought of Riley anywhere near him.

'They found the contract,' said Anderson.

'Fuck,' said Jed. 'How?'

'It was printed off, shredded in the girl's bedroom.'

'Paper. Fucking paper.'

The sick, twisted feeling was coming back. The pressure was tight in his chest, in his head. How could that have happened?

'Relax, sir. We'll deal with it.'

Jed pulled a bottle of whisky from his desk. He needed another shot to calm him. He'd finished off a bottle the night before, trying to medicate himself to sleep. It only worked to help him pass out.

'How do we get the video to Riley, then?' he said, filling a tumbler on his desk.

'Rourke,' said Anderson. 'That way, there's nothing to link back to us.'

Jed smiled. Yes, Karl Rourke. The desperate fool.

Jed felt another muscle relax, the breathing come more easily. Rourke could deal with Riley; she was only a woman, after all. How good could she possibly be?

Chapter Sixty-nine

Kate was in the conference room with her team. Zain was wearing shades, to allegedly cover dark circles and tired eyes. Kate was fine with it, though; she wanted to avoid looking into them, seeing the night before reflected back at her.

Where was her head? He was working for her. Why him? She couldn't cross that line, not with a work colleague.

The drive back to the London HQ had passed in silence, no music, just the news on Radio 5. Ruby was still headline-worthy, the search in Hampshire the lead item. So far, Kate had avoided the press. She didn't want to appear on TV, or have her picture in the papers. She wanted to keep her cover.

She wondered what she would look like to someone from her past. The blonde girl gone, a brunette woman in her stead.

'I've seen stuff like this on *CSI*,' said Rob Pelt. He was chewing a plastic spoon that he'd used earlier to stir Sweet'N Low into his decaf coffee. Out of all of them, he looked the most freshest. He seemed so unconcerned all the time. How did he switch off?

'How do we pin it down? Show that he strapped her to the chair, led her into the woods?' said Zain.

'Do we have anything from Forensics?' said Kate.

'His partial prints are on the tape, the one used to strap Ruby to the chair. On the boat, they found fingerprints, and some hair,' said Rob.

'Circumstantial,' said Zain. 'He owns that place, and the boat. Everything would potentially have his prints on it.'

'How did he restrain her with just tape?' said Stevie.

'It's specialised, made from nanotechnology. Silica atoms, blasted to a millionth of an inch, then hammered back together. It would be like being restrained by steel.'

They all turned to stare at Zain.

'What?' he said, noting their surprise. 'They make it at UCL; they have a nanotechnology department. I was there on a case, once, learned a few things.'

'How do you know it's the same stuff?' said Stevie.

'Saw the roll on the kitchen table,' said Zain.

'We back up the forensic evidence with the text messages, the emails,' said Kate. 'His lack of an alibi is key. We have a strong case against him. Hope is keen for us to proceed. That means he's cleared it with the lawyers.'

'Over golf or pints at his club,' muttered Stevie.

'Don't think they do pints in his club,' said Rob.

'Whatever,' said Stevie.

She skulked down into her jacket, her hands in the pockets. Her legs were stretched under the table, her boots tapping the floor as her legs bounced. She concentrated better by using up her excess energy that way.

'What we need is the body,' said Rob.

'Plenty of people get convicted without a body,' said Stevie.

'When he gets nailed in court, and banged up, to become some guy's bitch, that's when I'll celebrate,' said Zain. 'Because I've seen too many guilty bastards walk.'

'Cynical freak,' said Stevie.

'What is your fucking problem?' said Zain.

'It's speaking to me? I mean, what the hell, Harris. You think you're in *Heat* magazine? What are the shades for?'

'Get a grip,' said Zain.

'You guys are making me turn to religion,' said Rob. 'And drink.'

'It's true, though, come off it,' said Zain. 'Your case – remember the guy who arranged to help his brother-in-law kill his love rival? Got off with a crap excuse. That's what happens. Fucking judges.'

'That was harsh, took me ages to get over that,' said Rob. 'How did you know about that, anyway?'

Zain froze.

'I wonder what else he knows,' said Stevie.

'Whatever it is, I hope it's related to this investigation,' said Kate.

She felt tired, suddenly. She had let them all start work late that morning. Zain had dropped her off at HQ, giving her enough time to head home, check in on her mother and Ryan. Both were in a mood but she couldn't unpick why, and she didn't have the time. Something had happened.

'I have to go early today,' Ryan had said.

Kate agreed to be home by six-thirty.

'And I need some time off,' he had added.

Kate had felt her world shift. What was going on? She would have to speak to her mother that evening. With no Ryan, she didn't see how she could manage her life.

There was a knock on the door. Lia told her Karl Rourke was in reception, needed to speak to her urgently.

Michelle played the footage Rourke had brought with him. He was nervous, a layer of sweat on his face. He was touching his hair a lot, smoothing it down, wiping at his nose.

On the screen, they saw a man in a hoodie walking through a council estate.

'Where is that?' said Kate.

'Carsdale,' said Rourke.

Carsdale estate was notorious, set over six blocks in Peckham. It was standard London council estate, solid bricks, white-framed windows.

The man walked past parked cars, a group of young men huddled together.

The camera angle changed, catching the man from the front, his face visible, even though his hair and chin were covered. The eyes. They were huge, distinctive.

Kate sat down, her legs shaking.

The man was next caught on camera inside D block. He looked at them for a second, an involuntary stare, but not one that meant he was aware of his image being captured. He was caught side on, pressing for the lift. It came, and he disappeared inside.

The video spooled; it was a shot from inside the lift. It was looking down at the man, his face, the upturn of his nose, clearly seen. There was a timestamp on the CCTV at the bottom of the image, the seconds running along, the twenty-four-hour clock.

The next shot was in front of the lift. The man walked past the camera, turned left, and was caught walking to a flat on floor six, according to a sign on the side of a pillar. He knocked, looked around, went inside.

The picture cut again to the man leaving the flat, some hours later. He wasn't walking in a straight line. In fact, Kate noticed, he wasn't walking straight at all through any of the film. He looked as though he was dragging one of his legs behind him.

'Why does he have that limp?' she said.

'He's had it since childhood. An accident. Made him a target at school, suffered quite badly,' said Rourke.

Was there accusation behind those words?

The last shot was of the man walking across the estate again. It was 9 a.m. According to the CCTV monitored by Lambeth Council, Dan Grant had spent the best part of the time Ruby disappeared at a flat on the Carsdale estate.

'How did you get hold of this?' said Kate.

'Privileged sources,' said Rourke.

Kate looked at him, and then stared back at the frozen face of Dan. Her case unravelling.

'If this is where he was, why didn't he tell us? Why didn't he give up his alibi?' said Kate.

Rourke couldn't meet her gaze.

'It's fucking obvious,' Zain said.

Chapter Seventy

The Carsdale estate was no less bleak in the daylight than it had appeared on the CCTV footage.

They passed a group of young men dressed in estate uniform: hooded tops, baseball caps, low-slung jeans, expensive trainers. They might have been the same gathering from the other night, or the same gathering that was a staple of these places.

Kate didn't make eye contact for too long with any of them. They were a problem for another day.

'This is why I parked outside Tesco's,' said Zain. 'I have no problem handling myself, but my car isn't going to be at risk from these dicks.'

They entered D Block, Kate looking up at the cameras placed high on the wall, secured with more than just cable wires. They had solid steel reinforced cages around them, the lenses popping out.

Inside she smelled what they couldn't on the video footage. It was ingrained, familiar. Cigarette smoke, urine, beer, sweat, dirt, desperation and despair. More than anything else, poverty.

The lift doors creaked open slowly, then shut just as sluggishly. It took off, shaking, feeling like a bronchial attack on a treadmill.

'I bet no one comes if we press the alarm on breakdown,' said Zain.

The lift stopped, and the doors began their unhurried opening routine.

They walked along the same corridor Dan had on the video they'd seen, stopped outside the door he had entered. It was red, with the number D63 on it in hopeful gold metal symbols.

'Do we knock?' said Zain.

Kate rapped on the door. There was no answer. From inside, she could hear the thudding of loud music.

Zain checked the front windows, banged his fists against them. Someone lifted dirty yellow netting. A face peered out, mouthing, 'What the fuck?'

Zain took out his badge, flattened it against the window. The face panicked, disappeared.

'Is there a back way out?' said Kate.

'No, just a six-floor drop,' he said.

'And if you thought the cops were here and had something to hide?'

'Ah, fuck this shit,' said Zain, running back down the way they had come. He shouted back to Kate: 'The idiot's hanging out of the window, about to jump.'

Kate walked quickly to where he stood. It was a balcony by the lifts, offering them a view of the back windows to the flats. She could see the man half out of his window, looking down, calculating the drop, looking back at her.

'It's at least a forty five foot drop,' she said. 'You really want to risk it?'

He turned black eyes towards her, spat out of the window. Calculating how long it would take to land on the grass?

'We're not here for you,' she said. 'We want to ask you some questions about Daniel Grant.'

The face creased in anger.

'We don't have a warrant; we won't be searching your apartment. We just need to talk.'

The face was pensive, staring down at the grass. The man moved a fraction forward, building up courage. He glared at her, scanned his chances of survival. Spat again. Then disappeared back through the window.

The flat stunk of grease, fish and curry. The front room was bigger than Zain's, he thought bitterly. How did someone on benefits get a better place than him?

'What's your name?' said Zain.

He looked Somalian, or from some other part of North Africa. Dark skin, but delicate features.

'Barry,' he muttered.

'Barry?' said Zain. 'Joker.'

'Barry is just fine, for now,' said Kate.

Zain shrugged, inspected the room. It was furnished with a single couch, orange, and a unit where the TV, DVD player, satellite box, and various games consoles were kept. The room was muggy with sweat and the distinct smell that young men manufactured. He felt his skin crawl, perched himself on the arm of the sofa. Kate was sitting on it. Zain saw stains on the material, didn't want to take the risk.

Barry sat cross-legged on the floor. He was emaciated, his bony frame visible in joggers and T-shirt, both too big for him. Both emblazoned with 'Moschino'.

'Why you here?' he said. 'What you wanna know?'

It was a south London accent, the ghetto version, but identifiable.

'We need to speak to you about Daniel Grant,' said Kate.

'Yeah, I know him. He's good people.'

'We believe you might be able to provide us with some vital information about his whereabouts, the day before yesterday,' said Kate.

'Don't know nuttin' 'bout dat. Saw it on da net. Dan ain't no killer.'

'How can you be sure?' said Kate.

'He got balls like a cockroach, tiny little coward balls. He don't have it in him to be killin' jack.'

'You seen his balls?' said Zain.

'You got jokes? Naice,' said Barry, spitting from the side of his mouth. Zain realised he had khat in his cheek, was chewing it while he spoke to them.

'Barry, we have CCTV footage placing Mr Grant in your apartment from about 10 p.m. on Tuesday the tenth of November, until approximately 10 a.m. on the morning of Wednesday the eleventh of November.'

Barry gaped at them, a blank expression on his face.

'What were you doing for those twelve hours?' said Kate.

'Nuttin', he wasn't here,' said Barry.

'We saw him enter and leave. Unless he jumped out the back, he didn't leave your flat,' said Zain. 'So what were you doing? Checking out each other's bollocks?'

'You callin' me a fag?' said Barry, swearing at Zain in Arabic.

'I prefer women to dogs,' said Zain.

Barry blinked wildly, his pillow of confidence removed.

'I have to make assumptions,' said Zain. 'Unless you say what went on here.'

Zain knew what was going on inside that tiny brain. He knew Dan had been here getting high, playing computer games. Barry was no supplier, though, just a user, a middleman. He was providing Dan with the drugs; someone else was Barry's source.

'We just chilled,' said Barry.

'Did you partake off any narcotics or stimulants?' said Kate.

'No drugs,' said Barry. 'I'm a good Muslim.'

Zain felt the immediate spike of red mist and rage. He felt himself go into tunnel-vision mode, Barry at the end of that dangerous lens.

'If you were both here relaxing, then why is Dan so reluctant to let us know?' said Kate.

Barry shrugged.

'What did you talk about? What did you do, while together?' said Kate.

'This and dat. Played games, innit. Yeah, computer games, we played those,' said Barry enthusiastically.

'Again, why was Dan so reluctant to tell us this? There is nothing incriminating in anything you've told us,' said Kate.

Barry shrugged. 'Got nuttin' else to say to you,' he said. 'You know where da door is.'

Zain felt the sensible side of him being pushed off a ledge. The other side took over. He knew it had happened. And he knew what was going to happen next would probably wreck his career. Still, he couldn't stop.

Chapter Seventy-one

Kate only caught a blur of movement. Zain had jumped up from the arm of the sofa and grabbed Barry, pushing the frail figure against the wall. Suspending him five inches from the floor.

Zain had his hands carefully arranged, she observed. He had scrunched up Barry's top, used it as leverage. It would mean no finger marks on his neck – bruising possibly, but no marks. And no skin-to-skin contact.

Harris was no raw recruit; she had to remember that. Two weeks in her team didn't discount everything he had learned over the last few years.

Zain's face was close to Barry's, his teeth bared, spittle landing on the man's face as he spoke. Barry's skinny fingers tried to release Zain's grip. Kate was torn between reprimand and an opportunity she fully recognised.

'Now listen to me, Barry. You start by telling us your name. And then you tell us what you and Dan got up to. And then you don't have your neck broken.'

Barry choked, kicked out, but Zain used his own body to pin the man's legs back.

'You see, I'm an expert at this. I won't leave a mark on your body, and she won't say a word. Us cops stick together. You understand? Nod if you understand.'

Barry did so. Even Kate felt herself nod, such was the intensity of the exchange.

'Name,' said Zain.

'Abdu Basit Mahboob,' he said.

'Good boy,' said Zain. 'Now, what were you guys doing?'

Barry shut down until Zain yanked him further into the wall, which made him drop all attempts at concealment.

'I don't wanna go to no prison, please!'

'You're not in a position to negotiate, because you either tell me or you get hurt,' said Zain.

'Just Kaching and Blocaine.'

Legal highs, chemical stimulants, easily available.

'So why was Dan so scared to tell us?'

'I told him – he tell on me, I whack him,' said Barry.

Zain let go of Barry, let him fall to the floor. 'That wasn't so hard, was it?' he said. 'You even think of what just happened again, let alone say it, and I will have you in a prison cell so quickly, your head will spin.'

'Prison cell for what? You ain't got fuck all on me. Dis is po-po harassment.' Barry rubbed at his chest and neck, spitting, getting some confidence back.

'Watch him,' said Zain, leaving the room.

Barry got up to follow him, but Kate blocked him in the doorway. Zain came back within minutes, flinging a clear polythene bag at Barry's head.

'What the fuck is this? Baby powder? You lying little prick.'

'Dat ain't mine. You planted it, you cunting pig.'

'Don't fucking swear at me, you piece of shit,' said Zain. He kicked Barry hard on the elbow. Barry howled in pain, scrabbling across the floor to get away from Zain.

'Enough,' said Kate, pushing Zain hard in the chest. He tried to get past her, but she held him off. 'Get out of here. Now.'

'Thank you for your time, Mr Mahboob,' said Kate. 'We will need a written statement from you, confirming what you just told us. That Mr Grant was here on the night in question.'

Barry turned black eyes on her.

'If you play ball with us, I'll overlook the class A drug possession with intent to supply, and the verbal assault on a police officer,' she said.

The implication that he also needed to keep his mouth shut about what Zain had done to him came across loud and clear.

'Save it,' said Zain, when they were in his car, heading back to HQ.

Kate kept her rage under control, her voice neutral. Bit back the desire to do to Zain what he had done to Barry.

'There was no cause,' she said calmly. 'He confirmed Dan's alibi, that's all we needed.'

'Tells us what a scumbag Dan is, though, knowing about the drugs.'

'It was illegal what you just did,' she said. 'Thanks to you, we can't charge Barry for the cocaine. And slow down, for Christ's sake.'

'I don't believe in respecting dicks like that. Fuck.' He stopped the car, banged his hands on the steering wheel. Cars behind them beeped their horns. 'Go fuck yourselves,' Zain shouted out of the window. 'Police!' he added, when the verbal abuse started to come back.

'Park up there. That's an order,' Kate said.

He glared at her; she held his gaze. He blinked first, shifted the car into gear and pulled over. Drivers gave them daggers as they went by; Kate waved at them in apology.

'I don't want a lecture,' he said. 'Either fire me or leave it.'

'What happened back there?' she said.

'Does it matter? I fucked up, fine, but I got a result.'

'Is it usual for you to lose control so quickly?'

'I didn't lose control. I just got sick of the prick. Him, Dan, Rourke. All of them. Ruby is dead; Millie is in metal splints. And these fuckers walk around unaffected, and there's fuck all we can do about it.'

'Why has Millie affected you so strongly?' said Kate. 'I almost feel as though she's got a hold on you deeper than Ruby does. Ruby is our priority.'

'I know that. But you didn't hear what Millie said, the way she said it. He treated her like garbage.'

'She knew what sort of risk she was placing herself in.'

'Why? Because she's a slut? A hooker? She doesn't walk the streets. She's not like that.'

'Aren't they just points on a scale?'

He punched the car door to his right, undid his seat belt.

'What set you off back there, Harris? If you're going to work with me, if you're going to be part of my team, I need to know. Am I placing any of us at risk? If Brennan pushes a few too many buttons, or if Michelle does, will you strike out at them as well?'

Zain rubbed his face with his hands, breathed out.

'It was him, Barry. Fucking ridiculous name, stupid man. He just reminded me of something. And he was driving me mad. Him and Dan and all of it.'

'What did he remind you of?'

'It was the khat. The stuff he was chewing. When I was . . . taken . . . when they held me, one of the men was Somali. He kept chewing khat all the time. It's like they say, when you lose one sense others compensate? They had me blindfolded, so I could smell that rotten stuff.'

'And you are going to racially profile the entire British Somali community forever because of it?'

Zain didn't seem to hear her, he was so engrossed in telling his story.

'The khat guy, I never knew his name then. Afterwards I did. And he kept saying, 'Call me Bob.' Jihadi Bob. I laughed the first time he said it. That got me a punch that nearly broke my nose. And his real name . . . well it doesn't matter. Only he was the one that tortured me.'

Kate held her own breath as Zain's became more laboured. He was sweating at the temples, and his voice was thick with emotion.

'And he would spit. Right before he pulled out my toenails. He would spit that stuff into my face. And the first time I didn't know, he just spat, and then fuck . . . I blacked out. And the second time, he spat in my face, and I knew what was coming. And I screamed. From the moment he spat, to the moment I fainted from the pain, I screamed like a fucking coward. And the third time, he came towards me, and I could smell the khat. And I started screaming even before he spat. Each time I blacked out from the pain, and I cried out, begging them to stop. I am so ashamed of myself. I gave them what they wanted. Only, when they got to the seventh time . . . I didn't black out. I was awake all through that pain.'

'I can't imagine how that must feel,' said Kate. She heard a slight tremor in her voice.

'You know how I remember all that? Because the bastards filmed it. Every fucking painful second. They filmed it and they laughed. They were going to post it online. They couldn't get a signal in that container or they would have done. And I got hold of the videos. Afterwards, I mean. And I saw them . . .'

'You shouldn't have watched them,' she said. It was a whisper almost. She reached out and touched the back of his hand.

'I'm sorry. It was all I knew to do in that moment, she said.'

Kate let silence mark time as she thought about what to do next.

Harris was good. He had shown flashes of his brilliance already. The technical assistance he had given the team, the support he had provided to her. Even Hope was encouraging about him. And against that, he was obviously still damaged from his experiences. He had acted out, done something she had been tempted to do many times. Only she was clear about boundaries. She knew what happened when men stepped over them.

And then another thought. She now had leverage over Harris. Something that potentially ensured she could trust him. She would write up the incident, officially, on an EIR2 form, and keep it filed.

If she ever needed it, she would use it. Compassion would be given the upper hand, for now at least.

'Let's go back to Regus House,' Kate said. 'This isn't over. Only, your mental health is low on my list today. We're running late to meet Dr Sandler, the cyber psychologist. If Dan isn't behind Ruby's disappearance and murder, we need to find out who is. Before we end up with another dead body.'

Chapter Seventy-two

Dr Eric Sandler was in his mid-thirties, attractive in a preppy way, Kate thought. He was wearing chinos with a blazer and pastel-coloured polo shirt, his hair long and dark blond. He worked for Cambridge University as a forensic cyber psychologist, a new but booming field.

DS Harris was in the conference room with them. Zain was much calmer, having cooled off. This meeting would be a way to try and salvage their working relationship. She needed to solve this case; she needed his expertise. Reprimanding him could take place another day.

Kate had a sudden recall to how he had tasted, the smell of him on the hotel sheets in the morning. Again, she felt shame burn inside her. What was she thinking? Imagine if she had gone through with it, and there was an official investigation into how he had treated Barry?

'So it's Locard's principle?' she said instead to Eric, sipping at a black coffee. Both men were drinking water, she noticed. 'The forensic principle that every contact leaves a trace?'

'Yes. It's the same with online crime scenes. Every interaction online, no matter how innocuous, or forgotten, leaves a trace. I have a paper I can send you if you are interested. It was something I published last year.'

'Great,' muttered Zain.

'That would be useful,' she said.

On the scant details Kate had sent Eric, he had managed to come up with an analysis for her.

'The psychology of Ruby's viewers is simple enough. Teenagers looking to be part of something, needing friends and validation.

People like Ruby offer them both, someone to call on when in need. The videos are intimate, Ruby is speaking to them alone, she is their friend, they matter to her. The psychology of online creatives themselves is complex, though. Their motivations, goals, ambitions, are as individual as they are.'

'What do you think of Ruby's motivations?' said Zain.

'Calculating by your information about her present age, I guess she was around fourteen or fifteen when she started going online. At that age, her primary focus would have been to form peer-to-peer relationships. SNS are used by adolescents for forming friendships.'

'SNS?' said Kate.

'Social networking sites,' said Zain.

'Precisely,' said Eric. 'Facebook, mainly, but a whole host of others now exist in its shadow.'

'What about real-world friendships?' asked Kate.

'SNS allow young people to cement those relationships, and to widen their circles. The downside is that young people are so desperate to make these bonds, they open themselves up to risk. Adolescents and young adults are more likely to add strangers who request to be their friends, for example.'

'Ruby was deliberately looking for a wide audience; it was a business for her,' said Kate.

'The dichotomy between public and private is blurred online. In real life, you can choose who to have in your personal space, say your bedroom . . .'

Zain choked on his water, causing Kate to feel embarrassed heat in her face.

'Sorry,' he said, not looking at her.

'And you choose who to have in your public space, or at least you are aware of it more,' said Eric.

'Online you can't make that distinction?' said Kate, trying to ignore Zain's outburst earlier.

'Ruby seems to have been typical of her generation. Her tweets sometimes say very personal stuff, deep emotional thoughts. Other times they are aimed at her audience. For some reason, people think the tone of their tweets or online comments is enough to differentiate between public and private. Ruby was the same.'

'So potentially she was tweeting personal messages into a public arena?'

'Exactly. SNS are great – hey, I make my living from them – but they have a lot of downsides. They cause depression, especially in young people, who think they should have more friends if peers have more Facebook friends, or Twitter followers. They feel inadequate if peers are posting messages about all the fun they're having; they feel left out, less interesting. Adults feel that way when friends post about how many kids they have, or how well they're doing at work. Nearly forty per cent of girls have a blog or a vlog, and fashion, beauty and lifestyle are the most popular topics. Ruby took a private activity and became part of a public network.'

'It just doesn't fit with what we know about her,' said Zain. 'Her parents say she's introverted, nervous, quite sheltered. And then there she is, making a splash, posting her videos all the time. I don't get it.'

'It is confusing for many,' said Eric. 'In my experience, though, individuals that focus so much on their online persona ... well, they struggle with reality. They are usually trying to get away from something. In our day, we would sit in a room, blast music, isolate ourselves, scribble in our diaries. Ruby and her generation don't have to skulk. Cyberbullying may be an issue, but the freedom to connect online is revolutionary, too.'

'So Ruby may have been lonely, isolated, possibly bullied?' said Zain.

'It's only conjecture, but that might have been the cause of her isolation.'

'Her ex-boyfriend told me she was bullied at school,' said Kate. She made a mental note to follow up on these thoughts with

Ruby's parents. So far, they had closed off at any suggestion that Ruby might be unhappy. 'Somebody like that, she might be susceptible? If a skilled person knew what they were doing?'

'Yes. Ruby left a trace every time she posted online. Somebody could follow that, like a trail, and know everything about her. Details she probably didn't think important, probably couldn't recall, somebody could read them and make sense of them.'

'Interpretation of a young woman,' whispered Kate.

'What's that?' said Zain.

'A theory I came across,' she said. She didn't say it was from her own PhD. 'The interpretation of an object by a psychopath.'

'I think that's very possible,' said Eric. 'Even likely. For example, you talked about MINDNET, the company she was affiliated with . . . Is someone out there thinking she sold out? You mentioned her boyfriend . . . Is someone feeling betrayed because they want Ruby for themselves? What about the products she used? Is someone watching her, and has Ruby used something they object to? Animal rights groups? The diet industry is worth billions; Ruby regularly criticised them. Are they protecting their interests? Or is it envy? Somebody whose own life isn't going the way it should, resentful for what they perceive to be Ruby's perfect life. And it does look perfect. When all you see is a random sequence of fifteen-minute video clips, YouTubers and vloggers can create a high level of perfection. It's the best form of air-brushing around.'

'You're frying my brain, doctor,' said Zain.

'Ruby online is key to this, that much I am sure of. The videos were posted online, posted into her public and private sphere. It means something.'

'What exactly, though? That's what I'm struggling with,' said Kate.

'I'm here to advise; I leave the dot joining to the professionals,' he said. 'And if someone else, like you said, is in imminent danger, then you need to join those dots quickly, detective.'

'What did you make of the message at the end of the last video? "You're next",' said Kate.

'It's personal. If whoever posted that video wanted us all to watch, they would say something like, who's next, or watch this space. They didn't, though. Somebody watching that video was being targeted. The killer sent out a clear message.'

'And yet no one has contacted us, scared for their life.'

'They might not have worked it out yet. It's not a generalised threat though, that I am sure of. It's directed to someone in particular.'

Kate dreaded that call; a new video has been uploaded, someone else is dead.

'Alternatively, and this is just free, out-of-the-box thinking; it could be a diversion. The killer might be frightened – maybe you got close, without realising it? They are distracting you, making you look over your shoulder for a second attack.'

'Messing with the cops,' said Kate. 'Hardly atypical.'

Chapter Seventy-three

Susan was waiting for him. The warning signs were clear as soon as he walked into the house. He dropped his car keys into the glass bowl on the cabinet by the front door. He removed his jacket, rolled up his sleeves, ready for a fight.

The air was thick with wood polish, bleach and, above it all, the unmistakable aroma of red wine. It was what she did. Drank, cleaned and then argued.

She was wiping the walls when he went into the TV room. One wall was covered with a projector screen, his home movie experience. A repeat of *Come Dine with Me* was playing, muted. The faces on screen screaming laughter with mouths wide open, then bitching about the food when alone in the host's bedroom.

'Where were you?' Susan said, not missing a single scrub on the magnolia wall. She was a suburban Mr Miyagi, he often joked. There was no break for humour tonight, though.

'The office. Lots going on. Dan's been released; I had to sort it out.'

He put his jacket on the arm of a sofa, went to the drinks cabinet. He caught his reflection in the shine on the wood. He poured himself a whisky, spilling a bit on purpose.

'They let him out?'

'He's innocent. Was holed up with his drug dealer pal during the crucial time frame. Silly arse.'

'Why did he call you? Don't Byrne and his lot have any decent lawyers?'

'He trusts me. Old time's sake I suppose.'

'You just can't let them go, can you?' she said. There was accusation there, but also chastisement. 'And Ruby?'

'Still not found her,' he said, sitting down and taking his phone out. 'Dan's trending on Twitter. Hashtag DanIsOurHero, DanIs-Free. DanILoveYou. Crazy idiots. If only they knew.'

'Yes, well, he's not the only one. A lot of people have a lot to hide,' she said.

'What's that supposed to mean?'

'I think you know.'

'Come on, baby, let's just relax,' he said.

The cloth whacked him on the head. Unexpected, hard, on tar-get. His glass flew from his hands, landing with a quiet thud on the furry white rug at his feet. The golden-brown liquid seeped into the layers of cotton.

'Don't patronise me,' she said.

'I wasn't. Do we have to fight? I'm tired.'

'Tired chasing her. Always her. You know, when she signed up with MINDNET, I was so fucking delirious with happiness. I thought that's it, it's over, she's away from you. I don't have to compete with her anymore. Ever since you met her, you've been obsessed with her. Even after she dumped you, because that's exactly what she did, you just couldn't leave her be, could you? Getting involved with Dan again, keeping your grubby fingers on Ruby. But she didn't want you, did she? She's nearly young enough to be your daughter, for fuck's sake.'

'She's hardly a child,' he said.

'You disgust me.'

'It's all in your head, Susan, always has been.'

'Really? I saw the way you fawned all over her at her launch party. You cried when she thanked you in her speech. It's on You-fucking-Tube. You hanging on her every word. I don't even know why you were there. She's not your client anymore. Except I do know exactly why you were there.'

'Stop watching things and reading your paranoia into them.'

Rourke picked up the empty glass, licking drops of whisky from the rim. He refilled it, swallowed half of it.

'You better start treating me better, Karl,' she said, coming up behind him. Rourke felt the hairs on his neck prick up.

'I treat you the way you deserve,' he said. His voice was tight; he shouldn't have said that.

'You bastard,' she spat. 'I can destroy you.'

He should have let it go, let her go. He didn't, he turned to face her, the words pushing out of him, goading her. 'Do your worst,' he said.

'I mean it. After everything I've done for you . . . treat me right, or else . . .'

'Or else what?' he said.

'Otherwise I'll tell the police how your alibi is a lie. How you weren't really with me, and how you disappeared the night your precious little Ruby did.'

Rourke drained his glass, left Susan to her rage. He was shaking when he tried to undress. Out of nerves or fear, he didn't know.

PART FOUR
HEART OF DARKNESS

Chapter Seventy-four

DS Stevie Brennan was still bemused by the army of girls that had threatened her outside Southwark police station. How could they be so enamoured with Dan Grant that they turned into mindless zombies? Stevie had dealt with enough drug dealers, murderers and gang members. She'd done a stint with psychopaths, even. And yet she'd never felt so nervous as when confronted by eight hundred screaming girls, baying for blood. Police blood. Her blood.

A police constable had sat and watched all three hundred of Ruby's videos posted online. Those of interest had been forwarded to Stevie, who was now looking through them.

This petite girl, very conventional in some ways, the sort of polished middle-class white girl she had once thought she should aspire to be. She laughed now, thinking how she would have hated that skin. Stevie was meant to be something else, and she was thankful she was just that.

The office was quiet. Michelle was at her computer. Riley and Harris had gone to speak to Jed Byrne. Riley was pursuing every tentative lead she could, Justin Hope having called her in and bollocked her that morning. Pelt was out with Hampshire police again, seeing if they could expand their forensic search.

Ruby seemed so alive, looking into the camera directly, her smile easy and her voice soft.

Hey, guys, how are you? So this video is a bit serious, but I think it's important I make it. I've talked before about the way I feel, the days when I wake up sometimes and don't think I can face the world. I'm so glad it's helped some of you; your comments always make me think this is worthwhile. So today, I wanted to talk about when things go really badly. And you guys are all so supportive, and it makes this whole thing easier.

Ruby is in her bedroom, the camera picking up her bed, the blinds down on the windows behind her.

I just wanted to say, there's no shame in feeling like this. When sometimes things are getting so bad that you feel all alone, lost, and think you might not be able to cope, there's no shame in getting help. I let the girls that treated me so badly have a hold on me for years. I remember the fear of waking up every morning, dreading going into school to face them. All the harsh words they ever said, the taunts about my weight. I try to block it out, but it comes back in flashes, and I can picture it. All these years later, I know exactly where I was, and what they said. And it makes me angry, that they had that control over me. And for what? Because I wasn't some silly size for a girl to be anyway?

Ruby runs her fingers through her hair, shakes lose strands into the air. Her rage, her upset falling away with them. Her voice is calm again.

But all that hatred, it was only hurting me. I was tormenting myself, making myself ill. The people that made me feel like that, they will never be sorry or ashamed for what they did. So why should I give them power over me now? Wanting to hurt them, get them back, destroy them, all it does is raise my own stress and blood pressure. Makes me anxious and angry. I am killing myself slowly if I let them win. So I wanted to say to them that I forgive them. Not for them, but because I want to let this poison go.

And I can do that because of you guys, always there for me, whenever I need you. You draw the poison out of me, and I feel safe and secure in this space. This little place we share, where it's just you and me. Alone.

Stevie, despite her revulsion at the cosmetic front, felt herself warming to this girl. She was doing something useful, she supposed. And the vulnerability of being watched by millions, and still having a crisis of self-esteem. And to tell the world that, not trying to portray an image of perfection.

'Fuck this. I'm being sucked in,' Stevie commented to Michelle.

'Anything useful?'

'I just feel for her. Stuck in that cellar, out in the woods. Her mental state must have been shit; she must have been terrified. Poor cow.'

'You think someone else is already missing? The next victim, I mean. What if they're already locked up, or being killed right now?'

Stevie pulled up another video. This one was Ruby speaking about her successful make-up launch, Any Size. Stevie cringed at the obsession with objectification.

Hey, guys, just little old me, Ruby. So just had my launch for my new make-up range. And it was amazing. I know I use that word a lot, but actually it was amazing. So thank you to you all, and thank you for your support and getting me to here.

I love make-up, and I've called it Any Size because that's what make-up is. It doesn't matter what size you are, how old you are, what colour you are, if you're gay or straight, make-up is yours to use. Anyone can enjoy it, and I hope with the tips I've given, you will use it to make yourself feel amazing as well.

Ruby is in a hotel room in the video, with her boyfriend. Another girl is there, Clarissa, another YouTuber.

Anyway I'm having a bit of an after-party with some of my besties, just having a bit of a break from the main events. Aw, guys, that was an amazing night. I had a great night, didn't you, guys?

Clarissa agrees, congratulating Ruby on her success.

Didn't you?

Her boyfriend looks at the camera, doesn't answer, but instead puts breadsticks into his mouth, doing a walrus impression for the viewers.

'I don't think the boyfriend liked playing second fiddle to Ruby,' said Stevie. He couldn't bring himself to congratulate Ruby like Clarissa had, instead was doing tricks to pull the attention back to him. And why walrus? Was he trying to say something to Ruby about her weight?

'Dan's just posted a video,' said Michelle.

Stevie walked over to Michelle's terminal, pulled up a chair. The video was shot in Dan's bedroom. Why were they so obsessed with their bedrooms? Girls must have been fascinated, curious to know what a boy's personal space was like. Good job they didn't have smellovision yet, thought Stevie. And Dan was hiding his mess.

Yo, thanks for watching this. It's a bit more serious shit than I usually like to post. I thought it was important though, after everything that's gone on. It's been a crazy few days, what with Ruby gone, and then the police involvement. How they could think it was me, I can't believe it. I mean, I love her. Loved her.

Dan blinks at the camera, wipes his hands over his face, as though holding back his emotion.

But you know, despite how they treated me, I get it. I understand. They were just doing their jobs, right? Trying to eliminate everyone, so they can find out where Ruby is. And I believe they will find her. I can't believe she's dead, I just can't . . .

Sorry, it's too difficult for me right now. I just wanted to let you all know that I'm cool, and that I'm OK. Thanks for all your messages and Twitter hashtags, it's been humbling. Anyway, I might go offline for a bit. And just hope Ruby is OK. Even though I know she might not be.

Peace out.

'Oscar-worthy,' said Stevie. 'Prick. He makes me so angry,' said Stevie. 'Look at that! He's acting as though he's blameless. I feel like posting his drug habit online.'

'The dealer only testified to the fact that Dan was with him, not what they were doing,' said Michelle.

'Give me a few minutes alone with him, and he'll be testifying to anything we say.'

Stevie went back to her own computer. The next video was odd. It was Ruby, just woken up, no make-up, sounding hoarse.

I think everyone goes through this, questioning themselves. What am I doing with my life? What is this all for? For so long I was on the outside, so alone. And now, with you guys all out there, supporting me, I feel finally as though I'm not an outcast. I feel normal. You've all taught me normal is so mixed, it's so many things. I just need to figure out what to do now, what to do next. I don't want to take you all for granted. Things have happened, and I need to really think about what my priorities are.

Ruby looks into the camera, there are tears forming in her eyes.

Sorry for being so raw with you all today. But I know you understand me. No one else does, I really believe that.

Stevie made a note of the time and date: it was the week before Ruby disappeared. What was she so worried about or conflicted about?

The next video had Ruby sans make-up again, her eyes swollen.

'I know that look,' said Stevie. 'Before I decided men were all shits and had to be kept at a distance.'

'Ouch, poor men,' said Michelle.

'Whatever,' said Stevie.

Ruby was dressed in a jumper too large for her, comfort dressing as Stevie liked to call it, her hair pulled back into a ponytail.

Guys, I might not post a video for a while. I just need to clear my head. Please keep commenting, and I will check your messages. I just need to go quiet for a while, just a few days. I'll miss you guys, but I'll be back. I have something important to tell you, and I just need to make sure I do it right. Love you always. I can't say at the moment.

A bitter laugh at this.

But I know you will all still be there when I'm back. And I know you'll support me, whatever I tell you. No one understands me, no one really gets me apart from you.

Stevie checked the date, and then checked her list. She logged on to Ruby's channel. It was the last video Ruby had posted.

Chapter Seventy-five

Michelle was on the phone to her daughter's school. There had been an incident; her daughter had just bitten another child.

'I assure you, Mrs Hadley, she has never exhibited this behaviour in the past. And has never bitten, any other child. Was she provoked?'

Michelle listened as the deputy head teacher told her how offended she was, thinking she would allow children to provoke others.

'I wasn't suggesting you don't have a safe environment, I am just curious what made Maya bite this boy.'

More official speak.

'Yes, of course, I will come in this evening with my husband.'

Please don't ask me to come and collect Maya now, she thought. Luckily, the school agreed not to insist her daughter go home, but would keep an eye on her.

'Trouble?' said Stevie.

'Yes. I hope it's not my fault. I missed saying goodnight to her last night, because I was so busy here. I really hope that's not what caused this.'

'She's tough, just like her mum. A slipped goodnight won't be affecting her. What happened, anyway?'

Michelle explained. Stevie grinned.

'Don't worry about it. I used to bite boys in class all the time. They're so fucking annoying, even aged five. Maya will be just fine.'

Michelle didn't like to say how she didn't want her daughter growing up to be like Brennan. She went back to what she was doing. It was what Riley had instructed: making sure everything was covered. Michelle had pulled up the CCTV from Windsor Court, and was spooling through it. It had been watched up to the time Ruby had supposedly left, when she didn't appear on camera. It hadn't been watched after that.

Figures came and left, residents Michelle had no interest in.

But then, at midnight, there was a visitor. He came in via the back entrance. Michelle replayed the video, just to be sure. She called Stevie over.

'Fuck me,' she said. 'What's he doing there?'

Michelle uploaded the clip to an email and sent it to Riley and Harris.

Jed Byrne was a type. Kate imagined his clones in executive boardrooms across the world. Men burning with ambition and their own self-importance. Used to getting their own way, the thrill of screwing over their opposition as great as the satisfaction from winning. A hit that lasted as long as that from cocaine, and then the craving started again.

Kate had known too many men like that. They had burned her. She felt the resentment and antipathy travelling through her veins.

'So you think demanding seventy per cent of her revenue was justifiable?'

'Yes, I do. We got her those deals, the lucrative contracts. We told her how to demand her worth. Before MINDNET, she would advertise products for free. Under Karl Rourke, he didn't have a clue, and in consequence neither did Ruby. We made sure that every time she mentioned a product, she got paid for it. And when she did a whole segment just using one product, we got her more than one of your officers probably earns in a month.

We did the production, promotion. We got her on TV, in every worthwhile magazine. And you should see the money we bring in, bribes from diet companies, for example, asking Ruby not to use their products and lambast them.'

'I might be naive, not part of your corporate world, but it seems to me that Ruby was crucial to all of it. Without her, you would have nothing?'

Jed's face was reddening; mixing with his tan, it looked like a type of wood she had once seen. 'We can replace her.'

'Is that what you plan on doing? Replacing Ruby? Is she that disposable to you?'

'I'm not sure why you are here, detective. Why aren't you out there finding Ruby, and finding whoever killed her?'

'I am,' said Kate, casually.

Jed's brows lifted, his jaw began to pulse. 'You think MINDNET are involved?'

'I'm curious . . . If Ruby refused to sign your new contract, what would you do? It seems to me that she is essential for your brand. And if your star isn't playing ball?'

'You think we would kill her off? It doesn't make sense.'

'Like you said, Ruby is replaceable.'

'You're being ridiculous.'

'I bet you already have a hundred potential girls lined up to fill her space. A targeted campaign at Ruby's subscribers. That on top of rebranding Daniel Grant as a broken-hearted, misused-by-the-system hero. It seems to me MINDNET are the only winners in this sad situation. And I can't help wondering, who else in the MINDNET stable is rebelling? Who else might need to be kept quiet?'

'I think we're done,' said Jed.

Kate wasn't. There was more here, she could see it in his face. She had broken through his confident veneer, his shield of privilege, and she had made him tremble. The nerves, the sweating, the ticks.

'Not yet,' said Kate. 'Where were you on the day of Ruby's disappearance?'

Jed's mouth opened, ready to attack her, then closed quickly.

Chapter Seventy-six

Zain was locked away with Bill Anderson, going over the data MINDNET had collected. Riley had painted Anderson as a Neanderthal. Zain took offence on two grounds.

'You know that Neanderthal image is a load of crap,' he'd told her back at the office, when she'd updated him about her latest encounter with the MINDNET staff. 'They found skeletons that were old with arthritis when they died; one had a damaged leg. And from that they concluded they were all bent over and dumb and aggressive. They could speak, looked nearly the same as us. Had culture and religion, and it was probably us who butchered them. So, I get what you're saying. Anderson is a man's man, probably a misogynist and difficult, but don't insult our cousin species.'

The look on her face.

Anderson was his sort of man, similar to his own father. Zain understood him, his mentality. He saw it in the groomed cleanliness that wasn't obvious but was military grade. Short, hair, clipped nails, smart clothes. Shoes the colour of liquorice, they were polished so well. A man who took orders, followed orders.

Zain got that. He took orders. Didn't always follow them, though. Probably where he and Anderson would diverge.

'Training recruits. It's what they make men like me do. Once they have no use for us. It's our version of horses for glue,' Anderson said.

'Inspiring the next generation?' said Zain.

'Hardly. They make you into a highly specific engineered machine. A trained killer. Then they expect you to sit in a classroom and teach?'

'They probably expected you to die early,' said Zain.

'Yes. Surviving sometimes isn't the best option.'

'You turned to the dark side?' said Zain – jokingly, he hoped.

Anderson narrowed his eyes, pulled his head up, nostrils enlarged. Not in a joking mood, thought Zain.

'I make use of my skills, that's all.'

'You married?'

'No. Men like me don't really get married. Even when we do, it's only a half truth.'

Zain nodded. Another similarity. 'How did you find out about Ruby?'

'I got a call from Mr Byrne, about 5 a.m.'

'How did he find out?'

'No idea. Ask him.'

'DCI Riley is probably on it. You alone when you got the call?'

'Yes. I work long hours. And I'll save you the trouble. I have no one that can verify my whereabouts. If I am of interest. Between 8 p.m. and 8 a.m. when I started work again, I was alone. Didn't speak to anyone.'

Window of opportunity, thought Zain. Here was a man admitting he had one. What was the motive? There had to be one before that time frame became important.

'Not of specific interest, Mr Anderson. Just asking everyone Ruby might have come into contact with. Expanding our investigation.'

Riley's words.

'Now your prime suspect is no longer viable, you mean?'

'You've met him, haven't you? He's not right.'

'You shouldn't judge him so harshly,' said Anderson.

'I judge as I find,' said Zain. 'I would've thought Dan rubbed you the wrong way. He's ideal material to get into the army for a year and get the wrongness trained out of him.'

'I understand Dan. His leg was damaged in a fall. It left him with a limp, from aged five or six. He went through years of torment at school, never allowed to take part in games, the usual stuff boys get up to.'

'Some boys,' said Zain. 'My cousin liked dolls.'

'Gay?'

'No, has had two wives and seven children.'

'Dan was always on the margins. That sort of outsider status builds up an anger inside, a rage. He turned to the net for his sanity. Although I think it was already too late; he was damaged.'

'How do you know all this?'

'He invited all his school pals to his birthday party.'

'The party? The one at chrome?'

'Yes. He invited his pals, who weren't really his pals. He had no friends; these were his classmates, year mates. He rubbed their faces in it. How they had come crawling to his party, were drinking his champagne and getting off with the women he'd hired.'

'You make him sound like a character out of *Carrie*.'

'When you're so hated for so long, I don't know if you can ever be right again.'

Anderson tapped on his keyboard, brought up the files Zain wanted to see.

'We checked the trolls, the threatening comments. The majority are from young girls, aged twelve to seventeen. Some older. The pervs, the old men pretending to be teenage girls, they don't really troll. They send arse-kissing messages, usually, and they were targeting other young girls, fans of Ruby's, not Ruby herself.'

'Yeah, let's all get online, so perverts can get access to our kids,' said Zain. 'Makes me sick.'

'We gave details to the police, when we found them. It's difficult. Anyone can open a YouTube account; you don't need a credit card.

Unless you want age verification, but none of Ruby's videos were adult.'

'How did you find out, then?'

'Guesswork, instinct. Checking the email addresses used, checking IP addresses. If there are no kids in the house, then we know. Like I said, very few were found.'

'And the ones threatening Ruby? There must be something?'

'I sent a list to your colleague, Michelle Cable. Mainly trolls, jealousy reeking from every typed letter. No stalkers sending her messages saying they want to lunch on her kidneys.'

Except for Dan, thought Zain.

'I think your investigation is probably going to stall, detective. I can sense it. I'm also guessing, right now, a second victim might be just what you need.'

Zain needed a leak on his way out of the MINDNET offices, although Anderson seemed reluctant to let him loose in the building.

Zain was washing his hands. Even the Gents had bottles of Molton Brown soap and moisturisers. That's when you knew a place had money.

The bathroom door opened, and a man came in. Zain watched him check the cubicles, the urinals.

'I need to speak to you,' he said. His voice was shaky, as though stuck in his gullet. 'Not here, though. You know the British Museum? The Montague Place entrance. Where the stone lions are.'

'What's this about?'

'It's about Ruby Day. You need to know something; it might help.'

'When?'

'Today. Nine p.m.'

They heard the outer door being pushed open as someone else came in, and the man ran into one of the cubicles. Zain swore he could hear the first man's heart beating, although it was probably his own.

Chapter Seventy-seven

Kate watched the video in the conference room back at Regus House. Michelle circled the figure on her tablet in digital red paint, the image transferring to the plasma screen.

'It's the back entrance to Windsor Court,' she said.

Kate watched the figure, at first shaded by night and then bathed in the fluorescent security light, until he was out of range. The lights went off, and there was darkness again. She checked the timestamp at the foot of the screen: 00:34.

The images spooled forward and, thirty minutes later, he left. In his right hand he was carrying a folder full of paper.

'I think he must have dumped the contents – the stuff we later found in the rubbish bins – out of camera shot.'

The figure was recorded by the immobile camera as he walked through the back gate of Windsor Court. The screen flipped to another shot, this time taken from a traffic cam by the overpass on Edgware Road.

'That's his car. I checked against the DVLA database.'

'Excellent work, Michelle.'

Kate turned to Zain, who was slouching forward in his chair, tapping his fingers on the table.

'I knew it,' he said. 'Ruby's bedroom was just too clean, too ordered. Too paperless. The bastard must have cleared it out.'

Kate pictured the scene Harris was painting, imagined Karl Rourke rummaging around Ruby's bedroom. Hours after she had disappeared, just before her parents made the call to the police.

'This makes his alibi a load of bullshit. His wife said he was home from about seven, until he went back to work around eight-thirty the next day,' said Zain.

'He was also the signatory on Dan's place out in Hampshire,' said Kate. 'Michelle, I need you to trace Rourke's car. See if you get a hit of it leaving London, heading out towards Winchester. And contact Pelt, he's still with Hampshire police. See if he can get them to do a trace at their end.'

'The parents must have lied as well,' said Zain. 'The whole lot of them have been messing with us.'

'The Days must have known he was there at their flat. They must have invited him,' she said. 'The question is why?'

'Let's haul his arse in, and find out,' said Zain.

'Bring Mrs Rourke in as well. I want to know why she lied about his alibi.'

Susan Rourke was leaking information. Her wedding ring was being pulled off her finger, twisted around the knuckle, then pushed back in place. She did it repeatedly as Kate spoke to her.

Susan was dressed in a cream jumper, striped collar poking over the top, and tight coffee-coloured slacks. She looked like the sort of woman who lived in a commercial for a ready-made suburban housewife.

Apart from the eyes. They were leaking information, too, her pupils contracting and expanding as Kate spoke of her husband.

'I have to remind you how serious this is, and that I recommend the presence of a legal representative,' said Kate.

Susan shook her head.

'You are waiving the right to counsel?'

'Yes,' she said. Her voice was quiet.

'When we questioned you about your husband's whereabouts, you said he was with you from 7 p.m. the night Ruby disappeared. That he was at home throughout the evening and night, not leaving the house until eight-thirty the following morning. You were certain he hadn't left.'

'Yes,' said Susan.

'Mrs Rourke . . .'

'Call me Susan,' she said, snapping. A sliver of anger across her face, in her eyes, the ring on her finger tugged.

'Susan, we now have evidence to show that Karl Rourke was not at home during the hours you claim. We have him on CCTV, at Windsor Court, arriving at approximately twelve thirty-four. This would suggest he left the house you share somewhere around eleven-thirty at night. Is that correct?'

Susan stared into Kate's eyes, deliberating. Balancing.

'Lying to the police is perjury, Susan. We can already prosecute you. I don't think that would be to our advantage, though. Honesty would help us clarify our next steps.'

'Karl wasn't home. He didn't come home after work. He came back at about 2 a.m. I'm sorry. He asked me to lie; he said he couldn't explain. He asked me to do it for the sake of the children.'

'You have no idea where he was between the times he claims he was with you?'

'No.'

'Does he do this a lot? Not come home, not tell you where he's been?'

Susan laughed. 'I sound pathetic, don't I? I bet if your husband did that, you would ask him, wouldn't you?'

'Have you never questioned him?'

'No. It's work. He always gives me that generic excuse. And, like a fool, I accept it.'

'Where do you think he might be when he doesn't come home?'

Susan chewed the inside of her cheek, her eyes wandering around the interview room, resting on Kate when she was done taking it all in.

'I try not to. I cram my days with so much that I don't have a place for paranoia. What would take over my thoughts otherwise? Karl with another woman? Gambling? Or is he genuinely so busy he needs to work odd hours? I don't fully understand his business, and I don't pay attention to it.'

'Do you think there might have been another woman?'

'Sometimes. When I let myself dwell on it. Most of the time, like I said, I'm kept busy. With the house, the children. His children, his perfect house, our perfect life.'

'Do you have any idea who the other woman might be?'

'It's obvious, really. There was only ever one woman he was obsessed with. I thought when he sold out, when he gave up his list to MINDNET . . . I was a fool. I thought he would give her up, that she would be out of our lives. It didn't happen though. His obsession just grew.'

'Who are you referring to, Mrs Rourke?'

Susan turned eyes of steel to Kate, and the wedding band was pulled right to the nail, where it could fall off.

'Ruby Day,' she said, letting the ring clatter on the table, and roll off the edge.

Chapter Seventy-eight

Karl Rourke was nervous, sweating, pacing the interview room. He didn't want a brief, he said; he was a lawyer, he could handle anything they accused him of. He sat down, but his body was dancing in the chair.

'Karl, you claimed that on the night of Ruby's disappearance, you were at home with your wife, Susan Rourke. At the time, Mrs Rourke backed up this claim.'

Kate was reading from her prepared opening gambit.

'Since that time, CCTV footage has emerged of you at Windsor Court approximately five hours after Ruby disappeared. You were there for thirty minutes, after which the CCTV shows you leaving.'

Karl looked surprised. The CCTV to the back gate was not as obvious as the one to the front entrance. He probably hadn't picked up on it.

'I don't have anything to hide,' he said.

'The video footage calls into question the alibi you provided us with for the night Ruby disappeared. After confronting your wife with this new evidence, she has now withdrawn her version of your alibi.'

'Bitch,' said Rourke, almost spitting the word.

'She claims you were not at home until 2 a.m., having left home at 8 a.m. the day before. Meaning we currently have no idea where you were during the time Ruby disappeared.'

Rourke's face was salmon-coloured. He wiped the sweat forming around his nose, before it dropped onto the table in front of him. His jacket was off. Kate saw the sweat stains expanding under his armpits.

'My wife's a liar, detective. I was at home from 7 p.m. I left the house just before midnight, once the Days had called me to ask me where Ruby was. And then I returned home again at 2 a.m., after I left Windsor Court.'

'Your wife is very clear that you didn't go home after work, that she didn't see you until 2 a.m. Why would she lie?'

'Because she's being . . . she's just having a turn. She's got OCD. She's pissed off I work so hard, and this is her axe grinding.'

'You expect me to believe your wife is lying to the police?'

'Yes. I told her to keep quiet about me leaving when I did, I admit that. I went to see Ruby's parents, to see if I could help them out. That's all.'

'Why? Ruby was no longer your client. Did they invite you over?'

'Yes. They were going crazy, wondering where Ruby was. I went round to help calm them down.'

Kate pressed a button on the laptop sitting between them.

'Have a look,' she said. 'You are carrying a file of some sort in your right hand. When you left the building. We also found letters and documents from Ruby's bedroom in trash bags, dumped in the waste area. What was in the file, Mr Rourke?'

'Nothing. Just paperwork I needed. Business stuff.'

'You have to do better than that, Karl. She was with MINDNET. What possible business documentation could she have that would be of interest to you?'

'It's the truth. Just some old invoices. I asked her to get me copies, she had them in a file. I saw them when I was at the flat. And I didn't dump her stuff. Ruby must have done that herself, before she left.'

'I don't believe you,' said Kate. 'I want to see that file, I want to see what these documents are.'

'Why? I was at home when she disappeared.'

'Just you and your wife?'

'Yes.'

'What about the children?'

'They were at a sleepover, or something. Or school trip.'

'Was it planned? Them not being at home?'

'I know what you're doing. I did it on the night they wouldn't be home. You know I should just say "no comment" until you realise you've fucked up. I'm helping you, though. I hope you appreciate that.'

'Where were you on the evening Ruby Day disappeared, Karl? And don't say at home.'

'Look, check my mobile, it will confirm where I was.'

'Mobiles can be left anywhere; it doesn't mean you were with your phone,' said Kate.

Michelle was working on getting a trace of Rourke's phone. That would help them to at least work out which of the Rourkes was lying.

Chapter Seventy-nine

Zain looked out over the gardens of Buckingham Palace, his eyes needing a break from his screen. He wondered how secure the royal residence was, if someone like him could get a view like this. The sort of view a sniper could use.

He sat back down at his desk. Only Michelle was in the office, working away at trying to get a trace on Karl Rourke's phone, and on his car registration. She was following protocol, asking the relevant agencies for help. Zain felt his fingers itch. He could crack Rourke's phone within minutes, see if his internal GPS gave him away. He also missed access to the software that could trace a car through the thousands of cameras across London.

The F&M toffee had managed to raise a cordial hello to him today. He let his antsy tendencies dissipate, left Michelle to her methods. They would find out what they needed to, even using her simple techniques.

He chided himself then. He heard how arrogant he sounded, even to himself. He didn't mean to; he just believed that if there was a smarter way to do things, they should take it. They owed it to the people they worked for. People like Ruby.

Shut up, Zain, he said to himself, and tapped away, trying to work out MINDNET's internet presence.

Everything was linked to Jed Byrne – all internet articles, *Financial Times* reports, even their Wikipedia entry. Because that was always factual. He needed a spider web diagram to work out who MINDNET were. They couldn't just spring up, a company like that, with the sort of resources they had, the offices they had.

And that man in the bathroom. He was so nondescript, so ordinary, like millions of men in offices. If Zain had to pick him out of a line-up, he'd fail. Yet he had set his mind reeling. Zain hadn't spoken to Kate about it. She would have insisted he do things properly, bring the man into the office. Scare him away.

'How you getting on?' he called over to Michelle.

'Slowly,' she said. 'Just waiting for his network to release his cell tower positions.'

Zain scrolled through more pages of data on Jed Byrne, and MINDNET. The same self-glorifying pieces about the YouTube stars and their power. Eventually, after scrawling through what seemed like hundreds of articles, Zain found something of interest.

He checked the directory for internet sites. MINDNET's website was protected, ex-directory, no ownership details available. He next checked Ruby's personal website. This was registered to her. He then recalled she had a number of sites, and so did Dan. So did the other stars tied in to MINDNET.

Zain checked their websites; most of them were personally registered, until he hit one that wasn't. He checked the name the website was registered to. It wasn't MINDNET; it was a firm called DORF Finance.

Zain did a search for them, and found they were a subsidiary of something called KANGlobal. DORF acted as the accountancy arm, the glorified petty cash tin, really, for KANGlobal, referred to as KNG in its abbreviated form.

Zain checked for KNG. They were an international conglomerate with interests in a number of ventures. Their primary sources of income seemed to be conservation research and sustainable exploration. Drilling down further, he realised that they were in fact a mining company, with a focus on oil and minerals, with operations across the world. Specifically West Africa.

Zain checked in with Lideo. It had a record of every company in existence, or so it claimed, with a breakdown of their last financial statements, if known, and who was behind them. Zain used the PCC login details.

He scanned through for MINDNET, which listed Jed Byrne. Then checked KNG.

'Well, fuck me,' he said, reading through the skeleton details. Detailed under the entry for KNG was a list of companies they had control of.

'What is it?' said Michelle.

'MINDNET. They're owned by one of the largest conglomerates in the world.'

Zain turned back to the KNG links he had found. The company was listed as being run by a board, a list of names. They didn't mean anything to him. He checked Wikipedia for some of them; only a couple turned up. Professional board members, previously with banks.

'Damn,' said Michelle, interrupting the cogs that were making links in Zain's head. 'Karl Rourke was home when he said he was.'

'Why would his wife lie?'

Michelle shrugged, turned back to her screen.

'Still doesn't explain what he was doing at Windsor Court,' he said.

The image of Rourke with the files. The shredded contract. The dumped paperwork.

Zain started to see a pattern in his head. He needed to speak to Riley. And he really needed to speak to the mysterious MINDNET employee.

Chapter Eighty

Kate took her shoes off at the door, enjoying the blast of heat as she walked deeper into the house. Her mother was in the lounge, watching a film she had watched numerous times. It was always the same. She liked to watch films she knew well: she could keep track more easily if she knew what was meant to happen.

Kate felt an instinct to make contact. Kiss Jane on the head, touch her hand to her mother's face. In her head, the gesture was so easy. In the room, the few metres between them were full of invisible walls. She had no energy to surmount that level of emotional barbed wire tonight.

Ryan was in the kitchen, washing his hands. His jacket was already on.

'Coffee before you go?' she said.

'You know I swapped coffee for camomile tea,' he said.

'Just a quick chat? Please?'

Ryan nodded, and sat down with his hands in his pockets. He reminded her of someone, but she pushed the thought away.

'I'm sorry,' she said. 'Is it ever going to be enough? Just saying that?'

He shrugged.

'She just worries about me. And I do too, about her. All that gets me through is knowing you're here with her. I've had a day that just makes me want to quit, and if I had to think about her with someone . . . well, I need you. That's what I'm trying to say.'

Kate reached her hands across the kitchen table, hoping he would meet them with his own. He didn't, kept them deep in his jacket. He started to bite his lip, though. He was at least affected by the gesture.

'Will it be so bad if we stop?' she said. Yes, she thought. For me it will be.

'I don't know. I quite like the benefits package,' he said, only half maliciously.

'I wonder if she heard us? I'll try to come home earlier more often. And the spare room is yours.'

'I get it, no more knowing each other in the Biblical sense. You don't have to make it so obvious,' Ryan said.

'So you'll stay?'

'I don't know. I need some time. It's not so easy. Her condition . . .'

He unsheathed his hands, let them fall on top of hers. Kate felt the atoms in her rise up to meet his touch, the familiar desire. She swallowed, hoping the gesture would send a signal to her brain. Ryan was now in a different box, only to be recalled as friend and carer.

'I thought she was managing on her own?' said Kate.

'She is. The cell phone you gave her – so simple, why didn't we think of that before? She calls me if she gets overwhelmed.'

Kate had given Jane a mobile. It enabled her to go shopping, for walks, to appointments. An app on it gave away her location wherever she was. In her pocket was a letter and next of kin form, in case the dementia reared up. The mobile was always unlocked; Kate and Ryan both had their details in the contacts list.

'How did she get it? The prosopagnosia, I mean?' he said.

Kate felt winded by the unexpected question. She had asked Ryan never to broach the subject. Was this his trade? Secrets from her past in exchange for a commitment to her future?

'That word is so clinical, meaningless. Prosopagnosia. How does it say what it is?' Kate heard the thickness in her voice, the pain, self-pity. 'What it means,' she went on, 'to say that my mother can't recognise faces. Not even mine. Her own daughter? That I have to wear a blond wig, because I stupidly changed my hair colour. That I have to wear scarlet when I approach her, because she panics and thinks a stranger is in the room if I don't. And as if that wasn't punishment enough, she's now going to suffer from dementia?'

'I thought the specialist said it was temporary? Just a side effect of the face blindness?'

'I can't tell you how much I hope that is true.'

'How did she get it, Kate? If you want me to stay, I want to know. Let me help you. To do that I need the truth.'

Kate looked at him, the sincerity in his eyes. Could she trust him? She hadn't trusted anyone for so long, not with this. And yet, she left Ryan to look after her mother. Maybe she had no choice but to trade now.

'She was attacked. By my father.'

'Jeez,' said Ryan.

'My father, he was involved with politics. Man of integrity, power. Impeccable public image. Only behind the scenes, he had corruption running through him like blood. He took bribes to help pass laws, backhanders to sway local politics. A phone call in the middle of the night, and some lowlife the cops had spent years chasing would walk free. And when I joined law enforcement, he tried to use me. He told me what he wanted from me. I mean, he pulled strings, got my career moving. Only so he could manipulate and use me.'

'Let me guess. You refused.'

'He made me sick. When I found out what he had been doing. He thought it would be genetic, that I would be like him. Bastard. I went along for a bit, got to know what he was up to. Turned evidence for the FBI, was their star witness in the end. He got sent away. But before he did, he hired someone to deal with me. I can't prove it, but I know it was him. Only I wasn't home, and they attacked my mother. Beat her to an inch of her life.'

Kate stopped, her breath catching. She would not cry, not ever, not because of him.

'We had to go into witness protection. In case they came back for us. And my brothers, they took his side. They said my mother was attacked by someone I had messed with, someone I had arrested. They called me a liar, said I had betrayed them and our father.'

'Fuck,' said Ryan. 'How did you keep all this to yourself?'

'I have to. I'm trusting you with my life, Ryan. With my mother's life. I chose not to stay in hiding in America, living a half-life. I came here, took a new name, and I relaunched my career. Officially, me and my mother are in witness protection in Key West still. Nobody knows I'm here. Nobody I don't trust, anyway.'

That was all she would share. That seemed everything, but it was just a sketch. There was no need to reveal who she had been. Kate would keep her birth name, Winter, a secret from Ryan. For now at least. With a name like that, she would be too easy for him to trace. To find out who her father had been.

There was silence between them, as Ryan poured them whisky.

'Well we're both British now,' he said, clinking glasses with her. 'Although I think this stuff is Scottish.'

It seemed late when Ryan left.

'I'll stay,' he said at the door. 'For now.'

The street looked like a film set. It was empty. Dark.

Zain rested against one of the stone lions on Montague Place. They were a pair that guarded the back entrance to the British Museum. Trees shone under a moon that reminded him of a communion wafer. He thought of his Catholic grandmother competing with his Hindu grandmother and Muslim grandfather. Zain smiled at memories of that tug of war.

A few yards away were Russell Square and Southampton Row. Zain loved these corners of London. When everything seemed to stop, as though the soul of the city was resting.

He checked his phone. It was ten minutes past nine. He shivered. Cold breathed up his trouser legs, down the back of his jacket, around his ears and against his nose. He stamped a couple of times, started to pace between the statues.

He waited an hour. That was reasonable, right? London could hold you up in its arteries, like blood clots, delay you. An hour was OK to be late. He should have driven here; he could have waited in his car.

Someone else drove by, slowly. Zain felt hope, but the car went past, and a woman was driving.

Another half hour. Zain checked his phone. His father had called. He should call back.

Zain waited until 11 p.m., then gave up. Two hours was enough. The man wasn't coming. Zain felt something bitter inside him. He needed to know what the man had to say. Thoughts started to turn into phantoms. Had the man been caught out? Were Byrne and Anderson involved now? Was the man being dealt with, held somewhere? Or had they simply threatened him to keep quiet?

Zain walked into the traffic rush of Southampton Row, towards Euston. He waited at a bus stop outside Age UK, got on the number 68 and headed home.

He was worried, wondering why the man hadn't turned up. And more interested than ever in what exactly MINDNET and KNG were hiding.

Chapter Eighty-one

Kate sat drinking black coffee, letting her eyes adjust to the dimmed lighting and the plasma screen in front of her. Harris was explaining to the team what he had found. He was wearing a blue shirt – royal blue, she thought. Why did she know that? A memory, a present for her father? A sudden hit of sadness, over quickly.

'So I did some searching on the net, simple stuff, got a link between MINDNET and KANGlobal. They call it KNG, which makes no sense. Until you realise most of their mining licences are in the Congo.'

'Is it a secret?' said Kate.

'You see, the more I researched, the more I think it is. Companies are usually easy to find information on. Take Unilever or Glaxo or L'Oréal. A bit of research and you know what companies they own, who their board members are. MINDNET, I couldn't find any link to KNG. It was by accident, and then only on one site did I find them linked officially. I checked, and the web page hadn't been updated by Google's search bots for over eight months. What I saw was a cached version of the page. The current website has the link between MINDNET and KNG removed.'

'Someone has deliberately had it removed?' said Kate.

'Yes, or so it seems.'

'Why go to the trouble? Why is KNG such a big deal?'

'I'm not sure. What I do know, mining in the Congo, it's like testing on animals or using kids to glue trainers. It's one of those areas that's murky, full of corruption and greed and sheer terror. Firms involved in that part of the world have a lot of ethical question marks over them,' Zain said grimly.

'Ethical question marks someone like Ruby Day wouldn't be OK with?' said Kate.

'That makes sense,' said Stevie. Her arms were folded on the table in front of her. 'I saw Ruby's videos, the ones of interest. She made one on animal testing. She said she would name and shame any company sending her anything that had been produced using those techniques.'

'So she was ethically aware?' said Kate.

She knew people called it instinct, but in reality it wasn't. Just the brain pulling bits of evidence from drawers of stored information, and making sense of them. She felt it now, something falling into place, something that would make sense in a law court.

'Yes. There was something about Fair Trade in another video. It's just hit me,' said Stevie. 'I didn't pay attention at the time, but now you've said that. She kept going on about Divine chocolate and some coffee brand. And it was all about Fair Trade.'

'Fair Trade, animal rights? She was more than just a pretty face,' said Rob.

'Don't be facetious,' said Stevie.

'Just stating facts. She had depth, then. A conscience.'

'Don't fall for the glossy face and soft voice,' said Stevie. 'She had issues, and she put it all out there. To help others. And I believe her. Stars do it after they're famous, and I think they're after the column inches. Ruby started it when she only had a few people watching.'

'This is fucking ridiculous. But it's starting to make sense, right?' said Zain.

'What do you mean?' Kate asked.

'KNG. My big reveal. What I was leading up to,' he said.

Kate swallowed her cooled coffee; she had a sense she would need the caffeine hit today. 'Go on,' she said.

'I checked in with a pal of mine, at Inland Revenue. Wanted to make sure I had it right. And he confirmed that MINDNET and

KNG are linked. KNG syphoned off a load of money into MIND-NET; investments which they weren't taxed on.'

'Greedy fucktards,' said Stevie.

'Clever, greedy fucktards,' said Rob.

'It gets better. I asked him what the link is between the companies. Why were KNG interested in a lightweight media outfit like MINDNET? And he said he'd look into it.'

Zain moved his fingers over his tablet. He pulled up a list of names, and focused in on one. 'Innocuous, right?' he said. 'Just random names?'

Kate stared at the plasma screen on the wall and tried to see a pattern, or find something familiar about them. She couldn't; there was no relation to anyone she had dealt with so far in the case.

'Until I do this,' said Zain.

He tapped and a red circle appeared around one of the names. He tapped again, and there it was. Two images flashed up on the screen. And Kate knew then that they had something.

Chapter Eighty-two

Stevie Brennan felt the raw emotion in the air. Palpable. That was a good word for it.

Mike and Laura Day were like actors, left without a script, forced to ad lib. Only they had nothing left to say.

Mike hadn't shaved, his skin was greasy and whiteheads were dotted around his face. He was wearing calf-length shorts and a T-shirt. Laura had her hair tied back, the classic not-washed look. She was wearing a loose jumper, and pyjama bottoms.

When Stevie spoke to them, they seemed to take forever to understand and reply.

'Why was Karl Rourke here?' Stevie said. It was blunt, but she had to cut through the sheer human misery she was faced with. 'We saw him on CCTV, entering and leaving. The night Ruby disappeared.'

'I called him,' said Laura. 'When we couldn't find Ruby, I tried him. In case he knew where she was.'

'Why would he?'

'They used to be close, when he represented her. I think that stayed, even after she moved to MINDNET. I was reaching out, hoping he could help.'

'What did you say to him?'

'I told him we were going to call the police. He told me to wait until he got here.'

'Why?'

'I have no idea.'

'Yet you did as he asked?'

'It was a strange time; my head wasn't here. Mike was out looking for Ruby again. I needed someone to tell me what to do. I can't explain it. I wanted to curl up in a corner and cry, because I knew, even then. I knew . . .'

Laura trailed off, and her eyes filled up.

'What did Karl do when he got here?' said Stevie.

'He told me to call the police. That was all.'

'Why was it OK then? Why not when you spoke to him on the phone?'

'I don't know,' said Laura.

'Did he do anything else? When he left, he seemed to have a file with him?'

'He had a look around Ruby's room,' said Laura. 'I don't remember a file.'

'And he didn't fill up trash bags with paper statements from Ruby's room?'

'No. I think she did that, had a clear-out,' said Laura.

'Why didn't you tell us?'

Laura shrugged.

'Karl asked me not to,' she said.

'Didn't that strike you as odd?' said Stevie.

'I didn't know all of this,' said Mike.

'Yes. Now, afterwards, of course it does. At the time, though, my focus was on Ruby, getting her back. That's all,' said Laura.

Stevie didn't understand. Ruby disappears, and her ex-manager asks her mother not to call the police until he gets there. He then asks her not to tell the police about his involvement. Why would you not disclose that? Karl Rourke would probably have been their prime suspect if she had.

'I need to speak to you about a company called KANGlobal,' said Stevie.

The Days showed no reaction at all to the name.

'They are the parent company that own MINDNET,' she explained. A vague nod; they weren't interested. 'KANGlobal are an international mining company. They have licences in a number of conflict areas, especially in the Congo.'

Laura knotted her eyebrows, and Mike put his head to one side. She had their attention then.

'How do you think Ruby would feel if she found out MINDNET were part of a corporate from that was involved in questionable mining practices?'

'She would be appalled,' said Laura.

'Do you think she had an inkling of KANGlobal's relationship to MINDNET?'

'No, she would have said. She wouldn't have kept that to herself,' said Mike. 'I agree, she would have been unhappy, to say it politely, if she found out.'

'She would have felt betrayed, completely,' said Laura. 'More than that, she would have done something about it.'

Stevie considered Laura's words. It seemed too big, complicated. Then again, the last video Ruby had posted, she said she was about to reveal something to her fans.

Was Ruby just something KNG had to deal with? Had she threatened to do something that meant she needed to be silenced? Had she confided in somebody? Somebody who was now in grave danger?

Chapter Eighty-three

Graveyards. Tombstones. That's how he tried to explain it.

It was the road they were walking down. Unlit, air sharp with the smell of rot, concealing terrors. Things were falling into place; something was emerging. A man visits the mother of a missing girl, lies to the police about it. Gets his wife to lie. A fixer man who was working on someone else's orders. Why? What power did they have over him? A man who took a file from a missing girl's bedroom. What was in it? Something damning him, or the company? You follow the silvery threads, and you see the underbelly of the beast.

Zain was backtracking. They had focused on Dan. He had focused on Dan. He had obsessed over him. It was a basic rule: switch off your own distaste. Like walking through a sewage pipe. Rank, full of crap, maggots. Don't let the stench overpower you, and he had done just that. He had let his own dislike of Dan take over.

He felt like a dick.

The green pills were good, but redemption was beyond them.

Zain was going over Ruby's hard drives again. He had done cursory examinations earlier in the investigation, pulled emails he needed. Michelle had done the rest, but they had focused on the evidence they'd thought they needed. Dan's messages were what they'd wanted to find. The evidence that fitted the man they wanted to lock up.

Zain was looking deeper now, running tests, algorithms and software that Forensics would take weeks to run and deliver on. It meant Michelle was sitting with her spine angled like a broad sword. He would have to visit Fortnum & Mason again.

He had an idea. He needed her. He could have looked online – would have been easier – but this would be an offering. In binary.

'Michelle,' he said, trying to feign charm. At what point did you stop being charming and become creepy?

She didn't turn around, and he thought he sensed the features on her face twist.

'I need some help,' he said. 'Can you take a look at something for me?'

'You need help? I thought you were the great Oz. You can do anything?'

'Oz was faking it.'

'Is that what you're doing?' she said, still with her back to him, banging her keyboard hard.

'Will you take a look at something for me? I'd appreciate it.'

'What?'

'I need to send you some code. It's software that looks at deleted memory that's been overwritten.'

She turned around. She was a nerd at heart. They both knew it. He had just given her the equivalent of a 'show me yours'.

'Are you saying what I think you are?' she said, arching an eyebrow.

'I'm not sure. Look, I'm good at running scripts, following procedures and functions others have written. I don't code. I'm not like you. What I do know is that you can't delete stuff anymore, not in a basic way. Memory holds deleted files, waiting for them to be overwritten. It's why our forensic teams have it so easy recovering data.'

'Yes, I know.' There was an excitement to her voice, waiting for him to go on and reveal what she wanted him to.

'Only, the criminals are becoming more sophisticated. They've developed a way to delete files and immediately overwrite them. Sometimes with genuine files, sometimes with background files. So you lose the ability to easily pull what was there before, because the empty placeholder is now full of something else.'

'And you're telling me you have software that pulls away the new data, and tells you that a placeholder was empty, not because it was unused, but because the data in it was deleted?'

Zain shrugged. 'It's all zeroes and ones, but yes, I think that's what it does.'

Michelle rolled her chair across the office to his desk, her fingers going to his keyboard, her eyes roaming the code on his screen.

'It's falling over,' said Zain. 'I don't think I copied it correctly?'

'Yes, there's a secondary file structure it's calling. It's going around in a loop; it needs input, or will keep crashing.'

'Can you work out what the secondary file structure might be?'

'Give me a few minutes. Where's the rest of your software? You must have copied this from somewhere?'

Zain hesitated. Did he want to give her an in to his secret places? He pulled a USB stick from his pocket, plugged it into his desktop base.

'That's all I have,' he said. 'Like I said, I can do protocol and pro-cedure. I can hack, and I can get results. Using what others make.'

'Go and get me some tea. Jasmine green tea.'

'Sure,' he said, smiling at the change in her.

An hour later, she had created what he needed. His software called her file as part of a crucial bit of code, and it ran. They watched as the secrets of Ruby's computer opened up to them, the bits some-one had purposely overwritten.

'Do you think she did it herself?' said Michelle, sitting next to him as he drove. The air still carried the fresh smell of her tea.

'Possibly. She was computer savvy. But this is high-grade cyber security awareness. Why would she need something so sophisti-cated – unless she had something to hide?'

They split the results between them, opening files and seeing what was inside them.

'This is odd,' said Zain.

Michelle came to his desk, her arms folded across her, but her head bent close to his shoulder.

'What the hell is that?' she said. 'I don't believe it.'

'Tombstones,' he said.

'A graveyard of them,' she whispered, going back to her own desk.

He clicked through some more files, but found nothing significant. Michelle called him over.

'I think this is it,' she said.

She clicked on a generic icon, which her computer opened up in Media Player. It was a film of Ruby, in her bedroom. She had candles lit on either side of her, but her face was without make-up, her hair tied back. There was a silver chain around her neck, a pentagram hanging from it. Her fingers twisted it as she spoke.

Hi, guys, how are you all? I said last time I was going through some things. I still am, but I'm getting closer now to being able to share it with you. The world is a sad place sometimes, and it broke my heart what I found out. I turned in on myself, and my depression really peaked. I got past it, though. And now, well I think I'm going to share it with you all. I think what I tell you will affect lots of you. I hope you are sensible about it, and I hope you work positively and make a difference. You will be shocked. I know you will be. Because I was shocked. In fact, it really shook me up. But I trust you, I always have. You got me through the times when my own head was against me. This is important, though. And those involved need to be exposed.

The screen fades to black.

Chapter Eighty-four

Kate was parked up outside the MINDNET offices. Jed Byrne had tried to avoid her with the excuse of having an important meeting. Kate had read out two names to him, and he had agreed to meet her. After not breathing for a few seconds, she thought.

Zain called when she was just about to leave her car.

'There's a video you need to see,' he said.

He emailed it to her, and she watched it on her phone.

'It's a first cut,' he said, when she had finished. 'The way they put their videos together, they do them in segments. So even though the ten-minute videos on YouTube run like a single shot, they're edited like any other film on TV or the cinema. This is Ruby's first take, and the first segment. The rest of the video has disappeared.'

'How? Didn't you say you found this by running software that found invisible files?'

Kate hated technical explanations; her mind switched off at the early stages. She just liked to know who did it and what they had found. Harris and Michelle had done this together: great; finally, he was working successfully with someone else in her team. Ruby's video had been found; again, brilliant: result. What she didn't need to know about was the coding loops and file calls and syntax errors and missing algorithms.

'Yes. That's just it. Her hard drive has been double-whacked. Someone has not only deleted and overwritten memory, but they've then gone in and deleted it again. So what we're left with is a series of markers.'

'I'm not sure I follow,' she said. Get the hint, please, she mentally pleaded.

'OK, it's like you're in a graveyard. And you see all these tomb-stones – you know, with all that stuff about who died and who their family was. So you know someone was buried there, because of those tombstones, right?'

'Yes,' she said. This was better. She liked analogies; they made sense to her. They made sense to a jury, too.

'Imagine, then, if when you came to one of those tombstones, and you saw the grave hadn't been messed with. You would assume that everything was OK.'

'Reasonable assumption,' she said, thinking she knew where he was heading now.

'Until you start digging. And realise that someone's taken the body, and replaced it with someone else.'

Kate watched the shock fall over her face in the wing mirror.

'Someone deleted Ruby's files, replaced them with empty files. They then deleted those rubbish files, and replaced them with something else. So we have deleted tags which refer to files that are no longer there.'

'A professional would have to have been involved,' she said. 'A very expensive professional, with a lot of resource and a lot of contacts in the security world.'

'Remind you of anyone?' said Zain.

'And the deleted videos, they would probably tell us what Ruby was so upset about?'

'It's not just videos missing. A lot of data has been deleted twice over.'

'Can we not retrieve it?'

'*We* can't,' he said.

'How did this video survive?'

'Usual "cops catching a break" stuff.'

'I don't understand.'

'Ruby deleted this herself, it's the first take of a segment. Who-ever went into her system wasn't expecting that. They probably found the completed version, went to town getting rid of that.'

'It might be enough,' she said. 'This coupled with what we know about MINDNET and Jed Byrne, it should be enough to get someone opening up to us.'

'Good luck,' he said.

She needed more than luck. She needed Jed Byrne to be scared. Scared people cracked more easily. And in her head, Jed's features, contorted, turned into those of her father. His lawyers. Her brothers. The faceless men that had ruined her mother's life.

Kate breathed out slowly. Battles for another day. Today she had Jed Byrne in her sights. She called Harris back.

'I'm changing strategy,' she said. 'Prepare the interview room. I'm bringing Jed Byrne in for questioning.'

Chapter Eighty-five

The house was echoing its size as each empty room mocked him. Karl Rourke watched his glass fill with brown liquid, then empty, then fill again. He lost track. Did he refill it?

Susan had gone. She had taken the kids. How could they fix this? She was supposed to back him, lie for him. Not lie about him. How had he missed this? Had it been obvious? Had she been pulling away from him, resenting him, hating him, while he'd been busy gliding images across his tablet? Or FaceTiming his clients? Didn't she realise he did it all for her?

'You fucking love Ruby more than you ever loved me.'

Her words. Painful. Damning. True?

He swallowed, and the glass was empty again. Where was the gun? Why had he thought that? It came to him. A subconscious whisper, dragging itself up from the sewer of his brain, where all the other shit stuff festered. Where was the gun?

Fuck. No. He wouldn't let it solidify, and he wouldn't let it take over.

Karl flipped up the lock symbol on his phone, tapped in his passcode. Dialled. Anderson picked up straight away. Anderson. The viper. He wouldn't sleep. Not tonight.

'You set me up,' said Karl.

Good thing about mobiles. You didn't have to say who you were. Not when the other person had your number.

'And I have no idea why anymore,' said Karl. 'I am not taking the fucking blame. Do you fucking well understand me?'

Bill Anderson's breathing was heavy in his ear. He was mulling it over. Trying to work out what to say to Karl. It's why Jed Byrne paid him a bastard fortune.

'Look around you, Karl. Look around your detached house, your expensive furniture. The whisky I can tell you've been drinking. The designer watch on your wrist, the clothes your arse is wrapped in. That's why you do what we tell you.'

'I don't need your money,' said Karl.

'I think you do. I've seen your accounts. You pissed away all the money you sold your clients for. You have no income. And expensive tastes. So look around you, Karl, and know this. You are one call away from losing it all. Cash the cheque from MINDNET, and crawl away again. Understand?'

Karl dropped his phone into his whisky glass. The glass was empty.

Money. Kate was looking at it. Not the dollar bills, precious stones or status symbols. But the men. The men that embodied money, their every pore reeking of it. It was their veneer of confidence, threaded through everything they wore and smelt of.

Jed Byrne, in his casual jeans and open shirt, a baseball cap on his head. His lawyer, Tim West, manicured nails. There wasn't a stray piece of dandruff between them; they were so polished. Slick, like skid marks. Her father used to say that. And that's what they were. Slick like skid marks.

'No comment,' said Byrne.

His arms weren't locked over his chest: one was hanging over the side of his chair, and the other was resting on the table in the interview room. He could have been in a sports bar, checking out the game with one eye, the talent with the other.

West had instructed his client to say no comment, and not directly answer Kate's questions. She was pissed off, always was when faced with assholes with that attitude, but she kept the bile low, swallowing it back. She was damned if she'd let these walking examples of privilege faze her.

'Jed, we did some investigating of MINDNET. We found that there was a registered link between MINDNET and KANGlobal. Can you confirm this is the case, that your company is a subsidiary of KNG?'

'No comment.'

'We also found some interesting names sitting on the board of KNG. In particular, we found Harry Cain, current CEO of KNG. The man who built the company.'

'No comment.'

There was no emotion. His voice had trembled slightly when she had spoken to him about it on the phone earlier.

'Come on, Jed, are you going to use that line when I tell you we've worked out that Harry Cain is your father?'

'No comment.'

It had been Zain and his checking that had unearthed the revelation. Harry Cain was never married to Jed's mother, Elizabeth. He had been married four times with kids from each union, so Jed got lost in all that. There were rumours, though, picked up from online gossip and an old newspaper cutting. Elizabeth was cited as potentially the reason for Cain's second divorce. And a check on Jed's birth certificate confirmed it.

'A deliberate effort seems to have been made to hide the link between MINDNET and KNG, including your use of your mother's maiden name in all official documentation pertaining to MINDNET.'

'Conjecture, you don't know that,' said West, without even looking up from his laptop. He had taken it out at the start of the interview.

'Was it to keep a separation between yourself and KNG? A global mining corporation, specialising in a political hotspot like the Democratic Republic of Congo, would hardly go down well with the media-savvy clients you have?'

'No comment.'

'Ruby Day had made videos about ethical standards in the products she used. She also made a video, just before her disappearance, saying she was about to expose something to her audience. A video that was deleted, remotely, by hacking into the wireless network in her apartment. A sophisticated act of sabotage. Were you afraid a public link between yourself and your father's company would be damaging to your client base?'

'No comment.'

'Did you authorise the hacking of Ruby's computer to hide evidence of this?'

'No comment.'

'Ruby claimed in her video that when she revealed the information she had, people would be shocked. What did she know about you, Mr Byrne? It can't simply be your relationship with KNG?. Was it something bigger? Something that KNG has done?'

There. She saw it. A smile forced its way across her face; she couldn't stop it. Jed Byrne's jaw had pulsed, his fingers, tapping on the desk, had stopped moving, and his right shoulder had come up. Slightly, but enough.

'No comment,' he said.

It was too late. She knew what she was looking for. The motive for getting rid of Ruby.

Chapter Eighty-six

'We have him until tomorrow, but there's nothing to keep him here,' said Kate.

She was at her desk, briefing her team. Zain was in the chair nearest to her, Stevie leaning against the back of her own chair. Rob was sitting at his desk, with his back turned to his computer screen. Michelle was listening, but was busy with her computer.

'It was always a bit of a piss in the dark,' said Zain.

'My aim's pretty good,' said Rob.

Stevie's top lip pulled back, disgust setting over her face.

'He let himself down, told me what he was most afraid of. Nothing fazed him, not the information I presented about his father or the links between the two companies. Or the fact they've been hiding those links publicly as much as possible. Only the suggestion that Ruby was about to expose something his father's company were doing.'

'It could be something to do with their mining,' said Zain.

'No shit, Miss Marple,' said Stevie.

'There's all sorts going on in the Congo. Conglomerates and their dodgy work practices. Villagers dying, pollution of the environment. Deals with corrupt warlords. KNG must be caught up in that. You can't take a dump in Kinshasa without some bloodthirsty warlord involved,' said Zain.

'You need the toilet, mate? You're dropping the analogies,' said Rob.

'It's a good theory, but I need more than that. I need evidence,' said Kate.

'I had a look online, couldn't really find anything. Not even a whiff of exploitation involving Byrne and his dad,' said Zain.

'Probably means they did a clearing-up act,' said Stevie. 'When there's no evidence, it means someone's gone over everything with bleach. At a crime scene, I mean. So online it would be the same?'

'Has to be,' said Zain. 'And that's only possible with lots of dosh, and a shit-hot lawyer. Which we know they have.'

'And what are we saying? Harry Cain and Jed Byrne did a job on Ruby to keep her quiet? Why? What's that worth to someone?' said Rob.

'I'm not sure,' said Kate. 'It might explain the threatening message at the end of the video. Ruby may have had an accomplice, a confidante. I still don't understand Rourke's involvement. Why would he remove documents for Byrne?'

'We'll find out, when we get the bloody search warrant,' said Rob.

Justin Hope hadn't responded to Kate's requests yet. She had two warrants she needed his Masonic or club friends to authorise. He had acted immediately with warrants for Dan Grant, but nothing so far for Rourke or Jed Byrne's properties.

She tried to push away the unbidden thought, but it kept pricking at her. It was the second name Harris had discovered during his search into the board of directors at KANGlobal. Thinking of it, and what it might mean, was overwhelming. She had to stay focused on the detail, the evidence as she could see it.

'I think I might know,' said Michelle, her voice low but getting their attention.

'What have you got?' said Kate.

'Come and look,' said Michelle, rolling her chair away from her desk to give Kate access to her screen.

Kate skim-read the report. It was in the *New York Times*; a small piece but containing all the salient facts.

'You asked how much silencing Ruby Day might be worth,' said Michelle. 'According to that, an estimated two billion dollars.'

Chapter Eighty-seven

Justin Hope tore up the paper, then tossed the pieces over his head. It fell around him, like the first snow, almost artistically. A segment of a music video.

He leaned forward, lacing his fingers, forming a battering ram with his hands.

'I take it the warrant requests didn't meet with your approval?' she said.

'Jed Byrne is being released at this very moment,' said Hope. 'It was a mistake bringing him in. His father has been on the phone to the PM. Do you know what that does to us? To me?'

Kate didn't move. Harry Cain was calling the prime minister? What was this? The Nixon era?

'Harry Cain is one of the biggest donors to the PM's party. He is also the man giving a grant to the Home Office to bolster policing in inner-city London. Specifically, areas where his offices are located. And do you know what the Home Office did with a substantial part of that money?'

Kate could guess. She wanted Hope to say it, though. She wanted the dirty words to actually leave his lips.

'They created this office, my role, your team. Our wages are paid by this initiative. Investigating the son of the man that bankrolls us? Do you have any idea what a massive fuck-up this is?'

Kate felt her lungs fill with tension, oppressive and suffocating.

Then she felt the anger push upwards, forcing out the stalled breath, and felt herself bolstered by the action.

'We know that Paul Newton's brother sits on the board of KANGlobal,' she said calmly.

Hope said nothing.

'Paul Newton, our friendly junior Home Office minister – the man who interviewed me, alongside you, for this position,' Kate pressed. 'The man signing off on your budget. Supposed carte blanche for everything we do. The go-to man, the one who smoothes things over for you with the home secretary and the prime minister.'

There was no reaction from Hope as she needled him, patronising him with the information he already knew.

'We've discovered that his older brother, Mark Newton, is on the KNG board. Six degrees of separation, have you ever heard of that? I think I can link you to Harry Cain and KNG in three.'

Hope sat back, relaxed his arms, and his face grew slack. What was it with men like Hope and Byrne? Men like her father. They seemed so comfortable when faced with difficult situations. As though they revelled in the challenge.

'Did Paul Newton persuade his big brother to influence Harry Cain to siphon funds to our unit? Is SOE3 a bogus front for a corrupt system? Is that what I wake up for every morning? What have you involved us in?' Kate asked heatedly, riled by Hope's lack of response.

'I would control that unnecessary speculation, Riley. Harry Cain is a man who wants to see London a safer place for business to operate. That's all there is to it. It's unfortunate there is a tenuous link to the disappearance of this young girl.'

'Tenuous? KANGlobal is about to float with an IPO of two billion dollars. London, Hong Kong and New York. And Ruby Day goes missing when she is about to expose something that might jeopardise that?'

'Your evidence is scant, Riley. If you repeat everything you just said to me outside of this office, you could probably be sued, if nothing else. Slander and conjecture, that's all this is.'

Conjecture? She was sick of that word being hurled at her. Had Hope been briefed by Byrne's lawyer? Kate's fingers began to feel numb as blood pumped to the parts of her body where anger burned.

'Then let me search the MINDNET offices, and let me search Karl Rourke's home,' she spit out.

'Jed Byrne has an alibi. He was with his assistant, Siobhan Mann, on the night of Ruby's disappearance.'

How did he know that? She hadn't disclosed that to him. Who was updating Justin Hope apart from her?

'A woman in his employ, on his payroll? How watertight is that alibi? Besides, a man like him wouldn't get his hands dirty.'

'DCI Riley, I am closing myself off to anymore theories from you. Jed Byrne is free to go. I will apologise to him and his father on your behalf. And there will be no warrant approval to search any property that might lead you to harass that family or their confidantes even more. Is that clear?'

Kate maintained her dignity by not replying, instead walking out as calmly as she could. She had to leave the building, and stand in the crowds on Victoria Street, letting people jostle her.

How had this happened? What had just happened? What the hell had Ruby Day found out?

Kate tried to think of who she could turn to, who could support her through this. Harry Cain had the ear of the prime minister. How was she going to fight that?

Only, she had been here before. Powerful men, impossible men, trying to force her to back down, to close her eyes. Her father used to brag how he had the ear of the president. Kate didn't care, she wasn't scared off. Kate had refused to back down then. And she sure as hell wasn't going to back down now.

Chapter Eighty-eight

Paranoia. It had gripped her. She looked around the office after her meeting with Hope, and all she saw was open space. Random faces, strangers, admin staff, electronic devices. Any of it could be watching her, reporting back to Hope. Her voice could travel, evidence folders left lying around, screens not locked when her team popped away from their desks for a few minutes.

Were their phones being tapped? Was every keystroke on her computer being mapped?

Her mouth had gone dry and she had felt herself grow lightheaded. Enough to make her write her Skype address on pieces of paper and discreetly drop them onto the desks of each of her team.

It was 7 p.m., and the three of them were logged on. Small faces on her screen, as she spoke to them in hushed tones. It felt exciting, like a rebellion. Also daunting, and how could she be sure none of them were relaying information to Justin Hope?

She hadn't involved Michelle. She knew it shouldn't matter, and she was acting like a man from the 1950s, but she thought of her husband and kids. It seemed unfair to place her in this bracket of risk.

Kate explained the situation to Harris, Brennan and Pelt, telling them what Hope had said. Her fears that what had happened to Ruby involved KNG, and that their investigation was being locked down.

'Officially, Harry Cain and Jed Byrne are now off limits. That means our investigation is restricted to the forensic search down in Hampshire. How is that progressing?'

'Slowly,' said Rob. 'Detective Lowe is still managing the team, but they're winding down. Very few resources involved now, and it's all a bit searching by numbers, going through the motions. That sort of stuff.'

'Which means fuck all is happening, right?' said Stevie. 'We have nothing. Hope is a jerk. I knew Paul Newton was shady. That day I spent interviewing with them. Misogynist fucking throwbacks.'

'It's obvious,' said Zain. 'It all fits. We need to follow the money. They must have hired a hitman.'

'I'm not sure,' said Kate. 'The kidnap videos felt too personal, too staged. I think a stranger hired for the kill wouldn't do that, necessarily. They had to be more directly involved.'

'Hit men have changed since the eighties,' said Zain. 'They do what the hell they get paid for nowadays. They're all clued up on forensics as well.'

'This is fucking insane,' said Stevie. 'I mean, what the hell? We're talking about professional assassins? I need a drink.'

Kate saw Stevie's image blur on screen as she drank deeply from a bottle of something.

'It's a lot bigger than we thought,' said Kate. 'This feels like a cover-up, and we have nowhere to go. We have to keep this between ourselves.'

'Men are such bollocks,' said Stevie.

'Cheers, love,' said Rob.

'Fuck off,' said Stevie. 'You're not a man.'

'Ouch,' he said.

'What do you suggest?' said Zain.

'I want you to act like your normal annoying self,' said Kate. 'I want you to hack away at MINDNET and KNG, anything you can find. Ruby's computers, you said files had gone missing? I need you to find them. Do whatever it takes.'

'You're sanctioning him fucking Michelle off,' said Stevie.

'I'll handle her,' said Kate. 'And you, I need you to interview Ruby's friends again.'

'I'd rather stick rusty bottle tops in my eyes,' said Stevie, demonstrating with the top of the bottle she was drinking. Her right eye displayed a Coors logo.

'They can't be that bad,' said Rob.

'I know who Megan Trainor and Ariana Grande are. And when 5SOS trends on Twitter, I know what it means. My brain cells have committed fucking suicide in protest, the amount of crap her friends have filled it with.'

'This time you need to find out if Ruby mentioned her concerns about MINDNET to anyone, or concerns over the treatment of employees used in mining. Target your interviews, it should clear the junk.'

'And me?' said Rob.

'You've got the boring job. You're my public face of the investigation, the smokescreen. You act as though we are only interested in finding Ruby, in Hampshire. Means you get to spend more time with Detective Lowe.'

Kate saw a grin spread over Rob's face.

Chapter Eighty-nine

Zain was sweating. The storage heater in his flat had been on the night before, his small lounge now heavy with the warmth. He sat in gym shorts, exposing every part of him that could be naked. It was November. This shouldn't be happening.

He was lost in *Assassin's Creed*, thoughts of captivity in his head. They always came when he played this game. Sometimes they came when he could hear his heart beating. He remembered that sound, locked away in silence. It marked time. Thinking of just how many times it beat a minute, an hour, a day. It was an impossible thing, a breakable thing. He felt so mortal, so temporary.

Occupational Health had said he shouldn't be alone. Dr Pat Michelson, responsible for assessing him, had been a big help, had given him some good advice. She said she went home every evening and she had four dogs, her husband, three kids and her mother. She would unload on them, share her stress.

Zain lived alone, was alone: who could he share his stresses with? How should he unload? Dr Michelson said he needed someone to do that with. That would be fine, he thought, if you were normal. Normal people shouldn't be alone. If you could, you should find someone to share your life with. Marriage, kids, co habiting, whatever the fuck you wanted to do. All good. He celebrated it. His own mother was testament to the rejuvenating power of marriage.

Not for Zain, though. He was existing in a crease of humanity, and who could find him there? Only someone as damaged as him.

Zain walked barefoot to the kitchen; food would distract him. Turkey – ham, bits of salad, some light mayo. He made himself a sandwich, sat down to eat it while catching up on the headlines.

Ruby was no longer a main story. Only online. Although Dan the victim of police brutality, the hero risen from the ashes, was the talking point even there. It made Zain's insides twist with anger.

He muted the TV, unsure at first. He put his plate down, walked to stand behind the front door. He put his ear against it, heard a faint shuffling. He was right. Someone was out there.

Zain jumped, his heart thumping, when the knock came.

He opened the door, and looked into a face he didn't recognise at first. Then he knew. It was the man from MINDNET. The man who hadn't turned up for their meeting outside the British Museum.

'Not here,' said the man. 'Don't bring your phone. Meet me in the park opposite the Old Vic.'

He left, covering his face in a scarf as he walked to the lifts.

Chapter Ninety

Kate stared out into the darkness. She had seen the face again, through her kitchen window. She felt watched. The unease was creeping over her, her inner voice of logic not strong enough to shut it down.

She checked the locks, made sure they were turned. Why did a house need so much glass? The door leading to the garden; the windows above the sink. The windows in the lounge, in the TV room. They were all so big. You could smash them and walk through.

Kate pulled back the curtains that blocked her view of the main road. Nothing moved; cars so still they could be rusting and part of a film set. The moonlight turned their metalwork into treacle.

No man, no face. Kate let the curtains fall back into place. She shivered, despite the central heating. That's what fear did, once it got hold of you. It chilled you somewhere inside your head, the nerves in your brain sending the ice to every other part of you.

Kate checked the alarm. It was set so the doors and windows were guarded. She would set it to pick up any movements downstairs when she headed to bed.

'Winter?'

Kate couldn't hide her shock as her mother came up behind her. She refused to use the name 'Kate' when they were alone. Kate worried one day she might let it slip in front of Ryan. And the name, Winter, reminded her all too well of their shared past.

Winter Moorhouse. The name she had carried all her life.

'I thought you were asleep,' said Kate.

'No, I was restless.'

'Do you want a drink? Water or hot chocolate?'

'Yes, hot chocolate would be nice.'

They sat at the kitchen table, letting their hands warm on their mugs. Kate tried not to, but she kept glancing towards the window. The darkness was forming outlines, her eyes moulding them into phantoms. She blinked them away, fixed a weak smile on her face.

Her mother may not recognise her face – prosopagnosia was face blindness – but she could make out her emotions. The way her mouth quirked, what emotions were in her eyes.

'I need to speak to you about something. I didn't want to. I don't want you to worry, OK?'

'Mother?'

'Promise me you won't fuss,' said Jane. 'Ryan said I should tell you, but I refused. Now, thinking about it . . .'

'Mother, tell me,' said Kate.

Jane took a sip of her hot chocolate, letting her tongue work around her mouth, tasting the sugary coating. It was a habit her father had hated. Kate wondered if that's why she did it with relish now he wasn't around.

'I was out for my usual,' said Jane. Her usual was a trip along the high street, or a visit to a museum or gallery, or even a day sitting on a park bench. Anything she could do in the daylight, independently.

'Where did you go?'

'Just to Primrose Hill,' said Jane. 'It was warm in the sunshine today.'

'What happened?'

'There was a man,' said Jane. 'He asked me if I was your mother. And he asked me about you. Asked how you were.'

Kate felt as though someone had just plunged her head into freezing water. She started shaking, but tried to still herself. If it had been anyone else sitting in front of her, she would have asked what the man had looked like. Not her mother, though.

'What did he sound like?' she said.

'It was that broad English accent. I couldn't place it; it's the one they all have.'

'So not regional, then?'

'No. I couldn't say if it was. I couldn't tell his age. Under fifty, possibly.'

'That's a big range,' said Kate. 'What did he say, Mom?'

'Asked me if I was Detective Riley's mother. I said yes, asked whom was I speaking to. He said he was a friend.'

'And?'

Kate couldn't breathe.

'That was all. He said he was a friend. And then he left.'

A stranger had just approached her mother, her vulnerable mother, asking about her. Kate's eyes searched the darkness outside the window through the crack between the curtains again. She wasn't imaging things, was she? She couldn't let her mother see her panic.

'You know how it is. Probably someone who doesn't realise about your . . . situation, was most likely a bit upset you didn't recognise him.'

'Yes, that's what I thought, too,' said Jane.

It was a common enough occurrence. People who she had met before would meet her mother, and be put out when she didn't recognise them. Usually her mother was honest, told them, and asked them to explain who they were.

This man, though, he hadn't given her that chance.

He had stopped long enough to send Kate a message. They knew her weakness; they knew how to get to her. And then that overarching thought. Was this it? Had someone leaked her location? Had her father found her again?

Fear turned into anger. A familiar anger. When she found out who they were, Kate would ruin them.

Chapter Ninety-one

Waterloo Millennium Park was a small area of grass opposite the Old Vic. It was fenced, by trees and metal bars. One side was buffered by the noise of traffic heading down to Elephant and Castle, the other shaded by council flats.

Zain knew it well, had used it on summer days and early evenings.

'Why didn't you just call?' said Zain.

'Don't trust them,' said the man.

They were seated on a bench under a tree.

'I waited two hours,' said Zain.

'I couldn't . . . I tried, but I was too scared.'

'Of what? What's your name?'

'Deep Throat,' said the man.

'I see you haven't lost your sense of humour, at least,' said Zain. 'I know what you look like; I'll hack into the MINDNET database tomorrow. Get your name that way. Or you could just tell me. I'm a police officer. You can trust me.'

'Richard,' he said. 'That's all for now.'

'OK, Richard. Why all this cloak and dagger shit? How did you get to my front door?'

'Just followed someone into the building,' he said.

'Let me go further back. How the fuck did you know where I live?'

'I followed you back, the night we were supposed to meet. I knew your building from there.'

'What about my flat number?'

'Electoral register. I have access to it for work.'

'What do you do?'

'I work in IT.'

'I see,' said Zain.

Fucking databases. They were wrecking his privacy as well. It felt like payback a bit, the number of data hits he'd been authorised to do. And done illegally. Other people's information felt cheaper than his own; maybe he should respect it a bit more.

'Why couldn't we just do this at the station?'

'I don't want it to be official.'

'Why not?'

Richard's eyes glared at Zain, his face clearly visible in the artificial light surrounding them. Blackouts in London must have been a bitch, back in the day.

'I'm on a leave of absence, from MINDNET. Two weeks, just annual leave, nothing out of the ordinary. I thought it would be enough time.'

'For what?'

'To tell you what I have to. And then to leave. Hide.'

'What are you afraid of?'

Again the accusatory staring.

'Have you not seen what they did to Ruby? And that message, at the end of that video, the one they blew her brains out in. That message. "You're next". That was meant for me.'

Kate was awake. She thought she would be awake for ever. How had this happened? She had come to London to get away from this sort of bullshit. And now here she was again. Scared for her mother, spinning wild theories about those who were putting them both in danger.

Was it her father? Or was this Harry Cain and Jed Byrne? Was Justin Hope involved? Had they paid someone to speak to her mother? Was she being irrational? Nothing had happened. It might just be an innocent conversation. Only, coming on the back of everything, it was just too convenient to be a coincidence.

Kate sat up, keeping her light off, listening. The house, the heating. She had her bedroom door open. Any noise her subconscious didn't recognise, she wanted to be jolted awake.

It didn't seem to matter, though; sleep was not coming for her tonight.

Chapter Ninety-two

Zain felt sweat dripping down his back, even though it was a cold autumn night. He'd only had time to put on his jeans and a T-shirt before he left his flat, hoping his jacket would be warm enough. The excitement of speaking to Richard was enough to keep his blood pumping.

'You think they know it's you?' said Zain.

'If they don't, they'll soon work it out. I'm not waiting around for them to link it back to me. They know Ruby had someone on the inside. That's why they posted that threat. And when they find out it's me, that's it. I'm fucking dead.'

'I can help you,' said Zain.

'Not against them. Look at how Ruby ended up. Fuck.'

'Stay. I can get you Witness Protection.'

'I'm here because I owe Ruby. After I'm done, I have a morning flight out of here.'

'Where are you going?'

Richard didn't reply.

'When did you meet Ruby?' said Zain.

'September. I contacted her online first, asked to meet with her. She didn't respond, probably thought I was a crazy or perv.'

Zain wondered if either of these labels might fit. Richard was a mess, unshaven and unshowered. Zain offered him some chewing gum he found in his pocket.

'I called her, got her details from a MINDNET contact list. I took the risk. But said I needed to speak to her in person.'

'Where did you meet?'

'There's a lake in Regent's Park. We met there.'

'What did you tell her?'

'The truth about Byrne.'

'Which was?'

Richard put his head in his hands, took deep breaths. His leg started hammering nervously.

'You know about his father?'

'Harry Cain? Yes I do.'

'Cain had a crisis. Felt he'd neglected his son growing up. Fuck, he didn't even acknowledge him for most of his life. That's the office gossip anyway. MINDNET was like a bribe, a proof of love, if you like. A father buying his son's forgiveness.'

'Mine mumbled a sorry when he split with my mother,' said Zain. 'I think Jed did just fine.'

'Yes. And MINDNET has done well, even though it shouldn't. Byrne knows nothing about business. He just loves talking about his success when he's hanging with his pals in Kensington and Chelsea.'

'Good for him. I'm still not clear, though: what exactly did you tell Ruby? And why did you?'

'I came across something. I wish to God I hadn't, but I did. And once I saw it, and once I knew for sure, I couldn't ignore it.'

'What exactly do you do for MINDNET? IT is a vast field.'

'Systems administrator,' said Richard. 'I manage the entire network infrastructure. The hardware, software, I purchase it all. I manage the teams responsible for IT services across MINDNET.'

'I'm guessing you looked at something you shouldn't have?' said Zain.

He was always shocked at how trusting people were of their IT teams. These men and women had the ability to access everything you did at work, from emails to your personal drives. And it didn't take more than a few clicks for them to do it.

'Not at MINDNET. The systems got hit at KANGlobal. DOS.'

Denial of service. It was usually spamming a website to make it crash, but sophisticated hackers could use web servers to access the protocols internal to an organisation. Crashing the entire IT system.

'It was quite something; we still don't know where it came from. I was drafted in to help. The senior network manager developed appendicitis.'

Why didn't they use an assistant or something?'

'No one there was as qualified as me, or Stella Kapur, their network manager. I don't want to sound arrogant, but the threat was so severe, they wanted the best.'

'So what happened?'

'It was a fraught forty-eight hours. I was working twenty hours straight, sleeping in the office..'

'No one at home to miss you?'

'I have an ex-wife and kids I rarely get to see. No, there's no one at home.'

Zain saw the sadness of it in Richard's face. 'So you saved KANGlobal?'

'Yes. But we needed to upgrade their security software. Because the network was so badly damaged, some of the machines had to be manually upgraded. One of those was Harry Cain's machine.'

Zain felt expectation course through him. He pictured a stressed Richard in a plush office a CEO like Cain might have. Cain probably barely acknowledged him; men like Richard were minions, there to be ignored.

'The update took a while, twenty minutes or so. Cain left his office, so it was just me. Once the update was done, I got his PA to log in, using Cain's username and password. He asked her to, wanted me to check everything was working OK. She then got called away, an urgent phone call. She left the office door open, so I could hear her outside. It's crazy, isn't it, how something so small and insignificant can change so much?'

'So you were logged in, and left alone with his laptop. Then what did you do?'

'I shouldn't have. I was in a position of trust. But there I was, looking out of his floor-to-ceiling windows. He has views across London. And I felt some sense of power, and it was like being invisible. I thought, I can do this. I can have a look around the big man's computer. Curiosity, detective. So I did it. And look where it got me.'

The sweat had dried on Zain's back; he was beginning to feel the November chill creep into him. It reminded him of waiting outside the British Museum for Richard.

'What did you find?'

'I did some random searching at first. Typing in stupid things, pornographic search terms. Then I started to look through documents marked "personal". It was wrong, but it was also irresistible. And that's when I came across documents related to that place.'

'DRC?' said Zain.

'Yes. Democratic Republic of Congo. The temptation not to look at something marked classified, it was just too much.'

'So you clicked?'

'So I clicked.'

Chapter Ninety-three

Zain had persuaded Richard, who was now claiming that his last name was Brown, to relocate to the Duke of Sussex pub. It was at the far end of Waterloo Millennium Green, close to the council estate. It didn't feel like central London, or a stone's throw from Waterloo. It could be a washed-out pub on a corner anywhere.

The pub was ingrained with decades of smoke and cheap beer, giving off a distinctive smell. A masculine smell, sour. Zain thought of his father, the military man. He didn't smoke and didn't get drunk. Apart from the day he knocked up Zain's mother. Worst hangover of his life, he claimed.

Richard was in the bathroom while Zain settled in the pub's second room with their drinks. A pool table stood empty in the centre of the room. An old-fashioned jukebox against the wall. This could be a fun night out. Nostalgic, simple.

Zain missed his phone. He wanted to check his messages, update DCI Riley. Do some surfing while he waited.

Richard came back soon enough, looking more relaxed. He had removed his outer layers, revealing cords, a jumper and shirt. Zain saw the man clearly for the first time. He was younger than he'd first thought, probably late thirties, early forties. He had a short beard, a bit like Zain's, dark brown, matching his dark eyes. His hair was cut short, but slick on top, giving him a trendy look.

Richard sat down and emptied his glass, prompting Zain to get him another beer.

'You sure you don't want something stronger?' he said, returning with their drinks.

Richard shook his head, taking his beer from Zain and supping the top before putting his glass down. 'I just needed that to steady myself,' he said.

Richard looked towards the door leading to the main room before carrying on with his story. The customers in the main room were mainly old men and middle-aged couples.

'It wasn't all in one place,' he said. 'And I got about forty minutes on the computer, before his PA came back in.'

'What wasn't all in one place?'

Zain wanted to hurry the man, but he knew this was probably only the second time he had told his story to anyone. The first probably being Ruby.

'The documents were a bit cryptic. They referred to trucks, jeeps. Also supplies, food, steel. It wasn't anything that jumped out at me. But there was a lot of action over a three-day period. Dozens of emails saved in one folder. Some were short, confirming an action had taken place. Others more detailed, but again they kept referring to logistics. Numbers of vehicles used, supplies being moved around. They were all referring to the "Bunda project", the "Bunda action". I Googled on my phone, found it. Bunda is a small village near the Rwandan border. It's been through every level of hell. The genocide in Rwanda spilled over into it. Then the civil wars. The mass atrocities on its civilian population. I asked myself why anyone would stay there.'

'I'm guessing people have nowhere to go.'

'Yes. And it's their livelihood. The people were cheap labour for the mines surrounding Bunda. Mines rich in coltan. Do you know what coltan is?'

Zain shook his head.

'Columbite-tantalite. That's its proper name. It's a metal ore more vital than gold and diamonds. Coltan is in practically every electrical device there is. It has something called tantalum in it. That's what we use. Mobile phones, computers, Play-Stations, iPads. Whatever people use these days, it needs coltan chips. And most of us don't even have a clue where so much of it comes from.'

'The Congo?'

'They say about sixty per cent of the world's coltan is there. No one knows exactly how much, the place is such a mess. You don't go in and do geographical surveys. DRC is the third biggest producer at the moment, shipping its dirty gains all over the place. China, India, Europe. All the surging economies and developed countries, using metal picked from the carcasses of the poorest.'

Zain let his eyes wander around the room. The world was full of depressing, monumental crap. People got screwed over; the system was fucked. What was an individual against all that?

'How is KNG involved?' he said.

'They own coltan mines around Bunda. It's their secret little enclave. I found all this out afterwards, not while I was in Cain's office. What I found there was the name Pierre Sese. He had signed off on something. I did a search in Cain's files, and found a contract. Pierre Sese giving KNG access to the coltan mines. In return for money, trucks, food, steel, all sorts.'

'A business deal?'

'Of sorts. You see, I found afterwards that KNG bought the mines from Sese at a knockdown price. Less than ten per cent of their value in actual terms. What they gave him on top was what he needed.'

Zain could guess what Richard was about to reveal.

'You know why he needed all that? To help his militias. They went marauding around the countryside, butchering, enslaving, burning. They killed hundreds, everyone they didn't like, indulging in ethnic cleansing. It's all in a UNICEF report, Amnesty too. All official, documenting the crimes they are accused of.'

Richard laughed. 'You know there's a child, the only survivor of a small village. Fifty-nine people died there in one night. Apart from this nine-year-old boy. Jean Paul Motumbo. And they say he's lucky.'

'Lucky how?'

'He survived. He was hidden in the rafters of the roof, the only one small enough in his family to hide there. He watched as Sese's men butchered his parents. Jean Paul's three brothers – twelve, thirteen and fifteen – were in the room. Sese took them, to turn them into killing machines. And they say Jean Paul is lucky.'

Zain felt sick. Images floated through his head. Anger followed. He wanted to hurt the people that did this.

'Have you got these documents?' he said.

'No, only what I could print out. Cain's computers are all local area networked. Only an encrypted USB stick can be used on it, otherwise the system crashes. He has no internet connection to it.'

'How did his machine get hit, then?'

'The DOS attacked the network, like a domino effect. It hit the LAN eventually.'

'What about the emails?'

'They were sent to another computer, possibly his phone or a laptop. He must have uploaded them. Or his PA did.'

'So you couldn't send anything to yourself? Or save anything onto a memory stick?'

'No. I know from the documents that I saw that for three days in particular, KNG were driving those fucking bastards from village to village and supporting them as they tore that place apart. Sese's men and what they did . . .'

'How do you know for sure?'

'I tied it together. The emails, the contract. The reports. You know KNG sold some of the coltan mines back to the DRC government in Kinshasa? They sold them at a profit of twenty-three times what they paid for them. Robbery under the African sun, like fucking colonialism. The DRC government bought them back because, years ago, KNG were logistically helping the current government in their war, when they were militias. It's like a poisonous cycle, militias rising up, slaughtering everyone in their way, getting into power. And when in power, they help the men that backed them on their way up. And KNG? Companies like that hedge their bets, support every side. They buy their mines cheap, and then sell them back at huge profits. And it's done legitimately, for everyone to see. And nobody does anything about it.'

'What can an individual do against what you described?' said Zain.

'It's funny, isn't it? Here we are, two grown men. And neither of us can see a way to fight that, to change it. Insurmountable. That's what it felt like to me. The more I researched, the worse it got, and the more powerless I felt. And then I came across the Joseph Kony video.'

'I remember hearing about the video. *Kony 2012*, wasn't it?'

'It was made by an American director, Jason Russell. He and two of his fellow college students set up a charity, Invisible Children, Inc. Its main purpose was to expose the war crimes and recruitment of child soldiers by the Ugandan warlord Joseph Kony. That's what the *Kony 2012* video did; it got their message heard, started a momentum.'

'And you thought . . .'

'Yes. I thought of Ruby. And she had enough guts for a million men.'

Zain started to see it all then, as everything fell into place for him. He understood what had happened. How the anguished Richard Brown, too scared to go to the police, worried about getting directly embroiled in a situation that might put his kids in jeopardy, had instead turned to Ruby Day. And how that young girl, barely out of her teens, was ready to stand up in a way that had put her directly in the path of whatever had taken her. The people that had killed her. The same people that were going to kill Richard.

PART FIVE
THE DIRTY GAME

Chapter Ninety-four

Zain had driven through the rain, which started as a drizzle and soon became heavy. Car lights blurred around him, as though he was seeing them through refracted glass. It was midnight before he got to Regus House. The office was empty, the automated lights all off. They flickered into life as he walked to his desk, grabbed what he needed and headed back out.

DCI Raymond Cross, his old boss from SO15, was waiting for Zain outside Westminster Cathedral on Victoria Street.

Traffic was still flowing, and a crowd made their way to the all-night bus station on Terminus Place. This road would never see peace, or an hour when no one was wandering along its pavements. Imagine living with a neighbour that played loud music or banged on the walls 24/7.

DCI Cross and Zain sat on the steps leading up to the cathedral doors. Its red and white brickwork reflected shades of orange from the street lamps. Zain was wearing jeans, boots, a burgundy shirt and his short black jacket.

Cross was dressed in a dark suit, white shirt, tie done up neatly. Flasher coat. At least he wasn't wearing his trademark 'man from Del Monte' hat, his silver hair neatly combed. Strangers could never mistake him for being anything but a cop.

'How are you?' he said.

'Just fine, sir. Thank you,' said Zain.

'How are you getting on with Riley?'

'Everything's great, sir.'

'She's quite something. You slept with her yet?'

'No, sir. Not yet.'

'Working on it?'

'No, sir.'

'She knock you back?'

Zain didn't like to think it was him saying no. Objectively, Kate Riley was stunning. Not model beautiful, but the sort of beauty that was more about her attitude, the way she carried herself. The steel in her blue eyes. The respect she engendered in her team. There was something about women like that, women in control of their own destinies.

She was his type, completely.

'I have a lot of respect for her, sir.'

Cross laughed. He took out a cigar. Cuban, expensive. Zain remembered, as the familiar smoke surrounded him. He knew in daylight it would be blue-grey. It smelled like the old pub he had met Richard Brown in.

'What made you call me tonight, then?' said Cross.

'I need your help. I need experts, and I need them to do something quickly. I need SO15, and I need their . . . friends.'

'What have you got?' said Cross.

'Ruby Day's hard drives,' said Zain.

Cross enjoyed his cigar for a minute, the silence between them filled with the traffic and shouting voices.

'Harry Cain is involved,' said Zain.

Zain thought he heard the cogs in Cross's head turn. You didn't have to explain to a man like DCI Raymond Cross; he would put the pieces into place in his head.

It had been the same when he had recruited Zain.

Zain had been a radicalised, lonely teenager. He had been friendless, mixed-up and lacking identity, and gone to find one. Back then, 9/11 had just happened, and he was the first cohort to be brainwashed online. His mother had a choice between thousands of Hindu gods and the Muslim one, and chose none. His father was lapsed from his own Christianity. They believed in love and humanism.

Zain, the multicultural conundrum, was an easy target for men who knew how to prey on the vulnerable. Luckily for him, Cross had called. Zain had helped Special Branch, as they were. And in the process had saved himself, and let Cross rescue him.

He looked at Cross now, both men bonded by something deeper than they could ever articulate.

'You ever wonder what we do this for?' Cross said.

'Always,' said Zain.

'Look at that. That man is barely able to walk in a straight line and, look, there you go.'

Zain watched as the drunken man Cross referred to walked to a tree on the edge of the cathedral courtyard and pissed against it.

'Like a fucking dog,' said Cross.

The man started shouting to his friends, running after them before he had finished or zipped up.

'He had the freedom to do that, sir,' said Zain. 'That's worth something.'

'You still think we are free?' said Cross.

'In a way, yes. We are part of a system that suspends actual freedom, I am aware of that. On a daily basis, in the little parts of life, people have the sense they are free at least.'

'And you think it's a fair price?'

'Yes, I do.'

'I'm sorry I couldn't take you back,' said Cross.

Zain froze, the reference to his captivity and its aftermath like ice. 'I understand, sir. You fixed my occupational health report. Gave Hope glowing references. That was enough.'

'You're a good officer. You proved yourself. I just couldn't put you at risk again, not until you're ready.'

Don't feel it, he told himself. But it was too late. Cross had pulled the scab, and the fresh blood of hope was trickling out.

'It's fine. This team is a good place to be.'

'And Hope?'

'He knows. About the doctored OH report,' said Zain.

'Not from me,' said Cross quickly.

'He wanted a favour in return. I did some things for him, during this investigation.'

'Such as?'

'I changed a despatch call. And I gave him updates on Riley when he wanted.'

The cogs were turning again.

'You see, Zain, on one side of that coin, you have betrayed Riley. On the other, you now have something on Hope.'

Zain didn't reply. Instead, he reached for the plastic bags next to him. They were clear packets, containing metal boxes.

'These are Ruby's hard drives. From her laptop and her desktop. I need them analysed. There's evidence of someone hiding deleted files by overwriting them. I need them located, but don't have the right tools. And Forensics will take weeks, if they can do it at all.'

'What are we looking for?'

'A video or files. Anything relating to KNG and the Democratic Republic of Congo. Specifically coltan mining and Pierre Sese.'

'The warlord?'

'The warlord.'

Cross whistled. 'Are you sure?'

'I need evidence to be sure,' said Zain.

'What are you mixed up in?'

'That's what I'm hoping you'll find out for me. Before I can proceed against KNG, I need some hard evidence.'

The hard drives disappeared into inside pockets within Cross's coat. 'I'll get someone on it, see what we can find.'

'Thank you, sir. And another thing. The KNG whistle-blower, he needs protection.'

'My sort of protection?'

'Yes. Can you get him into a safe house?'

'Where is he now?'

'He's gone home to collect some things.'

'Let me know where you want him picked up.'

'Thank you, sir.'

'Come round for dinner sometime. Julia asks after you, occasionally.'

'I will, give her my regards.'

They shook hands, and walked off in separate directions.

Chapter Ninety-five

It was 3 a.m. Kate was still awake. Harris had told her he would Skype her later. He needed to explain where he had been earlier. She knew his lack of communication meant it was somehow connected to Cain and Byrne.

Her mother was asleep upstairs. The alarm was set, protecting the doors and windows. Kate had found her Glock, loaded it with bullets she kept in her safe. The gun rested on the computer unit next to her. Easy to reach. She hadn't used it for a while.

A friend in the US embassy had helped her acquire it. She loved those diplomatic pouches.

Harris's face filled her computer screen, his voice in her ears through the headset she wore.

'Are you certain it was the same man from MINDNET?' she said.

'Yes, of course. I didn't look at him for long, but it's him.'

Yes, because most people didn't have face blindness.

'What did he say?'

Kate listened as Zain told her about DCR, Pierre Sese, coltan mining and the logistical support KNG had provided for a massacre.

'Is there any evidence for this?' said Kate.

'Richard printed out emails and documents, but he had limited time to do it. He said he gave them to Ruby, didn't keep copies himself. He claims she scanned it all in, shredded and destroyed the originals.'

'Convenient,' said Kate. 'So we have the word of a man who won't even tell you his real name? We need more.'

'I'm working on it. It will be on Ruby's hard drives.'

'We've looked,' she said.

'Not deep enough. I met my old boss tonight. DCI Raymond Cross. Gave them to him. He's going to get someone to examine them for me.'

Another independent action, she thought. A mix between resentment at being left out of his working methodology, and admiration for his initiative.

'Why didn't your source go to the police? Or the press?'

'He said he was worried about his kids. They don't live with him; he hardly sees them. Loves them, though. He also knows about Harry Cain and his links with the PM. Newton is on his payroll, and that means Hope is.'

'Where is he now?'

'I've arranged a safe house for him.'

'Who signed off on it?' Zain couldn't meet her eyes. 'I see; DCI Cross.'

'Richard didn't see any other way to do this,' said Zain.

'There's always a way,' she said.

'His was to use Ruby. Do you remember the *Kony 2012* video?'

Kate said she didn't.

'It was a video made and posted online about the Ugandan warlord Joseph Kony. He was involved in recruiting child soldiers, mass atrocities. Anyway, the video has had a hundred million views on YouTube, and started a mass global campaign. Teens that had been obsessed with make-up and porn suddenly developed a conscience. Wanted Kony found and brought to justice. They say he's hiding out in DCR now.'

'I'm beginning to fear the power of open-platform video sharing,' said Kate.

'Everyone in the system is afraid, trying to control it behind the scenes.'

'It's the absence of a filter,' said Kate. 'What happens when somebody posts false allegations on there? We already had someone falsely accused of being a paedophile; they ended up dead at the hand of vigilantes.'

'Everything has its risks,' said Zain.

'So this Richard was trying to recreate *Kony 2012*, aimed at Sese and exposing KANGlobal?'

'Exactly. He contacted Ruby, told her what we know, gave her the files he had printed. He said she had already made the video talking about the issues. It would have been a nightmare. More so after what Michelle found. Richard confirmed it, too, said the IPO for KNG is two billion dollars.'

The initial public offering on the biggest stock exchanges in the world.

'And if Ruby had gone public?'

'The price would have plummeted and KNG would have lost hundreds of millions off their value. No one likes touching conflict mining, not openly. It's done behind closed doors, like coke snorting by celebs.'

That made sense. Conflict minerals and diamonds were still being sold and bought; the trade didn't stop because of moral or ethical issues. It just happened where nobody looked, and those involved had too much to lose by exposing their transactions.

'That's not all, though,' said Zain.

'Isn't that enough? If we can find evidence pointing to this, we can go after KNG and MINDNET.'

'I think we may have another option, even if we don't find the paperwork,' said Harris.

'How?'

'Have you ever heard of the ten-minute rule?' said Zain.

Chapter Ninety-six

The morning was fresh, but filled with the sweet decay of leaves and the smoky gunpowder from fireworks that people continued to let off even days after Bonfire Night. Kate breathed in the fall smells, closed her eyes. For a moment, she let herself remember. Life before her mother was attacked, before she'd had to run away.

'They kicked us out,' her mother used to say.

'No, Mother, we left of our own choice. They made it hard for us, sure, but we made the decision to go.'

Kate tried to hold on to that, because the idea of what had been done to both herself and her mother turned her blood into lava.

'You OK?' said Zain, setting his car alarm, startling her.

'Yes,' she said. 'Is she expecting us?'

'I said nine-thirty; she said to meet her here.'

The house was on St George's Road, a quiet street of white-washed houses near Elephant and Castle. Westminster was a brisk walk in the opposite direction.

At the front door, Kate heard a dog bark inside the house. The woman who opened the door was in her late forties, possibly early fifties. She had auburn hair, tinged with red, dark eyes and a friendly manner. She was holding on to the biggest dog Kate had seen in a while; it came to the woman's thigh in height. Like so many dogs that size, it had a smile on its face.

'Don't mind Benjy,' the woman said. 'Or I'll put him out in the garden if he bothers you.'

'No, it's fine,' Kate said.

Zain was already rubbing the dog's head, speaking to it in baby language.

They followed the woman into a spacious lounge. A real fire was lit in the grate. Benjy settled himself on a rug in front of it.

'He's beautiful,' said Zain.

'Yes, he is, isn't he? I needed something to fill the children-shaped holes in the house. My husband works away a lot; he's a consultant for the oil industry.'

Kate was surprised by this. Margaret Walsh was an MP who they were here to question about KANGlobal's mining. The link with oil production seemed ominous.

'He works on developing greener technologies for oil extraction and refinement,' Margaret explained. 'It's how we can afford to live so close to Westminster.'

'It's you we've come to speak to, Mrs Walsh,' said Kate.

'I only mention that because people always wonder, after the expenses scandal. I was one of the few untouched by it, but I stand by the others. I am lucky, damned fortunate. Without those expenses, others not in my fortunate position may struggle to enter politics. And if I hadn't married Gregg, I would have struggled. I was born in a terrace house in Bury, just above the poverty line. Getting out, moving up, it's never easy from those beginnings.'

'You live here during the week?' said Kate.

'Yes, and weekends back up north at my family home. My children are in Manchester, as are my siblings and my mother. Although she's in a home now.'

Kate wanted to pursue that. Understand when Margaret made the decision to move her mother into a home, what stage had her mother hit to prompt the decision. So Kate could be prepared . . . when it happened to her own.

'Your private life is none of our business, Mrs Walsh,' Kate said instead.

'Please, call me Maggie,' the MP said. 'You said on the phone that this is about Ruby Day?'

'Yes. I believe you knew her?' said Kate.

'Yes, she had been in contact with me recently.'

'Where are you the MP for?' said Zain.

'An inner-city ward in Manchester called Gorton and Longsight,' said Maggie.

She was wearing black trousers and a purple shirt, which revealed her curves; a woman comfortable with her body and sure of her appeal. Kate felt an affinity with her; this was a rare woman, she could tell. An MP that was in the job because she genuinely wanted to make a difference.

'Can I get you a tea or coffee at all?' said Maggie.

'No, I'm sure you have enough to do. We won't take up too much of your time,' said Kate.

'Why did Ruby approach you?' said Zain.

'I used to be a junior minister in the Foreign and Commonwealth Office. I resigned because I disagreed with a contract the FCO was overseeing, in Angola. For oil reserves, but the company involved was treating the Angolans unfairly.'

'You're on record as resigning over ethics in corporate affairs in Africa,' said Zain. 'Ruby would have come to you purposely, then?'

'Yes, she did.'

'What did you discuss?' said Kate.

'She told me she had evidence that a company was involved in illegal mining in DRC.'

'Did she name the company?' said Kate.

Maggie rubbed her jaw, her eyes filling with a hardness she had hidden from them up until now.

'Yes, she did. KANGlobal.'

'Had you heard of them previously?'

Maggie looked down at her hands, making a washing motion with them, before meeting Kate's gaze. 'My husband worked for them. He was a consultant, for a pipeline they were trying to run through Kazakhstan. And I came across their file, when I was at the FCO.'

'In what context?' said Kate.

'I signed off on their purchase of some coltan mines.'

'Was there anything wrong with the contract?' said Kate.

'No. I had some researchers look into it. It was all legitimate. A corporation in DRC was selling land to KNG, where a land survey suspected the presence of high deposits of coltan. The report said the area was unstable, that Pierre Sese was rumoured to be hiding out close by. But the DRC corporation and KNG were legitimate. The price was low, in their opinion, but there were no working mines. So I signed off on it.'

'Ruby had another story?' said Kate.

'Yes. She claimed the DRC firm was a front for Sese, that the land purchased already had working mines present. If that was the case, not only did KNG lie to me, but the researchers were also economical with the truth.'

'Who did the research?' asked Zain.

'Yoko Kosh,' said Maggie.

Kate knew the company. They were one of the big six, like Ernst & Young, Deloitte, Price Waterhouse.

'So, in essence, I oversaw the sale of mines at a fraction of their cost. Worse than that, I oversaw the sale and transfer of funds to Sese,' she said.

'Was there never an investigation? Did no one ever find this out?' said Zain.

'These areas of the world, they're not cities like London. They are lawless, forgotten corners of our planet. Who has the resources to solve the hell that is DRC?'

'And when you found out about the illegal mining? My source said you were going to use the ten-minute rule, or something?' said Zain.

'Yes,' said Maggie.

'Can you elaborate?' said Kate. 'What is the ten-minute rule, exactly?'

Chapter Ninety-seven

Maggie had gone to make them drinks. She insisted, as they'd been talking for a while. Kate realised there was a reason the woman had obviously cleared her diary this morning; she wasn't going to be a quick interview. There were layers to what she had to tell them.

'Do you remember what it was like when Ruby disappeared?' Zain asked Kate.

He was throwing a red toy for Benjy to catch, and bring back.

'It's only been a few days, but it feels so long ago, and too unreal,' he continued. 'At first I thought: young girl, gone clubbing, forgotten her phone or something. Then the videos, and I just thought, OK, I got it wrong. A psycho serial killer has her. And then her bastard boyfriend, I thought it was him. And now? Mining contracts in West Africa? Fucking warlords? How did we get here?'

Kate didn't know how to reply. Maggie came back with a tray of drinks.

'None for you,' she said to Benjy, as he came towards her.

Zain was drinking tea, like Maggie, while Kate had gone for her usual black coffee. She welcomed the instant hit from the caffeine, her body tired after barely three hours' sleep.

'The ten-minute rule is complex, but vital – although, for the most part, it can be ineffective,' Maggie started explaining as soon as she sat down. 'Every week after Prime Minister's Question Time, MPs are allowed to bring their own bills in for discussion. Most bills that are debated in parliament are party approved, part of the manifesto, so known in advance. They usually form legislation to honour election promises, or guide policy.'

'Cutting benefits or privatising the NHS?' said Zain.

'Don't be puerile,' said Maggie, but smiled as she said it. 'If a member wants something discussed that isn't part of planned policy, then they use the ten-minute rule. There is no system to get your ten minutes; it's not based on merit or who you know. It's whoever gets through the doors of the Public Bill Office first, three weeks before you want your ten minutes. It's a horrendous system, and you'll find MPs sleeping outside the PBO to get their place.'

'Is that what you did?' said Zain.

'Yes, two weeks ago. Ruby asked me to, to get the issue raised in the Commons and prompt an inquiry, and I thought it was important enough. From 4 p.m. the day before, I sat cross-legged, stood waiting and even slept in a sleeping bag my assistant had brought me. And I was first through the Public Bill Office door.'

'What happens now?' said Kate.

'It means that next week, three weeks after I went to the PBO, I get to speak for ten minutes in parliament after Prime Minister's Questions. That's the day most media attention is given to the House.'

'And you are planning to raise the issue of KNG?' said Kate.

'No. I'm intending to raise the wider issue of British companies investing in conflict areas in DRC, and call for a parliamentary committee to examine their operations, and a unit to be set up at the FCO, specifically overseeing their presence.'

'Why not just use the time to name and shame?' said Zain.

'I want the bill to be unopposed, so that it will get a second reading later on.'

'So, assuming you get your bill passed, and it becomes law, what then? You set up your watchdog unit at the FCO? And they investigate KNG?' said Zain.

'Not exactly. Private members' bills rarely become law. I will have been given a platform, though, and I will start people talking. Get the media to sit up and take interest, with any luck.'

'Why haven't you simply used the information Ruby gave you? Made it public?' said Kate.

'Because by now I would be sitting in a prison cell, probably, or at least facing a law suit for defamation,' said Maggie. 'The documents Ruby had, they were poor. In terms of evidence. Just printouts from Word documents, emails on paper. They could have been fabricated, for all I know. And she wouldn't reveal her source to me.'

'Yet you believed her?' said Kate.

'I believed her. And I hoped my bill would allow me the chance to get some hard evidence, to carry out a full audit on KNG.'

'If it doesn't become law, how might that happen?' said Zain.

'The interest that will arise from my ten-minute presentation should force the PM's hand. Make him set up an inquiry, call the CEO of KNG before a select committee. A trial by MPs. And as part of that, we would ask him to answer to all the allegations with concrete proof disputing them.'

'And Ruby? How would she fit into the inquiry?'

'Ruby was going to make a video, start an online awareness campaign.'

'And if Ruby's video had gone live, and her millions of fans had taken to the net in outrage, your revelations would have had even more impact?' said Zain.

'Yes. If her video had gone public, my allegations would cause even more of a storm. And I would be able to correct my oversight, the sale that I was responsible for.'

'Without Ruby, can you still have the ten minutes? The inquiry?' said Kate.

'Yes. It won't have the same impact, however. Do you remember what happened with phone hacking? Do you remember why it took off?'

'Because journalists hacked into Millie Dowler's phone,' said Zain. 'Public opinion.'

Kate could hear the thoughts in his head. She felt a sense of excitement herself.

'And if we could prove that KNG hacked into Ruby's computer? After she was kidnapped and murdered?' said Kate, in a whisper.

Maggie smiled, although there was sadness in her eyes.

'I'm curious,' said Kate. 'Do you think KNG would orchestrate what happened to Ruby? They have a lot to lose.'

Maggie considered her words. 'Knowing what I knew before I started with the FCO, I would have said no. And what I know now, afterwards? Yes, of course.'

'When Ruby hit the headlines, why didn't you contact us?' said Kate. 'We appealed for information.'

Maggie's face registered surprise. 'I don't understand. Isn't that why you are here?'

'What do you mean?' said Kate.

'I spoke to Commissioner Hope about my concerns. Did he not send you?'

Kate felt something close around her, and a tightness under her ribcage.

Chapter Ninety-eight

They were driving over Westminster Bridge, back to HQ. The tension from Maggie Walsh's revelations was still suffocating them both. Kate wanted to confront Justin Hope. So did Zain.

The word 'traitor' kept flashing into his mind. That was him. The notes of Puccini's *Un bel di vedremo* filled the car. His own emotions soared and fell in time with the strings.

As they approached Victoria Street, Zain took a detour, parking up on a quieter road running parallel to it.

'Everything OK?' said Kate.

'No,' he said.

He didn't know the best way to begin, so he just said it. 'There's something I have to tell you. About Hope.'

Zain kept his eyes on the car in front. Stationary and empty. Drilling could be heard from a construction site nearby.

'It starts before I was hired. You asked me after the Barry incident, whether I was OK. Truth is, not completely. DCI Cross, he sent improved health reports and gave me a reference he shouldn't have. The one you saw.'

'I remember,' said Kate. 'Very positive.'

'Yes. Only, Hope saw the original health reports somehow.'

'He knew you weren't fit for purpose?'

'He said he would overlook it. But he asked for something in return.'

'What have you done for him, Harris?'

'I gave him unofficial updates on the case.'

That was it, wasn't it? The bitter truth?

'It was the morning you disappeared, when we couldn't get hold of you. He was trying, and he asked where you were.'

Kate's face was impassive.

'And what did you say?' she said.

'I told him you abandoned your team. Had some kind of family emergency. Left us to it. He asked me to let him know when you came back, what state you were in.'

Zain tasted the bile in his mouth. How could he have been such a dick? And to Riley, who had protected him from her team?

'And Winchester?' she said softly. 'Did you tell him about that night? How did you spin it, I wonder? That I got you drunk, and made a pass at you?'

'What do you take me for? Of course I didn't.'

'And what about your assault on Barry? Did you mention that?'

'No. He didn't approach me again after that morning.'

'He was getting information somehow. He knew about Jed Byrne's alibi before I told him.'

'That wasn't me.'

'Why should I believe you? How do I know you weren't giving him little updates all throughout this investigation?'

Her voice sounded calm still. She couldn't possibly be calm, though.

'Why are you telling me this now?' she said.

'I think you need all the ammunition you can get today. And there is one thing. Something he asked me to do. We might be able to use it.'

'Why would you help me now? What can you possibly have done that Hope would worry about?' she said.

'The night when Ruby disappeared . . . Hope knew before we did. He was told by, I'm guessing, Harry Cain. He must have asked Hope to lead on the case, but asked him to hold off the investigation into MINDNET.'

'When did you find this out?'

'The day after Ruby disappeared. Hope asked me to alter the emergency call records. Anyone looking at the records would now think that Ruby's parents called 999, and that they contacted our office. In reality, Hope contacted the emergency despatch team and had the case assigned to his office. To SOE3. To you. And I hacked into the database, and I changed the record to conceal that. I didn't know about Harry Cain, though.'

'What evidence is there, apart from your testimony?' she said. 'It's your word against his.'

'I kept the original records, in electronic format. Any forensic specialist will be able to trace what really happened. And then Hope will have to explain why he assigned the case to himself. It's something at least.'

Zain held his breath. Kate was silent, before turning to look him in the eyes.

'Let's go and see Hope,' she said.

Chapter Ninety-nine

Justin Hope surveyed them with the calculating stance of a predator. His eyes flitted between them as each spoke. His face didn't betray a single emotion.

'Let me ascertain some facts, Harris. Are you threatening me, or blackmailing me? You know a black man doesn't take kindly to being blackmailed?'

He laughed. He actually laughed. An inappropriate joke, surely?

'The colour of your skin has nothing to do with this, sir,' said Zain.

'It has everything to do with this,' said Hope. 'You don't get it, do you? And yet you should, both of you should. Do you wonder how I got here? A black man born on a council estate? And now look at me. And do you know how I did it?'

Kate didn't trust herself to speak. Zain got in first.

'By breaking every rule there is?' he said. 'Why was I asked to alter the despatch database? Why did you want to hide the fact that you took this case on purposely?'

Hope studied them both at length. The tension was gut-wrenching.

'I am an impossible man,' said Hope. 'I hold the most senior position in policing for London. Do you know how many times I have had to compromise? You must. Riley, how many times have you been shut out?'

Kate understood what he was saying. It had been tough. Even in Washington, she'd had to fight to be taken seriously. Yet she could say her conscience was clear. Mostly.

'You can't justify this, sir. You have impeded our investigation; it's a criminal offence, perverting the course of justice. Who are you protecting?' Her voice was calmer than it sounded in her head.

'Why haven't you gone to someone? Why have you come to me?' said Hope.

'I wanted to give you a chance to explain,' said Kate.

'Redemption?' said Hope, laughing and drinking the bourbon he poured himself.

'I would like to know. I deserve that much,' she said. 'There is nothing else on offer here. Except to know the truth.'

'And if I tell you? Harris will keep his misdeeds to himself?'

'Yes,' said Zain.

She hadn't agreed to that.

'How can I be sure?' said Hope.

'You'll have to trust me,' said Zain.

Hope drained his glass, walked over to his window, staring out over Buckingham Palace.

'A man like me, looking into Her Majesty's back yard. There's a story in that, don't you think? You want to know what it's like, being me? I went to Oxford, worked my way up the ranks. And still I have to prove myself. I'm not one of them. And when I mess up, they see it as a failure for every black man out there. Do you know what that does? That sort of pressure?'

'It's not a free pass to do as you will,' said Kate.

'No, indeed. But playing politics, sometimes you have to stretch the law, even beyond its limits.'

'Is that how you interpret it?' said Kate.

'You've made your mind up already, then,' he said.

'I'm listening,' she said.

'The boundaries shift constantly for us all. Don't you wonder how this office was created? How, while budgets are being cut nationally, we are provided with state-of-the-art graphic interfaces? Think of the equipment you have at your fingertips. The best vehicles. Think about the cars you both drive. These premises. Look at that view!

'On top of all that, a carte blanche to act in a manner we choose. That kind of freedom doesn't just happen. I make it happen. I break corporate bread, and I drink networked wine. When I leave here, I rarely go straight home. I spend hours every day schmoozing, whether it be business contacts, politicians or security experts. And I put us on the map; I get us the money we need. The blank cheque the Home Office writes? It comes to us because Harry Cain and KNG wrote it.'

'And what did they want in return for their generosity?' said Kate.

'Nothing. At first.'

Hope sat down at his desk, steepled his fingers in front of his face, his familiar pose, his eyes making direct contact with Kate's and then turning to Zain.

'And then Ruby Day disappeared,' he said.

'And they collected their pound of flesh?' said Zain.

'Precisely.'

'Talk us through it,' said Kate.

'I got a call from Harry Cain. He said his son, Jed Byrne, had been in touch. Ruby Day had disappeared. Harry believed Ruby had information that could be damaging for his company. He asked me to lead on the case, to find Ruby and stop an information leak.'

'Harry Cain thought Ruby had done a runner?' said Zain.

'That's how Cain described it. He was in contact with me over the next few hours. And after the videos were released, he convinced me that Ruby's boyfriend, Daniel Grant, was unstable. He told me about the escort, the one he attacked at his birthday party. Insisted the investigation focused on that.'

'That's why you were pressuring us to pursue Dan?' said Zain.

'It seemed plausible,' said Hope.

'Only they used us,' said Zain. 'Harry Cain and his son. They turned Dan into a fucking saint.'

'Their strategic play is not lost on me, DS Harris.'

'What happened after that?' said Kate.

'Nothing. Cain and Byrne both went quiet, while you investigated Daniel Grant as instructed. And then you went after Byrne. Harry Cain was not amused. He contacted the prime minister, who in turn asked to meet with myself. It was made very clear to me that unless we had hard evidence, we were not to pursue KNG. Cain also threatened to withdraw funding for us.'

'How is it that someone with money can control you both? You hold the power, not Cain,' said Kate. She was angry and, more than that, disappointed. Hope and the PM needed a spine and some balls.

'I wouldn't have let him, if there was credible evidence. If KNG had turned out to be involved in wrongdoing over Ruby, I would have let you run wild over their offices. But there was nothing concrete. Bits of conjecture, possible motives, suggested sabotage. You don't bring down a multi billion-pound company, with links into the heart of government, on that pretext.'

'You weren't simply saving yourself?' said Kate.

'There was an element of that. Why risk this privilege I have to make a difference, risk one of the finest teams I have ever managed? And over what?'

'So when Margaret Walsh called you, what did you do?' said Kate.

'What could I do? She had nothing to substantiate her allegations.'

'When we find the video Ruby made, exposing KNG, then we'll see,' said Zain.

'When you find that video, yes, let's see how it plays out. The facts are that Maggie Walsh has no real evidence, only hearsay and documents that could have been fabricated. She herself isn't willing to name KNG next week; she just wants to start an inquiry. What was I meant to do with what she told me?'

'And if Harry Cain hired a hit on Ruby?' said Zain. 'While you've been buying time for him and his son?'

'Find me the evidence, and I will drag Harry Cain and Jed Byrne into a holding cell myself. I am on your side, detectives. I am not fighting against you.'

And how does that fit in with spying on me, Kate wanted to say.

'You've heard my side of events, my explanation,' said Hope. 'Now it's your turn. What do you plan on doing? What happens now?'

Chapter One Hundred

Zain was sitting in Julie Trent's desk chair, swinging it back and forth. Kate sat on one of the sofas set around a small table. It was Trent's informal corner, apparently.

'What do you think?' Kate said.

Zain shrugged his shoulders. 'No idea. Hope sounded sincere. Then again, he pretty much told us he's a player. He might have been acting all through that discussion. Cain and Byrne have gotten away with something bigger than murder. It's disgusting.'

'You think they're the first or that they'll be the last?' she said.

'Those others didn't happen on my watch, though,' he said. 'This *is* happening, and there's fuck all we can do. I can fall on my sword, and stab Hope in the back as I do it. Admit to tampering with the chain of evidence, resign. Then what are we left with? He's right, there is no evidence at the moment.'

'It fits, though, doesn't it? They have motive, means, opportunity,' she said.

'And two billion dollars,' he said. 'That buys you immunity, apparently.'

'They'll be called before a select committee with Maggie Walsh,' she said.

'Big deal. A bit of embarrassment, a few awkward questions. They might even apologise, and then what?'

'I guess the DRC government need to charge them with corruption. They haven't broken any laws in this country, even if they did support mass murder.'

Zain stopped rolling his chair around, instead put his feet up on Trent's desk. He felt his hamstrings and calf muscles stretching, enjoyed the sensation. He hadn't been to Krav Maga classes since starting this case, needed to get back into it. Staying fit was the first step to keeping the other stuff quiet. Well, keeping fit and his little pills from China.

Was he in a position to judge KNG? He was surfing using Tor, the dark web. Taking tablets that had no licence to be sold in the UK. No, that wasn't the same as giving Sese a truck to go and round up child soldiers.

'And Ruby is still dead. And we still don't know where her body is,' he said. 'It's bullshit.'

'Yes,' Kate said.

They were lost in their own thoughts for a few moments. Zain wondered what was going on in hers. In his own, he was thinking how access to Jed Byrne's account might show a payment sent to Bill Anderson to hire a hitman. Or would they simply have used cash on delivery? That had to be registered somewhere, though. There would be an online transaction or a physical one. Zain would find it, he was sure of it.

'What do we do?' he said.

'We wait. Let's see if DCI Cross can pull something from Ruby's hard drives. Let's get the ten-minute bill read next week by Maggie Walsh, and let the inquiry start. We can then angle for a warrant.'

Zain didn't like the idea of that. Waiting for things to happen.

Chapter One Hundred and One

When Kate's eyes opened, she was curled up on a sofa, in an office that was dark. No lights, the clouds outside blocking the sun. A fall day had turned into a winter one.

She must have fallen asleep, her body tired after a night where virtually no sleep had come. And the intensity of the morning. She had dreamed of forests, mines, mysterious black faces. And bodies lying bloody and covered in flies, piled up on the side of a ditch.

And then she was back in that New England forest, running. Her father coming at her, appearing from the shadows. A weapon in his hand, what it was she could never see clearly. But he used it with blunt force, smacked her across the face with it. The attack always woke her up.

Kate let thoughts of her father come freely. She had said it now. Ryan was the first person she had told since moving to London. Even her own mother didn't remember who attacked her. And Kate didn't tell her.

'He's dead, Mom,' she had lied.

It had helped convince her mother that a fresh start was needed for both of them. There was no need to explain that they were in a witness protection programme, until her mother had wanted to contact their relatives and friends.

Kate had lied then. Said Jane had been attacked by people who might come after them again. Jane couldn't piece it together. Instead, she grieved for her dead husband, and her sons, who she was told she couldn't see again.

'For their own safety,' Kate had said. Not a complete lie. They would never be safe from her.

Kate felt a surge of panic, hatred and rage when she thought of her brothers.

Most of it was reserved for her father, though.

Her phone rang; it was Harris.

'Cross just delivered Ruby's hard drives,' he said.

'On my way,' she said, slipping her feet into her shoes as she continued holding the phone to her ear.

'They found files about mining,' Zain told her. 'It's worse than we thought. People died from poisoning, from chemicals that might have come from KNG. As well as the logistical support for Sese. They're fucking scum. And there's nothing we can do, nothing's been proved.'

'Was there a video accusing them? Made by Ruby?'

'No.'

So there was no video after all. Kate knew that would be it, then. Unless there was evidence Ruby had been on the brink of going public, a few files related to events thousands of miles away . . .? They had nothing.

'It's not right,' Zain said. His voice was heavy, as though he couldn't breathe. Then there was silence on the line.

Zain sat in his car, watching. The office was in darkness, the autumn days short, the temperature falling as the sun died. He took a green pill from his glove box.

Zain swallowed, looking at each of the floors. The first two were occupied by the offices. Lights were still leaking out into the street from the second floor. He would take the risk if needed.

Jed Byrne lived on the top floors of the building, in his duplex suite. The windows were covered by blinds, but Zain could see the flashes of TV images behind them. Jed was home.

There was nothing Zain could do – Riley was right. Legally, anyway.

Zain shut his car door behind him gently, and headed towards the back of the building. There was a residential entrance, leading off from a stinking alleyway filled with industrial-sized rubbish bins.

Zain rang the buzzer for Flat 1. Byrne answered.

'It's Detective Sergeant Harris. I just have a few questions, if you don't mind?'

'I told you people, I'm not saying anything without my lawyer.'

'It's not about you; it's nothing official. I just have a few questions about Karl Rourke.'

'I'm not interested,' said Byrne.

'All off-the-record stuff. Please, it won't take more than half an hour.'

Zain heard the door buzz open and pushed it to go in.

Dan Grant was shaking. Barry had given him a new pill, one of his specials. So hot, so bad, it wasn't even illegal yet. Like a chase, the formula changed faster than the law could keep up. Banned substance lists were like viruses. You tackled the ones you knew about, while the real dangerous, mutated ones crept up and got you.

He needed it, though, after the shit that they had put him through. Fucking Ruby, stupid cunt. Still destroying him, even when she was dead. He should never have gone near her.

And that prick Karl Rourke? The bastard. He had left Dan to rot; he was crap in front of the cops. Dan was glad he had dumped that no-mark, gone with MINDNET.

Only Jed Byrne had come through. He had made him a legend. Except they were all feeling sorry for Dan, pitying him again. And he hated that. He had spent a lifetime being pitied, loathed and picked on. It all started with pity. He didn't want that; he wanted to be admired. His fans loved him, they saw him as something to desire. Not to pity. And now they were turning him into that again.

The phone rang with a withheld number. Dan thought he could walk through his window. The rain was smudging faraway lights, and he thought he was outside the glass. The phone rang again, withheld number.

After the fifth time, he picked up. He didn't recognise the voice.

'I know what happened to Ruby,' it said. 'And I'm scared. Can we meet?'

The voice wasn't one to be scared of. So Dan agreed to meet. Alone.

Chapter One Hundred and Two

Kate was reading through the files DCI Cross had recovered, the ones Zain had already seen. The poisoning led to the deaths of forty-three people, after they drank water polluted with mercury. There was never a link proved to any of the local mining corporations. KNG was the biggest one out there.

The other reports recovered from Ruby's hard drives included background on Pierre Sese, his armed struggle against the government in Kinshasa. The links he had to Ugandan warlords. The purchase of coltan mines by KNG in Bunda.

Richard Brown obviously gave the same stories to Ruby as he had to Harris, and Ruby had wanted to be sure; she had clearly done her research. Only in the video they had seen, the one never broadcast online, was Ruby saying she had evidence of something that would shake things up and shock people.

There was nothing here, from what Kate could see, that would achieve that.

She looked out of her window, the sky blue-black with a thread of moonlight behind thick clouds. She should be home. Michelle was at her desk, preparing to leave for the day.

'You done?' said Kate.

'Yes. Is Harris OK?' she said.

'What do you mean?'

'He was cut up when he went through the files he got back from his old boss.'

'There's not much in them, really,' said Kate.

'Maybe that was the issue?' said Michelle. 'Anyway, I'll see you tomorrow.'

'Listen, can you do something for me before you go?'

'Yes, of course,' said Michelle.

'Run me a trace. I want to know where Harris is right now.'

Michelle hesitated, but then sat back down and switched her computer on.

Zain sat on an ergonomic chair, without a back. Byrne's flat was all old brick outside, but the interior was more in line with the minimalist glass and steel front of the MINDNET offices.

Byrne was sitting on his La-Z-Boy chair, his legs sticking out, his back tilted. There was a dining table set with four chairs, and a desk with a computer station. A Bang & Olufsen media centre.

'You don't own a TV?' said Zain.

'I have a room for visual entertainment,' said Byrne, with a serious face.

He was wearing pale-blue trousers and a polo shirt, his feet bare. The scent of sandalwood was heavy in the air.

'You meditate?' said Zain.

'It helps,' said Byrne. 'Can we get this done? I have an event to go to later.'

'Yes, of course,' said Zain.

He pulled paper from his folder, and handed it to Byrne. The man's eyes widened, and his jaw started to tick. Riley had told him about that, how Byrne's face was crap for poker, gave him away too easily.

'You know that place? Bunda? Weird name, isn't it? Some backwater African place. Bunda.'

Byrne turned the pages, shook his head. 'Don't know what this is. I thought you wanted to speak about Karl?'

'Karl, is it? First name basis? For the man that stole files from a dead girl's bedroom for you? What hold do you have over him? Is it money? Do you think Daddy's money can just buy everyone?'

Byrne sat frozen, his hands clutching at the sheets of paper in them. He stared at Zain, swallowed loudly.

'You see, I'm not really here about Karl. I had a choice. Get you to open your door, or fucking well break it down.'

'I want you to leave now, detective,' said Byrne.

'You always get what you want? Rich, spoilt little Jed, with his billionaire daddy. You click your fingers and people do whatever you tell them to?'

Byrne stood, dropping the paperwork Zain had given him onto the coffee table in front of him.

'You need to leave,' he said.

'Or what? You'll call the police? Go ahead. Oh, look, we're already here,' said Zain.

'What do you want?'

'Just some honesty,' Zain told him. 'You know, I'm sick of all the lies and bullshit. Ever since I got involved with this, all I've got is men lying about Ruby and how they used her. And, just for once, I want someone to man up and be honest. Is that too much to ask, do you think?'

Stay measured, he told himself. Stay calm. Don't let the red mist fall; don't let it control you.

'You see, I know about Daddy's little secrets. About his mines in Congo, about him poisoning villagers. Just poor black faces to you, right? Don't care, do you? Collateral damage?'

Byrne stayed motionless, but his eyes were roving around the room. What was he looking for? His phone? A weapon?

'No comment,' said Byrne.

Zain stood up, and walked towards Byrne. The man started to back off.

'This isn't a fucking police interrogation, you dumb fuck. This is me and you, two grown men, and this is a time for truth.'

The back of Byrne's legs hit his sofa, and Zain stopped too.

'What did she say to you? Did she threaten to expose you all? You see, I know Ruby left her home about seven-thirty that night. And yet around midnight, or nineteen minutes after, to be precise, someone used her wireless network to hack into her computer. And delete these files. Now you tell me, is that coincidence? Because I traced what time Karl Rourke called you. It was just before midnight. Seven minutes to midnight, to be precise. So he calls you, and you get shit scared. Ruby's gone, is she going to go public? And so you hack into her computer and delete the evidence?'

'I have no idea what you're saying,' said Byrne.

'Or did it happen like this? Ruby was about to go public, and risk two billion dollars for your darling father . . . You know, the dick that abandoned you?'

Zain felt the cold, dark pain inside him start to leak out. A pain he wanted to inflict on others. On Byrne.

'And so what did you do? Always after his approval, so you hired a hitman, didn't you? Or got your little Rottweiler Bill Anderson to hire one. And while Ruby was being tortured and murdered, you were erasing your tracks. Only you didn't do it thoroughly enough. You didn't delete the data enough times. And I found it.'

'You're mental, mate, and you need to get out of my flat.'

'I'm not done yet, not at all. You see, I don't give a flying fuck about procedure and law and the proper way of doing things. I believe in justice. Three million people have died in that hellhole, because of people like you. And I think you think your money will protect you.'

Zain grinned, but his eyes were dead; he knew.

'Well, guess what, Jed, nothing will save you tonight.'

Chapter One Hundred and Three

Kate tried the door to the MINDNET offices, but they were locked. No security inside. That was odd; they must trust their automated systems. She tried the phone again, and this time it was picked up.

'This is Detective Chief Inspector Kate Riley. I'm outside, can you please let me in?'

Bill Anderson walked through the darkened lobby and unlocked the doors for her. He must have disabled the alarms before he got there.

'I need your help, Mr Anderson,' she said, standing in the lobby to MINDNET with him. 'I need to speak to Jed Byrne. It's urgent. I think he might be in some danger.'

'What's this about?' said Anderson, already walking quickly away from her.

'I just need to see him, for his own safety,' she said.

Anderson led her through the foyer, past the lifts, through what Kate had thought was a wall. It was a door covered with the same panelling as the rest of the wall, which in turn led to another lift.

This lift was small; only the two of them could really fit inside. It smelled new, but she could smell Anderson, too. It was an earthy scent. Clean, but not artificial.

The lift opened onto a door with Flat 1 in gold on it. Anderson raised his hand to knock. He stopped when they heard shouting. It was Zain.

'Can you open it?' she said.

Anderson took keys from his pocket and, finding the right one, turned the two locks quietly. They walked in, just as Zain's voice was reaching levels Kate had heard once before, in Barry the drug dealer's flat.

They opened the lounge door and found Zain with his hands reaching for Byrne's throat.

Zain turned to look at them, and stopped in mid-movement.

Anderson ran to put himself between Zain and Byrne, and pushed the former away. Zain stepped back, then rallied to go for Anderson. Kate grabbed his arm and spun him around.

'No,' she said, as though admonishing a child or a pet. 'That's enough.'

Zain sneered at her, but left the room.

'I apologise, Mr Byrne,' she said. She caught sight of the papers on Byrne's table, recognising them from the electronic versions she had seen earlier. 'I'm sure, though, that it's in both our interests not to pursue this. Shall we just pretend this never happened?'

'We don't tolerate people making threats to us,' said Anderson.

'Neither do I,' said Kate.

Stevie parked up outside James Fogg's house in Goodmayes.

She had interviewed Ruby's friends and family again, trying to pick apart and discover something new. Nothing had come of it.

Ruby's parents had been the most chilling. They were defeated, immobile. Nothing seemed to be left of life in them. They explained about Ruby paying the mortgage on the flat, about them having to leave it. They focused on that, the loss of their home. Because focusing on the loss of their daughter was too much.

'You don't know what I went through to have her,' Laura Day had said. 'It makes losing her so much worse.'

What could you say to that? Fuck all.

Stevie had covered most of the friends living in London, but James Fogg hadn't responded to her calls, so she decided to visit him. He had known Ruby more intimately than anyone else; he might have some random bit of information that might crack this.

Truth was, they'd exhausted everything else.

The house looked empty, with no lights on. No cars parked outside it. Stevie tried the doorbell first, then the letterbox. She sensed someone watching her from across the road. Curious neighbours? Did it count as curtain twitching if it was done with blinds?

Eventually, a light went on inside, and the door was opened by a young woman. She was rubbing her eyes, yawning. She was wearing a dressing gown, her feet bare.

'Who are you?' said the woman.

The way she said it, though. She seemed to be alert, suspicious. Looking Stevie over. There was nothing about Stevie that said police officer. She was dressed in black jeans, a hooded top, and a midi jacket.

'Detective Sergeant Stevie Brennan. Sorry I woke you. Is Mr Fogg at home?'

'No, he's away,' said the girl. 'We spoke before, didn't we? I'm Rachel, his partner.'

'Yes, I remember. Do you know where he is?'

'Family emergency. He had to go.'

'When will he be back?'

'I have no idea.'

'Where is his family?'

Hesitation. Rachel was thinking. Her sleepy head churning, calculating. Just a fraction, but enough.

'Not sure. Plymouth, I think,' she said.

'You've never met them?'

'No. They're not close.'

'What's the family emergency?' Stevie asked.

Again, a moment of hesitation. A lie being formulated?

'His grandfather is ill, I think,' said Rachel.

'Do you mind if I come in and speak to you?'

'About what?'

'Ruby.'

'I didn't know her,' said Rachel. Her voice grew cold. Jealousy at the ex-girlfriend?

'It won't take long. Plus, I'm dying for a piss.'

Stevie pushed past Rachel before she could object, her instincts screaming at her.

Chapter One Hundred and Four

They were in Zain's lounge. Kate was on the sofa, perched on the edge. She wasn't staying, wasn't interested in her comfort.

He stood in the doorway, looking down at her. She met his gaze hard, no flinching or insecurity. The random thought came again that she was stunning.

'What happened?' she said.

At least she was giving him a chance. Wasn't going to convict without a trial.

'You know what. The bastards got away with it. They used their money and their friends, and they fucking well killed a girl and got away with it. It makes me so angry, and makes me sick. Sometimes, I think this whole country is stitched up. Politicians, business, the media . . . they're all shagging each other, and no one stands a chance.'

'You make it sound so easy, so black and white,' she said. 'It's so much more complex.'

'Are you defending them?'

'No. Do you think Justin Hope is a bad person? Or is he just in a difficult, compromised position?'

He's a dick, thought Zain.

'I don't think I care anymore,' he said.

'You trusted him enough to do his dirty work, not so long ago. You must have had an instinct about him.'

He was ashamed of that now. He'd been desperate, though. Thought non-compliance would mean losing his job. The job that he hoped would rehabilitate him, get him back to Cross and his team.

'You want something to drink?' he said.

She shook her head, got up, ready to leave.

'Where does this leave me?' he said.

'If Jed Byrne brings charges, we can deal with it then.'

'As long as I take the fall?'

'I'm not clairvoyant. I don't predict how things will work out. I live in the moment.'

'That's what I was doing. I was frustrated, and I wanted him to confess to it. I thought, no, this is bullshit, I am not letting them do this. And I was going to make him say it, tell me what they did.'

'Has that ever worked?'

It worked on me, thought Zain. When the pain got extreme, so bad it was in that zone before death. What he said, he couldn't remember. But he hadn't stayed quiet. When his captives tortured him, when they were about to cut his head off. He told them everything he knew. There were no heroics then; there was no bravery. He was shit scared he was about to die.

'What you did was illegal and unprofessional,' she said. 'Understandable, yet wrong. And what worries me is that I don't think you truly accept that.'

She stopped at the door. 'My father, he was like Harry Cain. He was a man in a position of power. And he destroyed everyone around him. My mother, me. And in the end, I didn't take short-cuts. I brought him down, the right way.'

'Is that why you're really here? Thousands of miles away?' Zain countered.

'The right way isn't the easy way. Usually it's the toughest road to take, and that's why so many don't. They lack the strength and the courage.'

He stared after her, feeling as though she had just kicked him in the balls.

Chapter One Hundred and Five

Rachel was making Stevie some coffee, while Stevie was pretending to use the bathroom. She listened to the woman moving about, filling the kettle, letting it boil. Preparing cups, the fridge door opening for milk.

She didn't have long, maybe a minute. And her gut was on fire; something did not fit. It was the way the girl had obviously lied about, or not been sure of, where James was. And more than that, the way Rachel looked.

Stevie had spent so long in the company of Ruby's friends that she understood some things now. And she could see the rawness, the naivety, around Rachel. It was unsettling, and a thought was creeping into her. One that made her sick.

Images then flashed into her head. Ruby's launch, the video in which James had been more interested in playing a walrus than congratulating his girlfriend.

Walking up the stairs to use the bathroom, she had to calculate. Where would she find what she needed?

The bedroom was the obvious place. She scanned the room, opened dresser drawers. Then checked the wardrobe. She found a briefcase, but it was locked. She didn't have time to break the seals.

A second, smaller room. A study, a computer with multiple screens, hard drives. Why did people need intelligence-agency-level equipment in their homes? A bookcase with textbooks stood against one of the walls. And on the floor, she thought she might have found what she needed.

It was a satchel, light brown. Stevie tipped it out, letting the debris of paper, pens, make-up spill out around her. She put her hands inside, checked the front pockets, and there she felt it. A purse, small, functional.

Stevie flicked it open, and stared. She was right. She was fucking well right. She took out her phone, texted Riley.

Rachel had made their drinks, the smell of hot coffee hitting Stevie as she walked down the stairs. She sat down, and gulped the coffee back, burning her tongue and the top of her mouth. She welcomed the caffeine.

'Thank you,' she said, when she felt some form of control. She felt the thrill, tense but also aware of what this moment might lead to. 'How long have you and James been together?' she asked.

'A year maybe,' said Rachel. 'Just over a year.'

'When he broke up with Ruby?'

'Yes. We met soon afterwards.'

'Is he a good boyfriend?' Stevie asked.

'Yes. The best. Why?'

'I'm just making small talk. Did you know Ruby well?'

'Never met her. I knew her. Saw her videos online, and I was curious when I started dating James. I didn't know her, though,' Rachel said.

'What did you think? From what you saw?'

'She was a nice girl. I don't like her, though, for hurting James. She broke his heart. And for what? Daniel Grant? She made a mistake.'

'You said you're at university?'

'Yes. First year.'

Stevie considered how to approach what she had to say next. In the end, she went with Stevie style: straight up and to the point.

'You must have been clever. Getting into university early.' she said.

Rachel froze, then looked up to the ceiling, then back to Stevie. She was calculating. Stevie saw her weigh the filled cup in her hand.

Barefoot, in a dressing robe, she was still thinking of running. She breathed heavily, her words slow when they left her mouth.

'I don't know what you mean,' she said.

'I saw your driver's licence,' said Stevie. 'Your provisional licence. It says you turned sixteen just over seven months ago.'

'What were you doing going through my stuff?'

'So if you started university at sixteen, you must be clever.'

Rachel was silent, still. On conflict management courses, they always said that was the time to be really worried. Intense staring; no communication. Stevie put her drink down.

'Rachel, how old were you when you met James?'

No response, but Rachel started shaking. Stevie took the cup from her hands.

'I think I know what happened, and I think you aren't to blame. Let me help you. Where are your parents?'

Rachel stared into Stevie's eyes. They were black, melting, angry.

Stevie barely had time to react as Rachel reached under a cushion next to her and pulled out a kitchen knife. She stabbed Stevie, pain exploding in her chest.

'You fucking bitch, you've ruined everything,' screamed Rachel.

She was on top of Stevie, who pushed her backwards, trying to grasp her wrists, all the while feeling the pain in her chest and the blood soaking her. Rachel spat in her face and drove the knife towards Stevie's eyes.

Stevie turned her face away, while using all her strength to control the knife hand, but Rachel was pushing as hard as she could. The knife cut Stevie's cheek, and started to move towards the side of her eye.

Stevie felt her own anger build then. She was not going to let this be the way it ended; she would not let herself be damaged like this. Stevie heaved her body upwards, felt Rachel give way, and twisted the hand holding the knife until it was facing away from her. Rachel was like an animal, hissing, spitting, and trying to bite her. Stevie let go of Rachel's left wrist, which led Rachel to try and gouge her eyes out.

With her free hand, Stevie twisted Rachel's fingers until she released the knife. Stevie then punched her in the face, knocking the younger girl back. Stevie was now on top of Rachel, pinning her to the floor.

She reached for the handcuffs she'd carefully concealed inside her jacket, trapping Rachel's wrists in front of her chest. Rachel tried to scrabble away, get to her feet, so Stevie tripped her onto the sofa and ended up sitting on top of her as she secured the handcuffs and then called for back-up. All the while, her own blood was gushing from the open stab wound. Please don't let me black out, she thought.

PART SIX
THE RECKONING

Chapter One Hundred and Six

Kate had just showered, ready for a night watching a familiar movie with her mother, when the text from Brennan had come through. Left without someone to look after Jane, Kate had brought her with her, put her in Julie Trent's office.

Rachel was like a zombie, incommunicative and sullen. She was still in her dressing gown, had refused to change into the clothes that officers had packed for her. She was shivering constantly. Looking at her, knowing what Brennan had discovered, it was obvious. You could tell how young she was by the insecurity of her body language, the sheer panic she exuded.

She had stabbed Brennan, cutting through arteries and flesh, but luckily missing any vital organs. Brennan was in hospital recovering, but Kate couldn't see Rachel as anything but a victim. She had been fourteen or fifteen at most when James Fogg had met her. That was a sickening place to start. Rachel's parents had been contacted, were on their way from Bristol.

They confirmed that Rachel had left home four months previously, that she had been a child prodigy in some ways. Michelle had pulled articles from local papers in Bristol, Rachel passing her A Levels early, getting a place at King's College.

With Brennan in hospital, and Pelt carrying out a search of James's property, Kate was relying on Harris. Could she believe him when he said he wasn't the source of the on going leak to Hope? She didn't know. She needed him, though; he had been involved from the start, and the investigation was hopefully hitting its home straight.

She watched Rachel through the two-way glass, the tension and nerves buzzing through her. Her lawyer hadn't arrived yet. Kate knew the young girl wouldn't say anything. A psychiatrist was also on the way. Kate didn't let herself think of what James Fogg had done to her. And if their relationship had been sexual before her sixteenth birthday, then that was a whole other angle to the 'nice' boyfriend James.

Kate wondered how Ruby had managed to bag herself men like James and Dan. Was she that low on self-esteem? It made her blood boil, the way women could be broken down in that way. She thought of Laura Day's story; like mother, like daughter, she reflected with a mix of sympathy and sadness.

'James's phone is dead,' said Zain, coming up behind her. 'They can't track it. He must have killed it and be using another number. Probably pay as you go. Rachel texted to let him know she had company. He told her not to panic, to remain calm. That was it. He was a couple of miles north of Winchester when he sent that. We've put out an alert on his car. Nothing so far, though.'

'What's happening with his computers?'

'I left Michelle to look over them. Pelt secured them when he got there, put them in special bags. Brennan had them disconnected as soon as back-up arrived, just before she passed out. Hopefully, James has no idea what's happened, but when he doesn't hear from Rachel, he might guess. Still, he won't have had a chance to wipe anything.'

'You're assuming James wiped Ruby's hard drives?'

'It makes sense. They were wiped in two attacks. He must have, if he was behind this. Then I guess MINDNET were responsible for the second attack.'

'We have Rachel's phone, if James gets in touch. I'll send a text message from it.'

'I think he might be tracking it. She has GPS on it; he might already know where she is. It might explain why he's gone dark.'

Kate remembered the charming young man she had met. The man Laura Day had wanted her daughter to be with. And now?

Was it possible he had taken Ruby? What was his motive? Was it Rachel?

'She's not going to tell us anything. The way she attacked Brennan, she must be involved somehow. I feel for her. James Fogg has truly messed her up.'

'So what do we do?' said Zain.

'Find me something that will make her talk. I need to shatter the illusion that is James. And get DS Helen Lowe alerted. I want her leading the search for James in Hampshire. We haven't found the gun he used on Ruby, so he is potentially armed and he's probably desperate. Especially when he realises what's happened. And desperate people are always the most dangerous.'

Kate looked again at Rachel, the child woman who was tapping at her face, running her fingers through her hair. There was something so innocent about the gesture, so normal. Kate wanted to comfort her, let her know she wasn't to blame for what James had done to her.

Part of Kate was disappointed. She had wanted it to be Byrne and his father; she had wanted to bring them down for what they had done. Finish Ruby's work. Finish work she had started with her own father. Rachel didn't seem like a deserving villain, someone to punish for all this. The sympathy was too distracting, though. It had to be kept for later.

First, Kate had to run Rachel through the fire, make her reveal her secrets.

Chapter One Hundred and Seven

Zain felt odd being back in Regus House. Everything felt like it was happening for the last time. There was no coming back from the things he had done. Hope, Barry, Jed. He had acted out too many times. Kate would have no recourse but to get rid of him.

'How's it going?' he asked Michelle.

She turned a pale face to him, her eyes red. She shook her head, and he thought she was about to cry.

'What did you find?'

'I can't even . . .' she began, and pointed to the printer instead.

Zain picked up the stack of documents, went back to his own desk, started reading through them. He understood then why Michelle was in such a bad place. She had kids. Zain thought of his own step sisters. The same age as the girls on the pages he was reading.

'Fucking hell,' he said. 'I'm going to rip his balls off when we find him.'

'I'll help,' said Michelle.

Zain was in the conference room with Kate and Michelle. Rob was on Skype from the house James and Rachel shared.

'It's not easy listening, this,' Zain warned everyone in the room.

'You never are, mate,' said Rob.

'Michelle asked me to deliver this, so hope that's OK,' said Zain.

Michelle looked away, and for a moment Zain thought she might be physically sick.

'James Fogg's computers have revealed some disturbing things. For starters, there are files on there going back years. This isn't something new. All of it behind passwords, so even those living with him wouldn't be able to access it without knowing his security. And I doubt he shared any of this.'

'What are we looking at?' said Kate.

'Messages. That's the first thing. From his YouTube account, from his Instagram and from his Twitter. He's been interacting with his fans. You see, even though he's no longer doing videos, he still gets hits. And young girls are still contacting him. And he's replying to them. And it's not just a thank you for watching and liking. He's sending them personal messages. Most are deleted, but the recent conversations are all on there.'

'He's a paedo?' said Rob.

'Looks like it. There are girls as young as ten we've found so far, that he's sent suggestive messages to. It's the teenage girls, though; they're the ones he's been messing with. Sending them inappropriate pictures.'

'We're all adults here,' said Kate. 'I want to know what we're working with.'

'Usual crap. Selfies, torso shots, dick shots. He's then asked them to send him revealing pictures back. Persuading some of these girls to send him pictures of their breasts, of their . . .'

'I don't want to know. I'm in the fucking pervert's house,' said Rob.

'And they respond to this?' said Kate.

'He's groomed them, sent them multiple messages daily, made it seem as though he's having a relationship or something with them.'

'Is it all virtual? Has he met any of these girls?' said Kate.

'Yes. It's clear from the messages he's swapped numbers online. Then it goes quiet online. Only a couple of girls have messaged him afterwards saying how great it was to meet him.'

The room was quiet. They were all probably conjuring the same images as he and Michelle had. This was the worst. No matter who you spoke to, anything involving kids was always the crappiest part of their job. Luckily, he had mainly dealt with men threatening to release smallpox onto the tube system. None of it made him feel as sick as he had felt reading through James Fogg's hard drive. All the time he was transposing the faces of Holly and Lucy, his step sisters, onto those of the girls involved. If someone did this to them, Zain would tear them apart. And these girls were someone's daughters, someone's sisters. He would do the same on their behalf.

'We also found pictures he kept. And videos.'

He didn't want to explain; he didn't need to. No one asked him to.

'Is there any evidence that Ruby knew?' said Kate.

'No. We looked. There are no messages. We do have the texts and phone calls to James. She asked to meet him a few times, saying she really needed to speak to him. Nothing to say it was about this.'

'Then we keep looking,' said Kate. 'Pelt, I know it's not pleasant, but I need you to check for anything that might be a keepsake. And I want his clothes bagged and checked. Rachel and Ruby are not the only victims in this.'

Zain felt bile rising up his throat.

'Now we just have to find the fucker,' he said.

Chapter One Hundred and Eight

Kate sat opposite Rachel, who was calmer now. She had her lawyer with her, Augusta Khew, who specialised in cases of child abuse. It was a dirty job, dealing with paedophiles.

Augusta had explained to Kate that she had started off with lofty ideals at one time. Only, as a woman back then, she found it difficult to break through. The biggest cases she got were the ones nobody else wanted, so experience made her an expert at dealing with the worst dregs of society.

With Augusta was Melissa Sweeney. She was a psychologist, working on the opposite side to Augusta. She dealt with the victims, not the abusers.

Rachel was both in a way. She was a victim without doubt in Kate's eyes. She might also be a criminal, though, if she had helped James.

Augusta had advised Rachel to answer any questions put to her that she felt able. 'No comment' was never a good option when the charges were serious, she told her. Juries always took it as a sign of guilt.

'When did you and James first have sex? Can you remember?' Kate asked.

'No,' said Rachel. 'I was old enough. I was sixteen.'

'You can't remember the date you first had sex? Was he your first?'

'Yes.'

'I don't know, Rachel. I'm probably three times as old as you, nearly,' said Kate. 'And I can remember. Girls don't forget. I could give you the date, time, place and who it was with. Even now. And you can't remember such an important thing that happened within the last seven months? Because you only turned sixteen then, right?'

'It was in May sometime,' she said. 'Yes, May the fifteenth.'

'What day was it? Was it in the morning or evening?'

'I can't remember the day . . . it was in the evening . . .'

'At his home?'

'Yes.'

'And you were already living together by then?'

'No. I didn't move in until September.'

'So in May, you were still living with your parents?'

'Yes.'

'So you came down from Bristol? For the day?'

'No, I stayed over.'

'With James?'

'Yes.'

'How did you get here?'

'By train.'

'How did you buy the ticket?'

'Cash.'

'What did you tell your parents?'

'I said I was meeting a friend in London.'

'And they just let you go?'

'Yes.'

'So you can remember how you paid for the train, how you got here and what excuse you gave your parents, yet you struggle to recall the date? I don't believe you, Rachel,' Kate said.

'Steady on, detective. My client has answered your question. She probably just needed time to remember the date under pressure,' said Augusta.

'Do you remember your first time?' said Kate.

The lawyer arched an eyebrow, didn't reply.

The interview room was stuffy when Kate went back in. Melissa had asked for a break when Rachel had started crying. Kate had pushed her on alibis for herself and James, the evening Ruby disappeared. Asking her to describe what they had done in detail, what they had watched.

Rachel hadn't been expecting to be in this situation, and she wasn't prepared for being scrutinised. Kate had confused her, causing her to crack.

It had been thirty minutes now. Kate had checked in with Harris, who said they still had no trace on James. He might be driving with his licence plates hidden, he thought.

Rachel was drinking water when Kate sat down and spread her paperwork over the table between them. She switched the recording device back on. A digital camera capturing image and sound, and time stamping the interview.

Kate knew Rachel was under a spell, devoted to James Fogg and caught up in some misplaced, ill-advised sense of love and loyalty to him. She wanted to break that, and she had a feeling she knew how.

'Rachel, we pulled these documents from James's computers. The ones we took from your home. I'll give you a few minutes to read through them.'

Kate watched as Rachel turned the pages, her eyes speed-reading the messages. The shaking started up again. Augusta and Melissa both read their own copies, both keeping their faces impassive. Augusta locked eyes with Kate at one point, gave a subtle shake to her head.

'They are messages, some sent only yesterday. One this morning. To other girls. Children. We found messages to some as young as ten. Did you know James was communicating like this?'

'It's not him; it's these girls. They're crazy, they stalk him, send him messages all the time, say they love him. He doesn't do it, and when he does, it's only to be nice to them.'

Kate handed over copies of the next batch of messages.

'These are from girls he's met. There's a girl there, lisauk99. We checked her account. She was born in 1999. She's fifteen. James met her last month. Were you aware of this?'

Rachel stared at the page in front of her, at Lisa's message, no doubt, saying how she enjoyed them meeting up. How she loved him and couldn't wait until they were together properly.

'Do you think he's sleeping with these girls when he meets them?' said Kate.

Rachel opened her mouth, but nothing came out. She must be crumbling inside, thought Kate.

Kate slid over some more documents, pictures this time.

'We pulled these from James's computer, from his Instagram, Twitter, Snapchat, Vine. These are images he has asked for from these girls. This one, she's only thirteen. He sent her eighty-seven messages over two hours, until she gave in. And when she sent him one, he threatened to expose her if she didn't keep sending more.'

Rachel's shaking led to tears now.

'Rachel. How old were you when you met James?'

No reply.

Kate swiped her tablet, handed it over to Rachel.

'There are a number of videos on there. You can hear James in the background, directing these girls, telling them what to do. We found messages to most of them. There's a pattern. He tells them he loves them, and then he sends them pictures of himself. He then persuades them to send him pictures, and as soon as they send a compromising one, he then asks for a video. I'll leave you to watch these, shall I?'

Kate needed to breathe, needed some space between what was happening and herself.

Chapter One Hundred and Nine

Kate checked in on her mother in the break. She was asleep on the sofa in Trent's office, exactly where Kate had napped earlier. It seemed like another day, but it wasn't. Time was in a vacuum. The morning had started with Maggie Walsh, the MP. And even then, she'd had no idea how it would end, where this case would lead her.

It was approaching 11 p.m. Kate was tired, but she was close, she knew. Rachel was processing exactly who James was.

In the interview room, Rachel was being comforted by the psychologist, Melissa. Augusta had a hard set to her face. That could be good or disastrous.

'I want to remind you, Rachel, that you are facing charges of attempted murder and assault separately to anything we discuss here. This is extremely serious. Your parents should be here soon,' Kate added.

At the mention of her parents, Rachel looked worried.

'They don't know anything yet. Just that you have been brought in, and that they should probably come down. Did you watch the videos?'

'Yes,' she said, in a whisper.

'And how do you feel? Do you still think it was those girls harassing James?'

Rachel was free-falling, her eyes searching the corners of the room. Then staring at Kate.

'He cheated on me, didn't he?' she said. 'All these other girls. He's been cheating on me.'

Kate felt something inside her ache. She didn't think preying on young girls deserved to be labelled with anything as normal as 'cheating'. That's what boyfriends and husbands, girlfriends and wives, did. It's what she did with Ryan. Grown adults making the decision to stray – that was cheating on someone.

There would be time to heal Rachel later. Years, possibly, if there ever was a time she could be whole again. For now, Kate picked away at her delusion, joined in the act.

'Yes. He lied to you, and he betrayed you.'

'He kept saying that to Ruby. *Traitor*. And all the time, it was him. He is the traitor.'

'When did he do that?' said Kate.

'In Dan's house. In his basement. I tied her wrists. All that time, she thought James belonged to her. And he didn't. Even when he was with her, he was still sleeping with me.'

'How did you know about the cottage?' said Kate.

'James knew, I don't know how.'

Ruby possibly told him, thought Kate.

'How old were you when you met James?' said Melissa.

'Let Detective Riley conduct this interview,' said Augusta.

'I have a duty of care,' said Melissa.

'Do you feel the detective is pushing my client too hard and we should terminate the interview?' said Augusta.

Melissa did, Kate could see it in her eyes. She answered in the negative, though; she understood what Kate did. Now was the time for truth, for justice, for harshness. Rachel could be mended later.

'Rachel, answer Melissa, please,' said Kate.

'Fourteen,' said Rachel. Her eyes were still, staring at a place where she was conjuring up images of her past. 'That's when we met. He took me to Patisserie Valerie in Soho, for my birthday. I thought it was so grown up, so special. I'd never done anything like that before. I was always the boring one, the model student. And he told me I was beautiful, and clever. I still remember having my first latte. I loved him so much, before we met.'

'Did your parents not realise?'

'I played truant from school, got the train to London. James paid for my ticket. And I was back home before they realised, faked a sick note the next day.'

'How long had you been messaging each other? On YouTube?' said Kate.

'Maybe six months. It wasn't a fling, or anything; we had a proper relationship. And when he dumped Ruby, finally, we could be together.'

'I know this is going to be difficult for you to answer, Rachel, and it is a hard question. When did your relationship become physical?' said Kate.

'I was sixteen,' she said.

'Rachel, if you want us to help you, we need you to be honest. If James did nothing wrong, then we have nothing to worry about, do we? With these other girls – he won't meet them and harm them, will he?'

Rachel stared, and she deliberated, and she broke down. Then she raised her head, and through sobs, she told Kate the horrible reality.

'It was four months before my sixteenth birthday. Exactly. I do remember the date. He came to Bristol, and he booked into the Ramada Hotel.'

Chapter One Hundred and Ten

There was still no sign of James. He had no car registered to him, and Kate guessed he had hired a vehicle using false ID. Rob had found fake documents, including passports and a driving licence, in James's Goodmayes house.

Zain had found complex software programmes on the hard drives, code ripped from the most extreme hacking sites on Tor. James even had bitcoins, and a history of travelling down the silk road – the illegal trading routes hidden from most web users.

'Rachel, can you talk me through what happened the night you took Ruby. Why did James need Ruby out of the way?'

'He said she had hurt him. That she was flaunting herself and Dan all over, and he wanted to hurt her back. And I helped him, because I thought, if she's not around anymore, then I won't have to worry. She was messaging him, you see. All the time leading up to it. Messages, all the time. He said she wanted him back. And I couldn't let her. You see that, don't you? But I think she knew.'

'What do you mean by that?'

'This, what you told me. She knew. She kept saying it, when we had her. She kept saying she knew what James had been doing, and telling me he had brainwashed me, and I was being used by him. And the way we got her . . . it fits now. Now I get it.'

'You got her? How?'

'I called her. And I said I had information on James for her. I knew she was collecting it secretly, and I had some for her. So we agreed to meet. At her flat. I said I didn't want anyone to know. And the thing is, I didn't even know myself. James just told me what to say. But now I understand; it all makes sense. Because Ruby, she never asked me what the information was. She already knew, and she thought I was one of them – these young girls – and that I was scared.'

Kate wanted to say how Rachel *was* one of those girls. The worst one, the one he had ruined the most. She drank from a glass of cold water instead. Coffee wouldn't do; she needed the hard chill of iced water. Rachel was doing the same. Mirroring each other, finding a bond. Augusta and Melissa were transfixed, thankfully not interrupting. It was vital they heard this. Augusta would have to rescue Rachel, and so would Melissa.

'So you arranged to meet Ruby?'

'I called her at four, and told her to meet me at seven-thirty. She agreed. She said she had some paperwork to sort out, and would be home. She met me then. I was in a car, I had told her the make already. She got in when she saw me, and that's when James . . . he put a gun to her head. And I took her mobile phone. I took the battery out. And then I used plastic tags and I tied Ruby's wrists and ankles. Only it didn't matter, because James injected her with something. Into her neck. And she just slumped. I thought she was dead, but she wasn't, she was just asleep. So he shifted her to the back seat, and then we drove to Dan's place.'

'We checked the CCTV to Windsor Court. We didn't find any footage of you going to Ruby's flat, nor did we see Ruby leave.'

'James hacked into the system. He changed the camera feed. He deleted images of us.'

'We didn't find your number on her phone records.'

'I used James's phone, withheld the number.'

James had planned this carefully, thought Kate.

'Can you tell us what car it was?'

'It was a Peugeot, black. Small. He rented it. I'd never seen it before.'

Kate brought up the entire Peugeot range on her tablet. She scrolled through until Rachel identified the right one. Kate uploaded the details into an email and sent it to her team. Rachel couldn't recall the number plate.

'What happened then? When you got to Dan's cottage?'

'We strapped Ruby into a chair in the basement. James already knew it would be there, like he had been there before. And he used this really strong tape on her. When she woke up, she was scared. And we –'

Rachel stopped, the movie in her head playing out whatever role she'd had.

'What did James do?'

'He hurt her. He was angry. He taped her mouth up, so she would stop saying things. She kept calling him sick, a pervert. And he punched her, and he kept grabbing her hair and yanking it, and Ruby kept screaming . . .'

Rachel was crying now; ashamed, probably. The hair-pulling. Kate thought that was something a girl would do. Rachel had done that.

'And he filmed it?' said Kate.

'I filmed it. Yes, that's what I was doing. I was filming it all. And then . . . well, he let her go. I argued with him, said she was going to tell the police. That we needed to deal with her. He let her go, though. And she thought she was free, and she ran from there. She wasn't free, though, because we went after her. James had night-vision goggles, and he gave me a pair, too. We could see Ruby, and she couldn't see us. And I kept filming, watching her run, and stumble and fall. And I laughed.'

Rachel's face was wretched now.

'And she kept screaming, "Help me, somebody help me." There was no one, though. And we caught up to her, and James tied her up again. And then he left us.'

'Where did he go?' said Kate, already picturing in her head what had happened next.

Chapter One Hundred and Eleven

Rachel was wiping her face with tissue Kate had asked to be brought in for her, but the tears wouldn't stop. She talked through them, breathless, eager to get out the rest of what had happened. Her version. And Kate knew this was her version, the version she could say. And that was fine, because in Kate's mind, Rachel was not going to get the blame for this.

'He moved the car. I'm not sure where he went. And then he took Ruby. He made her walk through the trees, through the forest. I saw them from the cottage windows, and then they disappeared. It's funny, but I hated that place. It was so creepy, so dark, and I was left alone. I kept hearing things from the basement. And James used to tell me Ruby was a witch, and I thought, what if it's true?'

The pentagrams; Ruby's search for spirituality. She wasn't a witch; she was just like so many other people. Kate formed the word 'journey' in her head – such a cliché, but it fit.

'What happened then?'

'He came back. It was an hour, I think, that they were gone. And he came back, and they were in the car together. Ruby was tied up, and her lip was bleeding, badly. I think she tried to run, and he must have . . .'

The trail the bloodhounds had followed, through the foliage, the fields and to the road. James must have parked his car there, ready. Forced Ruby through the woods, and then returned to pick up Rachel.

'Where did you go?' said Kate.

'I don't know. We just drove. Ruby was struggling, so we stopped. And he put her in the boot. And then there were just roads, it was so dark. He knew where he was going, though. And we came to an outhouse, I think. It was a building with no roof, just walls. And he told me to wait in the car. So I did. And then I heard the . . .'

'What did you hear, Rachel?'

'The gunshots. There were two or three. So loud. And then he came back.'

The video, Ruby's brains flying from the back of her head.

'How long were you driving for? Do you know what direction you took?'

'I can't remember. It was less than an hour. It was dark. I don't know.'

'I need you to describe the journey. I need you to think back. Anything at all. When you got in the car, was it facing the cottage or not? Did James turn right, left, drive straight ahead? Any details you can recall, and the place he took you to. There must have been traffic signs, features that you picked up. I'm going to get somebody in to talk you through it. Is that OK? And then you can speak to your parents. They're here.'

Rachel panicked, her head jerking up, her eyes turning to the two-way mirror. As though she could see them, or sense them.

Kate wondered at the lies she must have told them. Had they known about James? How could they? They would have put a stop to it, surely? Then again, how many parents really knew what their kids got up to online? They thought they were secure and safe in their bedrooms, obsessing over internet personalities, the way they would over posters of a musician. Instead, they were being silently and stealthily groomed and betrayed.

James Fogg was the one that would get caught. Kate thought about the others out there, the Rachels of the world being slowly turned until they didn't know who they were anymore. Broken down to be nothing more than dolls, twisted to do the bidding of others.

James Fogg would be a start, though. Kate would find him, and then she would find others like him. She was going to bring justice down on these sick fucks, because that was who she was and what she did.

Chapter One Hundred and Twelve

Kate was fidgety, her chest hurting. It was a dull ache, the build-up of energy or lactic acid. She needed to release it, to be moving, doing something. She had ordered other people to do things, kept her team busy. She had dozens of police officers looking for James Fogg, checking CCTV, speaking to anyone in the vicinity of his house. Hampshire police were out in force scouring the directions Rachel had put together for them. It wasn't enough.

'This is crazy,' said Zain.

They were both in Trent's office, Kate's mother still asleep on the sofa. Dr Eric Sandler, the cyber psychologist, had called in via Skype.

'You got a live one, detective,' he said. 'This is the fear, what we've been dreading all along. And it's so tough to warn people. When you're lonely and reaching out, you sometimes don't know what's reaching back until it's too late.'

'Like a virtual ouija board?' said Zain.

'Something like that, yes. And you have to remember, at that age, young adults just want to be liked, be normal. On top of which, they have hormones racing through them. It's why they originally developed manufactured pop stars, especially for girls – they go wild for them. Release all their hormones on beings they'll never attain.'

'These vloggers – these internet stars – they aren't pop stars,' Kate said.

'Worse, in a way. You see, with musicians, actors, the usual pretty boys, they come with a fortress around them. Managers, PR, security. And they have a lot of media scrutiny watching their every move. They snort cocaine in a nightclub toilet, or get off in the back of a limo, and it's online within minutes. No escape. So that all acts like a barrier; it stops them messing around with their fans.'

'And these vlogger guys . . .' said Zain.

'It's the same relationship: the fans worship them, obsess over them. They fill every aspect of their lives with them, and that barrier just isn't there. It's direct contact with your idols, and no one is watching. It's a potential minefield. And the wrong people get involved, and that's it. You have something like this happen. I'm just surprised it's not more common.'

'Maybe it is and we just don't know?' said Kate.

'Yes, there is that,' said Dr Sandler. 'I think for these girls it's like having Harry Styles message them directly. They would do anything – these substitute boyfriends could ask them for anything.'

Her mother's eyes were open when the Skype call had finished. Kate went over to her, holding her hands, telling her it was OK, where she was, and that despite the lack of blond hair, it was Kate.

'Hi,' said Zain, when she was done. He walked towards Jane, held out his hand. 'Detective Zain Harris. Apologies if we woke you. Can I get you anything?'

'Some water would be good,' said Jane.

'Sure, no problem. You want me to order you some food?'

'Yes, please, if you don't mind,' said Jane.

'No worries, I'll get someone in with a menu, or something. I'll be back in a bit,' he said, leaving them alone.

'You have no idea what he looks like, Mother, so don't even start,' said Kate.

Jane grinned.

'I can tell he's polite. Might be the one.'

Kate groaned inside.

There was a knock on the door. Zain burst in.

'Sorry, they need you. Now.'

Michelle was in the conference room, the screen playing a video.

'When did this happen?' said Kate, her skin goosing and crawling with adrenalin.

'It was uploaded a few minutes ago,' said Michelle.

'Fucking mental, isn't it?' said Zain.

'Yes,' said Kate.

The scene was familiar. It was a figure strapped to a chair. Kate couldn't tell if it was at the cottage. It shouldn't be – that place was crawling with police officers. There was no sound, no message. The picture was the same grey-green tint used on Ruby, bruising visible as shadows on the face.

The figure was crying, shivering. And Kate knew they wouldn't find him in time. That Daniel Grant was about to be murdered by James Fogg, in the same way Ruby had been.

"You're next." She finally knew who that message was for.

Chapter One Hundred and Thirteen

Kate oscillated between frustration and compassion as Rachel ran fingers through her hair and nervously touched her face. Her eyes were roaming the room again; she was worse after meeting with her parents. After Melissa had spoken to her, and Augusta had advised her.

'You see, I wonder why Dan would put himself in a situation where James could get hold of him?' said Kate.

'He can manipulate anyone; you don't know him.'

'Yes, but Dan hated him. I don't think he would willingly want to meet him. Rachel, I think there is something else happening. And I need you to help me, and be honest.'

Rachel broke down again. Her tears – the sobbing, body-wracking, limb-shaking crying – were beginning to grate on Kate. She needed answers, and clarity, because somewhere she pictured James putting a gun to Dan's head and creating the same montage he had done with Ruby. And however she felt about Dan, she would not allow this to happen.

'I don't know anything,' said Rachel.

'My client is clearly distressed, and has told you she has no knowledge of Mr Grant's disappearance,' said Augusta.

'Rachel, where did you tell Dan to meet you?' said Kate.

'I resent the accusation,' said Augusta.

'If you tell me, we can find him. Or do you want to be responsible for another death?'

'No,' said Rachel; it was loud – a scream, almost. 'No, I don't. Please. Save Dan? I won't survive it, knowing James did that again.'

'Help me, Rachel, and I won't let him,' said Kate.

'I called Dan. I told him I knew who killed Ruby. And I told him to meet me by Trinity Square. It's near his flat, and that's where . . . He got into the car, when he saw me, and then James –'

'What time?'

'I told him to meet me at 6 p.m., so it was then. And when he got into the car, on the back seat, James stabbed him with a needle. It was the same thing he'd used to drug Ruby.'

'Where did he take him?'

'I don't know. He didn't want me to go, this time. He told me to go home, get a taxi and go home. He said that our alibi had to look real, you see? I had to speak to the neighbours, ask them for something. And stand at the front door, and shout into the house. So it looked like he was there.'

James must have known that with Dan gone, he himself would become a bigger focus. So James hadn't expected to be caught. Dan wasn't an escalation; his capture was just his next step. No wonder his hard drives hadn't been cleaned.

'Did James say where he was going?' said Kate.

'He said he was going to let them be together. Ruby and Dan.'

The same place; to do the same things. Dan was probably already dead, she thought.

Zain was waiting for her when she left the interview room.

'We had a breakthrough,' he said. 'We ran the fake licences James had made. None of them registered to any hire cars. So we broadened the search, ran some of his aliases from the student IDs and a passport. One of them hit. He used the name Derek Childs to hire a car the day before Ruby disappeared, returned it the day after. And he hired another vehicle yesterday. We've got a hit on traffic cameras.'

Kate looked at the excitement on Harris's face, the energised sound to his voice. If he had done this himself, he wouldn't be so enthralled by it.

'Let me guess, you spoke to DCI Cross?'

'I'm resigning in the morning anyway,' he said. 'Before you fire me.'

'No, that's not what I mean. I was going to commend you on your adeptness. We need all the help we can get right now. No rash decisions, OK?'

'Right. I got your mother some food, too. She seems settled.'

'Are you OK to go to Hampshire and start the search?' she said.

'Of course,' he said.

'Take a chopper,' she said. 'You might as well splurge Hope's budget, while he still has it. I'm sure once the PM finds out that his party's biggest sponsor is cutting them off, this place will soon start counting Post-it notes and paperclips just like every other police unit.'

Chapter One Hundred and Fourteen

Zain was suspended in mid-air, his head feeling light, as though there was nothing holding his skull up. Seventy-two moving parts that could malfunction. Why did people use helicopters?

'Rubberdingyrapids,' he muttered, quoting from *Four Lions*.

He hadn't been the same with hovering in the air since the shipping container.

The helicopter set down in a field a couple of miles from Dan's cottage, near to the farmer who owned most of the land. He caught up with DS Helen Lowe from Hampshire police. She didn't seem all that enthused to see him, probably not as much as she would have been if he were Robin Pelt.

'Thought it better you land here,' she told him. 'There's some phone reception, at least. I have a car waiting for you, and Michelle Cable called. Said it was urgent. You better call her back before we head off. Near Dan's cottage you'll get no signal.'

'Thanks, sergeant. Do we have any idea yet where James might have taken Dan? Rachel provided us with a route which might give us some clues, at least.'

'In the pitch dark? I doubt it,' Helen said. 'We tried out the route, but the clues were too vague. We have a helicopter searching the area, and patrols are out. There's an alert out on the registration plate and car. It's just too massive an area, though.'

'At least we know roughly where he might be, from the traffic cameras.'

She shrugged.

Zain called Michelle.

'Listen, something weird,' Michelle said. 'Rachel put her battery back in.'

'What do you mean?'

'When she was left alone in the cottage, she got scared. So she put her battery back in, and switched her phone on. And she didn't switch it off when they took Ruby for a drive.'

'That's brilliant,' said Zain. 'But out here, there's probably no phone masts anywhere.'

'No, there aren't. Coverage is archaic; they might as well have just left their phones off.'

'I'm guessing we have a rough idea of where they went?'

'Better than that,' said Michelle. 'Rachel has an app on her phone, one that records her food and then works out the calories. Weight loss as well.'

'I'm not following,' he said. What did dieting apps have to do with this?

'The app is a sleeper,' said Michelle. 'It masquerades as a weight loss app, but it's actually collecting location data.'

Zain felt his heart start hammering.

'If you tell me that the app is tracking this to a satellite, I will bathe you in that expensive toffee shit.'

'Well, get your overdraft ready, because that's exactly what it does,' Michelle told him. 'It locks into a GPS satellite. I'm sending you the route they took.'

Zain jumped into the VW Helen Lowe had given him and started driving even before Michelle could tell him where he was heading.

The outhouse was four walls made from white stone, with an open doorway. A rusted door was off its hinges, pulled back by force. The floor was covered in flagstones. There was no roof; Rachel had been right.

In the centre of the structure was a cylindrical pile of stones. Zain edged towards it slowly, saw that a metal cover had been kicked over. He was using his phone as a flashlight, the glow weak but enough to see his immediate surroundings. He sniffed what smelled like sulphur. He picked up a loose rock, and threw it in. There was a splash, but it was shallow. He heard the rock hit hard ground as it rolled away. Obviously, a well that had nearly dried out.

Zain turned his phone to shine inside. Was Ruby's body down there? He peered into the shaft, but there was just darkness.

He thought someone was behind him, and jumped when he saw two figures.

'Fuck,' he said, as DS Helen Lowe came into view with one of her team.

'Did you wet yourself?' she said. 'Anything?'

'Can't see, but we need it searched. Are you two it? I thought you were going to provide full support to this?'

'They're about an hour away, most of them, heading this way. We uploaded the directions you sent.'

Zain had forwarded the same route Michelle had sent to him. The satellite tracking had sent back signals from Rachel's phone, leading him practically to where they were now.

'We need to spread out. You got the backbone to search for them in the dark?' said Zain.

'Only men need balls to show how tough they are, DS Harris. Us women have toughness inbuilt.'

Zain realised DS Lowe's colleague was also female.

'I didn't mean it like that,' he said. 'I work with Riley and Brennan, remember? Toughest cops I know.'

'We got you a proper torch,' said Lowe, tossing him a flashlight.

'Cheers, my phone battery's dying,' he said. 'Shall we?'

They headed out of the outhouse, and chose a direction to go in. He knew they should wait for back-up, but he was too close to not follow a trail. Dan was somewhere nearby, he was sure of it. James wouldn't know about Rachel switching her phone on; he would be secure in the fantasy that he was still safe.

Zain was convinced he was close.

Chapter One Hundred and Fifteen

Grass, trees, fallen branches and mulched leaves. Like treading in slush. Everything was covered in a layer of darkness he wasn't used to. This was night in the country, no artificial lighting anywhere. He was reluctant to switch on the torch he'd been given. It would be like a beacon. At least he was as invisible as he was blind without it.

Zain twisted his ankle, misplacing his foot on what he thought might be solid ground but turned out to be a dip covered by leaves. He stopped to check, but it was just sore. And all around him the suffocating feeling, like being blindfolded. Like being trapped, not knowing who was looking for you, looking at you.

He spun around; something snapped behind him. How could black have so many shades? How could he see phantoms when he could barely see his hands? And then there was a glow over everything. The moon had escaped, and was gliding across the sky.

Where was he going? There was no destination, just a rough idea to keep moving, heading in a particular direction. The thought that this might be a waste of time crossed his mind a few times. He wondered if DS Lowe and her colleague were faring better. They had headed down a path parallel to his route, but further off.

His phone buzzed.

It was a number he didn't recognise. A text message. A link. There was no internet connection, barely a signal. He must have wandered into the path of a stray tunnel of connectivity.

He should have plugged into a satellite, got DCI Cross to sort him out.

The message was a map. Zain was a blue dot. A red dot was to his right, about half a mile away. Zain knew who it was from. He was being dragged into someone else's drama, with a role assigned to him.

And he was ready to play it.

Zain was sure he was near. It had looked like half a mile on the phone. Whoever sent it must have known where the mobile signal would catch, where Zain would pick it up. Was it meant for him? How could they have been sure he would pick it up? Or was it meant for anyone heading that way?

Zain checked the map again. He realised the blue dot had moved. He hadn't noticed it before; he'd been focused on his target. Zain had moved, and the map had recorded it.

'Fuck,' he said.

Something was reading his location. The same satellite that had read Rachel's location? The text message must have contained malware; he must have uploaded an app or code that broke into his phone.

Zain felt a trace of admiration for James. The man was a genius. A sick, twisted fucker, sure, but still a clever bastard.

So he was reeling Zain in, and Zain was swallowing the bait.

The woods came to a natural end, bordering an orchard. Trees in neat rows, branches curling and intertwined like unruly warriors.

Zain scanned them, trying to see his destination. The map on the phone was still, as he didn't move. The red dot was only a few yards away, but he couldn't get a visual on it.

Zain breathed deep, and stepped out from the covered position he was in. Go on, then, he thought, take a shot. Nothing happened, and he walked to where the map told him he would find whatever was there.

He walked down a path, between the battling trees, looking into the shadows, trying to see anything that might be human, or might be watching him. He jumped enough times, movement in the breeze shocking him.

He needed to head right, thought he'd walk to the end of the path he was on and then do it. Fuck it, he thought, and headed into the tree line itself. He fought his way through, tearing his clothes, his skin. He got stuck, broke away whatever branch had trapped him, and fell into the next line of the orchard.

He ran across it, did the same with the next set of trees, and fell into the grassy path again. He was winded, adrenalin running through him. His face was cut, and he felt bruises where he had bashed himself.

It took him a few seconds to be sure; he blinked, refocused. No, it couldn't be. He saw then. He wasn't alone.

A figure was kneeling up ahead. Zain gripped his torch, missing the weapon he had carried as part of counter-terrorism ops. He walked slowly, looking at the figure, aware of how exposed he was.

As he got closer, he saw the shape of the head, the hair falling down the back. He recognised the sackcloth. How could this be? It was impossible. Zain was close now, but his eyes were drawn to something else.

Kneeling opposite this figure was another one. Zain could see the outline, and knew it was Dan.

Zain reached out a hand to the figure nearest him, rested a hand on her shoulder. She turned to him, trembling, bloody, dirty. Grey under the moonlight, like a spectre, like the dead risen. And she was.

'Ruby?' he said.

Chapter One Hundred and Sixteen

Ruby nodded. Her hands were behind her back, tied with plastic. Zain pulled out his penknife and started to cut at the bind, but it wouldn't budge.

'Can you walk?' he said, helping her stand. 'Where is James?'

'He's watching,' she said. Her voice was dull, etched with insanity. She must have been kept chained, possibly in the empty well. He could smell the same sulphurous odour around her that he had smelled when he'd looked into it.

'What does he want?' whispered Zain.

'Immortality,' she said.

Zain shivered, as though iron was being dragged across his teeth. 'Is Dan all right?' he asked.

'He's alive,' she said.

Zain searched the shadows, trying to work out where James might be. He needed to get Ruby and Dan to safety, hidden among the trees or back into the woods. Provide them with some cover. How was Ruby alive? He had watched her brain being blown out dozens of times.

'Ruby, I need you to make it to that space there, directly in front of us. Where the trees are growing in front of each other. You can hide between them. Can you do that?'

'He can see in the dark,' she said simply.

Zain let her rest her weight on him, and she shuffled along. She was so frail, barely registered physically as he helped her. He tucked her in between the trunks of the trees he had identified, and tried to cover her with branches. There might be some concealment, but not if James got close and had his night-vision glasses on.

Zain went back into the orchard path, and walked quickly to where Dan was. He was just reaching him when his phone buzzed again. He took it out, and he saw it was another map delivered to him by satellite.

He opened it up. This time there were three red dots. Two were overlapping. Himself and Dan, obviously. One was nearby, Ruby. Then the map started to shake, and into the screen came a yellow dot. Something was heading towards them.

'Fuck me,' he said, grabbing Dan. 'Can you walk? Fuck that, can you run?'

Dan nodded, whimpering.

'Head that way, into the woods, do you understand?'

Dan nodded again, and started walking as fast as he could. He was dragging his left leg behind him, his limp too pronounced. James must have damaged it further in some way.

Zain ran to where Ruby was, and bent down, telling her to get on his back. He had given piggy-back rides to his step sisters, and Ruby didn't weigh more than them, he was sure. She gripped his throat with birdlike hands and bony arms as he started running in the same direction as Dan.

He should have checked his phone, seen where James was, but he needed to put distance between them, fast. He caught up with Dan quickly, but he couldn't carry him as well as Ruby.

'Keep going, Dan, you're doing great,' he said.

He could get Ruby into the woods . . .

He stopped, let Ruby slide from his back, and took out his phone. James was close, nearly on top of them. Zain threw his phone in the opposite direction to them. It would at least give them a few seconds, and James wouldn't be able to track them into the woods.

He let Ruby get onto his back again and headed into the woods, Dan panting and struggling behind them.

Zain was safely past the border of hardwoods, dropping Ruby and then hitting the ground himself. He was still catching his breath when the first shot rang out.

Chapter One Hundred and Seventeen

The H145 helicopter that had earlier delivered Zain landed close to her rendezvous point. Kate switched on her satellite phone as soon as the rotor blades came to a standstill. Her signal clear in the dark but open expanse of the South Downs National Park, it buzzed almost immediately.

'Finally – have been trying for the last five minutes,' said Michelle.

'Literally just landed and switched it on,' said Kate. 'The Hants Tactical Firearms Support Unit are already here waiting for me. I need you to guide us to where we need to be. Did you get in contact with Harris?'

'Not yet, his phone has no signal. And he switched his GPS off.'

A man in his early thirties came up to her, his helmet off, but the rest of his body armour in place.

'Detective Riley? I'm Detective Tom Pierce, designated aenior officer for TFSU.' TFSU was the Hampshire police version of SO19. Kate had tried to get the Met's team, but logistics and distance had meant outsourcing again.

'Thank you for the quick response, detective. We believe the suspect, James Fogg, is armed. He has used his weapon before, and we believe he will use it again. I'm afraid he may feel backed into a corner, so is extremely dangerous.'

'We have eight armed officers ready to go when you say. All specialist firearms officers. I have an ambulance and medical aid on the way as well.'

'Thank you, detective. My team back in London are trying to track the location of one of my officers already in the field.'

I just hope we find him before James Fogg does, she thought.

*

They were parked up, sheltered by some trees, not moving. The armed officers were inside the van, but Kate stood outside with a now-helmeted Detective Pierce, to allow better reception to her sat phone. Pierce looked eerie, like an alien life form, in the darkness. Huge goggle eyes staring down at her.

She had been given body armour to wear, but despite being licensed, and trained, she wasn't allowed to carry a gun. She had also been told to keep a back seat when they were called into action.

The buzz of her phone made her jump. She noticed Pierce stayed still. Good to know armed police could hold their nerve when the unexpected happened.

'Michelle, what have you got?' she said.

'Something odd. There's scant mobile phone reception in the area, but there are a couple of hotspots. I located Zain's phone to the one you are at now.'

'Did you find where he is yet?'

'No. But there was a data packet delivered from a satellite phone.'

'What do you mean?'

'I think a virus was uploaded onto Zain's phone, piggybacking onto a text message or some other form of communication. I think that's why his GPS is broken. It's been maliciously disabled.'

'Did you run a trace for where the packet was delivered from?'

'Yes. It's unlisted, and the satellite companies are harder to get data from than Google. I'm sure it's that sick James Fogg, though. It's too much of a coincidence otherwise.'

Kate felt a thrill, a possible ending. If they could get a lock on James's location, she could get to Zain and see what was left. Dan might still be alive.

'It might be a random app delivering something, but highly unlikely they would use satellite technology. For one thing, it's not particularly secure.'

Kate didn't respond. She heard Pierce breathing heavily through his mask next to her. She felt her own blood rushing behind her eyes.

'Tell me, Michelle,' said Kate. 'From everything we know about James Fogg, the highly skilled technical genius he is, do you think he would use a satellite phone and not know that it wasn't secure?'

Michelle was calculating, unwilling probably to say what they both knew.

'It might be the only sort of reception he could get out there. He might have been forced to. Alternatively . . .'

'Alternatively he chose an unsafe form of communication, knowing full well we would find him. He wants to be found. This is his end game. How close can you get to him?'

'They have a six-mile radius,' said Michelle.

'That's what, ten kilometres almost? Get me something better than that.'

'I can send a signal to the unlisted number that hit Zain's phone, see if I can get you a direction.'

'Get me whatever you can, but ten kilometres is not good enough.'

Kate signalled Pierce, filled him in as they loaded up into the TFSU van. She felt foreboding now. In the dark, with such a wide area to search, the chances of finding Zain or Dan were minimal.

She did something then she never did. She prayed she was not too late.

Chapter One Hundred and Eighteen

The night silence was shattered. The gunshot had done it, followed by Dan screaming. Ruby was sobbing. Zain crawled over to her.

'Ruby, listen to me,' he whispered. 'Look at me. This is going to be OK. We are going to live. The world thought you were dead, and you're not. I will not let James Fogg do that to you tonight. You have to help me, though. You have to stay quiet and still.'

Her sobbing subsided into hiccups and silent shivering. Zain took his jacket off and put it around her. He piled up wet leaves against her, trying to cover her as much as possible. The night-vision goggles wouldn't be able to discern her if she was hidden.

Her hands were still tied behind her back; he tried cutting through the plastic again with his penknife, but it was hopeless and he grazed her skin in the darkness. His best chance to save her was to stop James.

Zain crept along the ground, tasting rain-sodden soil and decaying autumn, until he was at the edge of the woods. He peered into the orchard, lit weakly by the scarred moon, remembered where he had left Dan.

There was silence. Only the sound of his heart hammering against his ribcage, and the loud rasp of his breathing. He wanted them to be silent. Another time, another prayer. Let it be still, so they can't hear that I'm still alive.

He moved forward, inch by inch. Exposed, wondering what James was doing to Dan.

It felt like an hour, but must have been a few minutes at most, as he finally reached the first line of trees of the orchard. Zain crawled into the tangle of branches, squinting, hoping he could see something that would let him know where Dan and James were.

A second shot, and Dan screaming again.

Zain captured the moment in his head. The shot had come from that direction, but the screams from over there.

They weren't in the same place. If Dan had been hit, he was probably dying already. Zain had to get to James, stop him moving on to find Ruby.

He followed the memory of the shot and pelted into the darkness. Running, falling to the ground, moving haphazardly, avoiding being an easy shot. A third shot rang out, and the bullet grazed his jacket. He ran faster, memorising where it had come from. A fourth shot, this time closer, his shoulder. He didn't stop, and then he was through a line of trees, and there he was.

James Fogg was wearing a balaclava and his night-vision goggles. He had a camera fixed to his shoulder, and a sniper rifle.

Zain ran towards him; he was too close now for James to get a good shot. But he tried anyway, and the gun went off, directly towards where Zain was.

The bullet tore through him; he felt it like burning and pain. He fell to the ground in agony. James Fogg was standing over him then, the gun thrown aside. He had a knife in his hand, a proper hunting one, scratted edges. They would slice his flesh like meat, he knew.

Zain looked up into the face of his death, but made his muscles taut. He would not go without a fight. He kicked out at the still figure of James, tripping him. The unexpected action made the knife drop from James's hand.

Zain coughed, tasting blood, but started to scramble for the knife. A last desperate attempt. But James grabbed it first. He punched Zain in the face, then straddled him. James put the knife to Zain's throat.

Zain pushed as hard as he could, but his body was weakened, losing too much blood. And then James started to press the knife in, making a guttural animal sound as he did. Zain kept his eyes open. He would not die a coward.

Chapter One Hundred and Nineteen

Kate was chomping at the bit, she was being held back physically by Detective Pierce now.

'My officers will fire when they have a clear shot,' he said.

'He will be dead by then,' said Kate, exasperated and desperate.

'Sir,' one of the officers shouted over.

Kate walked quickly with Pierce and looked at a laptop set up at the side of the TFSU van. The small screen showed images from the camera on the shoulder of one of the SFOs, zoomed in. Images of Zain and James Fogg tussling.

'Can you get a clear shot?' said Pierce. He was speaking into a comms app the unit were all hooked up to, aiming his words at the SFO whose camera images they were watching. Kate had been allowed a listening channel, but had no option to broadcast herself.

'Honestly, sir, they are moving around too much. I could shoot DS Harris accidentally,' said the SFO, her voice calm but showing the edges of nervousness.

'Then we wait,' said Pierce.

Kate bit back her response, watching Zain and James on the screen. James punched Zain, and was sitting on top of him. He had a knife in his hand.

'Now, quickly, shoot the bastard,' screamed Kate.

'Detective, this is not your call,' said Pierce, but it was too late. Kate had run to where Zain and James were.

'Sir?' said the SFO.

'Take the shot,' said Pierce.

The knife cut across his throat. Only it made the sound of a gun being discharged when it did. That wasn't right. James slumped forward, his body falling heavily onto Zain.

In a moment he was dragged off, and Zain thought he was in some dream space. Kate Riley was there, shouting for help, her hands pressing into his stomach and covering his throat.

'Open your eyes, Zain,' she was saying. 'Can you hear me? You've been shot, but help is close.'

Kate took off her jacket, balled it up, and pressed it against him. She wasn't touching his throat anymore. Did that mean it wasn't cut?

'Stay with me, Zain, don't close your eyes. I need you to stay awake, and stay alert, OK? Look, I can hear the ambulance now.'

Zain listened, but all he could hear was his heart slowing down. He started to lose focus, he knew it was Kate but he couldn't see her clearly anymore. He tried to make sense of her, but he gave up, his eyes closing.

'You will not die on my fucking watch,' Kate shouted. 'I will not let you.'

Zain opened his eyes, and he wanted to live. And he realised then Kate was the one person he would trust with his life. And he didn't want to die, not after knowing that.

He tried to speak, but coughed up more blood.

'You just look into my eyes, and you just stay alive. Where the fuck is that ambulance?'

And then he heard it. Over the sound of his heart, and over the sound of her shouting. The darkness was broken by blue lights and, in the distance, he swore he heard a helicopter come to life.

Chapter One Hundred and Twenty

The room was warm, causing Kate to remove her jacket before she sat down. She breathed in, the familiar but unpleasant smell she associated with hospitals. Decaying bodies, detergent, medicine and food. Get Well Soon cards were lined up on the bedside table, Kate recognising the one Michelle had organised from the team. The others made her curious. How many people did he know? Who else cared about DS Harris enough to get a card to him?

'Boss,' he said, catching her unawares. He was noisy as he tried to prop himself up on his bed, the plastic mattress making squelching noises. He was naked above the waist, bandages covering his abdomen where the bullet had gone in. He had an IV line protruding from his arm, attached to a bag of clear liquid on a stand.

'Pain relief,' he explained, following her eyes.

'Is it working?' she said.

'Morphine can only do so much,' he said, showing her a hand pump that let him self administer.

She smiled at him, willing herself to keep her eyes on his. She failed, and took in the plaster around his neck, covering his stitches.

'They said I'll have another scar,' he said. 'I've got a bit of a collection going. Don't need tattoos, I guess.'

Kate tried not to think of the missing toenails. When Zain had been rushed to Southampton General that night, they had stripped him of his bloody clothes. And despite the blasted skin from the bullet, the vast amounts of blood and bruising, it was when they removed his boots and socks that she was most shocked. It was the last image of him she had before he was rushed into surgery.

'Stevie sends her love,' said Kate, trying to remove the thought from her mind. They both laughed at the idea. 'She asked how you were anyway. I think that counts as progress.'

'How is she?'

'Doing great. Should be back at work in about six weeks, once Occupational Health sign her back on.'

'That soon?'

'If she's well enough.'

'And me?'

Kate looked away from him. She wasn't ready to commit to anything with Zain just yet.

'Get better, and then we'll talk,' she said.

'I understand,' he said. His face set hard, and his eyes darkened. 'How's Ruby?'

'Back in London. She's been helping us get some closure on this. With James ...'

'Dead,' said Zain.

'Yes, well, we need to try and figure out what happened, and why.'

There was a danger of anti-climactic lethargy infecting the case as a whole, she felt. James Fogg had died from the bullet of the Hants SFO. A clean shot, more on target than James's own attempts to kill three people. And James may be dead, but there were enough victims to fill the gaps he had left. Ruby, Dan and especially Rachel. And the countless others. Kate and her team were now supporting the Met in tracking down the girls that James had groomed over the years. The ones they knew about, and the ones that were too scared and ashamed to get in touch. A helpline had been set up to try and encourage them to come forward. The ones she worried about the most, though, the ones that were truly damaged, were those that were disbelieving. They considered their encounters with James, their idol, to be nothing short of love.

Kate could see years of broken women coming to terms with what they had been through, and what had been done to them. Sickeningly, a fan page had been set up on Instagram, glorifying James and defending him. Teenage girls worshipping at the shrine of this fucked-up psycho. Some argued he was too good-looking to have to force himself on anyone, that women would come to him naturally. The anger at those comments hurt Kate. It reminded her of women writing to serial killers on Death Row.

But set against the density of the dark, were the girls that were being helped. The girls that were being saved, and the ones that had been saved by him not being alive anymore.

'I can't believe I'm going to ask you this, but what about Dan? Is he OK?'

'Dan's still here. James shot him in the spine, and at the moment he has no movement below his waist. The diagnosis isn't positive; they don't know if he will ever walk again.'

'I feel sorry for the dude,' said Zain. He started coughing, and winced from the pain he had caused himself.

'Do you need anything?'

'No, I'm fine. I just have to remember a bullet tore through me, and I have a shattered rib.'

'You were lucky, DS Harris,' she said.

'A few millimetres and it could have been fatal,' he said. 'Yeah I know, they keep telling me. How's Dan taking it all?'

'Surprisingly well. He's very grateful to you, keeps saying you saved his life.'

'I know how he feels.'

Kate held her breath, she knew what he was about to say. There was no need, but he would anyway and she would have to listen.

'I feel that way about you,' he said. 'The nurses don't know much, but they know about the DCI that risked her life to save mine. I don't even want to say thank you, because even when those words form in my head, they just feel inadequate.'

Kate nodded at him. She was uncomfortable at being seen as some sort of saviour. She had reacted that night the way she always did. Instinct and the pursuit of truth.

Her phone beeped, a text message alert. It was from her estate agent. Following her mother's encounter on Primrose Hill, she had decided to sell the house in Highgate and move elsewhere.

'Got a date?' said Zain. He looked embarrassed after he had. 'Sorry, ignore me. I'm high, remember.'

'No, just work. Not important,' she said.

Chapter One Hundred and Twenty-one

Zain closed his eyes as pain shot through him again. It would be time for his top-up soon. He looked at Kate as she typed a reply to whoever had just messaged her. It definitely wasn't work. She had a different look in her eyes when it was about work. A hard focus he couldn't describe fully.

'Do we know why he did it yet?' said Zain. 'I don't mean why he was such a fucking pervert, I mean why was he trying to kill Ruby and Dan. Did Ruby say anything?'

'We might never really know,' said Kate. 'Ruby said when they were alone, without Rachel there, James had broken down and accused her of ruining his life. He blamed her for how his career online had ended so quickly, blamed her and Dan in fact.'

'So it was about revenge?'

'It was about more than revenge. Ruby said he wanted to be remembered for eternity.'

'Twisted fuck,' he said.

'It was premeditated and carefully planned, that much is clear. He ordered fast-acting anaesthetics online, the night-vision goggles and his gun as well. We traced transactions on his credit card to a firm called Razerbill Limited, and pulled as much as we could from his hard drives. He was using Tor, obviously, and had a number of purge programmes installed.'

Zain bit back a cough at the mention of Razerbill. It was the front company that carried out the financial transactions for his own green pills.

'I thought it was because Ruby knew. About what he was doing online. He was trying to silence her?'

'It was a set-up. James sent Ruby messages pretending to be a young girl asking for advice, because she was starting a relationship with him. It was a convincing exchange, according to Ruby. Pictures and messages. James even managed to arrange a Skype call with Ruby pretending to be this girl.'

'How?'

'She said the picture quality was very bad, and there was no sync in what was being said on audio and what was on the screen. It helped convince Ruby this girl was real.'

'How old was he pretending to be?'

'Seventeen,' said Kate. 'Ruby's concerns weren't that James was sleeping with underage girls, but that he was abusing his position with his fans. And to Ruby, whether you were fourteen or eighteen, James exploiting his position online was unacceptable.'

'That's why she went into meltdown,' said Zain.

'Yes. She holds the relationship between vlogger and viewer as sacred. The idea that James was abusing that trust, it was enough. She confronted him about it face to face, and started digging online, mainly on fan forums. That's when she started to discover younger girls saying things that really made her worry.'

'And then James got Rachel to call, with a smoking gun,' said Zain.

'Yes. When he was ready.'

'I don't get it, though, why did he only pretend to shoot Ruby?'

'This wasn't going to be a moment in the sun for him. James wanted to make an impact. The game was on as far as he was concerned, his end game, and he wanted to prolong it for as long as he could. He told Ruby he wanted her and everyone around her to suffer. It was an attempt to rile Karl Rourke and MINDNET too, by taking their assets and destroying them. Dan was supposed to be another drawn-out victim. He wanted Ruby and Dan to suffer before he got rid of them.'

Zain felt his throat constrict and dry up. Nausea or anger, he couldn't tell. It was followed by a wave of complete emptiness. What had he done to himself, where was his life going? He didn't have a clue. He let it pass, anchored himself to Kate instead.

'James told Ruby that he wanted her to believe she might sur-vive. When she saw Dan, he wanted Ruby to think that she had a chance, that maybe she could escape with him. Or that people would redouble their efforts to find them both. He laughed as he told them that they would be found. Together. Dead.'

'Until Stevie messed up his plans,' said Zain.

'Yes. That's why we found so much still on his hard drives. Why he panicked at the end. And possibly why he failed. He was fine while he was in control, while his plan was being executed. When we forced his hand, he fell apart.'

Zain could resist it no longer. He pressed the morphine pump in his hand. The clear liquid shot down through the IV line, and felt cold as it entered his system. The pain will pass, he told himself.

'So what was I?' he said.

'Right cop, wrong place. He knew it was over for him, and he wanted to be caught that night. He was using an unencrypted satellite phone, and he downloaded a virus onto your mobile when you came into range to lure you to where he was. He was willing to take the first officer that came close. We found cameras set up around the orchard at various points, and he had the new static body armour cams from America strapped to himself. They hold fairly steady even when you are moving around.'

The pain wasn't easing. And doubts started to come into his mind. It was the same when he had been kidnapped. They said he just happened to be the one the terrorists got, it wasn't planned that way. It wasn't personal. Well it felt fucking personal then, and it felt just as personal with James. It was Zain who was left with the wounds, the scar tissue and the invasion of his sanity.

'He went to all that trouble because people stopped watching him on YouTube,' said Zain.

'He was a sociopath and a narcissist, and a paedophile. There was more going on in his brain than I want to bring into your hospital room. But yes, the loss of his perceived status and fame, that really affected him. He suffered a breakdown. We accessed his medical records. He was on suicide watch for a couple of months after his break-up with Ruby.'

Zain wondered how far away he was from having his own break-down. They called you a hero because you were wounded in service, then left you while the rot set into the gaping tunnels where the bullet had travelled. And if you were to have any chance of coming back, you couldn't let on how the damage inside your head was so much worse than anything they could see on your body.

'He valued fame over his own life? I don't understand that. What a waste.'

'I don't think I agree on that last point. No one is going to miss him.'

'What about his parents?'

'Normal middle-class parents. Mother is a teacher, father works for an insurance firm. He blames himself, apparently spent a lot of time away from home while James was growing up. His mother feels the same, long hours with school work.'

'I don't think they can take responsibility for what their son became,' said Zain. His own parents weren't always present in terms of time. And he had turned out all right. OK, not really.

'Some people are just wired differently. And given the right circumstances, anything can happen,' she said.

Zain felt as though she was addressing him, like she could read his soul.

'What about KNG and MINDNET?' he said. 'Is Ruby going to help Maggie Walsh?'

Kate's eyed widened slightly, and she looked away from him.

'Ruby wants to help James's victims. It's what her focus is on at the moment.'

Zain understood that. He also realised what it meant for Jed Byrne and Harry Cain. They would get away with it. The thought weighed him down, made him feel exhausted.

'And Hope?'

'Justin Hope is a symbol of something, a realisation of an idea. They need him to succeed so they can roll out the PCC programme across London.'

Zain didn't say anything. The tone of Kate's voice conveyed exactly how pissed off she was about the whole thing. Hope would be protected no matter what they accused him of. The public sector were great at protecting their own, and closing ranks when they wanted.

Kate took her leave soon afterwards, promising to visit again if she could. And reiterating her promise to touch base when he was discharged. There was no mention of his determination to resign prior to the night he had been shot. He took that as a sign that there might be a way back. He didn't know who else might take on the further damaged and broken Zain Harris if she didn't.

Epilogue

The wind was cold, blowing into his face, so he pulled his hood up and crossed his arms. Since leaving hospital, he had noticed the weather play havoc with his body more. He felt tired and frail on some days, light-headed on most. Night sweats, nightmares, uncontrolled shaking. Panic attacks.

He was back on the green pills.

He looked up as two joggers went by, laughing as they did. Were they laughing at him? He hadn't shaved in weeks, and was dressed in dark colours. He looked like a rough sleeper, he knew.

Why Kate had chosen to meet in St James's Park rather than the office – that irritated his paranoia further. She was making it obvious. There was no way back for him, she didn't even want him in the building, let alone back on her team.

He pulled his phone out, to see if she had texted to cancel. There was nothing. From anyone. His parents usually messaged once a day, but that only made it worse. Zain didn't realise how alone he was, how much he had cut himself off, chasing a career that kept biting him back, until his discharge from hospital.

And in that loneliness, he felt as though he had nothing left. Unless he found something worth waking up for soon, what was the point in any of it?

A swan glided across the river, heading towards Buckingham Palace, as pigeons crowded around his feet. He kicked out at them.

Zain pulled up the internet browser on his phone, the last page he had looked at still displayed. It was an article about Maggie

Walsh and her parliamentary commission looking into corruption by British business operating in the Democratic Republic of Congo. She had managed to get that at least from her ten-minute speech. There was no mention of KNG, MINDNET, Jed Byrne or Harry Cain.

He had read elsewhere that KNG had stopped their IPO, stating uncertainty in the commodities market, and that they would reassess and float on the stock market at an opportune time. PR bullshit and spin. They had been hurt financially, at least. It just didn't seem enough. People had died, and no one was being held accountable. Maggie's commission would take ages to get going, and probably end up delivering nothing. It was the political equivalent of sabre rattling as far as he was concerned. A smokescreen the rich and powerful used to get away with their shit.

Still. He knew where Jed Byrne lived. Maybe he should give him some personal payback? It was an alternative way to exist. If doing things officially didn't work, take to the shadows.

He shivered as the wind cut through him.

It was a fantasy, though, he knew. They were too powerful, too well connected, for him to do any significant damage. And he could easily be got rid of. Zain was very aware of just how mortal he was. He felt as though he was living on borrowed time.

A shadow crossed over him.

'I bought you a coffee,' she said.

Kate was wearing a long black coat, her hair pulled back on top of her head. The aroma of latte filled the space between them. He took it, as she sat down on the bench next to him. It tasted good. He hadn't eaten anything for two days, burnt his tongue as he gulped it down.

Walking back, Kate decided to take a detour around the park. She had been shocked at Zain's appearance. Not just the unkempt beard, but the haggard look in his face, the deadness in his eyes. He looked like a poster image for someone that had given up.

Yet when he started to talk about KNG, and how they were going to get away with murder, there was that old fire and determination back in his voice, his eyes were alive again. It was manic. She knew then that her decision was the only one possible.

He had been certain she was going to send him on 'gardening leave' or, worse still, just terminate his contract completely. No longer fit for duty. Truth is, she still wondered if that might be the right course of action, especially seeing the state he was in. Instead, she had told him she would be giving him another chance. He had proved himself the night he saved Ruby and Dan. She just needed to know she could trust him.

Queen Anne's Gate was empty as Kate walked down it, the post-lunch crowds all gone. It was an early afternoon lull, before the commuters started their journey home. Kate's own journey was now cut to fifteen minutes of brisk walking. She had moved her mother into a riverside complex with twenty-four-hour security, and an on-site shopping arcade. Ryan was reduced to housekeeping, but his need was gone. Her mother was safe to walk around three acres of landscaped gardens, and Kate was secure in the knowledge she was being watched by the doormen, CCTV and nosy neighbours.

Another temporary belief she was safe. Until something happened to make her believe otherwise.

That was the problem with severing ties with your history, and all those in it. They became ogres, and you lost all sense of what they were really doing. Where they might actually be.

She thought again of Zain. He seemed to lose the ability to breathe when she told him he was coming back to work for her.

'I won't let you down,' he had said. 'This means everything to me.'

Everything. She could believe it, and she understood how the job really could be so all-consuming. In Zain Harris, she saw herself. Nothing else would ever match up to what they did. They were wired to be who they were.

Yes, she told herself. She had made the right decision. Everyone deserved the chance to live again. She of all people knew that truth.

Acknowledgements

It has been a 'journey' to get here and there are some people I can only describe as dream merchants that have helped me along the way.

The best agent in the world – Luigi Bonomi. Legend.

Alison Bonomi for finding me, keeping me going when it got really dark, and treating me so well. I owe you gunpowder potatoes at the very least.

My phenomenal editor Kate Parkin. Thank you for sharing my vision; your words are always surprising, never taken for granted, and make me feel ten feet tall.

My other amazing editor (yes, I realise how lucky I am) – Kate Ballard. I think I was your trial by fire right from your first day, but it's worked out so well. Thank you for your support and understanding always (and for letting me blabber away on e-mail!)

Thank you to Katherine Armstrong, for letting me indulge in my obsessions and just general support fantastic-ness.

I lack the courage to shout about this novel to the world, but luckily for me I have the awesome Emily Burns in my corner to do that for me! So thank you to you and your team!

Sam Bulos and Martin Fletcher for taking a hammer and chisel to my drafts.

Everyone at LBA Books and Bonnier. Nicest people ever.

The Twenty7 gang – Anadin has never met such suportive/ wonderful people, thanks for the laughter, advice and great novels.

God, Mum, my family and friends – the essentials to my life that I can't do without.

DISCOVERING DEBUT AUTHORS
PUTTING DIGITAL FIRST

Twenty7 Books is a brand new imprint, publishing exclusively debut novels from the very best new writers. So whether you're a desperate romantic or a crime fiction fiend, discover the bestselling authors of the future by visiting us online.

twenty7